PRAISE FOR
WILLIAM BAYER
AND HIS BESTSELLING
NOVELS . . .

"Bayer goes right on my 'look for' list."
—JOHN D. MACDONALD

"The pounding pace keeps the reader panting!"
—*Kansas City Star*

"Sharp . . . satisfying . . . richly detailed intrigue . . .
with plenty of twists and double twists."
—*Milwaukee Journal*

"Terrific page-turner . . ."
—*Cleveland Plain Dealer*

"A world of murder, blackmail, double crosses and
redouble crosses, all against a backdrop of obsessive
sex, plain and kinky . . . Its pace is fast, its temperature high."
—*Los Angeles Times*

"Dazzling, fast-paced action."
—ROBERT DALEY, author of *Prince of the City*

WALLFLOWER

WILLIAM BAYER

A Janek Novel

JOVE BOOKS, NEW YORK

This Jove Book contains the complete
text of the original hardcover edition.
It has been completely reset in a typeface
designed for easy reading, and was printed
from new film.

WALLFLOWER

A Jove Book / published by arrangement with
Villard Books, a division of Random House, Inc.

PRINTING HISTORY
Villard Books edition published July 1991
Jove edition / May 1992

ISBN: 0-515-10843-X

Jove Books are published by The Berkley Publishing Group,
200 Madison Avenue, New York, New York 10016.
The name "JOVE" and the "J" logo
are trademarks belonging to Jove Publications, Inc.

PRINTED IN THE UNITED STATES OF AMERICA

10 9 8 7 6 5 4 3 2 1

For Paula

Flower in the crannied wall,
. . . if I could understand
What you are, root and all, and all in all,
I should know what God and man is.

— *Tennyson*

1
She
Remembered

Even years before, when it first came to her, she had relished the idea for the sheer cunning of it, treasured and cherished it for its craft and guile.

She remembered: It had been a sour, rainy day, much like this one, in Cleveland, smelly old Cleveland where the air always stank of iron and dust. She'd been sitting in the window seat, the one on the landing that broke the stairs in the gloomy old Tudor-style house—sitting there, knees drawn to her breasts (such as they were), arms wrapped about her legs, looking out at the rain spattering the sidewalk below. Thunder was rumbling in the distance, and an old kindergarten chant was running through her brain: "Rain, rain, go away/Come again another day. . . ."

Then, suddenly, lightning struck, a real bolt that zigzagged, crack!crack!crack! across the sky.

She sat up straight, and the singsong chant was forgotten, for she saw something then, something dark and scary she would remember all her life. There was a moment, just a split second really, when the tight gray fabric of the sky was torn. And then she caught a glimpse of the inky black—the other side. She would never forget that shade of black.

A second later the thunder clapped, and the rain poured down furiously as if a huge bladder had broken open and was emptying itself upon the earth. It was before that, just an instant before, between the bolt and the clap, that the idea was born. It was a very simple idea yet most profound. Only later would she come to understand how there was a cosmic view implicit in it.

She remembered: She had been fifteen years old when the concept came to her. Every day after that she harbored and nurtured it. And now, many years later, it was about to bear fruition.

She smiled as she remembered, smiled at the sheer cunning of it.

The cunning.

2

Janek
in Love

There was in Frank Janek a certain imperturbability as the speedboat raced out of the dawn mist, then cut hard across the lagoon. A slapping sound, water against wood, as the boat sliced the tiny waves. A faintly rancid smell, too, seaweed and shellfish, hung on the vapor that rose from the salt marshes just touched by the morning sun.

The shadowy form of an oil tanker loomed on the horizon while ahead an islet fortress, deserted, trash washed against its seawalls, resolved out of the mist. He'd read about the place. He remembered now. It had been a lunatic asylum not too many years before.

The boat turned again, then charged forward faster, its sharp prow high and haughty, its wake a churning river in the smooth expanse of water behind. Then, in an instant, the fog broke, and his destination, pink and gold, was finally revealed. Towers, domes, arches, bridges, sculptures, pilings angled against a sinuous façade. The soft cries of men stroking long boats through the water merged with the muted tolling of church bells in the shimmering baroque city ahead.

She was there, all of her, all at once, suddenly, and as her remarkable presence hit him full force, Janek stood up in the boat and shuddered with rapture. He couldn't help himself. He had arrived, finally, in Venice.

It had been a dream to come here, a dream of seduction so long harbored he'd sometimes thought it would be better left unrealized. What if the legendary city, La Serenissima, failed to charm him with her wiles? She had fallen on hard times, he'd heard, was rotting, sinking, choked with tourists in her season, flooded and fetid the remainder of the year. There was a good chance, he knew, that he'd be disappointed. But rather than deter him, that possibility made him eager. If Venice had gone to seed, well then, hadn't he gone a little to seed himself? And if he was going to be disappointed, then perhaps disappointment was something he could savor. A depressed middle-aged detective with his greatest case behind him—might not a city well past her glory be the perfect place for him just now?

It had been ten years since he'd taken a vacation. And that was deliberate. "I just can't imagine myself doing nothing," he'd told people, "lying in the sun, broiling myself on some damn beach."

But there was a lot more to it. Perhaps, as he now suspected, he had been afraid of the feelings of emptiness a real vacation could expose. He had always considered himself fortunate: He had found his vocation early, had discovered the joys of investigating crimes, probing deeply into the motives of others. But the one kind of probing that was not pleasant for him at all was the examination of his own quite troubled soul.

Lately his despair seemed to have deepened, something he attributed to the Switch Case, which should have been his crowning achievement but which, instead, had left him feeling depressed, at times almost numb. Every case had its cost—he knew that, had been aware of that for years—but with Switch the price had been very high. No matter the glory, the fame, the adulation of young colleagues, and the respect of contemporaries, in Switch he had come face-to-face with a degree of blackness which haunted him even now, two years after the final trial.

After the book came out and the miniseries was broadcast, they'd tried to take him off cases. "We've got a thousand detectives to work cases, Frank," his chief had told him. "But you, you're something else, you've become a real asset. What do you say we put you on the fast track, get you ready for a field command?"

When he replied that he didn't want to go on the career fast track and that a command position wasn't for him, he saw the same skeptical expression he'd seen on superiors' faces since the day he'd come on the force, the look that told him he was being regarded as a maverick. He didn't care. Without cases to perplex him, taunt him in the night, he would begin to think about himself. And then he would have to deal with his greatest failing, his apparent inability to sustain a relationship with a woman.

For years he and his best friend and partner, Aaron Greenberg, had laughed over his "poor choices," his "bad luck," his weakness for "problem females." But lately the joke had stopped being funny. He had begun to fear the loneliness of middle age. Twice in the last six months he'd driven alone down to Atlantic City, walked into a casino, tanked up at the bar, bet and lost a week's pay at the blackjack tables. Then he'd driven back home in the dark, almost reveling in his loss of self-esteem.

Those episodes had frightened him. He didn't want to end up like so many detectives he had known, men who'd put in their time on the streets, done the job, retired after honorable careers to lead quiet, lonely, orderly lives. Until, usually on the eve of a winter holiday, the family next door would be awakened by a single shot in the middle of the night.

What he needed now was a chance to focus on who he was and where he was going with his life. And to consider, too, what form his redemption should take, redemption from his melancholy and despair. But it would never have occurred to him to combine that quest with his long-held dream of seeing Venice if Kit Kopta hadn't decided to send him to Lugano.

"You need a change, Frank. I've got just the thing for you," she said when he presented himself, obedient to her summons, at her office.

The room, large and square, seemed to dwarf her, for she was a small, lean forty-five-year-old woman with fine, sharp features, a mane of thick black hair, and dusty Mediterranean skin. Her eyes were her most prominent feature: big brown eyes that burned beneath dark Grecian brows. She'd been appointed Chief of Detectives three months earlier, the first woman ever to hold the position, the highest-ranking female cop in NYPD history. Now she was looking after her own.

"There's a detectives' conference coming up in Switzerland. A couple hundred of the top people from all over the world. We've been asked to send our best man. That's you, Frank. You're the one they want."

He squirmed in his chair. "Uh-uh, Kit. Please . . ."

She grinned, then shook her head. "You're not getting out of this one. They asked for you. They'll pay for everything. All you've got to do is give a little talk."

"About the Switch?"

She nodded. "I know you're sick of it. But a whole bunch of European detectives wants to hear how you solved it."

"I got nothing new to tell them. It's all in the goddamn book."

"Doesn't matter. They want to hear it out of your mouth. Face it, Frank—you're a star. So you might as well enjoy it instead of acting like it's a heavy burden you have to carry around." She squinted at him. "Anyway, it's not an option."

Janek laughed. "You're *ordering* me to go?"

"We take a bad rap here. Murder City. Five to ten fresh homicides a day."

She linked her fingers, then set her hands straight in front of her. *Just like a chief,* he thought.

". . . so if some big shot foreign cops want to hear what it's like playing detective in New York, we're going to accommodate them." She paused. "I checked your caseload. You've got nothing much going. When you get back, that's going to change. I want you to attend the conference, then take a vacation, two, three weeks, anywhere you like. The point is get some rest, come back here feeling good. A month from now I don't want to see you dragging your ass around. Okay?"

"Look, I appreciate—"

"This isn't charity, Frank. I need you in good condition."

"For what?"

"We'll discuss it when you get back."

Janek looked at her. He knew her well. They'd been lovers for two months twenty years before and then had parted bitterly. Five years after they split, they ran into each other at a police banquet, hit a bar together afterward for a drink, discovered they liked each other, and started dining out once a month. What had begun with sex, then soured to dislike had developed into a deep and mellow friendship. Janek thought of Kit Kopta as one of his half dozen closest friends in the department.

"Thinking of making me your special assistant?"

"Maybe something like that."

"People will talk, Kit."

"Let 'em talk. We won't give a shit, will we, Frank?"

Janek smiled. "Still the ballsy broad."

"I don't define myself that way. I like to think I'm . . . feline."

"Feline!"

Her eyes burned defiantly. "What's the matter?"

"Nothing. Just that in a Chief of Detectives 'feline' isn't what people expect."

She nodded. "People, as you call them, are going to have a lot of novel experiences now that I'm chief." She stood to signal the interview was over. "So it's settled. You're going to Lugano, then taking leave. Who knows, Frank? You might even enjoy yourself." She smiled. "Wouldn't that be different?"

"It would be," he said. "It sure as hell would."

Kit stepped out from behind her desk. "Give me a hug," she ordered. Janek hugged her.

"'Ballsy broad'!" She laughed. "You gotta be kidding, Frank."

He didn't much enjoy the conference, even though he was lionized. British, French, German, Dutch—every detective in Europe seemed to know about Switched Heads. "I'd give my left ball for a case like that," one Australian inspector confided.

His talk was well attended. After he finished, he politely fielded questions for an hour and could have gone on indefinitely except that the hall was needed for a symposium on computer crime.

Afterward a mustachioed Spanish police captain, famous for single-handedly tracking down a cell of Basque terrorists, asked Janek to join him for a drink. The Spaniard, proud of his own achievement, said he would have preferred to have solved a great psychological case like the Switch.

"The young ones here, all they talk about is DNA fingerprinting," he said, gesturing at a group of husky young detectives hovering around the busy hotel bar. "They don't understand that the great cases, the only ones that can justify living the best part of your life in the gutter, are crimes of the wounded spirit. And the detectives who solves crimes like that are men like us, men who have wounds of our own. . . ."

After dinner Janek walked by himself through the deserted arcade of shops facing Lake Lugano, then crossed the avenue and paused to gaze across the water, seeking out the farther shore. It was lost in mist. The lake's surface was smooth, like an expanse of black glass, and the lamps along the embankment, huge lanterns on bronze pedestals, burned gaseous and yellow in the murky night.

He thought about what the Spanish captain had said: "Wounds of our own . . ." *What are my wounds?* he asked himself. *How many have I got?* A long, loveless marriage that had ended in a bitter divorce, a few affairs that had ended badly, a lot of experience with the worst sort of people and the attendant law enforcer's disillusionment. A picture came into his mind, a network of scars, old and deep, crisscrossing his middle-aged torso. He shook his head; he didn't like the image. He turned away from the water and started back toward the hotel.

Once again under the arcade, the window of a travel agency caught his eye. He halted and stared in. A poster showed a gondolier in silhouette against sparkling water and the dark outline of a great domed church. The words below were few and to the point: VENICE THE DREAM.

The next morning he returned and bought himself a ticket.

It was a morose autumnal Venice he had come to. The first afternoon the air turned chilly; after that he wore a raincoat when he walked. It was mid-October, near the end of the season, and there weren't many tourists. The Piazza San Marco was inhabited mostly by pigeons, and Caffè Florian was deserted, its waiters lonely sentinels guarding neat rows of empty seats.

He bought a guidebook, then set out to explore in a studious manner, intending to work his way through a list of churches, museums, bridges, palaces of cultural importance. But he soon realized that it was not great paintings of the Crucifixion that interested him; it was the lore of the old republic, her hardness, her cruelties. He understood, with a start, that it was her crimes he wanted to understand.

When he learned, for instance, that state enemies were once routinely executed by being drowned secretly in the middle of the night, he hastened to the Orphan Canal, where the drownings were alleged to have taken place. And he was equally fascinated by tales surrounding the feared Council of Ten and the even more greatly feared

Three Inquisitors—tales of informers, night arrests, mysterious disappearances, undisclosed detentions, paid government assassins, official torturings, stranglings, knifings, poisonings, and beheadings, public and private, justified and capricious, the bodies often displayed without explanation between the "fatal pillars" in the Piazzetta. To live as a Venetian in the time of the republic, he understood, was to reside in a paranoid's nightmare. Stealth, vengeance, institutionalized terror—these, too, were among the traditions of La Serenissima. They were traditions he understood at least as well as the dignity of the churches and the grace of the bridges and canals.

As there was nothing to do at night, he went to an English-language bookstore, bought a copy of stories by Thomas Mann, and began to read *Death in Venice* after dinner in his room.

A dense and dreary tale, he thought, about a famous middle-aged German writer, hitherto tightly controlled, who finds his fate in Venice, intoxicated by a pale adolescent boy. The novel cut deeper than that, of course, was about form and formlessness, art and obsession, rationality and madness. Janek understood it, could savor its intricate design, but in the end he could not identify with its hero. Aschenbach, author of great books, and Janek, solver of a "great" case—both outsiders, lonely men, who had come to Venice on a quest. But while Aschenbach sought the abyss, Janek wanted only to crawl out of it, to be redeemed.

He noticed the woman several times before he really looked at her, and then, it seemed, he saw her everywhere, until, in his mind at least, their intersections became something of a joke.

She was a Northern European, most likely Austrian or Swiss, though possibly a German or a Dane. A stunning, stylish person, she looked to be in her late thirties. Very well put together, too: excellent figure, proud walk, handsome face, precision-cut blond hair. She wore exquisite clothes, well-cut slacks, elegant suede boots, and, over a salmon blouse, the finest, softest, blackest leather jacket he had ever seen. He liked the way she wore her silk scarf tied smartly at the side of her neck.

But it was far more than her style and grooming that caught his interest; it was, above all else, her eyes. Large soft gray-green eyes, sensitive, yearning—they reminded him of the eyes of the great French movie star of the forties Michele Morgan.

It became a game with him: Could he choose a church or museum at random, go there, and *not* run into her? There were other tourists trekking their way through Venice, but she seemed the only one on the same track as himself. How were they connected? Were their consciousnesses linked? Perhaps they should sit down and discuss it. But first she would have to recognize him and acknowledge the humor of their meetings.

For a while he was certain she didn't notice him, or else, he decided, she was the coolest woman in Venice. Then, while eating lunch alone in Harry's Bar, he saw her enter, pause, peruse the room, smile (or did he merely imagine that she did?) as she sighted him, then quickly turn away. He smiled back but was too late; she was on her way to a table at the opposite end. He watched to see if she was joining a companion, was relieved to see her sit down alone.

Relieved. What right had he to feel that way? The answer came to him almost at once. She was so damn attractive! Everything about her, her gestures, the way she moved . . . he knew he *had* to meet her. And the first step was to find out who she was.

In New York there would be no problem. He would simply follow her to her hotel, flash his shield at the clerk, and ask. But here in Venice he had no status, was but one of five thousand end-of-the-season stragglers in a centuries-long parade.

However, after three days of fortuitous encounters, he decided that he *would* follow her. A crazy idea, a little too close, perhaps, to Aschenbach's pursuit of the boy. But the notion appealed to him. He was a detective; he had the skills and also great curiosity. She certainly interested him more than any lifeless work of art. Let the tarted-up old whore of a city offer her meretricious charms to someone else. The lonely middle-aged detective from North America would track the live young beauty through her streets.

He picked her up outside Palazzo Ca' d'Oro. *How amazing,* he thought, *that I knew she'd come here!* He hung back, waiting, and then, as she wandered the galleries, began carefully to stalk her. She paused a long while before Mantegna's painting of St. Sebastian. Perhaps the naked, limp, pierced body of the executed saint excited her. Or else (and he hoped this was true) it aroused her compassion.

She boarded the No. 1 vaporetto. No difficulty following her onto the crowded ferry; he had only to linger among the workers to remain unseen. She disembarked at Pontile Sant' Angelo, and there he almost missed her; he nearly didn't make it off.

She began to walk down narrow alleyways and to cross little bridges, as if wandering irregularly without a plan. As he followed, he tried to stay a building's distance back. Once, when she stopped, he stopped as well. Then he watched as she consulted her map.

She entered an elegant women's store. Beautiful shoes and fine silk dresses were displayed in the window. She reappeared after fifteen minutes, and he was gratified that she carried no packages. Then she went into a tiny boutique that sold marbled papers and hand-bound note-books. When she came out, she carried a shopping bag embellished with a golden lion.

Look at what I'm doing: making up a personality for her, just the way I would for a criminal!

He was tempted to stop right there, leave her alone, retreat. But it was too late. He was fascinated. The game was on, and now he must play it out.

Seeing that she was following a narrow street that would dead-end on the Grand Canal and thus force her to return and meet him face-to-face, he cleverly moved to a parallel alley, then walked beside her, invisible though only a few feet away. Trying to match his steps to the soft thud of her boots upon the stones, he could not deny to himself that he was thrilled.

She carried a camera, a viewfinder Leica, but he didn't see her use it until she paused before a tiny violin shop near the Fenice Theater. Then she stepped back onto a delicately scaled footbridge and carefully composed a shot. After she moved on, he stood where she had stood and saw what she had seen: three fiddles hanging in the shop doorway reflected in the canal beneath the shadow of the bridge. It would make a fine picture, he thought. And then: *Perhaps I am beginning to know her a little bit.*

She looked more at home when she reached the Piazza

San Marco. She paused at its entrance, peered ahead, then crossed it with brisk, athletic strides. She paused again, to look up at the campanile, then moved rapidly into the Doges' Palace.

The Bridge of Straw; the Bridge of Sighs: he crossed them both close behind her, employing a small French-speaking group as his shield.

He followed her across the vast marble floor of the Sala del Maggior Consiglio and was surprised that she did not give even a glance to the huge Tintoretto on the wall.

Something was different about her. She seemed impatient, annoyed. Her forehead was creased, her stride anxious. She glanced at her watch. Did she have a date? Was she apprehensive about it? Was she meeting a man?

She backtracked to Santa Maria Formosa, then paused to study the stone head of a monster. Slowly he was learning more about her. Now, it seemed, she was interested in the grotesque.

Surely something was bothering her, for she abruptly turned again, and this time it was hopeless to avoid her. He walked straight past her, refusing to meet her eyes, circled, and deftly picked her up again as she headed rapidly back through the Piazzetta, then along the wide expanse that follows St. Mark's Canal.

Along the Riva degli Schiavoni, then, very briskly, tensely, across the Bridge of Wine and the Bridge of Piety to the open portion of the waterfront where old Venetians huddled on wooden benches trying to catch the faint heat cast by the brilliant October sun.

She was out of the labyrinth, in the open, and suddenly he knew why. *She's made me! Damn!* Too late now to retreat. A queasy feeling as he understood she was going to confront him. *Damn! Nothing I can do.* He would have to try to brave it out.

But when she finally turned on him, as he knew she would, she did not show an angry face. Rather, she smiled teasingly as she raised her camera and began to take his picture. Once, twice, then rapidly five more times, moving closer at each exposure, until, when she finally lowered the Leica, she was but three yards from his face.

"Do you speak English?" she asked with a German accent. He nodded. "I believe you're following me. You will please explain?"

She smiled as she waited for his response, and again he was struck by the beauty of her eyes. Also by her confidence. *She's got me, and she knows it. No choice. I'll have to own up.*

"I'm embarrassed. . . ." He grinned foolishly, feeling himself tongue-tied.

"American?" He nodded. "Do you know me? Have we met?" He shook his head. "I must interest you very much," she said, rolling her eyes in mock wonderment.

He grinned again, then caught himself. She was making him feel like a boy. "To tell the truth—"

"The truth! Yes, we must definitely have the truth!" she purred. "Because, you must know this, it is very rude to follow a woman through the streets. Adolescent Italian males do it, but a mature man and an American—that's quite unexpected. Frankly I would not have thought an American gentleman capable of such a thing."

She stared at him, levelly, waiting for his reply. And this time, he knew, she would wait until he gave her satisfaction.

"Yes," he admitted, "I was following you. I apologize. It was stupid of me and very rude. But please believe me, I intended no harm. I hope you won't call the police.''

"Why should I want to do that?" she asked with a slight smirk. She was amused now, enjoying his discomfort.

Fine with me, he thought. *Keeps it between us. I'll take any humiliation so long as she doesn't bring in the cops.*

"You took my picture," he said. "If you felt harassed, then I understand you might want—"

"But I didn't feel harassed. I was flattered. You have a kind face. I knew you wouldn't bother me. If I ask you now, you will leave me alone. Correct?"

"That is certainly correct," he agreed.

She paused, then introduced herself. "My name is Dr. Daskai."

A doctor! He would never have guessed it. "Mine's Janek," he replied, again feeling dumb.

She offered her hand. He took it. They shook.

"And what do you do, Mr. Janek?"

"I'm a tourist—"

She shook her head; she would not accept evasions. "You know what I'm asking. In your professional life?"

He hesitated. "I'm a New York City detective."

"Do you have credentials?" He nodded. "May I see them?"

He showed her his ID and shield. She examined both carefully.

"A New York City lieutenant of detectives following me through the streets of Venice." She shook her head and rolled her eyes again. "I would *never* have imagined this."

"It was a bad mistake."

"Really?" She was skeptical. "Did you think I was someone else?"

"I was attracted to you, I wanted to meet you, but I was too shy to approach. We kept running into each other, and you didn't seem to notice."

"Oh, but you're wrong. I noticed," she said.

Janek stared down. "Look, I'm really embarrassed. First, because I followed you, which I had absolutely no right to do. And secondly, because, well . . . I'm supposed to be able to follow people without their knowing I am."

"In New York perhaps. Here you stand out."

"I understand that now."

"Well?" She stared at him.

"I guess I'm not as good a detective as I thought," he offered humbly. Perhaps there was still hope; he could see another smile growing on her face. "I realize under the circumstances what I'm about to ask will seem like a pretty shameless question."

"What question?"

"You have every right to refuse." She stared at him curiously. He paused, then took the plunge. "Would you let me buy you a drink?"

She reacted with mock horror. "Now he wants to offer me a drink!"

"You're right. Enough is enough. I'm sorry." He stepped back, ready to withdraw. "I won't follow you again. I promise. I feel like such a jerk—"

"Actually I am thirsty," she said.

Startled, he studied her face. She was smiling broadly now. *What does she think of me?* he wondered. *Attractive and shy? Or a lonely American buffoon?*

"I'm staying nearby, at the Danieli. The bar there

seems very pleasant.'' She stared into his eyes. ''Shall we try it? Of course, I insist on paying for myself.''

Her first name was Monika. She was a psychiatrist. She lived just outside Hamburg and was a member of the medical school faculty there. She also had a specialized psychoanalytic practice—private patients she saw in the afternoons. She had written two books, one about the nature of rage, the other about narcissism and art. She was thirty-nine years old, widowed and childless. Her husband, an older man who had been first her teacher and then her mentor, had died of cancer the year before.

She didn't travel much; she didn't have the time. Her work was demanding, and she thrived on it. She had come to Venice on a private visit; she and her husband had taken their wedding trip here ten years before.

She had been hesitant about returning, afraid she would be haunted by memories, fearful she would slip back into the depression that had seized her after her husband had been buried and that had only begun to lift the last few months. So, in a certain sense, coming to Venice had been a test. Could she rediscover the city by herself, take pleasure in its beauty and art, or would it forever be tainted for her by nostalgia and regret?

He told her as much about himself as she had told him. And the longer they talked, the more he felt that there was nothing he would want to keep hidden. But then, on account of a few little things she let drop, he realized she knew more about him than he'd revealed.

''Yes,'' she admitted when he confronted her, ''as soon as I saw your credentials, I knew who you were. I read a book, *Tödlicher Tausch* it's called in German. I'm not sure what that would be in English. Maybe something like 'The Deadly Swap.'"

"Switch," Janek said.

She nodded. "Well, anyway, I knew you must be the same Janek who solved that strange case in New York. The one with the switched heads. But I can tell by the way you're looking at me that that's the last thing you want to talk about."

He nodded, pleased she was so intuitive.

"Perhaps you came here to escape it," she added.

My God! he asked himself. *Does this woman have any imperfections?*

"So, in a sense," she continued, "we have both come here to escape our pasts. Can the brilliant fire that is Venice burn away our ghosts?" She smiled. "I know it doesn't work that way, and I believe you know it, too. Travel is probably the worst form of escape. People carry their baggage wherever they go. But still, it's a wonderful romantic illusion, the idea of going to a place where the colors are bright, the light brilliant, the art incandescent. But now I am ashamed. I'm talking too much. I think I've spent too many hours as prisoner of my patients, listening, always listening, and now I am feeling free and letting loose. Poor you"—she gently touched his hand—"to be *my* prisoner now, to have to hear me babble on. . . ."

He looked into her gray-green eyes, eyes so full of yearning. Slanting beams crossed the barroom, found her irises, entered them, and broke into a spectrum.

"I love listening to you," he said. Then he turned away.

"Why do you turn from me?" she asked softly.

"Forgive me," he said. "I'm blinded."

"Then we must move to another table." She began to rise.

"No, no," he said, touching her hand. "It's all right. It's not the light. It's something else."

"What?" she asked, intense now, curious.

"You," he said.

"Me?"

He nodded. "I'm blinded by the beauty of your eyes."

To hold her, kiss and touch her—that was like a dream. His true dream of Venice perhaps, though he hadn't know it when, for so many years, he had dreamed of coming to this city. The way she made love was subtle, but he did not feel clumsy with her as he sometimes did with women whom he thought of as elegant or fine. She made it seem very natural that they should lie together in her room—her wonderful room, No. 13, where, according to the plaque outside the door, the great French novelist George Sand had lived for a brief time in the winter of 1833 with her lover, poet Alfred de Musset.

"They parted disastrously," Monika whispered to him as they lay together afterward, lightly tangled. "Musset fell ill; then Sand ran off with his doctor." She caressed him fondly. "Musset never got over it. It was the defining trauma of his life."

They made love again, more tempestuously the second time, and then Janek could not quite believe what he was feeling. Something in him was being released. The heaviness was lifting; a wonderful new buoyancy was taking its place. Her steamy skin burned against his body. Their sweat ran together and formed a seal.

"I haven't done this since . . ." She turned to him,

eyes glowing. "You're the first man I've been with since my husband died." Her fine eyes queried him. "It's been awhile for you, too, hasn't it?"

He nodded. "It feels good to make love again."

"Oh, yes. . . ." She showered kisses on his chest. "Frank, Frank. . . ." She made his name seem marvelous by pronouncing it in German. "It's very good. Very healthy. I think it must have been for this that I came to Venice." She licked his neck in long, even strokes. "But is this really happening?" She tenderly stroked his sex. "Yes, it is. And I *love* it. I'm so happy you followed me."

She looked up at him, her smile so bright, her eyes so brilliant—but this time he did not flinch, this time he drank in her light.

He took her to dinner at Antico Martini on the Campo San Fantin across from the Fenice Theater. There was only one other couple on the terrace, but they agreed they liked being in a nearly empty restaurant.

"Tonight Venice belongs just to us," she said.

He told her about himself, his marriage and divorce, his ambivalent affection for New York, how the Switch Case had changed his life, and how much he loved investigative work.

"You love it because you're good at it, isn't that right?" He nodded. "Tell me about it, Frank. What sort of detective are you?"

"Basically there're two kinds," he explained. "Scientists and artists. The scientists are puzzle solvers. They pore over evidence, figure out what's absent, then go after the missing piece. I'm probably more the artist type. I try to feel the case, identify with the perp, then generate the insight that will bring it all together. For me, the best cases are the psychological ones, where to solve them you have to go inside a mind and touch the madness."

"You're really a psychologist," she said.

"In a way—but I have no training in it. I operate on instinct. And often what I do isn't very civilized, Monika. Underneath I'm still a street cop. And New York is one very tough town."

She nodded. "Will you forgive me if I ask you a personal question?"

"I think we've been pretty personal with each other so far."

She smiled. "You're famous. You've been the subject of a book and a movie. I ask you this because I realize it must be your choice: Why are you only a lieutenant?"

Her question amused him, but he gave her a serious answer. "I won't take a field command," he explained, "which is what an officer above lieutenant is obliged to do. If I stay a lieutenant—well, I keep thinking I'll be able to work cases until I retire."

"Tell me why you like them so much?"

"First, the problem, then the fun of the chase, the joy when I get the flash, figure out who did it and, most important, why. You see, once I know that, I can usually persuade the person to confess, not just because I've got the goods on him but because my understanding of him usually makes him want to explain himself even more. Then through his confession I relive the experience of the crime. And once I've shared that, it's over."

"So you like confessions?"

He nodded. "Much better than building a case for trial. For me when a crime is committed, a wound is opened . . . and I want to be the one who closes it. An honest confession is the best kind of closure I know.''

She gazed at him. ''Perhaps then you are something between a psychologist and a priest.''

He shook his head. ''I can't absolve anybody. I haven't the right. But I always try to grant criminals their humanity. To help them? Partly. But I think it's really for myself. There's so much evil in this world, Monika. Perhaps a billion varieties of evil. The kind of work I do, and believe me it's very humble sometimes, puts me in touch with evil every day. And strange as this may seem, I think it's helped me gain a little wisdom. Though sometimes, I have to admit, I don't feel all that wise. Like this afternoon, for instance—following you around. That was very childish.''

''Boyish.'' She corrected him. ''I'm so glad you were boyish. It was exciting to feel pursued.'' She met his eyes. ''If you're not a cross between a psychologist and a priest, then what exactly are you, Frank?''

He shrugged. ''Just a detective,'' he said.

They spent the night together in her room. Early the next morning Janek moved out of his hotel near the Giardino Papadopoli and into a single at the Danieli, just down the hall from No. 13.

''Every morning I'll sneak back in and ruffle up my bedding,'' he told her.

She was amused. ''That won't fool the chambermaids.''

''I'm sure it won't, but I hope they'll appreciate my efforts.''

''What do you want them to think? That you're discreet?''

Janek shook his head. "I want them to know I am protective of the German lady's reputation."

She laughed, then hugged him. "You're a very funny man."

Janek hired a speedboat to take them to Torcello, where they lunched on grilled fresh scampi, then explored the island's little lanes. In the Cathedral of Santa Maria Assunta they stood in awe before the apse, meeting the grave gaze of the Teotoca Madonna, whose cheeks are laced with mosaic tears.

To eat, make love, experience the beauty of Venice— these things became their enterprise. She had much to teach him about art, and he had much to teach her about the streets. On golden mornings they wandered the city, strolling along her white and ocher walls, upon her stone and marble alleys, across her rainbow-hued canals. They watched glass being blown. They sat in cafés and made up tales about the people who passed. They told each other the stories of their lives.

Then, late in the afternoon, when the sweet fragrance of autumnal decay mingled with the saline scent of the lagoon, the heady aroma aroused their lust and drew them back to No. 13 and to her bed. Here, as the sun painted the walls gold and pink, they kissed, grew intoxicated, rolled together, and explored each other with their tongues. They made love lazily until darkness fell. Then they slept for an hour in each other's arms, showered, and went out to dine.

Monika's husband, Franz Daskai, was thirty years older than she. A handsome, athletic man with leonine features and a full head of iron gray hair, he had been chief of psychiatry at the Hamburg hospital where she had served out her residency. One day he stopped to watch her play tennis on the staff court behind the residents' dormitory. A couple of days later he called her to his office to invite her to be his doubles partner in an informal interhospital tournament. She accepted; they battled fiercely and to everyone's amazement won the cup. A few months later, when she began to see patients, she asked him to be her supervising analyst. A year later they were married.

Franz, Monika told Janek, was a wise, sane man who was an exemplar to all his students. The men worshiped him, and the women adored him, perhaps because he was one of the few people in the profession who lived the kind of rational life that is the supposed goal of psycho-analysis.

Over their ten years together he had taught her much, but she believed his most memorable lesson was the eloquent way he defined the mission of a therapist. At some point in every patient's past, he believed, there occurs a character-distorting moment when an emotion and an experience, normally incompatible, come together and lock. Abuse and love, shame and pleasure—no matter how contradictory, the pieces engage so the person can survive his fear and rage. It then becomes the task of the therapist to locate this hidden lock, analyze its parts, then gently open it up to set the patient free.

"He taught me how to be a healer," Monika said. "This was his greatest gift. When, that first evening, you spoke of crimes as wounds and your role as detective-confessor—well, I thought, you and Franz would have liked each other. I think he would have understood you."

"And that's very important to you?" he asked.

"Yes," she said. "I believe it is."

As Monika was due back in Hamburg the following Monday, she and Janek planned to spend their final weekend together visiting some of the famous villas of Veneto. Instead of reveling further in the marvelous stage set that is Venice, they would seek composure in the mainland in Palladio's rational geometry.

But very early Saturday morning, even before the dawn, the phone rang in Monika's room. The call, surprisingly, was for Janek. He began to complain: Although the management no doubt knew he was sleeping in Dr. Daskai's room, it really had no right to ring him there. . . . Then he stopped. A familiar voice had come on the line. Immediately he felt a portent of woe.

"Frank, it's Kit. Tough job to track you down. But the Venice police are pretty good. Course, we had to kick some ass."

Something was wrong. "There's trouble, isn't there?"

"Yeah, Frank." Her tone was grave. "There is."

"Please don't stall. Just tell me, okay?"

"It's Jess."

His goddaughter. *Oh, God!* "What happened?"

"Stabbed, Frank. She was jogging in the park, and someone, we don't know who—"

"She's going to be all right?" But even as he asked, he knew the answer.

"Uh-uh, she's not. She's dead. I'm so sorry to be the one to have to tell you."

Something piercing like a silent scream burst across his brain.

". . . listening, Frank? Laura Dorance called, asked

me to find you and let you know. She hopes you can come back. The funeral's tomorrow afternoon. What shall I tell her?''

''Tell her I'll be there,'' Janek said. Then he set down the phone, turned from Monika, faced the window, and wept.

''Jesus! She was just a kid! Twenty years old! A junior in college!'' They were in Janek's narrow room, Monika watching from the bed as, frantic and bitter, Janek paced and ranted while throwing his clothes into his bag.

Suddenly he stopped and turned to her.

''I can't believe it! I can't.'' He sat down beside her. She hugged him.

''I loved her, Monika. So much . . .''

In the lobby, after he had booked his flight, Janek gulped down three cappuccinos.

''Her father, Tim Foy—he and I were partners for five years. Then Tim transferred to narcotics, worked under-cover, was found out, and assassinated. One morning he went out to his car, parked as usual in front of his house. He turned the key, and the car blew up—twenty pounds of dynamite. Jess, who was five at the time, was watching from the kitchen window. He waved to her; she waved back; then her whole world exploded before her eyes. According to Laura, she didn't start crying for a minute, just stared, confused, at the place where Tim's car had been. Tim, you see, was something of an amateur magician. Maybe Jess thought he was playing a trick. Some trick! They never found all the pieces of him. Her tears, God! They flowed and flowed. Later we learned her hearing got damaged, too. . . .''

* * *

They entered St. Mark's. The cathedral was deserted. The aroma of the incense was cloying and thick. Janek fell to his knees on the hard stones before the altar. Monika knelt beside him and held his hand as he prayed.

Afterward they did a tour of the piazza. It would be their final walk together in Venice.

"My wife and I never had children. So Jess was like my own daughter. When Laura was struggling, I was over at her place all the time, helping with Jess, baby-sitting, assisting with homework, telling stories. I even taught her how to play baseball in Flushing Park. That's when I realized she could be an athlete. She turned out to be a damn good one, too. She's on the Columbia University women's fencing team. Or, I should say, she was. . . ."

Monika held tightly to his hand.

Even after Laura Foy went to law school, met and married Stanton Dorance, and she and Jess moved into Dorance's big apartment on Park Avenue—even then Janek remained close to the girl.

"What a waste, Monika. A fine young life like that! What a terrible waste." He paused, then spoke quietly. "I don't think I could have loved my own child more."

He sat with Monika in the rear of the chartered speedboat, racing for the airport, knowing that now his life would be forever changed.

"I headed up the team that went after Tim Foy's killer. Today they won't let you work a case that's personal, but back then you could swing a deal or two. Anyway, it didn't take us long to find the guy who built and placed the bomb. A scrawny little character; I can't even remember his name. Anyway, we caught him, turned him, and he gave us the guy who ordered it done, a slimy, rat-faced drug dealer. He's serving a life sentence now.'' Janek squeezed her hand. ''Sorry to make you listen to all this sordid stuff.''

''Keep talking, Frank. I don't find it sordid.'' She touched his face, then gently kissed his cheek. ''I want to stay with you as long as possible, stay close to you before you fly off.''

''I wouldn't have had anyone to talk to if I hadn't found you.''

''Well, we found each other, didn't we?''

Janek peered around. Venice was lost in mist behind. Ahead the lagoon was as still and flat and white as it had been the morning he arrived. The rising vapor carried the same faint sweet salt-marsh smell of decay.

''I wonder if I'll ever be able to come back here now. That call from Kit—I think I'll always associate it with Venice. The call . . . that broke my heart.''

He didn't turn away from her this time, didn't mind now if she saw his tears. And when she mopped his cheeks with her fine silk scarf, he kissed her hand and whispered, ''Thanks. . . .''

At the airport there was time to call Aaron Greenberg and arrange to be met in New York.

''Aaron and I work together,'' he told Monika in the coffee bar on the airport roof. ''He knew Jess, too. He says the tabloids are full of it. Stanton, Jess's stepfather, is a big corporation lawyer. He and Laura—I feel so sorry for them. They say the worst thing that can happen to you is to lose a child. You never get over it, they say. . . .''

* * *

Monika accompanied him to the security gate. There he put down his bags so they could embrace.

"This can't be good-bye. I don't want to lose you."

"We're not going to lose each other. Don't even think that," she said.

"You've been the best thing to happen to me in years."

"I feel the same. We'll stay close. Somehow we'll manage to see each other, perhaps sooner than you think."

"I'll phone you tomorrow night."

The final call for his flight was announced. It was time to go. He hugged her as tight as he could. Then, just before he reached down for his bags, she handed him a package.

"I bought this for myself, before I met you." She smiled. "Now I want you to have it. Please take it, Frank."

On the plane, somewhere between Venice and Rome, he carefully unwrapped her gift. It was a fine antique Venetian wineglass, pure Renaissance in style, nothing fancy, no spirals or wavy bands of color, just a simple graceful transparent cone set upon an octagonal base.

As Janek held it to the window so the wondrous light of the Italian sky could play upon it and fill it up, he knew, by the way it reminded him of the clear, yearning beauty of Monika's eyes, that it was the choicest piece of glass he had seen in Venice.

3

Conversation with Mama

"Can you hear me, dear?"

"I can hear you, Mama."

"It's getting to be time again."

"Yes, Mama."

"Remember, it's not enough to feel the pain and then the fury. You've got to do something about it. Got to fix them good."

"I understand, Mama."

"He deserves it. Doesn't he?"

"Oh, he deserves it! He surely does deserve it!"

"So?"

"I'll use Tool again."

"What will you do to him?"

"The same as to the others."

"Let's hear you say it."

"Fix him. Shut him up forever."

"*Why,* child?"

"Because of what he did."

"And what was that?"

"Must I, Mama? Please!"

"You *must*! You know you *must*! Now tell me what he did."

"He was unkind."

"*Ha!*"

"*Very* unkind!"

"Don't make me laugh."

"Well, he *was*."

"Of course, he *was,* you goose. But what did he *do*? Tell me!"

"*Insulted* me."

"Is that *all*?"

"*Hurt* me."

"Is that really all he did? Come on, child. Spill your guts."

"He *harmed* me."

"Can't say it, can you?"

"I can say it, Mama. I can say it all right. It hurts me to say it. But I *can*."

"Then say it, for God's sakes. *Say it!*"

"He—"

"*What?*"

"Humiliated me."

"Don't whimper, child. Say it loud."

"*He humiliated me!*"

"Yep, that's what he did. So what're you going to do about it?"

"Pay him back."

"How?"

"Use Tool."

"Use Tool to do *what*?"

"Kill him."

"And?"

"Fix him!"

"And?"

"Shut him up!"

"For how long?"

"Forever."

"Say it again."

"Kill him and fix him and shut him up forever."

"There, that's the ticket. You got it, child. Yeah, you got it now."

4
Jess

On the Van Wyck Expressway, peering out of Aaron Greenberg's beaten-up Chevrolet, Janek felt malice in the air. Traffic was heavy. People sat rigid and angry in their cars. Cold rain pelted the asphalt through noxious yellow fog, while all around he could hear the biting sound of horns and, in the distance, competing sirens, perhaps a fire truck and an ambulance at odds.

He touched the window. Ice-cold. The wiper slapped back and forth. The city ahead, toward which they were moving at such erratic speed, could not yet be seen, but Janek could feel it, could feel its nasty breath, its rancor.

He turned back to Aaron, who sat straight in his seat, concentrating on the road. A short, taut, wiry man with weather-beaten skin, his eyes and smile were sweet. *My partner and best friend,* Janek thought. Kit would gladly have sent her car, but only Aaron, he knew, would come out to Kennedy Airport on such a day to meet him and bring him in.

"New York's got no gender."

Aaron peered ahead curiously. "What?"

"Venice is a 'she.' New York's an 'it,'" Janek said.

"Well, what do you expect, Frank? I mean, Venice is pretty. New York's not supposed to be."

Janek glanced at him. "You haven't told me any-thing."

Aaron continued to stare ahead. "Been waiting for you to ask."

"How bad was it?" He held his breath as he waited for the reply.

Aaron exhaled. "I don't know how to put it quite."

"Try." The floor pads in the car smelled wet and old.

"Worse than you think, Frank. Worse than you think."

They rode in silence for a time; then Janek asked Aaron to give it to him straight. Never mind the niceties. Just straight, like they were starting out on a case and Aaron was filling him in.

"All I got so far is what I heard around. The detective in charge didn't get back to me yet."

"What's his name?"

"Ray Boyce."

"Never heard of him."

"Neither have I."

"Well . . . ?"

Aaron winced. "She was done with an ice pick in Riverside Park, not far from her dorm room at Columbia. It was early evening. She went out jogging alone. That wasn't approved; but she did it a lot, and she wasn't the only one. Plenty of other kids run alone in the dark. I don't know where they think they're living. Nicetown, USA? Anyway, it was about seven. No witnesses. Nobody saw nothing. She never returned to her room. She didn't have a roommate, so she wasn't missed. In fact, well I don't know if I ought—"

"Don't try and spare me, Aaron."

Aaron nodded. "Understand, Frank, this is just what I

heard. Seems she spent a lot of nights away. She had boyfriends. Again, she wasn't the only one. Other kids—''

"Okay, I get the picture. Go on."

"Every morning, early, the Columbia men's crew goes running as a group. They found her and called her in. Apparently nothing was taken, not that she was carrying much. But she had a watch and a Walkman. If it was a mugger, that's what you'd expect him to take."

"So it wasn't a mugger?"

"Doesn't look like it."

"Who was it then? Pack of animals on a wilding, like the ones smashed up that stockbroker a couple years back?"

"Doesn't look like that either."

"What does it look like?"

"Take it easy, Frank. You're closing in too fast. I don't know what it looks like. Like I said, Boyce didn't get back to me yet."

"Check him out?"

Aaron nodded. "He's okay."

"So-so's what you mean."

Aaron shrugged. "They can't all be stars, Frank. Boyce got the call. So it's his."

Aaron was right, that's the way it worked, and it was a stinking system, too, because a good 20 percent of the detective force was barely so-so, and when it came to Janek's goddaughter, so-so wasn't going to be good enough.

He turned to the back of the car. Aaron had spread the tabloids across the rear seat. Janek's eyes flew across them. The headlines shrieked.

"If it wasn't a mugger or a pack on a rampage, who the hell was it?"

"Could have been a mugger," Aaron said. "He could have gotten spooked."

"Mugger with an ice pick? Where did they find it anyway?"

"What?"

"The pick."

"It was left embedded."

"Oh, Christ!" Janek moaned. Just hearing that made him hurt. "You know how I felt about her, Aaron."

Aaron nodded, then paused a moment before he spoke. "Tell you what I think, Frank, just based on what I heard. There wasn't any reason. It was just, you know, one of those lousy goddamn things. We get them all the time. You know—"

"Yeah. . . ." Janek knew all right. He knew all about them, though they weren't the kinds of cases he ever worked. A unique phenomenon of American cities, of which New York, on account of its population, had a greater share than anyplace else, they were the homicides that were rarely solved because there was nothing about them to solve. They had no point. They were the meaningless murders committed by madmen stalking people alone at night in public parks.

There was a TV news unit with a transmitting device on its roof parked across the street from the James O'Hara Funeral Home. Aaron stopped the car; Janek ducked out into the rain, then wound his way between the waiting limos, past the cameras at the door, and into the lobby. A stand on the far wall was stuffed with wet umbrellas. A dour man in a cutaway stepped forward and asked if he was there for the Wentworth funeral.

"The Foy," Janek said.

The man looked him over carefully. "You're the godfather?" Janek nodded. "They waited long as they could. They're about halfway through it now. West Chapel, up the stairs, second door on the right."

When he got there, Janek stood in the back and listened. An intense, frizzy-haired young man in ecclesiastical garments was speaking with bitter scorn of the horrors of New York.

". . . this Cultural Paradise, once so gracious, now choked with the downtrodden and the homeless. This Imperial City, once so elegant, now ridden with rape and murder. Just this past week a grandmother was dragged to her death by a purse snatcher at midday on Madison Avenue. And a brilliant young intern, with a great future before him, was shot at dusk outside New York Hospital because he refused to hand over his coat. And now our dear Jessica, beloved daughter of Laura, beloved step-daughter of Stanton, and goddaughter of Frank, has been struck down . . . and we ask: What madness has been set loose in our city? Why must such a tragedy happen? For what reason? What cause? How can we allow it? What can we say? What can we do? And our voices are mute, for we have no answers. . . ."

It was a long, narrow, overheated room, crowded mostly with younger people. Janek recognized a few: Jess's friends from high school and college, her cousins on Laura's side, and Stanton Dorance's two older sons, children from an earlier marriage. He also saw Tim Foy's mother, a thin veiled Irish woman in her sixties who now had lost both son and granddaughter to violence.

Ten or so well-dressed middle-aged men with well-trimmed hair sat together in a row. *Must be Stanton's law partners,* Janek thought. Laura and Stanton sat at the front in the bent, broken postures of the bereaved. There was an empty seat beside them. Janek waited until the minister paused, then crept forward to it. He hugged Laura, shook Stanton's hand, then settled back in time for the final words of the eulogy, which ended unexpectedly, not with a plea for reconciliation but on a shrill note of inexplicability and despair.

Afterward Laura grasped his arm. Even in grief she was a beautiful woman. "Thank God you made it, Frank. You know how she adored you. . . ." And then clinging to him, sobbing: "What am I going to do without her? I can't imagine. I just can't imagine. . . ."

Outside, Janek hustled Laura into the lead limo, while Stanton walked over to the waiting press, stood stoically in the rain and addressed their microphones: "Please, ladies and gentlemen, please give us some room for our grief. . . ."

In Queens, at the cemetery, just after they left the car, Stanton motioned Janek aside. Gravestones covered the bleak wet earth as far as the eye could see. Stanton's face, always strong, sometimes arrogant, looked weak and blotchy in the rain. His gestures, normally poised, were angular and abrupt.

"Find the animal who did this, Frank. Promise me you'll find him and bring him in."

Janek became aware then of a new wave of pain. It rose out of the center of his belly and spread across his chest. He thought: *Just think of yourself as a detective and then maybe a little of this hurt will go away.*

"I'll do my best, Stanton. But you know how these things go."

As Stanton stared at him outraged, Janek felt ashamed; what he'd said sounded so impotent. But then Stanton nodded. He understood. To live in New York was to understand all too well the vagaries of the criminal justice system and the cheap price of young human life.

When Janek met Aaron at 6:00 P.M. in the lobby of the Two-Six Precinct, he didn't have to ask for his opinion of Detective Boyce. Aaron offered it by seesawing his hands. "Tell you this, Frank, he ain't no Sherlock Holmes."

Aaron continued imparting his impression as they mounted the precinct house stairs. "He's pissed off. He denies it, but I can tell. Chief Kopta told him you're the godfather, so naturally he's going to extend you every courtesy. But see, for Boyce a front-page homicide like this is a chance to make a big impression. Then the famous Janek walks in. He's afraid of you, Frank, afraid you'll steal his case."

Janek's own first impression was that Boyce wasn't so much dumb as slow. He had a beer belly and not much hair. He'd combed a few thin brown wisps back carefully across his skull as if he thought they might cover his baldness and make him more attractive—but they didn't. The base of his face had a kind of squared-off look that reminded Janek of the bottom of a paper bag. But though his manner did not proclaim great brilliance, Janek recognized a predatory look. Aaron was right: This was a mediocre detective inflamed by a stroke of luck. The Jessica Foy case could be just the break he'd been waiting for for twenty years.

"I understand your special relationship to the victim, Lieutenant," Boyce began, "but let's not start off on the wrong foot. She's your goddaughter, but she's my case. Long as that's clear, we'll get along."

Jesus! Janek thought, but he kept his anger to himself. He knew that sooner or later a man who talked like that would blunder his way into Kit Kopta's bad graces.

"What do you really know about her?"

"Me?"

"You're her godfather, so I figured—"

This time Janek didn't bother to control his temper. "What the fuck, Boyce! I know a million things about her. What are you looking for me to say?"

"Know much about her social life?"

"What *about* her social life?" Now Boyce was wearing a cagey look, as if he had knowledge and it wasn't nice.

Aaron casually picked up Boyce's nameplate and tested it for strength. "Way you're acting, Ray, someone might think you're taunting the lieutenant here. Not a good idea, Ray. Why not just tell Janek what you got?"

Boyce shrugged. "I got a diary." He reached into his center drawer, pulled out a stenographer's notebook, and tossed it casually on the desk. "Read it, Janek. You may learn some things about her you didn't know." He headed for the door. "I'm going around the corner for coffee. Stick it back in the drawer when you're finished, okay?"

After Boyce left, Janek stared at the notebook, then cautiously reached for it. The sight of Jess's handwriting brought back memories of the sharp, funny postcards she'd send him whenever she traveled. He handed the notebook over to Aaron.

"Sure, I'll read it, Frank," Aaron said.

Janek found Boyce hunched over a chipped Formica table in the back section of a dingy coffee shop around the corner from the precinct house. During the day the place was frequented by detectives. Now Boyce was the only cop there. Boyce didn't look up as Janek approached, which gave Janek a chance to observe him. Boyce looked older and more tired then he had in his office. Janek felt a tinge of pity. *He has to wake up every morning and know he's Boyce,* he thought.

"Okay, Ray," he said, sitting down uninvited, "I know you resent me. You saw the miniseries and you thought it sucked. Maybe it did. Who the hell cares? Right now I'm hurting. I've lost someone I loved. So tell me what's on your mind. Who did this to her? Tell me what you think."

When Boyce finally looked up, Janek wasn't sure he'd cut into him very deep. But he knew he'd broken skin; Boyce was ready to show a human face.

"She was an honors student." Boyce waited for Janek to nod. "And a member of the women's fencing team." Janek nodded again. "She was tops, okay? Beautiful girl, full of life, popular, ace student, competitive athlete— what more could you ask? But there was a side that was unexpected. A strange unstable personal life. Boyfriends, but they weren't quite her style, she being so fastidious and all. Okay, last spring she takes up with a rich kid name of Greg Gale. And he introduces her into his crowd, where they dabble in highs—a little dope here, a mind game or two there, weird sex all the time. To get in with these kids, you have to be initiated. The initiation is you have sex blindfolded with one of them while the rest of the group watches the ceremony. Reading her diary, you get the impression she got off on it, like she wanted to roll a little in the dirt.''

Janek nodded, but every word stung. Jess, blindfolded, having sex with a stranger before an audience—the image pierced his heart.

''. . . but then, see, over the summer, she decides to straighten out. So early this fall, she starts going to a shrink. Then, about the same time, she breaks up with Gale. Pretty bitterly, too, it sounds like. No, I haven't talked to him. You're thinking: *Why the hell not? That's the first thing I'd do.* I got no answer for you, Janek, except that's not my way. Call me methodical. I like to lay the groundwork. I don't like going in asking questions till I have a pretty fair idea what the answers are going to be. A guy like Gale whose parents have bucks—I may get one crack at him before the family lawyer butts in. Understand what I'm saying?''

Janek nodded again. He understood very well.

''Thing is, Janek, people dabble in weird sex, maybe they dabble in murder, too. So this group she was going with is going to get looked at. They're going to get a very close look from me.''

Janek sat back, shook his head. ''I don't get it. I thought this was a random park murder.''

''So did I at first. Now it turns out there's oddities.''

''Like what?''

Boyce hesitated. ''Something was done to her. Afterwards.''

''What was done to her?''

Boyce looked uncomfortable. ''Let's go back to my

office. I'll show you the medical examiner's report and the photographs.''

Janek declined. ''Just tell me about it, Ray.''

Again Boyce seemed hesitant. ''She was glued.''

''Glued! How?''

''Guy who killed her—maybe he had a little caulking gun. After she was dead, he pumped glue into her, into an intimate area, know what I mean? It's like he was trying to, you know—close off that part of her. . . .''

Close off! Janek felt sick to his stomach.

When they returned to Boyce's office, Aaron was waiting and Jess's notebook was back on the desk.

Janek gestured toward the notebook. ''Do me a favor, Ray. I want the family protected. Make sure nothing in there gets leaked.''

''Yeah,'' Boyce said, ''but you know how it is. Stuff like that has a way of getting around.''

''I'm asking you, don't *let* it get around.''

''Sure, I'll do my best.''

Aaron stared at Boyce fiercely, but Janek whispered, ''Thanks.'' He'd used the same weak I'll-do-my-best-but-you-know-how-it-is just hours before with Stanton.

When they got back to Aaron's car, it had stopped raining. They compared notes as they drove downtown. Aaron confirmed that everything Boyce had said at the coffee shop was actually in the diary. There was one additional thing, probably not too significant: Lately Jess had been having bad dreams.

''This thing with the glue,'' Janek asked, ''you didn't hear anything about it?''

Aaron shook his head. ''Hard to keep something like

that quiet, too. There isn't a reporter wouldn't kill to get hold of it.''

"So maybe Boyce runs a tight ship.''

"Isn't he a marvel! Thing is—can you trust him?''

"Hard to say. Like everyone else, he's out mostly for himself.''

"Well, I'll tell you what I think, Frank. I think the guy's a schmuck,'' Aaron said.

Aaron stopped in front of Janek's building, a gray stone apartment house, formerly a tenement, with exterior fire escapes on West Eighty-seventh. Then he went around to the trunk, retrieved Janek's suitcase, and offered to carry it upstairs. Janek refused.

"Thanks, but you've done enough.''

Aaron stood by the car awkwardly, as if he didn't want to leave Janek there alone. "I've been meaning to ask you, Frank. How was your trip?''

"It was going great till I got the call. I met someone. Someone terrific.''

Aaron grinned. "That's grand, Frank. Congratulations. When do I get to meet her?''

"It's going to be complicated. She lives in Germany.''

"Oh. . . .'' There was nothing Aaron could say to that. "We'll talk tomorrow, okay?'' Aaron put out his hand. Janek ignored it and embraced him.

"Thanks for sticking with me, Aaron. Thanks for everything.''

"Don't worry, Frank. Whoever did this, we'll get him for sure.''

Aaron spoke with such conviction that for a full minute Janek sustained belief. But then, as he stumbled into the gloom of his apartment, the notion faded fast.

It was a simply furnished place, mostly with pieces inherited from his parents, including the workbench from his father's accordion repair shop with a half dozen accordions in various states of disrepair.

When Janek entered, he turned on a couple of lights, opened a window, placed his bag on his bed, then went into the bathroom to splash cold water on his face. Unfortunately he splashed too fast; the water, unused for two and a half weeks, ran a nasty rusty brown.

After he unpacked, he placed Monika's wineglass on a table near his living-room window so it would catch the morning light. Then he rewound his answering machine, sat down in his easy chair, and listened to his messages.

There were the usual utilitarian calls amidst the hang-ups. Shoes he'd left for repair were ready for pickup. A friend had Jets tickets if he was interested. His ex, Sarah, complained he hadn't bothered to inform her he was traveling. Then, as a familiar voice came on, Janek felt a chill.

"Hi. It's Jess. Please call me soon as you get back. There's something I want you to—can't explain it now. But it's important. Call me. Please. Okay?"

It was the last message on the tape. He rewound it and played it again. She sounded worried but still in control, as if she had something on her mind and was turning now, as she had all her life when something bothered her, to her godfather, whom she trusted above all other men.

He played her message a third time, striving to decipher each inflection. Then he played it a fourth, at high volume, listening acutely to the background noise. After that rendition he felt fairly confident that she hadn't called him hastily from a public phone. And that meant she probably hadn't called him in a panic. When he played it a fifth time, checking for subtext, he heard the same basic message he'd been hearing all along: This is Jess; I need your help.

He removed the cassette from the machine and stored it safely in a drawer.

It was only eight-thirty, but he was too exhausted to go out and eat. And it was too late now to call Monika—past two in the morning in Europe. He'd read an article that said the best cure for jet lag was to go to bed the moment you got home. But now, with Jess's message running through his brain, he knew sleep would be impossible.

He dialed Kit's home number. There was only half a ring before she picked up.

"I've been waiting for your call, Frank. Feeling lousy?"

"Of course."

"Understandable." She paused. "I spoke to Boyce this morning. Did you see him?"

"About half an hour ago. Maybe he's okay, I don't know yet." He hesitated. "Hate to ask for favors, Kit. You know I've been careful about that. I wasn't that keen about going to Europe. And I'm not all that anxious to be your special assistant or whatever you have in mind."

"Hey! Hold it right there!"

"Uh-uh, Kit—let me finish. People know we have a past. Or whatever they want to call it. Who cares, right? So we bend over backwards, and I'd probably bend further than you just so people wouldn't be tempted to say anything. You know how much I hate office politics and all that kind of crap. Well, this time I'm asking because I think what we got here is a set of special circumstances. I was the one headed the investigation on

Tim Foy. So here you have someone just as close, in the same family, and it only seems right—know what I mean? Who'd complain? Nobody, except maybe Boyce, and you've got fifty cases you could assign him. And—''

"Stop it, Frank!" Her voice was sharp.

Janek shook his head. "What's the matter? Can't I even ask?"

"It's not going to happen, so you might as well forget it. No one's going on a case where they're personally involved."

"Oh, Kit, please, I don't need a lecture on department policy."

"Not department policy, Frank. *My* policy—it's the way I'm running the division."

"Jesus! You sound so fucking rigid."

"Is that what you think?"

"Maybe I'm out of line. I just feel—"

"Get some rest, Frank. You're not in condition to have a rational discussion. Cool down, and in a couple days, come see me and we'll talk. Meantime, stay away from the case. I mean it. Stay away." Her voice softened. "You know I care about you. So trust me. Please. Now try and get some sleep."

But he couldn't sleep. Not after that. He took a shower, changed clothes, called Stanton, told him he was coming over. Then, downstairs, he hailed a cab and asked the driver to drop him at Park and Seventy-second.

The Dorances lived farther uptown, but Janek wanted to walk a few blocks before he saw them. The rain had stopped, but it was chilly, a raw, cold October night.

The entrance to Laura and Stanton's building was guarded by a doorman with an outsize regimental-style mustache. He wore a parody of a military greatcoat embellished with silver epaulets.

The small lobby, lined in mahogany, contained four plush leather club chairs with a rare Persian rug in the center. In the elevator Janek could smell a recently extinguished cigarette. The elevator man had been smoking contrary to regulations and now had hidden the butt, probably in a box concealed beneath his uniform.

Janek got off at the sixteenth floor. The landing was decorated in a Japanese motif. Even after Janek rang the bell, the elevator man waited until Stanton opened up.

It was a magnificent apartment, a duplex with a huge sunken living room, a full dining room, and four bedroom suites on the upper floor. Stanton, who was wearing a maroon smoking jacket with silk sash and satin lapels, ushered him into a small paneled library and offered him a drink.

"Where's Laura?" Janek asked.

"She's pretty tired, Frank. I thought—"

"I want to talk to her, too, Stanton. Please ask her to come down?"

Stanton nodded and disappeared. While Janek waited, he fixed himself a scotch. Then he looked around. One bookcase was devoted to family photographs, each mounted in a different style of frame, which collectively suggested what it meant to live a life of privilege.

His eyes were drawn to the pictures of Jess. There she was in pigtails at the summer camp she'd gone to in the Adirondacks, grinning at the camera. Another photo showed her older, mountain climbing in Switzerland, and a third showed her smiling broadly the day she graduated from her expensive private school. She was a handsome girl, tall and leggy, with high cheekbones, short honey-colored hair, and the confident eyes of an athlete. There were several photos of her fencing. One showed her holding up a trophy like an Olympic champion.

For some years Janek had observed the Dorance family with a sense of wonder at their numerous entitlements. Stanton's million-and-a-half-dollar duplex. His weekend place in Litchfield County. The winter vacations in the Caribbean, Christmas in Aspen, the month they spent on Martha's Vineyard in the summer. Laura had come a long way, and Janek was glad for her. He'd wanted nothing but the best for her and Jess. But he was still upset by Boyce's description of Jess's "social life." Laura had never mentioned difficulties. He had come now to find out why.

When Stanton reappeared with Laura, Janek stood to embrace her.

"You're still one gorgeous lady," he said.

"Oh, Frank. . . ." She hugged him again.

"Sorry to descend on you so late, but I've got some real problems."

"What kind of problems?" Stanton's hands trembled slightly as he poured himself a cognac.

Janek had been dreading this conversation from the moment he'd decided he needed it. Now the only thing to do was plunge ahead.

"You know what was done to her?" Laura looked toward Stanton. "I'm talking about the glue," Janek said. They both nodded. "This afternoon we spent an hour together driving to the cemetery, but neither of you mentioned that. I want to know why."

"We didn't want to upset you," Stanton said.

"Excuse me," said Janek, "but could anything have

made me feel worse? I'm asking you again: Why didn't you say anything?"

"We were told—" Laura started to speak, but Stanton interrupted.

"We were asked to keep that to ourselves. Chief Kopta told us not to get you excited, because she said you couldn't go on the case. I don't know how the Police Department works, Frank, but when the Chief of Detectives tells us not to talk about something, I don't see that we have a choice."

"Well, that's just fine, Stanton. But at the cemetery you made me promise to hunt down her killer."

"Yes. . . ."

Janek shook his head. "You can't have it both ways. Was that rhetoric or for real?"

"I meant it. Jesus, of course, I meant it."

"Good." Janek nodded. "Now let's see how far you're willing to go." He turned to Laura. "What do you know about a young man named Greg Gale?"

Laura looked confused. "Just that Jess was dating him. Then she broke it off."

"Ever meet him?"

"I think we saw him a couple of times," Stanton said. "Maybe for a minute or two when he came by to pick her up. Why do you ask? Is he mixed up in this?"

Janek ignored Stanton's question. He'd decided to concentrate on Laura. She was softer, more vulnerable, more likely to talk.

"Know anything about Gale's friends and how Jess was involved with them?"

"A little."

"Pretty fast bunch of kids from what I hear."

"Goddamn it, Frank!" Stanton smacked down his

drink. "What're you trying to do? We just buried our daughter. Surely there's a better time."

"I'm a detective, Stanton. Good enough for you to ask for my help. But then you don't bother to tell me what was done to her or that she was moving with a fast bunch of kids who did drugs and played mind games and had group sex and I don't know what else. Better listen now: The girl was sexually mutilated. Doesn't take a genius to figure out she may have been killed by someone she knew. But you don't tell me anything, just leave me thinking she was a victim of a random park killer, and isn't that just awful! Isn't New York a terrible place! Why do we all live in this hellhole? Oh, dear! Oh, God! Oh, shit!" Janek steadied himself. "You've got two choices, Stanton. Tell me everything you know or withdraw your request. Because if you ever hold back anything from me again, I'm out of it. Forever. Understand?"

"Chief Kopta?"

"Never mind her. She's my problem, not yours."

Laura was crying now, softly into a handkerchief. Stanton stood beside her chair, one hand on her shoulder.

"All right, Frank. The hell with it! I don't know what we were thinking. Look, we didn't know exactly what was going on between Jess and Gale, but we got a few hints we didn't like. She was always boy-crazy. We assumed she, you know—fooled around. But we tried not to think too hard about it. What the kids do now, it isn't the same as in our day. If you're a parent, you can't do anything about it so you ignore it, maybe hope it goes away. I guess that's what we did."

Laura, obviously embarrassed, was staring at the rug. "Go on," Janek said. "Let's hear it all."

"There isn't much to tell. Early this fall, when Jess went back to school, she told us she wanted to break it off. We didn't question her. We just tried to be supportive. When she said she wanted to see a shrink, I told her to find a good one and not to worry about the fees. And that's just what she did. This Dr. Archer she started going to, a reputable woman, a clinical psychologist, seemed to help her a lot. As for not keeping you abreast of the details of her personal life, there were just some things we felt Jess wouldn't have wanted us to share."

Laura looked up. "She was a wonderful girl, Frank. But she wasn't perfect. No child is. She loved you very much, and she knew how much you adored her. More than anything she wanted your respect. I think she'd rather have died than disappoint you."

Janek shook his head. "Laura, Laura—she's gone now. We're past the time when you have to worry about my being disappointed."

"Yes, Frank. I know. Of course. . . ."

They both looked as if they felt they'd been awful and stupid. He didn't want to leave them feeling that way, so he decided to share the contents of their daughter's call.

"When I got home tonight, there was a message from Jess. She didn't leave the date or time, but it was the last call I got, so I know she made it no earlier than two days before she was killed. She sounded worried, said she wanted to talk to me, said it was important, urged me to call her as soon as I got back. What was it? What did she want? Think hard, because this is important. The girl's upset; then she's killed and mutilated. Maybe she felt she was in danger."

Laura stared at him. "I can't imagine."

"Could have been about her father," Stanton said.

Laura nodded. "It could." She turned to Janek. "A few weeks ago she started asking me questions about Tim. I was surprised. We'd barely talked about him in years. I thought, well, it probably came up in her therapy. I suggested she talk to you. I told her you knew Tim in a completely different way. She seemed pleased with that. She loved talking to you, Frank. So maybe that's why she called."

Janek thought about it. Did wanting to talk to him about Tim fit the tone of her message? Not likely.

"Well, maybe so," he said. He wound up the discussion, kissed Laura on the cheek, and started for the door. Stanton escorted him out to the hallway and stood beside him as he rang for the elevator.

"Well?"

"Well—what, Stanton?"

"I want you to promise me you'll hunt her killer down."

"I thought I already did."

"I want to hear you say it."

Janek looked at him. Stanton's eyes gleamed with a lust for vengeance.

"Yeah, I promise," Janek said. "I promise I'll hunt him to the ends of the earth. How's that?"

Stanton nodded. "Fine. That's fine, Frank. It feels good to hear you say the words."

The elevator arrived. Janek got in. The cigarette smoke was even more pungent than before.

"We'll stay in touch. Won't we?"

"Yeah, we'll stay in touch," Janek said to the closing door.

* * *

He was dreaming when, at six the following morning, his ringing telephone woke him up. As he groped for the receiver, he tried to recapture his dream, but the details were instantly lost to him, leaving him with nothing but a vague sense of dread.

It was Monika, and the fine clarity of her voice quickly drove away his demons.

"I was worried, Frank. You didn't call."

"Sorry. I got back too late. I figured you'd be asleep."

"I've been thinking about you, imagining what you've been going through. I wish I could be there with you now."

Wasn't she fabulous! Perhaps Venice had been more than a dream.

"I love the glass," he said.

"I hoped you would."

"I put it by my window. I want to look at it every day, to remind myself of Venice and how I met you there and what we found together." He pulled himself short. "Hey! I better shut up. This is getting sentimental."

"Don't be afraid of sentiment, Frank."

"No, Monika. But sometimes I'm wary." And then he poured out to her everything that was bothering him: the way Jess was stabbed, the gluing, the decadent boy-friend, and finally the diary.

"I couldn't bear to read it. I don't know why. First I thought it was her handwriting; then I realized I was afraid of what I'd have to read. Boyce almost leered when he offered it to me. I guess I didn't want . . . what? Disillusionment. Then, when he told me about her, that gang she was running with, having sex wearing a blindfold while the other kids watched . . . I don't know. I've seen a lot, maybe as bad as it gets, but I never connected Jess with anything sordid. Of course, it wasn't necessarily ugly. It all depends on how she approached it. She was a grown woman. She had every right to live her life. But still, I can't seem to come to grips with it. It's as if there was a part of her I didn't know.''

Monika told him she thought that if he just looked at it in a certain way, he wouldn't feel so confused. As for Jess's secrecy, she assured him that that was not at all uncommon in a young person, especially with an older person the youngster loves.

''I think she knew that to you she would always seem a perfect little girl. And I think it's a sign of her love for you that she didn't want to disturb your illusion.''

''Okay,'' he said, ''that makes sense. But this sex thing—''

''Don't dwell on it, Frank. She sounds to me like a fairly normal young woman, fully entitled to her secrets, insecurities, struggles, her groping expressions of sexuality. No one is obliged to be a moral paragon. And there's so much in her diary that sounds positive. The fact that she broke off with the rotten boyfriend and started seeing a therapist is an excellent sign. And the fact that she tried to reach you when she felt she was in trouble—that alone should tell you how much you meant to her. I hope you don't love her any the less for what you've found out.''

''Nothing in the world could make me love her less,'' Janek said. Then he started to choke. ''God! I don't want to break down again.''

''Please don't be embarrassed with me.''

He smiled. ''I just hate the cliché. You know: tough-New-York-cop-with-feelings.''

''I never thought of you as tough.''

"How did you think of me?"

"You were the big American I kept running into all the time, whom I lured into following me."

He smiled. She really was the best thing to happen to him in years.

There was a tremendous amount of mail waiting for him at the post office, so much that the clerk suggested he borrow a mail sack to carry it home. Junk mail, bills, magazines, and then, among the letters, one that didn't look right. He picked it out of the multitude and examined it carefully. It bore no return address. His name was handwritten in block letters on the envelope: "LIEUTENANT FRANK JANEK." The postmark, dated the day after Jess's killing, told him it had been mailed from Greenkill Prison. He ripped it open, read it quickly, then threw it down with disgust. The text, unsigned, was short and to the point: "JANEK, I SLEEP BETTER KNOWING YOUR GODDAUGHTER IS IN THE GROUND."

The road into Greenkill is as stark as the old red-brick buildings that comprise its campus. The complex looms upon a hill. Beneath its walls cows graze fields, a pastoral touch which, though meant to calm the inmates, only enrages them by mocking their confinement. Below the fields there is a moat, and below that interlocking rolls of razor wire. That October day, beneath stone gray clouds, Greenkill had a brooding presence. As Janek entered, he felt the screaming silence of the place and the stern essence of its gloom. But most of all, he felt the weight of unserved time.

He showed his badge, parked in the visitors' lot, then waited in the reception area until his visit was cleared by the warden's office. He checked his gun and ammo with the property clerk, was frisked by a gate guard, passed through the electronic barriers without setting off any alarms. Then he was escorted to a small plain attorney's room. Rusty Glickman, dressed in blue denim, was waiting for him in a cheap plastic chair set up before a battered wooden table.

"Pleasure, Janek," he said. But as he sat down, Janek responded only with a look.

It had been fifteen years since he'd last seen Glickman. Now he wasn't certain he'd recognize him if he passed him on the street. Glickman's tight black hair had mostly fallen out, replaced by a grayish fringe. His taut, lean body had gone to fat, and his breath stank of tobacco—not surprising since lung cancer, caused by excessive smoking of cigarettes, was the most frequent killer of lifers. But as Janek studied Glickman, he recognized the expression around his mouth. Even fifteen years of incarceration had not extinguished the sneer that said, "Whoever you may think you are, to me you're a total piece of shit."

"What brings you around? Social call? It's been what? Fifteen years?"

Again Janek didn't bother to answer. He reached into his pocket, pulled out the letter, and placed it flat on the table.

Glickman glanced at it. "So?"

"You wrote it."

"So what?"

"Why?"

Glickman shrugged. "Why not?" He smirked.

Janek slowly moved his head in close, deliberately invading Glickman's space.

"I know you're slime. But what could you possibly have against Tim Foy's daughter?"

"I got nothing against her. I didn't even remember he had a daughter till I read about her in the papers."

"So *why*?"

"You, the big shot detective from New York, got the balls to come up here and ask me that? I thought you were supposed to be smart, Janek." Glickman's voice was loaded with scorn. "I saw this shitty miniseries where this actor—what's his name, he's a lot better-looking than you—where he struts around making like he's so fucking brilliant. Lieutenant Frank Janek the character was called. What a pile of shit."

Janek stared at him. "Once a psychopath always a psychopath." He stood. "I don't need your abuse." He moved toward the door to call the guard.

"'Cause of you, I gotta spend the rest of my life in a rathole while you get to run around in New York playing Great Detective. You ask why I wrote you about the girl. I wrote you so you'd come up here and I could look into your eyes and see your pain. That's all I wanted. Now I'm satisfied. I've seen it. It looks pretty good to me. I *like* seeing you in pain, Janek. Like I said, it's a real pleasure."

"Guard!" Janek shouted, then waited facing the door. No matter what Glickman said to him, he vowed not to react. But Glickman was on a roll. He had only a few more seconds and nothing to lose.

"You call me slime. You're the slime, Janek. You and your buddy—what's his name?—Foy. And his little cunt of a daughter, too. That's what she was, wasn't she? A little cunt, a slut, running around, twitching her horny little ass in the park. Know something? I'm *glad* she's dead!''

The guard had arrived, was working his key in the lock, but Janek didn't care. Even as he yielded to his anger, he knew he was making a mistake. *But fuck it!* he thought. He turned, raised his foot against the leg of the table, and shoved as hard as he could, propelling the table straight toward Glickman, knocking him off his chair and onto the floor.

''See that!'' Glickman shouted to the guard. ''See what he did! Struck a prisoner! You saw it! *He struck a fucking prisoner!* That's grounds for a lawsuit! A big lawsuit! You're really fucked now, asshole! Probably cost you your fucking pension!''

Glickman was laughing, a sneering, bullying laughter, the kind you'd expect from a slimeball who'd order a bomb planted in another man's car. But Janek was already out the door. As he walked down the corridor, he could hear Glickman's laughter resound against the walls. By the time he reached the security gate he knew that he himself was now walking on a knife's edge of sanity.

That night, when he got back to New York, the craziness was really cooking in him. But being conscious of it and wanting to give it up were two different things. *I may be strung out,* he thought, *but I've still got control.*

Though emotionally exhausted, thoroughly jet-lagged, fatigued from his journey to Greenkill, he was nonetheless ready to do what Boyce was not: corner Greg Gale and squeeze him till he bled.

He called the number Aaron had provided and got a

taped answer off a machine. He didn't like the sound of Gale's voice, a snotty prep school whine.

Angry but composed, Janek taxied to a block on West Ninety-eighth between Broadway and West End. He found Gale's building easily enough, a subdivided gray stone town house. He rang the buzzer to be sure Gale wasn't in, then walked over to the garage across the street. Yes, indeed, the night manager said, he knew young Mr. Gale. He kept his car there, but it wasn't there now. He'd taken it out earlier that evening. Janek tipped him in return for permission to wait in the office until young Mr. Gale returned. Then he settled back into a beaten-up swivel chair and tried to get some sleep.

Two hours later he felt a light touch on his shoulder. The manager, hovering, gestured toward the garage drive. A well-polished red Porsche was angled in the entrance, and a lean young male, dressed in a trench coat, was making his way across the street.

"Thanks," Janek whispered, then hurried out. He reached the vestibule of the town house just as Gale was unlocking the inner hallway door.

"Greg?"

Greg turned. He had light, wavy hair verging on blond and the smooth, symmetrical features of a secondary lead in a soap opera. The only striking thing about him was his pallor; he looked like the kind of person who ventured out only at night.

Janek flashed his shield.

"This must be about Jess."

Janek nodded. "Got time to talk?"

Gale glanced around. He seemed reluctant. Janek tried to make himself vulnerable. "Been waiting quite a while,

Greg. Pretty cold out there.'' He rubbed his hands together as he spoke.

Gale nodded. ''Well, okay. Shall we talk down here?''

''Up to you.'' Janek rubbed his hands again to emphasize the chill.

The young man shrugged. ''Let's go upstairs.'' He grinned. ''I gotta take a leak.''

He was poised and he was handsome and the thought of Jess in his arms filled Janek with disgust. But he played along and smiled and followed Gale up the stairs, enjoying the thought of how the little jerk was shortly going to be sorry he'd invited him into his place.

Inside the apartment Gale excused himself, leaving Janek alone to look around. It seemed pretty lush for a college student, but then so did a red Porsche. There was black leather upholstery furniture, a sleek stereo, a top-grade TV with matching VCR, big collections of CDs and videotapes, a shelf of mystery novels, and, most striking, a large photograph hanging over the fireplace. Beautifully framed, it showed a muscular naked black male posed on one knee before a standing young woman. Dressed in white equestrian garb, she peered down at the black with a disdainful lascivious smile.

When Gale reappeared, Janek gestured toward the picture. ''Interesting,'' he said.

Gale showed his teeth. ''Like that, do you?''

''I didn't say I liked it. I said it was interesting.''

''I took it.''

''You're a photographer?''

''I fool around with it a little, yeah.'' Though the kid obviously wanted to sound self-deprecating, he came off as shallow and arrogant.

''Ever take any pictures of Jess?''

Gale ran his tongue across his lips. "A few. Want to see them?"

If they were anything like the kinky picture over the fireplace, Janek didn't think he did. He stared at Gale.

"I'll ask the questions, Greg. You'll answer them. Let's start off easy. What did you do to her in the park?"

"What?"

"You heard me."

"Hey! Are you for real? I want you out of here. *Now!*"

When Janek smiled, Gale looked confused. A slight vibrato in his upper lip showed that he was feeling fear.

"I know who you are. You're the detective she was always talking about."

Janek offered no response.

"Okay," Gale said, quickly adjusting his manner to eager-to-please, "you want answers. I don't know anything about the park. I didn't lay eyes on her the last seven weeks. We quarreled, and she kicked me out of her life. Naturally I feel real bad about what happened, but I don't know anything about it. That's all I'm going to say."

Real bad—shit! "Not good enough, Greggy boy."

"I want you to go."

Janek shook his head. "Not till I'm satisfied."

"Don't try to bully me, Detective!"

"Think this is bullying?" Janek laughed.

They stared at each other. Then Gale made a move toward his phone. "I'm calling the police."

He picked up the receiver, but his trembling betrayed his fear. Janek walked over to him and casually held out his hand. Gale paused, then surrendered the receiver. Janek set it down. He lightly pushed Gale into a black wooden chair bearing Columbia University's coat of arms. He pulled up a matching chair and sat down close, so close he could see a quiver in the young man's eyes.

"All right," he said, "here's how it's going down. We're going to have a polite conversation in which I ask the questions and you give me truthful answers. The alternative is you get mad and try to punch me out. That's an attack on a law officer, felonious assault, which yields your basic five-year sentence. Not to mention the fact that then I'd have to hit you back, which would probably cost you your teeth. If I had a pretty face like yours, I don't think I'd like that very much. Your choice. I can handle it either way. See, I'm mad. My goddaughter was murdered. So basically I don't give a shit."

Gale lowered his eyes. "I told you—I don't know anything."

"Let's get more specific. Jess rejected you?" Gale nodded. "You resented her for that?"

"I don't know if I'd say 'resent.' I admit I was pretty upset. But—"

"Yeah, yeah—you don't know anything. Now tell me about the sex club?"

Gale screwed up his face to convey perplexity. "What are you talking about?"

Greggy's not too good an actor, Janek thought as he tutted and shook his finger. "No questions, just answers."

"I don't know anything about any sex club."

"Your little clique. The ones who watch while the new kid fucks blindfolded."

"You *know* about that?"

Janek reached forward and slapped Gale lightly across the face. "*I* ask. *You* answer. Last warning. Okay?"

"Okay, okay. But it's not a club. It's more like . . . a group of friends."

"How many 'friends'?"

"Nine or ten, depending on who wants in or out."

"Percentage of women?"

"Half and half."

"Who started it?"

"My idea originally."

"You recruit new people?"

"Sort of. But it isn't exactly—"

"You brought in Jess?"

"Yeah. But—"

"You planned to bring her into the group from the moment you started dating her. You weren't interested in her as a girlfriend. You just wanted another body, right?" Gale shook his head. "I want a straight answer."

"Well, maybe that is what I had in mind."

"Damn straight it was. From the start, right? But you never told her, did you? You waited till you thought she was ready. Then you proposed it, in a slippery kind of way like 'I know this great group of kids, they're really far-out, but I think you'll find them interesting.'"

Greg lowered his eyes, resigned. "Maybe that's what I did." Then he looked up. "But she was a big girl. And she went for it. Believe me, she enjoyed it. The moment I broached it to her, her eyes lit up. Probably hard for you to hear this, but Jess liked sex. I mean she *liked* it. And there's nothing wrong with that. We played safe, took precautions, used condoms. That's why we formed the group in the first place, so we could have some variety and still play safe. The whole idea was to make it fun. Not nasty like you're trying to make it seem.''

''Did I call it nasty?''

''It's your tone. Your whole approach. You want to make me feel like a worm.''

That much was true, but Janek wanted to define his own attitude. ''I don't think sex is nasty. But I think someone who uses the guise of romantic involvement to entice a girl into that kind of thing is fairly low-grade slime.''

Gale twisted in his chair. He couldn't take contempt. ''That's pretty close to what she told me, too,'' he whispered.

Janek was grateful to hear that.

''She dumped on you?''

''I already told you.''

''You must have resented her.''

''I'm human. Wouldn't you?''

''Resented her so much you stalked her, stabbed her, and after you killed her, you attacked the part of her that mocked you the most, that mocked your manhood.''

Gale jumped up. ''What're you talking about. What part of her? Jesus!''

''The part you couldn't satisfy. The part that made you feel inadequate.''

''I don't understand.'' He paused. ''You mean, my cock? Is that what you're talking about?''

Janek smiled. ''Not your lousy little cock, asshole. A part of her. *Jess!*''

Gale was still confused. ''What part of her?''

''You tell me.''

''Are you saying she was—that someone did something to her? God! I didn't know! It wasn't in the papers. Jesus!''

Gale sat back down, then began to sob. At first Janek was certain he was faking. But as the sobbing turned to gagging and then to heaving, he began to believe it was for real.

He helped Gale into the bathroom, then stood beside him as he fell to his knees and retched into the toilet.

''It's okay, son,'' he said. ''Don't hold back. Let it out, let it out.''

When finally Gale was finished and turned to him with a grateful smile, Janek knew he had broken through. The bond was forged. The interrogator had become the friend. And now the truth would emerge.

''I was crazy about her, Janek. I swear to you.''

They were back in the living room in the university chairs, but Janek sat farther away this time. No need to sit close and apply more stress. All he had to do now was listen with sympathy as Gale, impelled to talk, regaled him with his story.

''. . . you got it right, I recruited her. Just like I recruited the others. And it was always a kind of victory for me, too. I'd pick a girl out, walking across the quadrangle, or sitting alone in a lecture hall, or jogging, or laughing, or coming out of one of the dorms. I'd pick her because she looked good, had a great body, moved a certain way, had a well-packaged butt, her lips were sexy, or there was something, you know, about the way she laughed, her mouth, her tits, whatever. Then it became a game. Get her name. Get a date with her. Kiss her. Get her into the sack. After that it was usually pretty easy to lead them to the point where, you know, they thought it was *their* idea. Then came the victory part:

putting the blindfold on them, leading them into the room, telling them to strip while everybody watched. We never told anybody who they were going to do it with. That was the game. Everyone liked it. Everyone wore the blindfold. The guys, too. Including me. That was the fun of it, to wear the blindfold, to strip and stand there until the selected person came forward, stood before you till you could hardly stand it anymore, then slowly reached forward and made contact. Fear and anticipation and the idea you were on display. Wondering who the person was, trying to guess, but preferring not to know because it was easier to let yourself go if you didn't. Plenty of time later to find out who and laugh about who you thought it was. To perform like that, be the object of so much attention—*I* loved it. Everybody did. Jess, too. You gotta believe me when I say this, Janek. She found it incredibly exciting.

"But, see, there was the problem, because when I watched her play with the others, a funny thing started to happen. It bothered me. I didn't like it. And I'd never felt like that before. So I said to her: 'Let's not do this anymore. Let's just go out as a couple.' She laughed, called me jealous, made fun of me 'cause I couldn't take it. 'You got me into this, Greggy,' she said. 'You created a monster. Now you'll have to live with it.'

"Over the summer we went separate ways. I had a half-ass job at my father's brokerage firm and was out in the Hamptons most weekends. Jess was with her folks up on Martha's Vineyard, so we didn't see each other at all. I called her a lot. She never called me. The few times I managed to catch her home she told me she didn't feel like talking. Then in August she went to Italy to some special fencing school. I wrote her, but she didn't answer. So okay, I figured when college started up again, we'd see each other and have a chance to talk. But come September she had a whole new attitude. Now all she wanted was to fence. She had ambitions, wanted to become an Olympic competitor. Her Italian coach had told her she had the potential for it but she'd have to give it everything she had. 'That's what I want,' she told me. 'I want to go all the way. I don't want to waste my energy anymore, dating people I don't care about or smoking pot and playing games with your chums.' 'Well, okay,' I said, 'that's fine. I'll go along with that. Let's start over, just the two of us.' But that didn't interest her either.

"We had a big fight. She told me she didn't care if she ever saw me again. She called me all kinds of stuff. 'Shallow.' 'Spoiled.' 'No backbone.' 'No integrity.' 'User.' 'Pimp.' And she was right. Maybe that's why it hurt so much. She saw through me clearer than anyone ever had. She saw me for what I really am, which is just what you're looking at now, Janek. Yeah, I think you see me pretty much the way she did. As a jerk. A zero." And with that he gave out with a forlorn little whelp and then a droopy self-pitying smile.

A nicely executed *mea culpa,* Janek thought, but he still had to be sure Gale hadn't gone after Jess in revenge.

"Okay, Greg. Pick yourself up. No law says you gotta be slime. That's a choice you don't have to make."

As Gale peered at him, searched his eyes for sympathy, suddenly Janek was sick of him. He was tired of people who made their confessions, then looked to him for solutions to their lives. What had he said to Monika that night in Venice? That he did what he did to gain wisdom, to comprehend the numerous varieties of human evil. But Greg Gale wasn't evil, at least not to a degree that mattered. He was smalltime-fuckedup-richkid-spoiled, and who gave a shit anyway? But somehow, some way this kid's life had touched Jess's, so no matter how sickening Janek found him, he still had to play out the string.

"You see yourself as decadent, but underneath you're pretty soft."

In return, as he expected, Gale gave him the warm, grateful, amazed look—the one Janek always got at this point in an interrogation—the look that said: "Thank you for understanding me so well."

"So you were hurt by her. She was a great kid, but she was capable of hurting. You don't decide to become an Olympic-class fencer if you haven't got some pretty hard stuff inside. In my experience women are tougher than men. Easy to forget that when they cry. But they can ream you out and backwards when they feel like it. Isn't that the truth?"

Still caught up by Janek's magical insights, Greg nodded solemnly.

"You were angry. It's okay, Greg. Admit it."

"Well, sure. Those things she said—"

"Made you feel like a worm. Pretty hard to take a beating like that without getting mad about it, wanting to hit the girl back."

Gale shrugged. "I didn't want to hit her. All I wanted was for us to, you know, hold each other."

"She rejected you, made you feel awful."

"Yeah. . . ." The spell was still holding; Gale was in a kind of dazed, suspended state.

"If she wouldn't go out with you, who would she go out with? You were jealous of what she did with the group. How about people you didn't know, sex you wouldn't be able to watch?''

"I didn't want to think about that.''

"Of course not. You'd go crazy if you did. But how could you be sure? Unless there was some way to . . . close her off. Prevent anyone else from getting what you couldn't get. That's when you thought of it, right?''

He looked into Gale's eyes, but all he could see there was confusion. No anger, no rage, no word forming to come out or being throttled so it wouldn't. This boy didn't know anything about glue; of that Janek was certain. Greg Gale hadn't stabbed Jess, and he hadn't mutilated her. He was lost in a reverie of his inadequacy as a man, not in a fantasy of stabbing and gluing up a woman.

Janek stood. "I don't know what to say to you. You messed around with my goddaughter's head. I'd like to think you couldn't help yourself, but still, it's hard to forgive. I'm not going to try. I think you've been honest with me. I appreciate that. No need to get up. I'll let myself out.''

But then, before he could turn, Gale stood up. He wanted to show Janek his photographs of Jess. Janek dreaded looking at them; he didn't want sordid images of her etched upon his mind. But he waited anyway while Gale dug the pictures out, and then he was surprised.

Gale's photos were not posed tableaux like the mistress/slave picture over the fireplace. Rather, they were superb black-and–white action shots of Jess fencing in tournaments, en garde, thrusting, making parries and ripostes and lunge attacks against her opponents.

He looked at them all carefully, admiring Gale's abilities as a photographer. Then he came upon a shot of

Jess so fine, so powerful, he could not tear his eyes away. Gale had caught her just at the moment of a victory. Having scored, ripped off her mask, she met the gaze of his camera with a great broad, beaming grin of triumph.

Gale watched him as he examined this picture. "Like it?" he asked. Janek nodded. "Take it. No, I mean it. I want you to have it." And before Janek could protest, Gale placed the print in a protective cover and presented it to him as a gift.

Clutching this image of Jess as he rode back to his apartment, Janek knew, no matter what anyone said, that he would have to find out who had killed her. The little girl he had nurtured had grown into the magnificent women in the photograph—and now she was dead. The wound this time was not just upon society, nor was it only upon Laura and Stanton. It was also upon himself, and it would not be closed for him until he had hunted her killer down.

Oh, Jess, he thought. *Jess.*

That night, his second since his return from Europe, Janek finally got a full ration of sleep. But it was total exhaustion, not peace of mind, that closed his eyes. His last thought, before falling off, was that Jess seemed to have been at a crisis point at just the time she was killed. Was that significant or merely a coincidence? He posed the question, then collapsed into a spiral of fatigue.

It was Laura Dorance who set up his appointment the following morning with Jess's shrink.

Janek arrived before the first-floor office entrance of a converted two-story carriage house on East Eighty-first. He pressed the bell, gave his name to a disembodied voice, and was buzzed in. He found himself in a hall. Through an archway to his left there was a sparsely furnished waiting room. He entered, took a seat, thumbed through an old copy of *Psychology Today*, while a small radio, tuned at low volume to a classical station, yielded a gentle flow of Mozart.

At precisely eleven o'clock Dr. Beverly Archer appeared in the doorway. A very short, fortyish butterball of a woman, she welcomed Janek with a sympathetic smile. Warm and friendly eyes, slightly rouged cheeks, curly, dull reddish hair, she had the kind of bland features one often associates with people in the mental health field. But her voice gave her away; it was throaty, low-pitched, intense.

"Please come in, Lieutenant. I have forty minutes before my next appointment."

He followed her into a comfortable consultation room. A desk, two easy chairs, an analyst's couch, and bookcases filled with psychiatric texts. On one wall hung a reproduction of van Gogh's sunflowers; on the other, a cluster of diplomas.

"Now what can I do for you?" Dr. Archer asked with a formal smile, after motioning him to one of the chairs.

"I'm sure Mrs. Dorance told you—"

"She said you were Jessica's godfather and that you're a New York City detective. But I must tell you from the start I'm most reluctant to discuss the contents of Jessica's sessions. Many people don't realize this, but the confidentiality of the therapist's office transcends even the patient's death."

Janek paused. The woman was more authoritative than he expected. He understood he would have to tread gently if he was going to get any information.

"Yeah, I've heard that, Dr. Archer, but her mother, her legal heir, has given consent."

Dr. Archer nodded. "So she told me. But you have to understand, there's a principle involved. If I make an exception, violate my pledge of confidentiality, then where do I draw the line?" She smiled. "My oath binds me to silence. Unless, of course, I learn that someone is about to commit an act of violence. And that I'm afraid, is not the case here."

Oh, shit! A real hard-ass! "I notice you call her Jessica," he said.

"That was her name."

"We all called her Jess."

"So did I, Lieutenant. But I'm not speaking to her now. I'm speaking *about* her, and as you can probably tell, I'm feeling just a little uncomfortable about that."

Dr. Archer, Janek noticed, pursed her lips into a little smile at the end of every sentence. It was a nervous habit, not unattractive or disconcerting, but he found it slowed him down.

"If it will make it any easier for you, Doctor, I already know a lot. We have her diary. We know about the sex group. I've already spoken with Greg Gale, and he's confirmed everything she wrote. If it's a question of protecting Jess's reputation, please believe that's foremost in my mind. I'm not going to repeat anything you tell me, and her diary won't be leaked. I guess what I'm saying is I hope you'll reconsider. My first priority, which I'm sure you share, is to find the person who killed her."

As he spoke, Dr. Archer nodded along. "Yes, yes, that's true, that's certainly true. And I shall certainly think the matter over." She paused, smiled. "Now why don't we start by talking a little about your own relationship with Jessica? I think that would help me to better understand your interest.''

She was such a nice woman, so clearly attuned to listening, that even though Janek was not in the mood to unburden himself, he soon found himself speaking of his sense of loss. He spoke, too, of his discomfort with thoughts of Jess's sex life, his overreaction when Glickman called her names, and the tight control he had had to exert upon himself with Greg Gale the night before.

''It's as if suddenly I have to deal with a side of Jess I never thought about before.'' Janek realized he was speaking to this woman much as he had on the telephone to Monika.

Dr. Archer nodded. Indeed, she understood. But then she wondered if it was really necessary for Janek to deal with that side of Jess at all.

''I think it is,'' he said. ''That's why I'm here. I need to know everything she did.''

''Do you really need to, Lieutenant?''

''I think so. I'm surprised you'd even ask.''

Dr. Archer settled back. ''You're saying that to pursue her killer, you must delve into every aspect of her character. I question whether that's true. My suggestion, and I make it with timidity and respect, is that you ask yourself why you're so disturbed by the intimate material you've so far uncovered. Is it Jessica you want to understand, or are you really seeking to understand yourself?''

Janek stared at her. It was an interesting suggestion, but he'd come for information, not therapy or analysis.

''What I'm saying,'' Dr. Archer continued, ''and I emphasize I do so without making any kind of value judgment, is that you possibly were and perhaps still are overly involved with your goddaughter. Perhaps you had unconscious fantasies about her. Perhaps you longed for her in some way you don't fully understand. And now that she's been so tragically killed, you use that as an excuse to delve into the most intimate aspects of her life. I suppose what I'm really asking, Lieutenant, is whether you're the right person to be handling this investigation. I certainly don't presume to know the answer. I merely raise the question."

A maddening, if fascinating, forty minutes, Janek thought as he emerged, somewhat shaken, on the street. Dr. Archer could not be faulted. She had acted professionally and shown herself protective of her patient. But instead of behaving in a cooperative manner, as is normally the case when a doctor is questioned by a detective, she had smoothly, even tenderly turned the interview around, with the result that it was not the victim but the investigator who had become its subject.

He knew he would return, and he had no doubt he would eventually persuade her to cooperate. In the meantime, he was captivated by her insights. Was what she'd said true? Was Kit right? Was he, Janek, too personally involved? Did he *have* to know everything? And how would the psychologist react when she discovered that his investigation was unauthorized?

Arriving at Kit Kopta's office suite, on the nineteenth floor of the police building, Janek did not receive the usual warm reception. The crusty redheaded sergeant, who kept Kit's appointments and supervised her secretaries, treated him with a correct but cool distance. The chief, he was told, was busy in a meeting; he was to take a seat and wait. Janek sat and waited for nearly an hour, watching people come and go through the inner office doors. Finally the sergeant deigned to notice him again. "Okay, Lieutenant, the chief'll see you now," he said without bothering to meet Janek's eyes.

Kit was seated behind her desk in a no-nonsense posture. She watched him closely as he walked in.

Her scrutiny made him feel awkward. "Am I in trouble?" he asked.

"What makes you think so?"

"Making me wait an hour. I can read the undertones."

"Screw the undertones, Frank. You've been working the Foy case after I ordered you to stay away from it, even after I begged you as a friend. You went up to Greenkill and kicked a table at a convict? You've got to know how stupid that was! Then you intimidated some snotty college kid whose dad's got City Hall connections. A few minutes ago my sergeant got a complaint from Ray Boyce. What the hell are you doing seeing the girl's shrink without clearing it first?" She took a deep breath; clearly she was uncomfortable with her anger. "So to answer your question, yeah, Frank, you *are* in trouble. And not just with those other people. You're in trouble with me."

"What am I supposed to say?"

"Stop carrying on, Frank. *Stay away from this case.*"

"You're serious."

Kit flushed. "Damn right I am."

"Boyce is a mediocrity."

"He's a competent detective."

"He's too slow."

"A lot of people think you're way too fast."

Janek peered at her. "Are you telling me there isn't a chance you'll turn it over to me?"

"Not a chance in hell, Frank. If there ever was, there sure isn't now."

Janek nodded. He hadn't anticipated this, but he'd prepared for it nonetheless. He reached into his pocket, pulled out his badge, and slid it quietly across Kit's desk.

She stared at it as if it were a piece of stale cake. "Is that supposed to mean you resign?" Janek nodded. She shook her head. "Cut the drama, Frank. What the hell's the matter?"

"*What's the matter?* Laura and Stanton ask me to get the guy who killed their daughter. I tell them I'll do my best. Then it hits me I have to get him not just for them but for me. A girl I loved, a girl I helped bring up from the time she was a little kid, was savagely killed and mutilated. I'm an investigator. I know how to track down the kind of people who do such things. That's my trade. If you won't let me practice it as a police officer, I'm perfectly prepared to do it privately on my own."

She studied him. "You were always convincing, Frank." She paused. "Know who you sound like?"

"Who?"

"Sam Spade." She grinned and, when he didn't return her smile, reclined back in her chair, her sharp Greek eyes fixing him.

They stared at each other, two people who'd known each other for twenty years. Then Janek remembered that tough as Kit was, she was no rigid disciplinarian.

"Something you're not telling me," he said quietly.

She peered at him noncommittally.

"You're much too adamant, Kit. Why ask the Dorances not to tell me about the glue? There's more here than you don't want me working on a case because it's, quote, personal. Better level with me now. Sooner or later I'll find out anyway.''

She stared across the room, as if weighing his suggestion. Then she focused on him again.

''You're right about Boyce. He's slow and mediocre. Two things you're not, Frank. If I put you on Foy, there'll be a serious investigation. And at this point that's not what we want.''

Janek leaned forward. His heart was pounding. ''Boyce's investigation isn't serious?''

Kit shrugged. ''Boyce doesn't know it, of course. But his investigation's bound to be a sham.'' Janek started to rise. ''Blow up at the end if you want to, Frank. But first hear me out.'' He sat back down. ''We're fairly certain we know who killed Jess. We don't know his name, but we know his work. He's done the same thing before. The FBI's been tracking him for a year.''

As she talked, Janek tried to concentrate. He didn't want to miss a word. But as hard as he tried, he couldn't shake off his fury. If he'd done as Kit had requested, played docile, stayed away from Glickman and Gale and Archer, he'd still be thinking about a random park killer.

She was talking now about a crack FBI team led by a specialist in serial murder cases, an inspector named Harry Sullivan. Sullivan believed the Jess Foy homicide fitted the pattern of his Happy Families killer, so named because several of the victims were apparently happy families killed together in their homes.

''They were all stabbed with ice picks. The stabbing's very specific. And the genitals of all the victims were glued,'' Kit said. ''I mean *all* the victims, Frank. Men, women, and children. Obviously we're talking about a psycho. So far the FBI's kept it quiet. You know how these sex killers like publicity. Fortunately no reporter's put it together yet.''

Janek could barely control himself. ''You weren't going to tell me?''

''Of course I was. After you cooled down. I didn't want you working on it, Frank. You were way too angry. You *should* be angry. But we both know an angry cop is usually not a very effective one.''

He was angry all right. For him the worst thing in the world was to be unknowledgeable. He never expected that Kit would deliberately keep him in the dark.

But now she was speaking pensively, as if she were having second thoughts.

''. . . okay, that's conventional wisdom. But sometimes anger can generate creativity. Maybe I was wrong.'' She looked at him. ''I've known you a long time. You've never been one for the empty gesture. When you tell me you're willing to resign—well, I know you're serious. I can't put you over Boyce. Not now, not after what you've done. But I can probably assign you as liaison to Sullivan.''

Janek frowned. ''I run investigations. I don't do liaison.''

''It's *their* investigation, Frank. You can only do what they'll allow.''

''You know that's shit!''

''It doesn't have to be. And please don't give me the old line about how you hate the feds. Right now the case belongs to the FBI. If you want to work it, and I mean Happy Families, not just Jess, the only way is to work it with them.''

''On what basis?''

"Why don't you go down to Quantico tomorrow, have a talk with Sullivan? If the two of you get along, I'm sure he'll find you a niche."

"And if we don't get along?"

Kit shrugged. "Boyce spins his wheels and Sullivan digs in. That's okay. We've had double investigations before. But a triple! Forget it, Frank. A triple's too arcane even for me."

"So it's take it or leave it—that's what you're saying?"

"Something like that." She paused. "I know you don't like it, but it's the best I can do."

He thought it over. "All right," he said. "I'll see Sullivan. But I want Aaron with me."

Kit gave that some thought, then agreed to it.

"So," she asked, "have we got a deal?"

They stood, shook hands; then she hugged him tight.

"I'm sorry, Frank. It was a close call. I did what I thought was best."

The morning he and Aaron flew down to D.C. the blue of the sky was so intense it made Janek's heart ache for Venice.

They rented a sporty Pontiac out of National Airport, then drove south for an hour until they reached the military base at Quantico; then they crossed through the reservation and entered the grounds of the FBI Academy. Here an oversize, rigorously designed glass and stone building was neatly set on a campus of perfectly manicured grass.

They were expected. The guard at the reception desk had their passes. While they waited for their escort, Aaron peered around the atrium.

"Sure all this is for law enforcement, Frank? Looks more like IBM."

Janek nodded. No crummy typewriters on rotten desks in roach- and rat-infested offices here. No drunks wandering in here off the street. This, he recognized, was law enforcement U.S. government style, practiced by men and women wearing dark suits and necklace badges working efficiently at computer stations. In this orderly temple of police science the windows were always washed and the floors were always shined and, when you needed something, you didn't have to beg; all you did was put through a requisition. Here, too, was the finest forensic crime lab in the world.

The Behavioral Science Unit, where Sullivan was headquartered, was a rabbit warren of windowless offices. When Janek and Aaron arrived, they were told Sullivan was in a meeting, but one of his staff assistants, a Nordic muscleman named Hansen whose shirt collar bit into his neck, had been delegated to take them on a tour.

Hansen led them down endless corridors, stopping from time to time to open a door and show them something dazzling: the director's paneled dining room; an Olympic-size swimming pool where agents were trained to swim while holding weapons; the world's largest, most efficient underground firing range.

After an hour of this Janek grew impatient.

"Look," he said to Hansen, "I don't mean to be rude, but I think we've seen enough."

"There's a lot more, Lieutenant," Hansen said. "Inspector Sullivan especially wanted you to see Hogan's Alley."

"What's that?"

"It's where we train police officers from all over the country in criminal apprehension."

"I think we can skip that," Janek said. "Please tell the inspector we've come a long way and now we're ready to work."

Hansen's face fell. He stared at Janek with uncon-cealed hurt, then dodged into a nearby office to use the phone. Janek watched from the corridor as, once con-nected, Hansen cupped his hand over the receiver.

"Probably telling Sullivan what uncouth louts we are," Aaron said.

Janek shook his head. He didn't like the setup. The tour had been laid on to intimidate. Sullivan wanted to soften them up, make them feel outclassed.

"All righty, Lieutenant," Hansen said, rejoining them in the corridor. "We're to go straight up to room two-oh-one."

Another march along endless windowed corridors, then up a stairs, around a corner, past hundreds of doors leading into hundreds of little offices until, finally, they reached the briefing room.

Sullivan was waiting for them. He was a stocky man about Janek's age, with an affable smile, beautifully coiffed iron gray hair, pink, well-shaven cheeks, and tiny, twinkling ice blue eyes. Though he spoke slowly with a slight drawl, this was no Ray Boyce. His gestures were sharp, his little eyes were quick, and he came off as shrewd and savvy.

But there was a cockiness about him that inspired in Janek a nearly instant dislike. He hadn't wanted to detest Sullivan. He'd come with the expectation that they would treat each other with respect. But the way the man stood, his back just a little too straight, his head angled upward, his chin stuck out just a little more than necessary, reminded Janek of a prison warden trying unsuccessfully to conceal his swagger.

He only hoped this first impression would be belied.

The briefing room was state-of-the-art with the latest in audiovisual aids. There was a polished white marble conference table with glasses, water pitcher, yellow legal pads, and sharpened pencils arranged like place settings for a banquet. Two tabbed briefing books, with Janek's and Aaron's names embossed on the covers, were centered perfectly before two deep upholstered swivel chairs with electronic gear built into the armrests. When Janek sat in his, he felt like a millionaire ready to deep-sea fish off the back of a yacht.

"Gentlemen," Sullivan announced, in a sonorous airline pilot's voice, "I thought the best approach would be to have members of my staff brief you on particular aspects of HF. Then, when you've got a handle on the cases, I'll rejoin you for the overview."

"HF—can you believe they call it that?" Aaron whispered.

Janek believed. The FBI was notorious for its abbreviations and acronyms. But he preferred HF to Happy Families, which smacked of a headline in one of the national tabloids: HAPPY FAMILIES KILLER STRIKES AGAIN.

The briefing that commenced, part lecture, part slide show, consisted of a procession of crisp, well-rehearsed young forensic analysts, each with his own area of expertise, doing his stint with pointer and easel, then yielding to the next.

They were shown detailed color slides of the five Happy Families crime scenes. People with stiffened limbs and ice picks protruding from their ears, eyes, and

throats lay at odd angles in domestic settings. All were
naked from the waist down, having been stripped in
order to be glued. Janek found himself turning his head,
then looking at the pictures obliquely with only one eye.
He wasn't certain why he did this; it was a habit he'd
acquired over the years. Perhaps, he thought, if only one
eye were exposed, the gruesome images would be less
deeply engraved upon his memory.

The agents used staccato tones to describe each set of
victims along with details of the abuses each had
suffered:

Miss Bertha Parce, an elderly retired schoolteacher, found murdered in her bed in a single-
room-occupancy hotel in Miami Beach, Florida

Cynthia Morse, a wealthy divorcée, killed over
Memorial Day weekend, with her two visiting
grown daughters, in her luxury condominium in
Seattle, Washington

James and Stuart MacDonald, two aging
playboy-type brothers, slain in their shared weekend
house in Kent, Connecticut

*The Robert Wexler family (husband, wife, three
children)* killed in their suburban ranch-style home
in Fort Worth, Texas

*The Anthony Scotto family (husband, wife, and
two teenage sons)* slaughtered in their Cape Cod–
style home just outside Providence, Rhode Island

There was also a homeless man who didn't seem to fit
the pattern, though he, too, had been stabbed and glued,
then left in an alley in the Alphabet City section of
Manhattan.

The presentation notably did not include anything about Jess. Janek wondered whether this was because the team was being considerate of his feelings or because it simply hadn't worked up that part of the briefing yet.

At exactly twelve-thirty a break was called, and Janek and Aaron were invited to join the analysts for a working lunch in the staff cafeteria. But as it turned out, the conversation there had little to do with the case. Rather, the agents solicited war stories from New York, for which they exchanged no personal revelations, only other war stories they'd heard from other visiting investigators.

Later, in the men's room, Aaron asked Janek what he thought was going on.

"They're looking to see if we're team players. Teamwork's what the FBI's all about."

Aaron laughed. "We're hotshots, ain't we, Frank?" Then, more seriously: "I feel out of place. Maybe it's the clothes. They all dress so nice. Even some of the ladies wear ties."

The afternoon session concluded the presentation of cases, after which their tour guide, Hansen, reappeared with another muscle-bound assistant to demonstrate the stabbing method. The men acted it out several times at normal speed and then in slow motion: a violent thrust with an ice pick from under the chin through the roof of the mouth, the ear hole, or the eye socket and then into the brain. The fact that the pick was always left embedded was, according to Hansen, "classic commando technique."

The star speaker of the afternoon was Dr. David Chun, brought in to explicate the killer profile. Janek had heard of him. The brilliant young Asian-American was not an

FBI employee but a forensic psychiatrist on the faculty at Harvard Law School, who had testified at numerous high-profile criminal trials around the country. From the flattering way Sullivan introduced him, it was clear he considered Chun a major asset.

The moment the doctor began to speak, Janek understood why he was usually so successful with juries. He had the kind of deep, authoritative voice that compels attention and belief. But there was something canny, perhaps even vain in his presentation, that fitted with the subtle swagger Janek had observed in Sullivan and the entire HF team. The way these people behaved spoke of arrogant pride. They saw themselves as the best of the best. And they'd made it clear at lunch that if the two shaggy, scruffily dressed detectives from New York wanted in, they would have to prove they had the stuff.

Dr. Chun stated his belief that the organized crime scenes and ethnic background of the victims indicated a white male killer most likely in his late twenties or early thirties. Further, he believed the neatness of the gluing suggested excellent hand-eye coordination, as well as a certain protective concern for the victims' "bodily integrity."

"Various facts," he continued, "such as the forced entries, clean escapes, and the killer's ability to take on multiple victims, suggest a particularly confident individual, probably one with a high level of martial arts training. The stabbing technique raises the possibility of a military background. The psychopathology is sexual-sadistic; I would surmise that the killer possesses a large collection of sadomasochistic pornography. The gluings and lack of semen at the crime scenes speak of sexual fear indicative of a loner type. But the most striking characteristic is the killer's lack of gender differentiation.''

The psychiatrist paused. Though his features remained composed, Janek picked up on something in his eyes. *It's almost as if he's afraid,* he thought as Chun continued in the same authoritative style.

''He glues up the genitals of men and women with equal thoroughness. Children, too, and, in the case of Fort Worth, even the family dog and cat. But beyond the genitals, all orifices seem to be fair game. With the Miami woman and the brothers in Connecticut we find mouths and anuses glued. In the case of Providence the wife's fingertips were glued together in a praying-type position. In the other cases fingers and toes were glued at random as if to create a webbed hand or foot effect. We call these variations subpatterns. They speak of something beyond conventional categories of sexual assault. In this case concepts such as straight and gay are useless, virtually irrelevant. We appear to be dealing with a man who engages in symbolic negation of any and all forms of human sexuality. One may surmise he has a disturbed relationship with a mother, who is possibly deceased. Finally, the killer is most likely sexually dysfunctional.''

This time, when Dr. Chun paused, his breathing quickened, and he screwed up his eyes. When he resumed speaking, Janek was certain. *Something about this definitely frightens him,* he thought.

''. . . there is one very unusual aspect. This killer chooses what we call difficult victims. With the exception of the homeless man and the young woman jogger in New York, the people he chose were not easy to get at, not easy at all. Most serial killers take an easy path, preying on hitchhikers and prostitutes. But not this one.

He set's himself extremely tough challenges. From this we must infer intelligence, a capacity for careful planning, and a streak of competitiveness rarely demonstrated in this category of crimes.''

After Chun was finished, he stared down at the floor, then raised his head as if he had something to add. He opened his mouth, then abruptly clamped it shut.

"Lieutenant Janek, Sergeant Greenberg—I thank you for your patience." Then he almost seemed to flee the room.

After Chun left, a full minute passed, during which Janek made out a short bit of conversation from the other side of the door. He strained to listen. It was between Sullivan and the psychiatrist. Chun sounded deeply upset:

". . . doesn't fit . . . diabolical . . ."

". . . overworked. Get some rest. We'll talk. . . ."

When Sullivan reentered the room, Janek was impressed by his sangfroid. He picked up the briefing just where Chun had left it off, dealing head-on with the issue of easy versus difficult.

"The homeless man was first and the Foy girl last," Sullivan began. "Both easy prey, both hit-and-run homicides committed outside at night in New York, and both glued quick and sloppy in the crotch. As you've heard, we find much more elaborate gluing when the killings are committed indoors. The killer goes in like a stabbing machine. But then he's careful, very, very careful with the glue. Squirts it in just right, makes sure everything's sealed up."

Sullivan paused for effect.

"All right, you know all that. We acknowledge the inconsistencies. In our discussions we've theorized a possible second killer, an outdoor killer, who murdered the homeless man and the jogger, as opposed to an indoor killer, who murdered the families. But the theory doesn't hold because there's another aspect to the signature. In all seven cases we find the weed.''

Aaron shook his head. "You talking about pot?"

"Not pot, Sergeant, I'm talking about a literal weed. We didn't pick up on it at first. Then our forensic people noticed that there was always some wild plant left at the scene, a dandelion or a dried-up field daisy, a junk flower like you'd find in a vacant lot. This isn't a mystery novel. No rose or carnation or orchid here. Just a weed. A crummy weed.'' Sullivan turned to Janek. "There was a weed left near your goddaughter's body, too. . . ."

They finally did get to see Hogan's Alley. Sullivan insisted on it. Color-coded students (red T-shirts for FBI; blue for police) ran around what looked like a movie set playing cops and robbers. The inspector watched, extremely proud, but Janek found it tiresome. *These FBI people,* he thought, *live in a world of their own, where technology and profiling and games are ends in themselves.* Meantime, city detectives like Aaron and himself worked sleazy cases out of dirty offices. He had no doubt as to which of them had a better feel for the criminal mind.

Janek arranged to meet Sullivan that night at a D.C. restaurant, then drove Aaron back to National Airport.

"I want to get him alone," Janek explained. "Really piss him off."

"I thought we were supposed to make nice."

"You want to work with him?"

"Be pretty tough," Aaron admitted. "But I'll give it a shot if you want me to."

"Maybe it won't be necessary," Janek said.

He dropped Aaron off at the Pan Am Shuttle, then drove into D.C. Though it was only five o'clock, the sky was already darkening. Affluent-looking joggers were running all over the place, and the rush-hour traffic was starting to build. He parked his car in a garage at the Watergate complex, then set out to walk. After a while he felt himself drawn to a center of energy. It was the Vietnam War Memorial. He knew it from pictures but had always wanted to see it for himself.

When he arrived, he felt no disappointment. The wall was everything he'd imagined. And it evoked in him a strong feeling, a bittersweet nostalgia for his own tour out there when, in 1968, he'd worked narcotics with Army CID in Da Nang. But as he stood in the shadows with the other visitors, staring at the black granite while the last light slowly faded from the sky, he felt a strong, sad anger for the awful waste of that war and the young American lives that had been lost fighting it.

The restaurant Sullivan had chosen, small, elegant, and expensive, was situated on the lower level of the Watergate Hotel. Even as Janek entered, he felt Sullivan's intention. The inspector knew he wasn't wearing the right clothes for such a place, so again he was trying to make him feel uncomfortable.

Janek waited a full fifteen minutes before he realized that, too, was part of the plan. And then he found Sullivan pathetic. The manipulation was so unimaginative, an exact duplication of the method used that morning at the academy. Sullivan had proven himself to have a small-time bureaucrat's mentality. Such a man would solve a major case only by luck.

By the time the inspector did arrive, smiling, solicitous, excessive with profuse apologies, Janek had decided to play the first part of their dinner at his most collegial.

"Here's how we see it," Sullivan said, after coaching Janek patiently through the menu. "The five indoor family killings were very difficult to bring off. The two outdoor single killings were relatively easy. But in all seven cases we see the same thrust, same brand of ice pick, same basic mutilation of the genitals and the weed. So what we're thinking—"

Janek interrupted. "You're thinking the homeless man was for practice. After him the killer went after desired prey."

"You're good, Frank. I'm impressed. So tell me— what else do we think?"

"You think Jess Foy was for practice, too. You think the killer lives in New York because that's where he practices. You think when he wants to kill a family, he travels outside the city until he finds one that attracts him."

Sullivan grinned. "You've pretty much got it."

"So tell me," Janek said, "if he likes happy families so much and has so much positive experience with them, what does he need another round of practice for?"

Sullivan clicked his teeth. "Who the hell knows? These sociopaths have their own twisted logic. Some of it we understand; some we don't. Maybe the guy's losing his nerve. Maybe he's just sharpening his skills."

Janek was not charmed by that little witticism. And he wasn't sure which notion he disliked more: Jess as random victim or used as a practice target by a serial killer.

Sullivan sat back, his pink cheeks puffed out. "I feel something in all this, Frank. Something that goes beyond cases I've worked before. It's like, I don't know, it's a . . . Great Crime."

Janek stared at him. "What does that mean, Harry? A 'Great Crime'—what the hell is that?"

"Like that big case of yours. That Switched Heads thing. A great criminal conception. A killer playing a dangerous game, taunting us while he weaves his pattern. He sees himself as an artist. To catch him, we have to understand his art. In the end that'll tell us who he is. Decipher the pattern." Sullivan held up his hand. "Then he's ours." He shut his fist to stimulate a trap.

"Any way you see me fitting into this?"

Sullivan smiled. "We stayed late, talked it over after you left. The boys think you could be a real asset."

"What about Aaron?"

"Not so clear. Don't misunderstand, Frank. I'm sure he's a terrific cop."

But with him on the team I'd have an ally, and you don't want that, Janek thought.

Sullivan leaned forward. He wanted to speak in confidence.

"I know it's tough. I know how cops feel. I know we're not the most popular guys around. But we've got the expertise, Frank. On a case like this we're the only game in town. Not just because we can coordinate on a national level but because we've been studying these guys, profiling them for years. After a while you get a feel for them. This one's tough, but I know there's a soft spot. There always is. With your help I think we can find it. I'd be truly honored, Frank, if you'd agree to join my team."

When the main courses arrived, they dropped discussion of the case. As they ate, Sullivan spoke casually of his ambition to write.

"It's what I've always wanted to do," he said. "Think about it—all the fiction writers out there who'd give their left ball for the kind of material we deal with every day." He took a bite from his plate. "Ever hear of Grey Scopetta?"

"No."

"A film director. Does these true crime things on TV. I figured with your miniseries and all you'd have heard of him."

"It wasn't *my* miniseries, Harry. I was just the police adviser."

Sullivan winked at him. "Don't be so modest." He gulped some wine. "Anyway, about Scopetta—he's been in touch with me about HF."

Janek put down his fork. "I thought the point was to keep it quiet."

"From reporters, sure. But the bureau likes filmmakers. Some way, we don't know how, Scopetta heard about the case and put through a request for a briefing. So we gave him one. Nothing like what you got. The smaller, simpler version. And nothing about the weed. Nobody knows about that, not even detectives in cities where the families were killed. Anyway, the two of us stayed in touch. So one day we're talking and he mentions I'm the guy maybe ought to write the script. I figured what the hell, why not give it a shot? So this past summer I flew out to L.A., took a crash course in screenwriting, one of those five-hundred-bucks-per-weekend seminar deals. Now in my free time, evenings and weekends, I've been writing away.''

Again Sullivan lowered his voice.

''Look, this is the kind of case that when it's solved, there's sure to be a movie. So I figured why shouldn't I, the guy who's going to solve it, get a piece of the action? Somebody's gotta write it. Why not me? That way, soon as there's an indictment, the script's ready to go. Nothing wrong with what I'm doing; I checked with our ethics guys. I'm not showing my script to anyone. Just getting it ready, that's all. See, Scopetta explained it to me: Screenwriting is structure. So that's what I'm working on, the structure of the thing. And lately I've had this idea that working on the structure of the script is going to help me solve HF. Because HF's got a structure, too. Know what I mean? Solve it as a story and I may solve it as a case. Anyway, it's an idea. . . .''

Jesus, what an asshole! Janek thought.

With dessert, they resumed discussion of Happy Families. Having trusted Janek with his writing ambitions, Sullivan was finally ready to expose the most sensitive aspects of the case.

''Okay,'' Sullivan said, ''you know what we've got. After a year of work, incredibly little. No prints. No fibers. No tissue cells. No DNA. The ice picks are common, sold all over the country, and the weeds are obviously untraceable. We believe the gluings were done with a standard caulking gun, the kind you can buy in any hardware store. He rams it into them, then shoots in potent animal glue. Now there was one thing we didn't get to in the briefing. Connections between the victims. Believe me, we searched for them. We have a powerful computer program designed to make that kind of search.

So far all it's come up with is a city, Cleveland, which ties together only two of the families. The brothers in Connecticut were from there, and the old lady in Florida taught school there before she retired. Coincidence? Probably. If it was a small town in southern Ohio, I might feel different. A serial killer fixated on Cleveland—I just don't see a story line there. . . ."

Janek cleared his throat. *Time now to rattle him,* he thought.

"Maybe it's not a serial case, Harry. Ever think of that?"

"You kidding? This is a classic. Of course it's a serial case."

"I'm not so sure."

Sullivan's pink cheeks began to redden. "What the hell're you talking about?"

Janek shrugged. "Call it a gut feeling."

Sullivan snorted. Then he turned sarcastic. "What else does your 'gut' tell you?"

"Now don't act offended, Harry."

"I *am* offended. You're questioning the premise of my investigation. What's bugging you?"

"No victimology."

Sullivan stared at him. Then he smiled. "Okay, you're good, you picked up on that. But see, even with the best software, the computer isn't perfect."

"Forget the computer. I'm talking about David Chun."

"David's upset about a couple things. But—"

"He talked about everything except what the killer found attractive, what he saw in his 'difficult victims' that made him decide to go after them. And that's the key, isn't it? If you've got that many victims and they don't tell you why they were attacked, well, then, what have you got? Far as I can see, nothing. Except''—he sneered—'' 'Happy Families.' ''

"You're mocking that?"

"I don't mock homicide victims, Harry. But tell me, between the two of us, what was so goddamn happy about all those people?''

"Oh, come off it! That's just the name we use. . . .''

"Sure. That's how it started. Because you couldn't read the common element. But now it's like the name's defining the case. 'Happy Families'—how do you know they were happy? Because they lived in nice houses, nice neighborhoods, Dad coached Little League, Mom baked apple pies, and kids were on the honor roll? Because their friends and neighbors told you they were? See, Harry, I never worked a case where I didn't hear the victims were just the greatest people, the finest, happiest people. And half the time it turned out they were just like everybody else, happy and unhappy, capable of hurting each other, even capable of killing each other if the stress got bad enough. I'm not saying your families *weren't* happy. I'm just asking how you *know* they were. Because I don't buy Happy Families. It's too vague. Show me a victim list of pretty blondes with hoop earrings or old ladies with hairy chins, then maybe I'll go along. But you don't have that. I think this goes deeper. I think these killings were victim-specific. I think there's an invisible thread connecting all these people and you and your team just haven't found it yet.''

"After a year of work we haven't found it, the best serial killer team ever assembled. But *you're* going to find it? Great! Maybe you'll even find it tonight!''

Janek sat back. Sullivan's sarcasm didn't bother him. It only made him want to push the needle farther in.

"Know what I think, Harry? I think working out of Behavioral Science has got you overinvested in the serial killer idea. I think you're so wrapped up in that you can't see beyond it to anything else."

Now Sullivan was staring at him, trying to push him with a hard cop's stare. "Man, you've got some kind of balls," he whispered. "If I were you, I'd watch my step. Someone just might come along and cut 'em off. Know what I mean, Frank?"

Janek smiled. He'd forced Sullivan to resort to vulgar, tough guy talk. When a cop started talking about cutting off another cop's balls, he was aroused to a highly competitive state.

"I've heard about you," Sullivan continued, not bothering to conceal his bitterness. "I saw the way they played you on TV. This genius cop who didn't need a team, didn't need backup, didn't need nothing except his brain, which we're supposed to think is so powerful it should be registered as a dangerous weapon." Sullivan grinned. His cheeks were quivering. His little ice blue eyes were sparkling with envy. "So here we sit, end of our first day together. I lay my case out for you, a year's worth of work, and now you slip to me you got a theory of your own."

"Yeah, I guess that's about it," Janek agreed.

"I think it's a crock of shit."

"Maybe it is. But the question is, Harry, how're we going to find out?"

Sullivan glared at him. "Suppose you tell me, Frank."

"My suggestion is since you're so sure it's a serial

case, you and your team continue working the way you
are. Meantime, let Aaron and me follow up on my idea.
We can set up a little two-man office in New York, in a
precinct back room somewhere. Of course, we'll share
what we find, but other than that, we'll stay out of your
way.''

Sullivan chewed on that for a moment. ''Nice concept.
Only trouble is . . . I don't see what's in it for me.''

''Come on, Harry! There's plenty in it for you. You
get the chance to compete.''

''Compete?''

''FBI versus NYPD, you versus me. Whoever solves
the case gets the glory: the book, the TV movie, the
whole enchilada. Right now you've got the manpower
and a year's head start. Pretty good odds.'' Janek smiled
as he appealed to Sullivan's weakness. ''You look like a
sport, Harry. What do you say?''

''I'll have to think about it.''

''Do that.'' Janek pushed away his coffee, tossed two
fifty-dollar bills onto the table, and stood up. ''That's for
the dinner. I'm going to try and catch the last shuttle. Call
me when you decide. But don't take too long, okay?''

New York was fogged in, so the late shuttle was
diverted to Newark. Janek exited the airport terminal into
a light and soothing swirl of softly falling rain. He shared
a taxi into town with a businessman from Taiwan who
admitted this was his first visit to the States.

As their cab approached the Lincoln Tunnel, the city
was suddenly revealed, a million lights in the towers of
midtown burning through the fog. It was a great romantic
vision of Manhattan, and the Taiwanese gentleman

peered at it, amazed. "You must be very strong to survive in a place like this," he muttered.

Janek nodded. *Yeah, you must be strong. And even then you may not survive.*

He dropped the visitor off at the Waldorf-Astoria, then asked the driver to take him through Central Park. There the fog clung strangely to the statues and hugged the glow of the sodium lamps.

When he finally got back to his apartment, he phoned Aaron at home, told him about his proposed competition with Sullivan. Aaron was surprised. On what basis, he wanted to know, had Janek come up with "victim-specific"?

"On no basis, except my feeling Chun had doubts and there was no way we could work under Sullivan. So I did the only thing that would shake the asshole up. Whatever he said, I said the opposite."

"But it *is* a serial case. I mean—isn't it, Frank?"

"Could be. I honestly don't know."

"Those guys seem so sure."

"Yeah, they're sure. But I wasn't bullshitting Sullivan. My true gut reaction is that they're all wrong." He paused. "Did you notice how bored they were? A year of grinding work, and they got nothing."

"Just a bunch of charts and a freaked-out psychiatrist. Still, if it *is* a serial deal . . ."

"Let me tell you something about serial deals, Aaron. When they're solved, *if* they *are* solved, it's usually because one night some hick town rookie pulls some guy over for a speeding ticket and happens to see a bloody knife on the seat. I say screw that."

"Fine, Frank. Fine. But where do we start—assuming Sullivan buys your deal and Chief Kopta approves?"

"We'll concentrate on Jess. She left me a worried message. Assume she knew she was in danger and was looking to me to help. If that's true, then the first question we've got to ask ourselves is: *What was Jess afraid of?*"

5

Mama
Again

"Listen carefully, child."

"I'm listening, Mama."

"I'm concerned about Tool."

"Please don't be, Mama."

"But I'm *very* concerned. Unless a tool like that gets regular use, it can easily lose its edge. Preventative maintenance is so important, you know."

"I know, Mama. And I keep Tool in excellent condition. I work with it every day, keep it honed. I want it to stay sharp. And always be ready."

"Still, I'm concerned."

"Please, Mama—leave it to me."

"It needs supervision."

"I give it plenty of supervision."

"You know the problem with a tool like that? A tool like that can get out of hand, can start to have a mind of its own."

"No. . . . Do you really think so?"

"I *definitely* think so. You must watch Tool carefully, child, see it doesn't get any ideas or forget its place."

"I just don't believe—"

"Better listen to Mama. Mama knows best."

"Yes, Mama."

"A tool like that needs tending. A tool like that is dangerous. You create a tool like that and let it get away from you, you lose control. The whole point of a tool like that is it works *for* you, does *your* bidding. A tool like that goes into business for itself, you gotta think about getting rid of it."

"Yes, Mama. . . ."

6
The Fear

Ray Boyce was steaming, his forehead popping sweat. The long, thin wisps he kept carefully combed across his skull were mussed, and the squared-off bottom of his face was trembling like Jell-O.

"I don't get it," he griped.

Janek watched Kit recoil; it was as if the back of her big chief's chair were sucking on her spine. Janek looked around the office, a cavernous space that spoke of the high status of its occupant. The windows were huge. On the other side of the glass large snowflakes fell softly to Police Plaza below.

"I'm sweating out the case, doing a pretty decent job." Boyce mopped his forehead. "Least I thought I was." He spoke with a whine. "Meantime, Janek here does all this unauthorized bullshit. And for that he gets—*rewarded*?"

Boyce's question hung in the overheated air. Kit stared at him with faint disgust. Janek, sitting beside him in the other chair facing Kit's desk, felt sorry for him. The poor slob was going to mouth his way straight into trouble.

"I don't know I'd exactly call it a reward, Ray," Janek said gently.

Boyce didn't bother to look at him. He stared straight at Kit, waiting for her to render justice.

"It wasn't a reward," Kit said finally. "Detective Janek is a specialist in this type of crime. His insights will prove helpful in solving it. As for his unauthorized activity, I've put a letter of reprimand in his file. Want me to read it to you?"

Boyce shook his head. "That's Janek's business. All I care about is my role. Am I supervising Janek or the other way around? 'Cause if it is, I can tell you right now, I'm not going—"

"I'm the supervisor here. You and Janek will run parallel investigations. If either of you finds anything, you'll bring it to me."

"What about duplication?"

Oh-oh—don't push it, Ray.

"I'll worry about that," Kit said.

"Sure, you'll worry. But what about the people we're going to interview? Two detectives coming from different directions—that'll get everyone confused." He glanced at Janek. Then his voice turned bitter. "Of course, Janek here's such a famous investigator they'll probably fall all over themselves they'll be so flattered."

"That'll be enough, Detective."

Boyce stared at her, nonplussed. "I may look dumb, Chief. But I can read the writing on the wall."

"What's that supposed to mean?" Kit's hoarse whisper should have cut straight to Boyce's ears. But the slob wasn't listening; he was too wrapped up in his self-pity.

"You don't want me in on this. You want Janek. I know why, too."

"Why?" Kit demanded.

"Because he's your . . . you know."

Oh, you poor hotheaded son of a bitch.

"My *what*?"

Boyce sputtered. "Your special friend's what I hear."

"Want a letter in *your* file, Boyce?"

"All I want is fair treatment!" But then something must have told Boyce he'd gone too far because suddenly he clamped his mouth. When he opened it again, his tone was different. "I respectfully ask permission to withdraw from the case," he whispered with restrained fury.

"Permission granted." Kit rose. "I've got work to do. Boyce, report to your precinct commander. Janek, stay. I've got a few choice words for you, Detective."

She walked across her office to the window, stared out at the falling snow until Boyce had shut the door. When she turned to Janek, her eyes were glowing.

"You're really a prick."

Janek shrugged. "You're the one who told me to go down to Quantico."

"And you played Sullivan just right, didn't you? I should have known."

"I don't see the problem . . . now that Boyce has so graciously stepped aside."

"The problem, my friend, is he's going to talk. It doesn't do anything for my reputation to have a pissed-off detective saying Chief Kopta's not a straight shooter."

"Everyone knows you shoot straight."

"Yeah." She looked resigned. "Well, you did it, Frank. Set things up just the way you wanted them."

"So punish me for it. Put another letter in my file."

She shook her head. "I hope I won't be sorry about this."

"You won't be." Janek walked briskly to the door. "Sullivan's the one'll be sorry."

Aaron had begged them space on the fourth floor of the Police Property Building in Greenwich Village between Fifth and University Place. The office was on the same floor as the narcotics storage room, past the detectives' lounge, down the hall, down three steps, up two, first door on the left. Aaron had borrowed two gray hard-rubber-top desks, two swivel chairs, a beaten-up filing cabinet, and an answering machine. When Janek appeared in the doorway, he was in the midst of sweeping out an accumulation of used Styrofoam coffee cups, empty potato chip bags, and cigar ash from the last special squad to occupy the space.

"I see we're slumming," Janek said.

"It's okay, Frank." Aaron gestured toward a dustpan. Janek handed it to him. "Remember last spring when the President was here? Secret Service unit used this for a command post. That's why we got so many phones. Connected, too."

Janek looked at the phones, six five-button models, three on each desk. Then he sniffed the air. The room was overheated and much too dry. He turned to the ceiling; the fluorescent lights buzzed. He peered around, noticed a disgusting crust on the far wall, most likely pizza sauce, he hoped not blood. A radiator hissed out steam. He looked at Aaron, who nodded back, mutual acknowledgment that though their office was a shithouse, it was at least their own.

He helped Aaron sweep out the remainder of the junk, then returned the brooms and trash can to the cleaning closet. The corridor smelled of stale cigarette smoke.

When he returned to the office, he noticed his rubber boots were leaking. He pulled them off and stared out the window. It had stopped snowing. On the street the buildup of perfect flakes was already turning gray.

He knew what he wanted to do: talk to everyone who'd had close contact with Jess, particularly the last few days of her life. He wanted to chart every hour of her final days: where she'd gone; what she'd done; the name of every person she'd spoken to.

He drew up a rough grid chart, showed it to Aaron, instructed him to get a police artist to paint it on their largest wall.

"And while he's in here with a brush," Janek said, pointing, "maybe he can do something about that crust."

He also assigned Aaron to talk to all the members of the Greg Gale group.

"Check them all out; get them alone; squeeze them hard. If you smell anything murderous or that smacks of a cult, let me know. But please keep the details of the fun and games to yourself. I'd just as soon not hear any more about Jess's sex life."

Aaron understood.

Janek had set himself another task. He taxied to La Guardia Airport, found a seat on the noon shuttle to Boston, then sat in the plane for an hour before it left the gate.

There were numerous announcements from the pilot: Air traffic was snarled up and down the eastern seaboard; half a foot of snow had fallen on Logan in Boston. Stewardesses prowled the cabin, offering tiny cellophane bags containing honey-roasted cashews. Then everyone was ordered off the plane. Then, suddenly, mysteriously, they all were ordered back on. And then, with undue haste it seemed to Janek, the plane revved up and took off with a roar.

When he reached Boston, it was nearly three o'clock. Janek took one look at the taxi line, found his way to the subway, transferred at Park Street, and fifty minutes later got off at Harvard Square. Some helpful students guided him to the Law School, an immensely long building, where numerous assistant D.A.s of his acquaintance had, in their student days, undergone excruciating torture.

Janek appeared in the doorway of Dr. David Chun's second-floor office just as the psychiatrist, already in his overcoat, was stuffing file folders into a briefcase.

Chun was not pleased to see him. "You should have called, Lieutenant. Unfortunately I can't talk to you now. I'm going home before the snow gets too deep."

"The snow stopped falling a couple hours ago, Doctor," Janek replied. "If you wait another hour, everthing'll be shoveled out."

Chun stared at him. "You know better than to show up here without an appointment. Please tell me why didn't you call."

"I didn't think you'd see me. So I came up anyway, took a chance."

Chun sat down. "Why didn't you think I'd see you?"

Janek sat, too. He'd gotten the psychiatrist's attention. Now all he had to do was hold it.

"You were upset down in Quantico. I had the feeling you wished Sullivan had never involved you in the case. Something frightens you about it, something you don't want to discuss. I need to hear you discuss it, Doctor. That's why I came."

Chun studied him. "You're different from Sullivan. You're a listener."

"I try to be."

Chun thought a moment before he spoke. "Okay, Lieutenant, take a seat outside. I'll give my wife a call; then we'll talk."

When Chun came out, he was carrying his briefcase and still wearing his overcoat. *Uh-oh,* Janek thought, *he's changed his mind.* But Chun was no less anxious to talk; he just didn't want to do it in his office.

He guided Janek across Harvard Yard. Students were walking briskly on the freshly shoveled paths, and some freshmen were putting finishing touches on a snowman that bore a vague resemblance to Fidel Castro. Janek watched while a rosy-cheeked girl in a white ski parka struck a piece of black wood into the effigy's mouth to simulate a cigar.

At Harvard Square the snow had turned to slush. A newsdealer hawked hometown papers. Chun led Janek through the Coop, past counters displaying Harvard running shorts and T-shirts with amusing slogans, then out a rear door and across a narrow street.

As they entered the dark lounge called Casablanca, Janek was struck by a throaty torch song rendition of "As Time Goes By." The place, dominated by a huge blowup of Humphrey Bogart, was empty except for a few student couples. Janek glanced at the jukebox. It offered esoteric selections, old love songs from the forties and fifties, renditions by Dietrich and Piaf.

"Oh, yes, something *is* bothering me, Lieutenant," Dr. Chun said after they were seated and the doctor had ordered himself a double martini. "But you see, there's a strange thing about these serial cases. You work with them awhile, you're bound to go a little crazy. It's quite common to become depressed. Dealing with killers, talking to them, interviewing them—that can bring you down a lot sometimes.''

He smiled, a crisp, neat little smile, then gulped from his glass. Waiting for the doctor to continue, Janek sipped some scotch.

''Those of us who do this kind of work are aware of that. Inspector Sullivan, too. He's a bright man, stubborn at times, but like yourself, he's a hunter, so for him there's always the challenge of the chase. Not for me. My job is to profile. And to do that, I have to go inside a killer's mind. I never had any trouble with that before. But this case is different. Please tell me, Lieutenant, if you will, why *you* think it's different.''

''I never said it was different.''

''But you believe it is or you wouldn't have come all this way.''

The same small, neat smile again. Chun lifted a toothpick from the holder on the table, used it to stab his martini olive.

Janek nodded. ''I found your presentation fascinating. A confident, organized, highly competitive killer, sexually dysfunctional and all of that. But I missed something important, an explanation of why the victims were chosen.''

Chun popped the olive into his mouth. ''You've seen the hole. You're a perceptive man.'' He cleared his throat. ''People who are murdered by a serial killer are not chosen for death by accident. In a sense, for which we must remember never to blame them, the victims select themselves. By the way they look or dress or talk they become attractive to the killer. Sometimes they become stand-ins for a parent or another person who has played a significant role in the killer's life. When we first started to work on Happy Families, we assumed that one person in each family, most likely a female, was the target and the the others were killed out of collateral rage or simply because they were witnesses. Then we found the case of the two brothers. So the gender thing broke down right there. To put it in a nutshell, I have analyzed these victims very carefully, charting every observable trait. And I cannot come up with a single common element of attractiveness. Except, of course, the families.''

"But everyone is a member of a family, Doctor. If that's the only common element, why these particular families? For me the idea of families doesn't pattern out.''

Chun swallowed the remains of his martini. "You're right, of course, and that, you see, is what frightens me so much about this case. That's why I wish Sullivan had never brought me into it.'' He screwed up his features the way he had in Quantico. "What I feel here is . . . I don't know quite how to express it. It's as if there's nothing here, nothing particular—do you follow what I'm saying? It's as if this killer doesn't care about anything. As if nothing attracts him. As if he only wants to kill. And as monstrous as a serial killer always is, usually there's some little thing, some small fascination with people no matter how twisted or perverse, that can help us to understand him, maybe even to sympathize a little bit. But here there's a void, a nothingness. I've never faced anything quite like it. It scares me, the blankness of it, the nihilism, the zeroness. Look at me, Lieutenant.'' Chun presented his face to Janek. "Can you see how terrified I am? Because where there is nothing, Lieutenant, no reason, no incentive, no caring, no human bond, then there is nothing to understand.'' Dr. Chun grinned helplessly. ''There's just . . . nothing.''

And with that the psychiatrist hung his head and stared disconsolately into his empty glass.

That night, back in New York, the snow was swirling around the streetlamps, almost, it seemed to Janek, like bugs on a summer's night. He phoned Aaron from the airport, was surprised to learn that Jess's things were still in her dorm room.

''The college wants the room back,'' Aaron told him. ''They've been bugging the Dorances to move her stuff out. But Boyce put a seal on the door, then never got around to inspecting it. Course, we already know what a dumb schmuck he is.''

They met in midtown, rode up to the Columbia campus together, then separated at 114th Street, Aaron to continue his interviews with the Greg Gale group, Janek to check out Jess's room.

The dorm was a modern high rise. A moody female student with badly bitten nails and stringy, unwashed hair manned the lobby security desk alongside a grizzled campus cop. An oddly mismatched pair, they screened visitors and checked student IDs.

When Janek told the girl where he was going, she gave him a curious look.

''Kids've been getting pretty spooked around that room,'' she muttered.

While he waited for the elevator, Janek perused the dorm bulletin board. It was layered with notices that collectively demonstrated the richness (or perhaps, he thought, the poverty) of American college life: a lecture on Icelandic poetry; a rally for Palestinian rights; a black lesbian tea dance; a plea for information on faculty-student sexual harassment, anonymity promised to informants.

On the twelfth floor he paused before Jess's door. The corridor carried a blend of sounds issuing from adjoining rooms: students talking, laughing; TV shows; heavy metal rock; someone practicing a cello far down the hall. It was the sound of young Americans, and it filled Janek with a bitter pain. A week before, Jess had lived within this sound, had contributed to it. Now her silent room "spooked" the other kids.

The room he entered was small, a virtual monk's cell, containing a narrow bed covered with an Indian blanket, a pair of matching bookcases crammed with books, and a clean white Formica desk with a laptop computer centered on its top. A small CD player and a pair of earphones she probably used late at night lay on a little table beside her bed.

Janek sat down on the bed. He wanted to feel comfortable, but he couldn't. He glanced at the walls, which spoke so strongly of Jess. Almost every spare inch was covered with items from her edged weapons collection: fencing foils; rapiers; swords; daggers; knives. It was an odd hobby for a girl, but Jess had clung to it since she was twelve. She had fallen in love with the romance of swordplay from the day he had taken her to a repertory movie house to see José Ferrer in *Cyrano de Bergerac*.

"Thrust home, thrust home . . ." she had repeated afterward on the street, exuberant as she mimicked Cyrano's elegant lunge.

Restless on the bed, Janek moved to the bookcases,

then knelt to inspect the titles. There were numerous volumes devoted to fencing and edged weapons and also martial arts, which Jess had taken up when she started college.

Janek remembered her words: ''There's so much crime around there, Frank. All sorts of muggings and stuff. A lot of the kids are scared to walk alone, but I want to learn to take care of myself.'' He remembered the way she'd tossed her hair when she'd added: ''I don't like walking around afraid.''

He sat for a long time on the bed, waiting for something to happen. The walls, the books, swords and knives—he waited for them to speak, to tell him what had frightened her. When they stayed silent, he knew it was time to take the room apart.

He searched the dresser first. He wept as he touched her clothes: neatly folded pairs of jeans, sweaters, jerseys, shirts, underwear. Her workout clothes moved him most, perhaps, he thought, because they seemed so intimate; within these garments she had moved, run, perspired. He examined everything, turned out every pair of socks, patted down every T-shirt, all to no avail. Aside from a comb, some costume jewelry, a pack of condoms, and miscellaneous coins, he found nothing.

When he was finished with the dresser, he went to work on the closet, checking the dresses, placing them lovingly on the bed, then exploring the interior of every sneaker and shoe. Behind the shoes he found a set of chromed weights and, inexplicably, a bow and a quiver full of arrows. When he had the closet empty, he stepped into it and peered around. Just above the door he saw a piece of cardboard. It was taped to the wall.

He hesitated. Behind that cardboard she had hidden something. Did he have the right to intrude?

But his role now was not that of a respectful godfather; he was a detective investigating a murder. He reached up and pulled the cardboard free. Several photographs floated to the floor.

He stooped to pick them up. They were Polaroids. A series of four shots, they showed Jess and another girl, wearing fencing pantaloons but also unmasked and, mysteriously, bare to the waist, fighting with sabers like duelists.

At first he couldn't bear to look at them. The exposure of Jess's flesh, the way her pert young breasts were pointed, their tips so eager and erect . . . he felt obliged to avert his eyes.

What the hell was going on with her? What the hell did she think she was doing?

She was playing some weird sort of game, he decided—perhaps some species of charades. Whatever it was it had shamed her or she wouldn't have hidden the pictures. But it had also meant something important to her or she wouldn't have bothered to keep them.

He wondered who had taken the photographs. Their existence implied an observer. Then he remembered that Polaroid cameras contain self-timers, so the camera could have been mounted on a tripod and set to fire off automatically.

What are these pictures about? Do they have anything to do with her call?

As much as he hated the thought, he knew he had to examine them. Sweat broke out on his forehead as he held them closer, searching their backgrounds for clues. They had been taken in an all-white high-ceilinged room.

No windows showed, but something about the slant of light made him think the pictures had been taken very early in the day.

The other girl had pale skin, short jet black hair, and icy blue eyes.

Who was she? What did she mean to Jess? Why on God's earth are they both bare-breasted? Were they posing, clowning around? Or were they really fighting?

From the intensity of their expressions they appeared to be duelists. In one shot, in a corner of the room, he could make out their discarded jackets.

Why were they fighting, risking disfigurement and injury? Were they settling some kind of grudge? Daring each other? Showing bravery? Exciting each other by the ritual of combat?

Janek sat at Jess's desk and held his fists to his head. First Greg Gale, now this. But the longer he thought about it, the more clearly he understood that Jess was no less enigmatic than other homicide victims he had investigated. So perhaps he shouldn't expect to understand her; perhaps, like every other human being, she would turn out to be unfathomable.

He took up his search again, combing through her notebooks. He checked her address book for coded telephone numbers. He pulled every book out of her bookcases and fanned its pages for hidden notes. He emptied her wastebasket, then searched each scrap for a revealing notation. When, at two in the morning, he finally left the dorm, a new security team was in place at the desk and he had to show his shield to get out.

He didn't sleep well that night. Images of Jess kept ricocheting in his mind. He recalled Dr. Archer's words:

"Perhaps you had unconscious fantasies about her. Perhaps you longed for her in some way you don't fully understand. . . ."

Was that true? He had interviewed Jess's lover, handled her underwear, searched out her secret pictures. When he'd found the pack of condoms in her dresser, he'd tossed them casually aside. But inside, he hadn't reacted casually at all. The condoms spoke of sexuality; if she owned them, she used them. And now, as whenever he thought of her engaging in sex, he felt something he couldn't define: a quick flush of excitement, followed immediately by a hard, harsh throb of despair.

Had he desired her, and, detesting his desire, immediately repressed it? Perhaps Dr. Archer was right; perhaps he had forced his way into this investigation in order to stay close to Jess. Was he after her killer, or was he really chasing something inside himself, some perverse aspect of his character he had hitherto denied?

The question tormented him until, with the dawn, he got out of bed, went to his living room, sat in his easy chair, and stared at Monika's glass. Then memories flooded back, memories of their carnal afternoons in room 13 with the sea smell drifting to them from the lagoon. Longing for Monika, her body, and her touch, he knew that Dr. Archer was wrong. It was Monika he wanted, not Jess. Feeling confident this was true, he knew he could go on.

He and Aaron spent the entire first week of November talking to people, then using what they learned to fill in the grid on their office wall. As is usually the case with students, Jess's schedule was rigorously defined. She went to classes, worked out with the fencing team, studied, ate, slept. No one took attendance at Columbia, so there was no hard proof which classes she attended and which she cut, but by putting together the recollections of her friends, they were able to reconstruct a large portion of her final days.

There were other less typical things she did, and they charted these activities as well: her midmorning therapy sessions with Dr. Archer; her late-afternoon classes in martial arts at a dojo on upper Broadway; her long, lonely early-evening runs through Riverside Park. But still there were gaps, often hours long. And they had no way of knowing what she did at night; students in her dorm came and went as they pleased.

When Janek met Fran Dunning, he felt a familiar glow. She was the confidante he was looking for.

Jess's fencing coach, Sergei Simionov, pointed her out in the fencing hall at the Columbia gym. Janek recognized her at once; he had seen her at Jess's funeral and at the cemetery, too.

"They were teammates and best friends," Simionov said. He was a stout, mustachioed, barrel-chested Soviet émigré, a onetime Olympic medalist in saber. "Fran's the one you want to talk to," he said.

Janek stayed to watch the workout. Women athletes fascinated him. He liked their poise, the way they moved, their ease and comfort with their bodies. Fran Dunning, a thin, willowy blonde with pert features and puffed cheeks, moved across the exercise floor with the smooth, liquid mobility of a dancer.

He waited until the workout was over, then positioned himself outside the women's locker room. When Fran appeared, he introduced himself, then asked if she had time to talk. She was on her way to a biology lab, but she invited him to escort her as she walked across the campus.

"I know who you are," she said on the steps of the gym. "Jess talked about you a lot. I saw you at the funeral. I wanted to say hi, but you were busy with the Dorances. I didn't want to intrude."

Janek liked her. She had the same direct look-you-in-the-eyes manner as Jess. Taller, thinner, she carried herself the same way, too, back straight, head high in the confident manner of an athlete.

"I miss her a lot, still can't believe she's gone. You read about these things, but you never think they can happen to anyone you know."

"What do you mean by 'these things,' Fran?"

"Getting attacked, suddenly, for no reason. Running in the park, just enjoying yourself, thinking your thoughts. Then suddenly a man appears out of the dark."

"Could Jess have known her attacker?"

"The way I heard it, it was one of those psychos, maybe a mugger gone berserk." Fran stopped walking, looked at him. "Do you think she knew him?"

"I don't know yet," Janek said. "Did you see much of her the last few days before it happened?"

Fran nodded. "The Sunday before. We spent the whole day together."

She and Jess saw each other daily at fencing practice and also spent time together on weekends. That particular Sunday was the last day of the Custom Knives Show, so they joined up in the morning, took the subway down to Grand Central, then walked over to the Hotel Roosevelt, where the show was being held.

"Jess got me started with knives. She had this great collection, mostly historical pieces, Italian stilettos, a couple of Japanese tantos, an Indonesian kris, a terrific French rapier. When I saw her stuff, I knew I wanted to collect, too. She was very generous with advice, and she steered me to the good dealers. That's how we became friends. On the fencing team we were rivals. We kidded each other about one of us switching to saber so we wouldn't have to compete. The joke, of course, was that neither of us was willing to switch.''

American-made custom knives were Jess's most recent passion. And as with the historical daggers and swords, she was the one who took the lead, learning to differentiate the work of the leading makers, then introducing Fran Dunning to the field.

''The knives some of those men make are remarkable,'' Fran said. ''They're like art objects, but still, you can use them. Hunting knives, bowies, fighting knives—Jess thought knifemaking was one of the few crafts at which Americans excel.''

The knife show was held on the mezzanine floor of the hotel. The main room was a large hall, filled with long exhibition tables arranged along aisles, occupied by hundreds of knifemakers from all over the country who had brought their wares to sell. At first Jess and Fran explored together; then they split up so each girl could look at the knives that most interested her. When Fran rejoined Jess, she sensed her friend was upset.

''I asked her if something was the matter,'' Fran told Janek as they crossed in front of Butler Library. ''She shook her head, said it wasn't anything. I went along. What else could I do? But I didn't believe her. As I'm sure you know, Jess was not a moody type of girl. But something must have gotten to her because she started out so exuberant, but when we met up at the door, she was downcast, almost sullen.''

''What did you do after the show?''

''Took the subway uptown, worked out for an hour with foils in the gym, then showered and went out to eat at a Chinese restaurant on Broadway and a Hundred and Nineteenth.''

''Anything unusual happen?''

''Nothing I can think of.''

''Did either of you buy a knife?''

Fran nodded. ''Jess did. A real beauty, a switchblade with an ivory handle. It wasn't legal. The man who made it was very cautious about showing it to us.'' She smiled. ''Jess told me you'd give her hell if you ever found out she bought it.''

A switchblade—why on earth?

''I didn't find it when I searched her dorm room,'' Janek said.

''Maybe she dropped it off at her mother's. If I knew Jess, she probably hid it someplace.''

Janek thought about hiding places. ''Something I want to ask you.''

Fran peered at him. ''I'll help you as best I can.''

''First, close your eyes.'' Fran obeyed. ''Now think of two women fencing. Imagine them topless, both of them.''

''Uh-huh. . . .''

''Think about it. Does the image remind you of anything?''

Fran shook her head. But Janek felt something tentative in her denial.

''Does it embarrass you?''

Fran blushed. ''It *is* kind of wild.''

She's not a very good liar, Janek thought.

"I found photos of Jess and another girl fencing like that. They were hidden in Jess's closet."

He stared at Fran, waiting for her to respond. When she looked away, he stopped walking and gently touched her cheek.

"Please understand," he said. "I need to know everything."

"Yeah. . . ." Fran took a deep breath. When she spoke again, her voice was agitated and her delivery faster than before. "There's a painting by a French artist, Émile Bayard. It's called *An Affair of Honor*. Jess found it in one of her books about dueling. It shows two topless women fighting with rapiers while three other women look on. Jess was intrigued by it—I don't know why. She was equally intrigued by a whole slew of stories she dug up on women duelists. She told me she wanted to write a paper about them for some feminist-oriented European history course she was taking."

"But there's more to it, isn't there, Fran? Did she ask you to fence topless with her?"

Fran nodded. "I didn't want to. For one thing it's dangerous. For another . . . I just didn't like the idea. So I told her: 'I'm a jock, but I'm not that butch.' I think she understood."

"Did you take her proposal as a sexual overture?"

Fran shook her head. "If Jess was inclined that way, she never showed it. No, I think it was just something she wanted to do. Fencing, fighting—those were things she loved. In some way, I guess, the image turned her on. And once she got it into her head, she wanted to act it out."

Janek showed Fran the Polaroids. Fran could not

identify the other girl, nor did she recognize the room where the pictures had been taken.

"I wonder if it's a fencing salon at the Ruspoli Academy in Italy. Fran was there last summer. It's certainly not any practice room we use around here."

"A final question," Janek said. "Did Jess do or say anything that Sunday, anything at all, that made you think she might be afraid."

Fran shook her head. "I don't think Jess was afraid of anything. That's why she was such a terrific fencer. I remember something she said to me once: 'I'll take life any way it comes.' I think if she saw someone running toward her with an ice pick, she'd have put up a terrific fight. She knew karate. She could disarm a man twice her weight. So whoever killed her must have come at her from behind, and the only reason she didn't hear him coming was that she had her Walkman turned up at the time."

Aaron's interviews convinced him that none of the members of the Greg Gale crowd had harbored any ill will toward Jess.

"They're not murderous types, Frank. Just your standard spoiled, overeducated, decadent, attractive young people with a hunger for dope and thrills. Actually they don't do that much drugs. Mostly pot, occasionally a little coke. To them the sex group's good clean fun, not a cult they'd kill to protect."

Aaron had looked into former boyfriends, too. Except for Gale they all seemed to be jocks.

"Maybe not the brightest guys, but most of them fairly decent. She didn't like pretentious or overstudious types."

Simionov, the fencing coach, had told Janek pretty much the same thing: "She talked straight and she fenced straight and she liked straight-talking people. If she'd lived, who knows how far she might have gone? Bronze medal, maybe even silver." The coach had shaken his head with grief. "She had everything: talent, will, strength and speed, and as fierce a fighting spirit as I ever encountered in a woman. Who knows? With a little luck she might have gone all the way."

Fran Dunning phoned Janek two days after their walk.

"You said I should call you if I remembered anything."

Good girl! "What do you remember?"

"Something Jess said at the Chinese restaurant. It's probably not important, but I thought I should tell you anyway. She said she might have to stop seeing her shrink."

Interesting. "Did she say why?"

"No. But I'm sure the reason wasn't financial because she once told me her stepfather was paying the fees. I wouldn't remember her mentioning it except the week before she'd been very positive about her therapist."

"Try and recall her exact words, Fran? Did she say she might have to stop or that she wanted to quit?"

"I don't remember exactly. But I had the feeling that she was disgusted about something, that whatever it was, it was gnawing at her, and that if she stopped seeing her therapist, it would be at her initiative." Fran paused. "I could be wrong, Lieutenant, but that's what I thought at the time."

Janek thanked Fran and reminded her to call him again if she remembered anything more. When he put down the phone, he thought about what she'd said. Jess's comment could have been a casual remark, but still he was glad he knew about it. He'd been looking for an excuse to see Dr. Archer again. This time, he resolved, he would limit the discussion to her former patient.

The therapist had set their appointment for 5:00 P.M. As before, she appeared at the door of her waiting room precisely on the hour.

"Nice to see you again, Lieutenant. You have fifty minutes," she announced with a sympathetic smile.

As Janek followed her into the consulting room, he noticed that her curly red hair was dyed.

"Now, how may I help you?" Dr. Archer began smiling again after they were seated in opposing chairs.

"Jess tried to get in touch with me two days before she was killed. Any idea why?"

Archer shook her head. "I have no idea, and I can't imagine why you'd ask me that."

"Her father and I were partners once. Laura Dorance thinks Jess might have wanted to ask me about him. Did she talk about him much in here?"

The psychologist looked pained. "As I told you before, Lieutenant, even though Jessica has passed away, I don't feel I can properly discuss her therapy."

"Look, Dr. Archer, I'm conducting a criminal investigation. Right now I need your help. If you refuse to give it to me, then I'm faced with a problem. I can write you off as an unhelpful witness or I can seek a court order to compel you to respond." The therapist was staring at him. Janek smiled to soften his threat. "I certainly hope that won't be necessary."

Dr. Archer sat very still. The office was silent except

for the muted sound of classical music issuing from the waiting-room radio. After waiting futilely for her to speak, Janek decided to take her silence as acquiescence.

"Laura tells me Jess began asking questions about her dad about the time she started seeing you. Laura assumed his name came up in therapy."

"His name did come up," Dr. Archer affirmed.

"Just his name? Or his character?"

The therapist tightened her lips. "I am truly mystified," she said. "Why are you asking me about this?"

"Please, Dr. Archer, I'm not your patient. I'm here to ask questions, not answer them."

She turned away, irritated. "And you expect me to respond without the right to ask questions of my own—is that how it goes, Lieutenant?"

Janek turned conciliatory. "Can't we try and work this out?"

Archer turned back to him, then folded her hands neatly on her lap. "I shall try to help you as best I can," she whispered, then clamped her mouth shut.

He found the next half hour trying. Archer kept her word, answered all his questions clearly, sometimes even exhaustively. But she made no effort to be pleasant. Rather, she replied to him in terse sentences while gazing at him as though she regarded him as a torturer.

Tim Foy: Yes, he was discussed; in therapy a patient's parents always are. Jessica had described watching her father get into his car and then seeing it explode. Her father's death had been the traumatic event of her early years, yet her long-term response to it had been surprisingly positive. Seeing him die had hardened her will. She was determined never to become a victim. She developed an aggressive personality that she channeled healthily into sports. All of that was entirely to her credit.

Bad dreams: Yes, Jessica had been having them lately. Nothing unusual about that. A patient often feels a requirement to bring dream material to her analyst, especially in the early stages of therapy. The content of her dreams varied, but they were typical college-age stress fantasies: facing an exam while blacking out all knowledge of the subject; finding herself naked in a room in which everyone else is dressed; letting her teammates down by stumbling during a fencing match and thus losing a tournament to a rival school.

Sex: Jessica had the normal longings of a woman her age with no indications of lesbianism beyond normal parameters. Again much to her credit, her initial exhilaration at the anonymous sex to which Greg Gale had introduced her gave way fairly quickly to feelings of inner emptiness and ennui.

The topless fencing episode: That could be viewed in a sexual context, although Dr. Archer saw it somewhat differently. Jessica had brought it up at their first session. It was her "presenting symptom." She was disturbed about it. She felt that by staging the scene with the other girl, a British fencer she had befriended at the Ruspoli School in Italy, she had done something forbidden, possibly even evil.

"The imagery of the Bayard painting embedded itself in Jessica's mind," Archer explained. "She was fascinated by the seminudity of it, the notion of women exposing their bared flesh to a steel sword. She equated it with the stripped-down costuming of male boxers. To fight bare meant to duel seriously, even to the death. We spent several sessions working through her troubled feelings about it, especially her guilt over having talked the English girl into trying it. In my analysis I tried to focus on the underlying meaning of the scene. What we came up with (and I emphasize we did this together) was that Jessica's strong attraction to fencing and to martial arts was based on her romantic notion of heroism. I called it the gladiator's syndrome, the idea that the highest, most noble way of life is the way of the warrior who regularly offers his body to injury or death for the delectation of the public. The gladiator's sacrifice is for the benefit of those who watch him. By engaging in dangerous fights, he fulfills the innermost needs of his audience, channeling its bloodlust into sport, stylizing its collective aggression into art. At the same time he, or she, in the case of Jessica, surrounds herself with an aura of glamour. It's close to the Japanese samurai ideal, but with the added component of exhibitionism. It's a hard, short life of intense experience—perilous, painful, and, ultimately, self-sacrificial.''

It was a brilliant analysis, and Janek was dazzled by it. He was also impressed at the way Archer seemed to come alive. But the change in her demeanor made him uneasy. The voice she used to explain the fencing episode was different from her voice when answering his other queries. It was more vital, authoritative, indicative of an inner power and confidence that didn't fit with her earlier pettiness. Now he felt he was listening to another person altogether, a strong, dynamic temperament hiding behind a bland, nondescript façade. But even before, he realized, Archer's eyes had betrayed her. Her relentless gaze should have warned him he was dealing with an extraordinary individual, far more passionate, forceful, and intelligent than her insipid professional manner and constricted body language would suggest.

But then another transformation, which Janek found equally surprising, took place. When he mentioned the Polaroids he'd found in Jess's closet, he saw an immediate pinching up of the eyes, followed by a grimace of anger. The reaction was fleeting, covered up almost instantly by a patient nodding of the head. But Janek was certain about what he'd seen: Jess had not told Archer about the pictures, and for that the therapist now felt betrayed.

"I take it you didn't know about them," he asked.

Archer shrugged the omission off. "A patient will almost always hold something back." Her tone connoted superior wisdom. "A little shield against the therapist, a small corner of privacy to be preserved."

"Do the photographs surprise you?"

"Not the photographs so much as the way Jessica hid them. I have to admit that surprises me a bit."

"Why?"

Archer raised an eyebrow. "You found them, didn't you?"

Janek squinted. "You're not suggesting she expected me to search her room?"

"Of course not, Lieutenant. But she didn't hide them all that well. A good hiding place is an irrevocable hiding place, one that stays secret even after the hider's death."

"So what does that tell you?"

When Archer began to speak, Janek recognized the same authoritative voice she'd used while analyzing the fencing incident.

"It tells me Jessica wasn't all that ashamed about partaking in the scene. I know from what she told me how difficult it was for her to set it up. I know she proposed the idea to a teammate here in New York and, to her embarrassment, was rebuffed. Still, she needed a confederate, in this case the English girl, and so she took a chance. By merely broaching such a bizarre idea, she risked exposing herself to the other girl's ridicule.''

"But this time the other girl went along."

"She did. And I think that that, ultimately, is what got Jessica so upset. Not that the English girl went along, but the *way* she went along, as if she took it as a seduction on Jessica's part and regarded it as a forbidden act.''

"But there's still something I don't understand, Doctor. You say Jess was troubled by the incident. If she was, why didn't she destroy the photographs?''

Archer paused to reflect. "Difficult to say. Perhaps for the same reason people often hesitate to destroy documentation even when it contains material that's painful for them to see or read. Jessica staged the duel. She had a large emotional investment in it. To destroy the photographs of the scene she'd worked so hard to set up would be to deny herself any chance to contemplate it in the future and perhaps even to revel in what she'd done.''

Janek smiled. "You're a fascinating woman, Doctor. It's very interesting to talk to you.''

The therapist smiled demurely, then glanced at her watch. "Which brings us," she said, "to the end of the session. Your fifty minutes are nearly up.''

"A final question.'' Archer motioned for Janek to ask it. "I have it from one of Jess's closest friends, who spoke to her just days before she died, that she was thinking about quitting therapy.''

"And you want to know what I think about that?'' Archer looked past him toward the opposite wall. "In this business we're used to sudden changes in a patient's feelings. In the therapeutic relationship the therapist often comes to represent important figures in the patient's life—parent, sibling, lover—toward whom the patient then acts out. So, you see, when a patient contemplates leaving her therapist, it's only a natural by-product of the process."

"So I shouldn't make too much of it?"

"You may make of it whatever you like," the psychologist replied, rising.

On their way to the door she turned to him again. "Have you given any thought to what I said last time?"

Janek nodded. "I thought about it."

"And dismissed it out of hand?"

"Not at all. But after I thought about it awhile, I decided you were wrong."

Archer grinned. "You work in a most dangerous and stressful field, Lieutenant. There's bound to be some distortion in your view of things."

Janek smiled. "Think I could use some therapy, Doctor?"

Her grin widened. "We can all use therapy, Lieutenant. In your case I'd say it certainly wouldn't hurt."

They both chuckled over that. Then at the door Janek thanked her for her time. "I hope we can talk again."

The therapist nodded. "Anytime, Lieutenant. Just give me a call. I shall always try to fit you in."

That evening Janek took a long walk. Leaving his apartment at six o'clock, when the rush-hour traffic was just at its crest, he headed up Broadway to merge with the throngs still surging out of the subways. On his route he passed stores offering high- and low-fashion garments; markets offering sturgeon and pastrami; Chinese, Turkish, Lebanese, and Ethiopian restaurants; bars catering to gays and transvestites; panhandlers; dope dealers; homeless people living in cardboard boxes; old people sitting on benches; and aggressive young people on the make. By the time he reached the Columbia University campus, he felt he had confronted a cross section of the human condition.

At 114th Street he turned into Riverside Park. Although it was a chilly November night, the joggers were out in force. He didn't see many lone runners; press and TV coverage about Jess was still in the public mind. But as he walked farther uptown, the number dwindled off, until, north of the Columbia Presbyterian Medical Center, there were none at all.

It was a basic principle of his trade that the first step in any investigation was to go to the crime scene and get a feeling for the place. Since he and Aaron had taken over the case from Boyce, he had been putting such a visit off. Now, approaching the spot where Jess's body had been dragged off the jogging path, he felt his heartbeat quicken.

The streetlamps were on, but in the long, narrow strip of parkland the foliage was dense and the shadows were deep. Despite the darkness, it didn't take him long to find the spot. Orange-tipped police stakes caught the ambient light cast by cars racing above on Riverside Drive. And then he was surprised. There were a good dozen bunches of flowers, mostly dried up but all the more poignant for being so, arranged along the bottom row of stones of an old retaining wall just behind the site. Stubs of candles were set there, too, in little hardened pools of melted wax. People had heard that a fine young woman had died in this place; they had been moved, had come and left tangible evidence of their caring. So now in the underbrush, amidst the jettisoned Coke cans and discarded sandwich wrappers, a small shrine had been erected at the Scene of Suffering. It would last until the first heavy snow.

The glue: Janek was obsessed by it. The ice picks were bad enough; they didn't reflect the caring of a knife, the quick dispatch of a bullet, the hatred of a poison. Leaving the picks embedded was bad, too. You didn't bother to use something fine to take your victim's life; you used a throwaway. Like eating your dinner off a paper plate or drinking your wine from a Styrofoam cup, it was a way of showing your contempt.

But the glue was worse; the glue was truly awful.

Janek had investigated many homicides in which victims had been bound. He'd seen handcuffs and rope burns and even barbed wire cutting into flesh. He'd seen his share of mutilations, too: cuts, slices, and, in the Switch Case, actual dismemberment, decapitation. But glue was different. Glue was made of animal wastes, old bones and hooves boiled down to a viscous jelly. Glue was what you used to stick pieces of wood together, not to bind the parts of a human being. Glue said: "I don't desecrate by cutting; I'm not a psychotic acting out my rage." Glue said: "I'm cool, patient. I go about my chosen task the way an undertaker goes about his. I'm neat and careful and whistle a merry tune as I seal up people's body cavities."

Janek thought he hated this killer more than any killer he had ever sought, not only because the man had taken the life of a person he had loved but also because he had done so with such dehumanizing scorn.

He was watching the late-evening news, trying to concentrate on an awful story about a ten-year-old boy set on fire because he refused to buy crack from a school bully, when his telephone rang. It was Monika calling with wonderful news. She would be coming through New York in three weeks' time, en route to a psychiatrists' conference in San Francisco.

"I hope you're planning to stay awhile," Janek said.

"Can I take that as an invitation?"

"You bet you can! How much time can you give me?"

"Two or three days. Maybe a couple more on my way home."

That wasn't very much, but it was better than nothing. "How about a couple of years?" he asked.

Monika laughed. "Why don't you come out to San Francisco with me?"

"Sure. And take a little room down the hall so the chambermaids won't get any funny ideas."

As they talked, he picked up the glass she'd given him, angled it so it caught the light.

"Maybe I ought to join you in Frisco," he said. "I've been spending so much time with shrinks lately I'm sure I'd feel right at home."

Monika was intrigued by his account of his meeting with Dr. Chun but was skeptical about something Dr. Archer had said.

"It's true," she told him, "that a patient who wants to leave therapy can be acting out against an analyst who reminds her of a difficult figure in her life. But your goddaughter wasn't in treatment long enough to develop that kind of strong transference relationship."

"How long would it take?" Janek asked.

"Several months at least."

"Can you think of any other reason why Jess may have wanted to quit?"

"There could have been a lot of reasons. Anxiety caused by her therapy or a personal dislike for her therapist. I lost a patient once because he saw me unexpectedly in a nightclub."

"What was so bad about that?"

"Normally nothing. But this man idealized me. When he saw me dancing with my husband in a sexy environment, he was thrown into such turmoil he couldn't relate to me any longer as his analyst."

"You say he saw you. Did you see him, too?"

"Yes, our eyes met," she said.

"How did you react?"

"I smiled at him."

"Ever occur to you he might have followed you to the nightclub?"

She laughed. "I never thought of that."

"It could make all the difference," he said. "To me the question is did he quit therapy because he saw you or because you saw him?"

"And therein," Monika said, laughing, "must lie the difference between a detective and an analyst."

Later he asked her if she thought Archer had deliberately misled him.

"I have no way of knowing," she said, "but her acting-out explanation strikes me as glib."

"Well, suppose Jess ran into her unexpectedly at the

knife show? Something happened there that changed her mood. But why would seeing Archer shake her up?''

"How did Jess feel about knives?''

"She was passionate about them.''

"Well, then, that could have been it," Monika said. "Suddenly there was her analyst infringing on her territory. But it's all conjecture, isn't it?''

"It always is," Janek agreed.

The next morning, over breakfast with Aaron at a Greek coffee shop around the corner from the Police Property Building, Janek described Dr. Archer.

"Tiny woman, built like a butterball, kindly smile, bland, self-effacing voice, a little fussy, a little too precise about time. But when I stoke her up, she turns difficult. Doesn't want to answer questions, wants to ask them. The end of our first interview she tried to turn things around, make me think I was probing because I had 'unconscious sexual fantasies' about Jess. Second time I put on some stress, and suddenly I started picking up on her anger. She's good at concealing, but the rage shows through, which tells me how strong it must be inside. She gives me a plausible but phony explanation as to why Jess may have wanted to quit on her, a lot of brilliant but tortured analysis about the fencing incident, and some strange stuff about a good hiding place being an irrevocable hiding place—whatever the hell that means. I don't know what the bottom line is on her, Aaron, but something about her isn't right.''

Aaron picked up a jelly roll. "She's weird, Frank. Ever meet a shrink who wasn't? You don't think she's the Happy Families killer, do you?''

He shook his head. "How could she be? But

still . . . I don't see Jess relating to a person like that."

Aaron put down his cup. "I know what you're thinking."

"What am I thinking?"

"That maybe the feds didn't conceal their case all that well. Maybe it leaked out. This guy Chun—he's a shrink. So maybe he spilled to another shrink, and Archer heard about it through the grapevine and did a copycat job on Jess."

Janek smiled. "Swear to God, Aaron—I never thought of that. But now that you bring it up . . ."

Aaron nodded. "Yeah, Frank—I'll check the little lady out."

Laura Dorance couldn't remember who referred Jess to Dr. Archer. "I think it was one of her friends," she said.

But when Janek called around, none of Jess's friends would admit to having made the referral.

That night, as he walked home from the subway, he noticed an unshaven man in a seedy suit lingering near the front door of his building. As he approached, the man stared at him.

"Janek?"

Janek stared back. "Who's asking?"

The man unclenched his hand. He'd been holding an old newspaper clipping. He showed it to Janek. It was a picture taken at the time of the Switch trial. *Oh-oh*, Janek thought.

"It's you, isn't it?" The man's breath stank of cabbage. There was dandruff on his shoulders.

"So what?" Janek said.

"You guys work long hours. I've been waiting here since five."

As the man put his hand into his pocket, Janek tensed, reached beneath his jacket, gripped the handle of his Colt. But when he saw the paper with the blue legal backing, he relaxed and let go of his gun.

"I am serving you, Lieutenant," the man said, offering Janek the document.

Janek snapped it out of his hand. One look told him what it was. He stared at the man with disgust.

"Great business you're in."

"Hey, don't take it out on me, fella! Just doing my job."

Janek brushed by him and entered his building. Inside his apartment he sat down and read the document. It was notice that a lawsuit had been filed by the firm of Streep & Holster on behalf of its client, one Clarence "Rusty" Glickman, wherein Glickman alleged unlawful assault resulting in severe physical and psychological injury, for which he demanded a jury trial and one million dollars' damages.

Janek didn't sleep well that night. Something— something he'd seen that could be important—nagged at him. Unable to recall what it was, he flopped from side to side in torment.

At two in the morning he remembered and sat up: *The arrows! I forgot to look inside the quiver!*

The next morning he phoned Laura and asked her if she'd saved it.

"A bow and arrow set—I don't remember anything like that."

"It was in her dorm-room closet."

"I never saw it. I couldn't even bear to go up to her room. When you called and told us it was all right to move out her stuff, Stanton went up there to collect her swords. He's put them out on consignment with a dealer. We decided to give away the rest of her things. Stanton phoned the Salvation Army. They sent over a truck."

"Do you happen to know if Stanton turned up an ivory-handled switchblade knife?"

Laura asked him to hold while she checked Stanton's list. A minute later she was back.

"Lots of knives but no switchblade. Sorry, Frank."

The Salvation Army sorted its pickups at its general warehouse in Brooklyn. Once inside the building, bulk donations were broken up. Toys went to one floor, furniture to another, clothing to a third, etc. Items such as archery equipment, unsuitable for general sale, were relegated to a special area.

By the time Janek found a friendly sergeant willing to help him, the bulk of Jess's stuff had long been sorted and shipped back out of the building, distributed to various sales outlets in and around the city.

"But there's still a chance on the bow and arrows," Sergeant Hunter told him as he led Janek rapidly down a long corridor lit by naked bulbs past cages filled with donations. The whole place smelled like a dry cleaning establishment. The sergeant's dog, an overweight dachshund named Clarence, scampered ahead. Hunter, dragging one foot behind him, strove mightily to keep up.

"We've got rooms here filled with anything you'd ever need," Hunter said. The sergeant had bloodshot eyes, wild hair, and a ragged gray-streaked beard.

"We've got a room of shoes, a room of crutches, a room of old dentist's equipment. We got pots and pans, lawn mower parts, old chemistry and Erector sets." Hunter rattled off other types of items processed at the warehouse: pinball machines; waffle irons; bathroom scales. "Would you believe we've even got a cage here filled with discarded artificial limbs? Strange maybe, but think about it. A guy loses his leg, say, in the war, and the vet hospital fits him out with a spare. Then he dies. So what does his widow do? Bury it with him is one possibility. Another is she calls us up. 'Can't stand looking at it,' she cries. 'Get it out of here.' And we take it, the way we take darn near anything. 'For every pot there's a top'—that's what my mother used to say."

The weapons room was not a cage. It had a solid door. "Don't want just anyone nosing around in here," Hunter said, working a key inside the outsize padlock while Clarence, the dachshund, dribbled saliva over Janek's shoes.

There were no actual guns inside the weapons room, though there were plenty of toy models and realistic replicas. The array of other weaponry was fascinating, ranging from the kinds of sticks with nail points used to clean up parks to a huge wooden sword with the word "Excalibur" burned into its blade. In between there was a hoard of tomahawks and African-style spears, assorted clubs, maces, cudgels, blackjacks and shillelaghs, sundry bomb and mine casings, numerous darts, slingshots, catapults, boomerangs, brass knuckles sets, and, in one corner, a homemade guillotine.

The archery equipment was positioned against one wall. Gazing at the crossbows, longbows, competition bows, and myriad quivers filled with arrows all bunched together in a vertical pile, Janek wondered how he'd manage to recognize the equipment that had belonged to Jess. He'd barely glanced at the bow when he'd discovered it in her closet and tossed it with the quiver into the pile of clothing on her bed.

But there was one important thing he did remember about it: The gear had seemed almost new. Scanning the bows before him, he reached for the one that appeared the least scuffed up. He pulled it out and examined it. The name DIANA was scrawled in blue grease pencil on the inside curve just above the handle. The handwriting didn't resemble Jess's, but the bow had an elegant feel to it that made him think it was the right one. He set it aside and knelt to examine the quivers.

He rejected ones made of wood or hide. The one he'd held that night had been aluminum. There were three of these, all relatively unsoiled. He took all three and emptied them out onto the floor, being careful to keep the arrows of each in separate piles. Then, with Hunter standing behind him and the dog, Clarence, sputtering through slobbering chops, he inspected each arrow, many of which were tipped with extremely sharp points, and, when he had done that, the interior of each quiver. Finding nothing, her turned the quivers over. On the bottom of the first he found DIANA written in the same blue cursive script. He stuffed its arrows back inside.

"This is it," he said, looking up at Hunter.

The sergeant shook his head, incredulous. "Got to congratulate you. All the years I worked in this dump, you're the first guy came around looking for something he gave away and ended up finding it." He pointed to his dog, vigorously wagging its tail. "See, even Clarence is amazed."

* * *

Diana: It was only later on the Brooklyn Bridge,
driving back to Manhattan, that Janek thought of Diana,
the huntress, twin sister to Apollo, virgin goddess of the
moon, usually depicted holding a bow.

What difference did the archery stuff make anyway?
he asked himself. And the moment he asked the answer
came to him like a blow. It was not that he'd forgotten to
look inside the quiver that had kept him up the night
before. It was the word connection between Jess's
possessing a bow and arrow and the name of her
therapist: *Archer.*

"Oh, she *is* a piece of work is Dr. Beverly Archer,"
Aaron said, shaking his head.

He read to Janek from his notes, compiled after five
days of investigation and surveillance, as they sat together in their office, the grid on the wall nearly filled in
now with the activities of Jess's final days.

"You've been to her house, Frank. You know the
routine. No receptionist. Patients ring and get buzzed in.
Two doors to her office, one to the waiting room, the
other opening directly to the front hall. That way nobody
sees anybody, conventional practice in therapeutic cir-
cles. But maybe there's more to it here. Maybe this one
doesn't want people to notice something not so conventional, from what I understand. Get this: All her patients
are young women."

"No guys?"

"Just females."

"Interesting," Janek said. "Tell me more."

"She owns the building, lives in the apartment upstairs, rents the basement to a young woman, a librarian.

I'd say the good doctor leads a tight, constricted life. All day long she sees patients. First appointment eight in the morning, last six at night. They all go in looking anxious and come out looking kind of dazed. Know what I mean, Frank? Glassy-eyed, smiling, but the smile's the shit-eating kind, like they're all wrapped up in themselves, their dear little egos so nicely massaged and all. Whatever she does to them in there, they all look like they feel better afterwards. Then, when the last one leaves, she waits a few minutes, comes out to do her errands. Usual stuff around the neighborhood—shoemaker, dry cleaner, grocery store, that kind of crap. And that's it. She's out for maybe half an hour; then she's back inside. Lights go off downstairs. Lights come on upstairs. Nine-thirty or ten, upstairs lights go off, too. And there she is, locked in, snug as a bug in a rug. No social life, no dates, no friends I can find out about. Her work is her life. It's girls all day long. Except for two other interesting little things she does."

Janek knew how fond Aaron was of turning reports into sagas. He used all the tricks of the tale-teller's trade: asides; digressions; embellishments; authorial opinions. Best of all, he liked to evoke questions. So Janek asked him one: "What two other interesting little things does she do?"

Aaron smiled. "Tuesday nights she teaches a class in 'Problems of the Adolescent and Postadolescent Female' at the Eisenberg Psychoanalytic Institute in Chelsea. I checked the place out; it's a reputable institution, no quack joint. They train laypeople, mostly Ph.D.'s, who want to be professional analytic-oriented therapists."

"And the second thing?"

"That's the goody. Thursday mornings she's picked

up by a car service, then driven out to a hospital called Carlisle in Derby, Connecticut. She's a one-day-a-week consultant out there. It's a special kind of hospital, Frank—a hospital for the criminally insane." Aaron tongued his lips to show how much he relished this juicy bit of information.

"So, an austere life devoted to work. That can be a rewarding way to live," Janek observed.

"So I hear, though I haven't tried it myself. But you were right, Frank. There *is* something about her. Maybe it's the expression on her face when she doesn't think anyone's looking. Lonely, desperate, tense, maybe even—"

"What?"

"I don't know." Aaron shrugged. "Angry. . . ."

He handed Janek her curriculum vitae and a photocopy of a professional paper she'd written for *The Review of Psychology*.

"I can't make head or tail out of it. Maybe you'll have better luck," he said.

Janek glanced at the CV. The first line in the personal background section sent a clarifying wave crashing across his brain: "Place of birth: Cleveland, Ohio, 5/6/50."

That night Janek read Archer's paper. He found it intelligent, coherent, and unusually compelling. In it she described three female patients: "Alice," "Wilma," and "Ginny." All three were in their early twenties, and each was tormented by an obsessive fixation upon what Archer called a "shaming incident," a traumatizing event in the girl's past that had inspired great shame and humiliation.

The patient Alice, a blond athlete from an affluent suburban family, could not go an hour without remembering in vivid detail the gloating expression on her younger sister's face while she, Alice, then ten years old, had been severely spanked by their mother for an act the younger sister had actually committed.

Alice was so obsessed with that injustice and the shame aroused by the witnessed punishment that she could barely function as a college student, often losing all concentration, once even in the middle of a final exam.

After describing the crippling effect of this memory, Archer went on to describe the treatment she had devised. This consisted of provoking the girl into emotionally reliving the shaming experience in all its humiliating aspects, but with the novel difference that in the reenactment the outcome for Alice was triumphant. This time, under Archer's guidance, Alice was able to "reread" the expression on her sister's face. This time it was not gloating that she saw but shame and deep remorse. Thus, by rewriting the script, encouraging Alice to devise a new ending in which she would emerge victorious, Archer had managed to vitiate the destructive power of the memory and even to assist Alice in increasing her sense of personal confidence and self-respect.

After describing two similar cases, Archer held out hope for patients traumatized by early shame. Though a successful treatment could not be guaranteed, the therapist was encouraged to be as creative as possible in devising ways wherein the patient could work through the insult to her ego.

"Above all else," Archer wrote in the conclusion of

her paper, "we therapists must never underestimate the debilitating effects and the haunting power of early shaming incidents. Often patients will carry the burden of such incidents as baggage through their lives, baggage, moreover, that possesses the surrealistic quality of becoming increasingly heavy as the patient ages. Eventually, unless a cure is effected, the load may become so heavy that the patient will suffer terrifying stress or even break down totally beneath its crushing weight."

Aaron, wearing one of his Hawaiian shirts, stood at the far end of the office, nursing himself from a mug of coffee. It was early the following morning. A cold rain, which had fallen overnight, had frozen on the ground, creating sufficient ice to turn the sidewalks into bobsled tracks.

"Tell me about it, Frank," Aaron urged. "Let's see what you got."

Janek, perched on the corner of his desk, spread his arms. "I've got nothing, absolutely nothing. You know that."

"So tell me about nothing. Worst I can do is laugh in your face."

"It involves a number of leaps," Janek said.

Aaron bit off the end of a jelly roll. "Go ahead," he said. "Leap."

Janek nodded. He stood and began to pace. "Two days before she was killed Jess tried to get in touch with me. Something was troubling her. About the same time she told her best friend she wanted to quit seeing her shrink." He turned to Aaron. "Leap number one: It was the shrink she wanted to talk to me about."

"Could be," Aaron said, biting off the center section of his roll. "I'll buy that. Go on."

Janek resumed pacing. "Jess was never involved with archery, but she had an unused archery set in her closet. Her shrink's name is Archer. Leap number two: The archery set's somehow connected to the shrink."

"Farfetched but . . ." Aaron made a wave motion with his hand. "Interesting," he conceded. "So far I got nothing to laugh at."

Janek nodded. "Try this. When Sullivan put his high-powered FBI computer to work on the Happy Families crimes, the only victim connection it came up with was that two of the people were from Cleveland. Now it turns out Archer's from Cleveland, too."

"So?"

"It starts to add up. I think Archer's involved. I think she did something or she knows something she's not telling. I think she found out Jess saw or suspected something about her and—"

"You think she's the Happy Families killer?"

Janek shrugged. "Well, I wouldn't go that far. Not yet."

Aaron gulped down the rest of his roll. "Now you've done it, Frank. That's a real stretch. Wanna know what I think?" Janek nodded. "It doesn't jell."

"Of course, it doesn't jell."

"So let's talk about it."

"It's impossible. I'm the first to admit that. This tiny fat lady, forty years old—she couldn't possibly break into all those houses, murder all those people. She doesn't have the strength to be a stabbing machine. She may have the hatred, but she doesn't have the guts. The Cleveland connection—that's meaningless, too, because, among other things, only two of the victims are tied together that way. Then there're other dangles, like why would she want to glue their genitals, and what's the meaning of the weeds, and what could Jess have possibly seen, and how could tubby little Archer get in and out so fast, so clean, never seen by anyone, slick without a trace. And I guess the biggest dangle is how could a trained psychologist with a full practice and a respectable career, who consults a day a week at a hospital for the criminally insane—how could such a person possibly be an insane killer herself? She's a healer, right? She specializes in helping young women traumatized by 'shaming events,' right?" Janek paused. "So it's impossible—right?"

Aaron grinned. "Sure, it's impossible." He looked into Janek's eyes. "But we know what we gotta do, we gotta satisfy ourselves." Aaron stretched. "The only way I can think to do that is check out the Cleveland-connected victims, see if either of them ever crossed paths with Archer. Another thing—Jess was Archer's patient, so I'll want to check if any of the other victims ever had her as a therapist. If it turns out even one of them did"—he grinned again—"then we'll really have something."

Janek nodded. "That's what I hoped you'd say. Why don't you get right on it? And while you're at it, make a low-level request to Sullivan's people for copies of the victim files. Not just the Cleveland pair, but all of them."

Aaron nodded. "I'll ask for the crime scene photos, too."

"To throw them off?"

"Partly," Aaron admitted. "And also because I think you ought to focus on the weeds. The weeds are a message. You're good at reading messages.'' He looked at Janek. ''What else have you got to do?''

Janek smiled. ''Nothing too important. I thought I'd try and put in a penetration agent, that's all.''

Early that afternoon Janek attended women's fencing practice. He found something tangy and enticing about the aroma of female sweat that wafted across the gym. Later he waited for Fran Dunning outside the women's locker room. When she appeared, her hair was still wet from her shower. Again he escorted her across campus to her afternoon biology lab.

''I'd like to take you up on your offer to help,'' Janek said. ''I need some information on Jess's shrink.''

''I already told you everything I know.''

''Of course, you have. But I wonder if you'd consider doing more.''

''What?''

''Going to Dr. Archer as a patient for a while. All you'd have to do is call her up, tell her you were Jess's friend, that you've been deeply troubled since she was killed and you feel you could use some help. I'm sure she'd give you an appointment. Of course, we'd reimburse you for your fees.''

Fran turned to him, her eyes curious. ''You think her shrink had something to do with it?''

Janek shook his head. ''I'm not going to lie to you, Fran. I don't know the answer to that. What I *do* know is there's something there I have to explore. I'm not asking you to do anything more than see this woman a couple of times, then fill me in.''

He could tell by the flush on her cheeks that the idea

attracted her. But she was also wavering, perhaps not certain she could bring it off.

"No spying, no snooping, no playing detective," he warned sternly. "You go in as Fran Dunning, with real feelings and real distress. If she asks about me, and I doubt she will, you can tell her all about our interview. The only thing you mustn't tell her about is this conversation we're having now."

"What do you want to know exactly?"

"How she acts, her manner with you, her feelings, if she reveals them, toward Jess. I've been in the waiting and consulting rooms, but I haven't seen any other parts of the house. So you might want to ask to use the bathroom, then let me know if you notice anything interesting on the way."

"What would you consider interesting?" He could see excitement in her eyes.

"Whatever strikes you. Believe me, Fran, if I thought there was any danger, I wouldn't ask you to get involved. This is a voluntary mission. If you don't want to do it, I'll understand."

"Oh, I *want* to do it," she said. "When do I start?"

Janek smiled, then handed her a piece of paper. "Here's Dr. Archer's number. You might want to give her a call this afternoon."

The next day Sullivan called.

"How you doing, Frank?"

"Fine. You?"

"Grand, just grand." Sullivan paused. "Understand you want to see some of our material?"

"Problem with that?"

"No problem. But I'm curious. Haven't heard a peep out of you since you started up there."

"Been busy getting organized, setting up an office, all that. NYPD's a little different from the FBI. We're the poor cousins, remember, Harry?"

Sullivan chuckled in response, a little roll of heh-heh-hehs. When the chuckling finally died away, he got to the point. "Actually I called you about something else."

"What was that?"

"Your surreptitious little trip up to Harvard Law School."

"I wouldn't call it surreptitious."

"Call it whatever you like. Chun has withdrawn as consultant on HF."

"So?"

"What the hell did you say to him?"

"What're you talking about?"

Sullivan's voice hardened up. "Don't bullshit me. You go up there, next thing I know he quits."

Janek laughed. "Don't be an asshole, Harry. Chun was uncomfortable with the case. Anyone could see he was."

During the ensuing pause Janek imagined Sullivan's mouth tightening to a line. But when Sullivan spoke again, his voice had turned cool and businesslike.

"We're pouching off the stuff you asked for. You'll get it by the end of the day."

"Damn gracious of you."

"Either of us finds out anything, we share it, right?"

"That was the deal."

"Well, good luck, Frank." And before Janek could wish him the same, Sullivan clicked off.

* * *

He spent the next three days studying the crime scene photographs.

When they arrived, he and Aaron tacked them up at eye level in neat, even rows on the office walls. Then, while Aaron worked the phones, trying to track down connections between the two Cleveland victims and Beverly Archer, Janek stood before each photograph, staring at it, trying to enter into it before moving on to the next.

He found this work extremely trying. He could not sustain it for more than a quarter hour at a time. When he felt he had sufficient command of his morning or afternoon quota of brutal images, he would leave the office to take long walks through Greenwich Village.

Sometimes he would wander as far as the Hudson River piers across from the strip of gay leather bars on West Street or, in the other direction, beyond Tompkins Square Park into the network of cross streets known as Alphabet City. And always on these walks, amidst these squalid surroundings, he would try to imagine the killings taking place. He did this with all the homicides except for one; he still could not bear to imagine what had happened to Jess.

The trick was to take the still pictures and turn them into movies. Horror movies, splatter movies—those were what he projected to himself. But hard as he tried he could not see tiny Beverly Archer performing a starring role. The intensity, the rage were there—of that he was nearly certain—but not the movements or the staging. He simply could not see her rushing into rooms, surprising people, thrusting at them with ice picks, then working on their fallen bodies with glue. Like most people in this world, Janek thought, the little shrink killed people in her dreams. But could she actually draw their blood? Could little Beverly wield the pick?

"It's getting interesting," Aaron said.

Janek had just returned from one of his walks. The moment he came through the door he could feel a certain cocky confidence in the room.

"Tie-in with Archer?"

"A very nice one." Aaron grinned. "Old Bertha Parce, the retired schoolteacher in Miami—seems she taught forty years at Ashley-Burnett, a snazzy private girls' school in Shaker Heights. And guess who happened to attend Ashley-Burnett during that same period?"

"Little Beverly Archer."

"You got it, Frank."

Janek sat down. He needed a few moments to think through the implications.

"So now it's not just Cleveland; it's a small exclusive school *in* Cleveland," he said. "Jess's shrink, Bertha Parce's student—" He looked up at Aaron. "It's almost too good to be true."

Aaron nodded. "I like it. It's starting to come together. But we're going to need a hell of a lot more. The subtle telephone approach can take me only so far. You know what I want to do, Frank: go out to Cleveland and make a real investigation into the lady's past."

Janek shook his head. "Too early. Expose our theory, and we run the risk of it getting back to her, plus we could screw ourselves permanently with Sullivan. Which wouldn't matter if we turn out to be right. But if we're not . . ."

"So what do you want me to do?"

"Keep plugging on the Connecticut brothers, the MacDonalds. Match them with Archer and you win a ticket to Cleveland."

"And if I can't match them?"

Janek shrugged. "We'll have to take another approach."

There was something about the weeds, a way they were connected, that haunted him on his walks. It was something that he'd seen but that hadn't registered yet, a binding metaphor that remained just beyond his grasp. He found that the harder he struggled to dig it out of himself, the stronger his resistance to giving it up.

Exhausted after three days of endless reruns of his self-made murder movies, he decided to try to free-associate. He remembered the moment the process began. He was walking in an area of old coffee and cheese warehouses on Desbrosses Street when, strangely, he detected the aroma of dead flowers in the air.

The weeds: No question that Aaron was right; the ugly dour little plants contained a message. But what was it? What did they say?

They had been left so they would be easily found; that could account for the fact that Sullivan's people didn't notice them at first. Left in plain sight, they were perhaps too obvious.

When, after four killings, Sullivan's team finally *did* notice them, the weeds from the earlier cases had long since been swept away. But research revealed that they'd been there as well, their presence validated by photographs taken by local investigators.

Once focused on the weeds, Sullivan's forensic experts were relentless. They carefully collected the scruffy little specimens, then sent them to the FBI lab for analysis. Alas, no secret writings were discovered inside, nor were any poisons or stains found upon their surfaces. So if the weeds did not conceal a message, then they must *be* the message. But again Janek wondered: What did they say?

Not orchids or roses or carnations, Sullivan had told them in Quantico, meaning, Janek supposed, not the noble flowers left by mystery-story killers, But if the weeds were, in fact, ignoble, could they then be taken as ironic comment on those elegant, glamorous fictional murderers?

That was one possibility.

Another was that the killer saw himself (or herself if it was Archer) as unglamorous, ignoble, homely. And with that thought the binding metaphor sprang suddenly into Janek's brain.

He mulled over his idea for a moment, then stopped on a street corner, stood still, and closed his eyes. Carefully he recalled the various crime scene photos in which the weeds appeared. Slowly at first, then faster and faster, he forced the pictures to flash successively on a screen inside his brain. Yes, the metaphor was pretty, but would it hold? He would have to go back to the office and examine the pictures again.

His heart was racing as he entered the Police Property Building, tore up the stairs, then down the hall. With sweat breaking out on his forehead, he rushed past Aaron to confront the pictures on the walls.

As he looked at each one in turn, the metaphor locked more firmly into place. But still there was ambiguity:

The killings had taken place indoors, inside rooms each of which had four walls.

It was time now, he knew, to look closely at the pictures of Jess. And when he did, the metaphor was validated. Up in Riverside Park the weeds had been left leaning against the same little stone wall where he had seen the remnants of candles and flowers left by mourners.

Exhilarated, he turned to Aaron, who, phone in hand, was gazing at him skeptically from his desk.

"It's the weeds," he said. "They're always placed beside a wall."

"So?" Aaron asked, waiting for the punch line.

"That's it," Janek said.

"What?"

"The meaning."

"Meaning? If you don't mind, Frank, please tell me what you're talking about?"

"It's how she sees herself, Aaron. It's her message, her calling card."

"So how *does* she see herself?" Aaron asked impatiently.

Janek turned to stare out the window. "As a shy and homely girl without a partner at the dance. As a wallflower," he added mournfully.

Later, when they pulled out the seven pictures and lined them up together, it was so clear Aaron wondered aloud how Sullivan's people could possibly have failed to see it.

"It was their own word 'weeds' that threw them off," Janek said. "They locked themselves in with that. If they'd started out calling them flowers, degraded, ragged flowers, they probably would have figured it out.''

But still, he knew, it was the placement near Jess that really was the clincher. And perhaps, too, before one could read the message, one would need to have a certain sort of woman in mind—a woman who could be considered a wallflower at the dance of life.

Janek met Fran Dunning at a coffeehouse around the corner from her dorm. It was one of those sixties-type places, with little marble tables, uncomfortable European café chairs, and a lone, slow, and very spacey waitress.

Fran had had three sessions with Beverly Archer. She found her a highly professional and compassionate shrink.

''She's really nice,'' Fran said, ''the way she makes you feel so comfortable and all. It was kind of intimidating to walk in there, not knowing what to expect. But then I started talking about Jess, and I could see she was moved.'' Fran paused. ''There were tears in her eyes, Lieutenant. She cared for Jess; I know she did.''

Fine, thought Janek. *It works better if Fran likes her.*

Fran hadn't seen much of the house. The lavatory was on the first floor, off the therapy room. On her way to it she'd passed through a small office containing a couple of locked filing cabinets and a framed poster for a Botero exhibition. She'd also noticed a burglar alarm system, keypad and siren, inside the coat closet off the front hall.

''Did you mention the knife show?'' Janek asked.

''Not yet.'' Fran paused. ''Want me to?''

Janek shook his head. ''You've done enough, Fran. No need to see her again. Thanks for all your help.''

Fran stared at him, concerned. ''I wish you'd tell me

what this is about, Lieutenant. I just can't believe Dr. Archer had anything to do with, you know . . .''

Janek nodded. He knew he had to give her a reason. "It's not a question of whether she had anything to do with it. It's more a matter of whether she knows something and is holding back. Whenever I ask her about Jess, she talks about patient-therapist confidentiality and how it applies even after death. I find that strange, don't you?"

"I guess so. I never thought about it actually." Suddenly the robust girl athlete seemed terribly fragile. Her smile was weak; her eyes were confused. Janek patted her reassuringly on the hand.

Aaron wanted to bust into Archer's house.

"Just for a look-see, Frank. Me, alone, on a Tuesday night, when she's teaching her class downtown. I'll slip in and out. She'll never know I was there. You won't either, 'cause I won't tell you about it."

"What good will that do?"

"If I see something, I'll say I'm strongly convinced there's evidence in her house. Then we'll figure out a way to get at it legally. That way at least we'll *know*."

Janek was familiar with the technique and its rationale: the illegal break-in or wiretap to assure yourself that you weren't wasting your time, that there was a real case to be made. He had never employed it and was contemptuous of detectives who did. It wasn't just the illegality, though that was bad enough. It was the chain of deceit that followed, that led inevitably to perjury in court. It would be one thing to acquiesce if Aaron wanted to go in for a look, another to state later under oath that he hadn't known anything about it.

Aaron understood. "That's what I thought you'd say. But if there was a way, Frank—a way that was, say, a little less direct, what would you think about that?"

Sounds like shading. But he felt he ought to hear Aaron out. Then, as he listened and began to feel seduced, he understood why Kit Kopta didn't like to assign detectives to cases in which they were emotionally involved.

They were in Aaron's car driving up Third Avenue. It was past midnight. They had long since passed Ninety-sixth Street, the infamous DMZ, and were now deep into the huge Hispanic neighborhood of upper Manhattan, where the store signs were in Spanish, the streets were crowded, bodegas sold live chickens, and pharmacists' wives told fortunes.

"In all my years with Safes and Lofts," Aaron was saying, "Leo Titus was the slickest burglar I ever met. Charming guy. I know you'll like him."

"I thought I wasn't going to meet him."

"Yeah. Sorry. I forgot. Anyway, if you did meet him, you'd like him. How's that?"

"Irrelevant," Janek said.

They passed a battered-looking storefront gym. It wasn't like a yuppie health club in midtown. Up here a gym was a real, sweaty, sour-smelling place where slick-haired Latino boys with names like Pedro and Paco slugged hard at leather bags and skipped rope with exquisite poise deep into the night.

Aaron was still talking about his favorite burglar: "Leo's got this corny MO, but it always seems to work. First he makes a point of going into the house legally in daylight. Comes on as a telephone or Con Ed repairman:

'Hey, lady, gas leak around the corner, gotta get into your basement,' or 'Line trouble, lady—gotta inspect.' He's got nice company credentials, and he's got his girlfriend working as backup. If anyone asks questions, he gives them her number. She's waiting on the other end to verify.''

''Yeah, slick,'' Janek agreed.

''On the first go-around he sees if there's anything worth taking, figures out how he's going to get in, and neutralizes the alarms.''

''What's he looking for?''

''Not the crap the addicts take. No computers or VCRs. Leo goes for the good stuff: money; gold; jewels; bearer bonds. He likes stamp and coin collections but won't bother much with art. Too cumbersome, he says, hard to sell. He likes stuff he can stick into his pockets.''

''I doubt Archer's got anything he'd be interested in.''

''You may be surprised, Frank. Anyway, it doesn't matter. Leo'll find something, and we'll take it from there.''

It was a complicated scheme, devious and tempting, which was why Janek had agreed to go uptown and take a look at Leo Titus. But he didn't think he'd end up going for it. *I'm much too true blue a cop for this,* he thought.

Aaron pulled into a space on the east side of Third, center of the block between 112th and 113th streets. He cut the engine and pointed toward a bar. A narrow red neon sign flashed BAD BOY. ''We're meeting in there,'' he said.

''Gay bar, isn't it?''

Aaron nodded. ''One of the esoteric ones. Whites cruising Latinos and blacks.''

''I thought you said this guy had a girlfriend.''

"Yeah, he does. But he's kind of a swish sometimes, too. Goes home occasionally with guys. He's gotten into some nice Park Avenue apartments that way."

"Shit!"

"Hey, Frank! This isn't about sexual preference."

"You know I don't care about that. But you make him sound, I don't know—undependable."

Aaron clamped his jaws. "Leo's highly dependable." He glanced at his watch. "Time I went in. I'll talk with him a few minutes, then bring him out and parade him up and down the block. He'll know someone's looking him over but won't know who. All I want is for you to get a feel for the guy. Watch his moves, see what you think."

Janek nodded. "Yeah."

As he waited, he asked himself what the hell he thought he was doing sitting low in a car in this none-too-elegant neighborhood, implicating himself in this thoroughly illegal maneuver. And the answer, he knew, was that he was at a point where he didn't care about legalities one way or the other. All he cared about was finding Jess's killer.

When Aaron walked out the door of Bad Boy Bar with Leo Titus in tow, Janek strained forward to peer. Aaron slouched in his usual manner, but Leo, a small, suave, coffee-colored man with neatly cropped hair and a debonair mustache, stepped forward with a stylish gait. And then, as they made their promenade down to the corner and back, Janek had to smile. It was impossible to dislike Leo. The lithe cat burglar moved with the bold grace of Fred Astaire. He almost seemed to prance.

"What do you have on the guy?" Janek asked as Aaron drove them back downtown. It was past 2:00 A.M.

The street life of Spanish Harlem gave way to the cold, silent, empty residential cross streets of Manhattan's Upper East Side.

Aaron glanced at him quizzically. "Huh?"

"He's not going to do this for charity, is he?"

"Charity?" Aaron shook his head. "Not Leo."

"So?"

"He owes me a favor, Frank. Let's just leave it at that."

Janek nodded. He knew better than to pry into the intricacies of a detective's relationship with an informant. Such alliances could be built upon almost anything from real affection and respect to manipulation and fear. This time, Janek suspected, it wasn't Leo who owed Aaron a favor; rather, it was Aaron who was about to incur an enormous debt.

"Here's the plan," Aaron said. "Tuesday night, soon as Archer leaves for her class at Eisenberg, we pull up to her place and wait. We're running a surveillance. After a while we happen to notice a black man with a briefcase enter the house. We sit tight. For all we know Archer gave him the key."

Janek nodded. "Go on."

"After a while the dude comes out. And now we notice instead of a briefcase he's carrying this over-stuffed satchel. We look at each other. 'Hey,' we say, 'maybe a robbery was committed in there.' So, having probable cause, we step out of our car and grab the guy. Leo's scared. He's done two tours in Attica, and he doesn't want to go up for a third. He starts to bargain. Is there any way he can get himself out of this mess? We don't take bribes, we're not that kind, but we're very interested in what he may have seen that could tie Doc

Archer to the Happy Families crimes. Well, seems with all his snooping around Leo came across some pretty interesting evidence. So he trades what he saw for a walkaway deal on the robbery. And on the basis of that, valid information from an informant, we get a warrant, go in legally, and impound whatever he saw.''

"Suppose Leo doesn't see anything?"

"Then he exits with an empty satchel. The satchel's the signal: If it's bulging with stuff, he's seen something, we move in on him and make the deal. Otherwise no harm done. He just walks away." Aaron looked at Janek. "What do you think?"

Janek stared ahead. "We never had this conversation."

Aaron shook his head. "That's right, Frank. We never talked about any of this."

Tuesday, December 1. All day Janek asked himself if he wasn't making an enormous mistake. Twenty-five years in law enforcement and he'd never done a deal like this. *Suppose Leo* does *find something,* he asked himself, *and they go in after it, and then Archer gets a smart lawyer who finds Leo's entry just a wee bit coincidental. The lawyer goes to the D.A., who opens Leo up with the threat of a perjury charge. Leo quickly gives up Aaron, but Aaron hangs tough.* Could he, Janek, live with himself if Aaron got in trouble for helping him out? No way! He'd turn himself in with the result that the doctrine of ''poisoned fruit'' would prevail, the evidence against Archer would be tainted and quashed, Archer would get away with murder, and he, Janek, could end up doing a year in the penitentiary.

Would it be worth it? Not if it went down that way, it wouldn't be.

But there was another scenario, far more succulent. With one bold stroke he might solve a case that could otherwise require years of orthodox investigation.

That, he was ashamed to admit, was a possibility he could not resist.

At seven that evening, fifteen minutes after Archer's last patient left her house, Beverly Archer herself emerged, bundled in a shapeless gray goose down coat.

It was teeth-chattering weather. Janek and Aaron watched shivering from their parking spot as Beverly seemed almost to be swept by the wind down to the corner of Eighty-first and Second, then attempted to flag down a cab.

Several passed her by. Perhaps they didn't like the look of the short, dumpy lady thrashing at the air with her arms. But then a large Checker glided to a halt, Archer hopped in, the cab took off downtown, and, a few seconds later, after Janek stepped out of the car, Aaron waved to him and took off after the cab.

For thirty minutes Janek waited on the corner, collar up, arms clutched to his chest, trying to avert his face from the wintry wind. "Knives-in-the-cheeks" was what he called the relentless, driven icy air that ripped into the sides of his face.

He was shaking when Aaron finally returned. He stumbled back into the car, then immediately began rubbing his hands while Aaron pulled into a fire hydrant zone directly across the street from Archer's house.

"Sorry I took so long. I thought I should follow her all

the way just in case she forgot something and came back.''

"She could still come back.''

"Harder now. Class started at seven-thirty. Which gives us a good hour and a half." He glanced at his watch. "Leo should be turning up. I talked to him this afternoon. Yesterday morning he did his utility man routine. No problems. The alarm system's disarmed." Aaron grinned at Janek. "Don't worry, Frank. No paper trail. I called him from a booth."

But Janek was nervous. *Still got time to cancel this madness,* he thought. He was about to call the whole deal off when Aaron gestured toward the corner. Leo Titus was crossing Third Avenue. "Good old Leo," Aaron whispered.

Later Janek would wonder if the reason he didn't cancel then was that he didn't want to cause Aaron to lose face.

Leo didn't even glance at them as he approached the house. And then Janek had to admire the man's cool. Leo walked straight up to Archer's front door, paused briefly, and two seconds later he was in, the door was closed again, and even someone watching would have no reason to suspect that a burglar had just entered the house.

"Guy's got moves," Aaron marveled.

Fifty minutes passed before Janek became uneasy. Then, when he asked Aaron if Leo wasn't due out pretty soon, Aaron responded with patronizing patience as if Janek were a rookie in need of a steadying hand.

"Keep the faith, Frank. This is our one crack at her. It's gotta be a thorough search. Leo's good. He knows how to look for stuff, and he knows how much time he's got left. Don't worry. If there's something in there, he'll find it.''

But that wasn't what Janek was worried about.

Twenty minutes later Aaron, too, started showing signs of nervousness.

"Class breaks at nine. Takes her a minimum of fifteen minutes to get home. Point of fact, she usually hangs around a while answering questions, stuff like that. So we're safe for another half hour at least.''

"Does Leo think he's got till nine-ten?''

Aaron exploded. "I'm not stupid, Frank! I told him nine max. He's got fifteen more minutes. He'll make it. Trust me—he'll be out of there in time.''

At eight fifty-five they turned to each other. "Should have wired him up,'' Aaron said.

But Aaron knew there was no way they could have wired Leo, though it would have been nice to listen to him as he worked. If they wired him and something went wrong, their role would be exposed.

At nine Aaron smashed his fist against the steering wheel. "That son of a bitch better not try a double cross.''

"*Could* he?'' Janek asked.

"If he found something really valuable—I don't know.'' Aaron paused. "I can't imagine it. Anyway, we would have seen him come out.'' He paused. "Unless there's some way he found to sneak out through the back.'' He hit the wheel again. "But he wouldn't. He wouldn't dare! He knows I'd come after him. I'd never rest!''

Ten minutes later Aaron announced he was going in

no matter the risk to the case. Janek gently put his hand on Aaron's arm.

"Yeah, you're right, someone has to go in. But this is my case. If it's going to get screwed up, I'll do the screwing."

"You can't go in there, Frank. You're a lieutenant, for Christ sakes!"

"I'll say I saw a thief enter and followed him in hot pursuit."

"Jesus!"

"They'll believe me."

"Leo's my boy. I feel . . . awful."

"Could be it's not his fault. Maybe he ran into whatever." Janek picked up a radio. "No talking unless you see Archer. Then just one squawk."

It was only on the doorstep of Archer's house that he wondered how he was going to get inside. He wasn't one of those detectives who excelled at opening locks. But when he took hold of the doorknob, turned it, and pushed, he was not surprised to find the door opening easily. Somehow he expected it to open, as if he had dreamed of the very sound it would make, as if everything that had happened and would happen on this night was familiar to him in some mysterious way.

The door, of course, was taped. Perhaps Aaron had told him Leo always taped his doors while describing the burglar's technique. Janek closed the door softly behind him, then stood very still. The hallway was dark except for a residual glow from the street that filtered in through the narrow leaded windows on either side of the portal.

The coat closet door was open. Janek glanced inside.

A tiny bulb on the burglar alarm keyboard burned red to show that the system was armed up.

But Leo had neutralized it the day before. There was no danger; motion detectors would not set off the siren. Janek listened but heard nothing. Then he thought he felt vibrations, a faint thump on the floor above. He glanced at his watch. Nine-eleven. He had four minutes to find Leo and get out. He headed for the stairs.

They were carpeted. He could barely hear his own footsteps as he crept up to the landing. He paused to listen again. This was the mysterious residential portion of the house he had been thinking about for a week. Janek waited until his eyes adjusted to the darkness, then continued to the second floor. Nine-twelve. Three more minutes. He noticed a reddish glow from an open doorway down the hall.

He passed a closed door, probably a closet, then a door that was partially open. A glimpse of floor tiles suggested a bathroom. He paused.

''Leo,'' he whispered. When he heard nothing, he whispered the burglar's name again and again heard no response.

He crept farther up the hall to the open doorway where he'd seen the glow. He stood there and peered into a cavernous high-ceilinged room strangely filled, like a photographer's darkroom, with dim red light.

It was a bedroom, but unlike any bedroom he had ever seen except perhaps in a movie. An enormous four-poster stood free, a foot or so from one of the walls. Opposite the bed there was a wide niche which once may have contained a fireplace. In this niche hung a full-length life-size oil portrait of a woman. A light extending from the wall above the painting shed red light upon its surface.

Janek stared at the picture, his eyes riveted to its dominating imagery. The woman depicted wore a low-cut silk scarlet dress and held a microphone in her hand. Posed before a dark velour curtain held open by a gilded rope, she appeared to be singing in a smoky ambience. But what was most striking about her was the halo of thick, glossy red curls that surrounded her head, her hard-edged alabaster white features, and the equally pale, lustrous exposed flesh of her upper bosoms, which swelled within the clinging silk of her dress. The woman made a striking figure, at once carnal and statuesque, sensual and unobtainable. And although the painter had worked in a standard academic style, he had caught something vibrant and alive in his subject, a moment when she projected herself, bursting with life-force, to the viewer.

But even as Janek was awed by the powerful image before him, his head began to whirl with a kaleidoscopic array of other images in the room. Below the portrait, arranged upon an odd piece of furniture set within the niche, he saw a number of anomalous objects he could not make out clearly in the red light. Something about them was important. He wanted to decipher them, and was about to move closer to do so, when his eyes, drawn around the room, fastened onto the curled figure of a man lying on the floor at the foot of the bed in a puddle of dark liquid.

Leo!

The moment it registered on him that Leo Titus was lying there, probably dead in a pool of his own blood, the radio strapped to his belt began to squawk. A second later he heard Aaron's voice.

''Shit, Frank! She's coming now, fast!''

Gotta get out of here!

Hearing a sound behind, Janek turned in time to see a short, slim, baldheaded figure, dressed top to bottom in black, ice pick in hand, poised in the doorway to the room. A second later the figure, weapon raised, was rushing at him through the reddish gloom.

Janek feinted to the left. At the same time he reached for the Colt strapped to his ankle. Too late. Before he could crouch, his attacker was upon him, plunging down the weapon.

He knew he'd been hit. No pain, but he could feel the steel strike the bone of his shoulder and then his right arm hanging limp. His only chance now, he knew, was to get to his gun with his left hand. He knelt and struggled for it even as he saw his assailant step back two paces, produce a second ice pick, raise it, and thrust at him again.

He ripped the Colt from its holster and, hand trembling, fired at the advancing figure. The pain was coming upon him now, a great wave of pain that filled his head with delirium. He fired a second time, directly into his adversary's body. And in that same split second, when he saw the body blasted back across the room and knew for certain that it was a woman, the pain smashed into him; he felt a wave of nausea and understood that on her second foray she had stabbed him in the throat.

He could feel the blood gushing out of him. And then, as his legs collapsed slowly, he was seized with the certainty that he was going to die.

* * *

He came to in an ambulance. He knew it was an ambulance because there was a white-coated medic leaning over him, working on his throat, a siren was blasting directly above, and Aaron was crouching by his head, whispering encouragement.

"Hang in there, Frank. Just a block from Lenox Hill Emergency."

"Aaron . . ."

"Frank?" Aaron's face was above him now, slightly blurry but recognizable.

"It was Archer, wasn't it?"

Aaron shook his head. "Wasn't her. But don't worry." Aaron smiled. "You got her. You blew the little bitch away."

"Then who?" But before Aaron could reply, Janek felt himself sinking back into a pit of pain. "Tell Monika—"

Oh-oh—I'm passing out.

When he woke again, he was on his back, naked beneath a sheet, being wheeled rapidly down a tiled basement corridor. Kit Kopta was by his side.

"Kit . . ."

"Right here, Frank."

"Who?"

"Don't worry about that now. You're going to be all right. The surgeons'll fix you up."

Surgeons. . . . Christ, it hurt!

Perhaps he dreamed it, though later he would tell people he woke up terrified during the operation, felt the heat of the lights on his face, saw the surgeons and nurses

in their pea green smocks and masks, felt the probe of
their instruments as they worked on his shoulder and his
throat. And then seeing something in their eyes that told
him he had a chance to live, he resigned himself and
slipped back into a fuzzy chemical-induced sleep.

Kit was beside him when he came to in the recovery
room. He could feel the tight grip of her hand.

"You're going to be okay, Frank. I've got some good
news for you, too. Aaron got hold of Monika. She's
flying in tonight."

"Great . . ." he murmured.

"Your arm should be all right. A week here, a week at
home, and that should do it. As for your throat—well,
another quarter inch and she'd have waxed you. She
didn't, thank God!"

"Who *was* she?" His voice sounded strange to him,
raw, hoarse, a mere whimper that sent pulses of pain
shooting through his brain. He tried to sit. *"Who?"* he
demanded.

"Take it easy, Frank. Lie back. She was the girl
downstairs, the one who rented the basement apartment.
She'd been Archer's patient in Connecticut."

Connecticut! What the hell was going on?

"But was she . . . the one? You know. Was she—?"

Kit was nodding. "Sure looks that way. I just got off
the phone with Aaron. They went through her apartment,
found ticket stubs, ice picks, caulking guns, glue. Sullivan's shitting in his pants. Because you solved it, Frank.
You did it, you brilliant son of a bitch! You solved
Happy Families!"

"Archer, she—"

Kit shook her head. "She didn't know anything. That's what she says. The girl was fixated on her, and . . ."

He felt his eyes starting to close. He struggled but couldn't keep them open. Kit's voice was distant now, as if in the back of a deep cave. "Rest, Frank. We'll talk later. Aaron'll be here soon. He'll explain. . . ."

When he woke nauseated and agitated in a darkened room, there was a moment of clarity. "You solved it." Had Kit actually said that?

Was it possible?

How could he have solved it?

How?

7

Wallflower

Diana Proctor, braced like a West Point plebe, stood rigid in the garden just outside the window. Back arched, eyes forward, head straight, chin down—in this exaggerated posture her nose was but inches from the glass.

Beverly Archer, sitting in the consulting room, glanced at her and smiled. The rain, running down Diana's young and ardent face, streaked her cheeks like tears. The girl's hair, cut close and butch, hung limp like wet black yarn. Her gray T-shirt, bearing the word TRAINING in small block military letters, clung sopping to her rib cage and chest.

What a sight! You'd think the poor thing would have to move, but there she stood still as stone just as she'd been ordered. She was shivering; no surprise, since she'd been standing out there for nearly forty minutes and still had twenty more to go. Rain or shine, a sentence was a sentence; an hour had been decreed, and an hour would be served. A fat little alarm clock, standing on tiny feet, was perched upon the windowsill. Diana's eyes were fastened to its taunting face, her features frozen, locked. That, too, had been ordered. If the eyes were permitted to drift, the strings of control would weaken. In a matter of this kind control was everything. Obedience and control.

To Beverly the glass between them, transparent yet impenetrable, symbolized their relationship: intimately bound yet separate and apart. Here she sat within, sheltered and warm, flipping casually through a magazine, while Diana stood less than a foot away, braving the elements as she performed her penance. The polarity was perfect, Beverly thought, and best of all, Mama would approve.

She remembered: Mama zippering her into an oversize snowsuit, then pulling the collar up above her head so her face was encased as well. "Better be good, Bev, or I'll zip you up forever. . . ."

She glanced again at Diana. Poor girl! But Diana craved hard discipline, reveled in it. It was discipline that had made her strong, that would make of her a perfect steely tool. With a person like Diana, discipline was the only way. Break her; control her; then build her up again. Take the raw killer rage and forge it to your need. Train her; teach her obedience; then she will serve you and Mama, too. Then she will be better than a bullet, better even than a knife.

She remembered: "Learn to be an archer, Bev," Mama said. "Find your arrow, sharpen it up, string it to your bow, and let it fly. It'll travel far and true, hit your targets again and again. . . ."

Beverly rose from the black Eames chair, set down her magazine, and moved to the window. She stared straight at Diana, trying to distract her, make her eyes flicker a moment from the clock. Not a blink. Good girl! Beverly was proud. Perhaps Diana's nipples twitched a little against the drenched gray cotton of her shirt, but her eyes, disks of sky blue ice, held firm.

* * *

Twenty minutes later Diana, trembling, stood before Beverly in the office. Her skin, so very pale, glistened with rain and sweat.

"Tonight you learned something," Beverly said. The girl nodded. "What?"

"That I can do it," Diana whispered, still shaking with chill.

"Do what? Go on, girl—speak." Beverly intentionally tightened her lips to make her mouth appear authoritative.

"That I can do as I'm told."

"And that's important. Why?"

"Because there'll come a time—"

"Maybe soon."

"—soon, when you'll order me—"

"To perform a mission."

"Yes. And then I must perform it exactly as you tell me."

"Without deviation."

"Without any deviation. And then I must return, stand before you as I'm standing now, and report to you everything I did."

"Everything, accurately, in scrupulous detail."

"In the most scrupulous detail," Diana affirmed.

"And so your task tonight—?"

"Was to show I can obey you without questioning, that I'm capable of doing what you tell me, exactly—"

"And correctly."

"Yes."

"To serve me and obey."

Diana nodded. "Serve and obey."

The girl drew in her breath. When she spoke again, she

lowered her eyes, as was her habit whenever she uttered
an opinion of her own. "I believe tonight I have shown
you I can," she offered hesitantly.

Beverly smiled, rose, stood before Diana, patted the
girl gently on the head. "Yes, my dear. We're coming
along nicely now." She toyed a little with Diana's
stringy, dripping hair. "Down to your room now, off
with those nasty garments, towel your hair, put on
something nice and clean, then join me in the bedroom
for a cup of tea."

At Beverly's gesture of dismissal, Diana raised her
eyes, gleaming with incipient tears. "Thank you, Doctor," the girl whispered, then, quick as a cat, scooted
from the room.

Afterward Beverly stood alone in the office, thinking
about the next phase of Diana's training, the next degree
of obedience she would instill. The control must be
remote, she thought. *Following orders with me hovering
about is easy. Total submission beyond my sight—that
will be something else.*

She had always believed that the concept came to her
on a certain rainy afternoon when she was fifteen years
old, came just after a crack of lightning revealed the inky
blackness that lay beyond the fine, tight gray fabric of the
sky.

A romantic fantasy most likely, although perhaps it
really had come to her then, at least in some rudimentary
form. She knew well from her studies of human psychology that life-changing ideas often seem to strike like
bolts delivered from above.

But it was not as if she were actually seeking some
means of reprisal at the time. Nor was she worrying over

one or another slight the way she so often did. Quite the contrary. So perhaps it was because she *wasn't* trying to figure out a way to squash her enemies that a method of revenge came to her, heaven-sent if you will, and then, of course, it was so perfect, so beautiful she had no choice but to devote the remainder of her life to seeing if it was actually possible to bring it off.

Get someone else to get them for you. There it was in a nutshell, so to speak, and, like so many great notions, startlingly simple once you thought of it.

But there was a special element to this particular notion, the craft and cunning of it that always made her smile. The thin, tight, knowing, masking, taunting smile that said she knew something the others didn't and was harboring a plan that would see them all in hell. No matter what you do to me, the smile said, no matter what you say, what insults you heap, what humiliations you force me to endure, in the end I'll get you back, and now, even as you torment me, I know exactly how I'm going to do it, too. Yes, that's what her thin, tight, knowing, masking, taunting smile said.

Mama knew. "Be an archer," she said. "Find an arrow; string it to your bow."

Mama, of course, had been playing with words, making a pun out of their name. What Mama meant was, go for the weak spot, which had always been Mama's way. But Beverly thought her own approach was far more cunning. *Find someone else to do your dirty work. Get yourself a human tool.*

It took her years to find Tool, and when she finally did, the moment she laid eyes on it was one of the most ecstatic of her life.

There she is! she said to herself. *That's her! I can see

it now, can see her doing all the things I've been dreaming of. Yes, no question, that's her, I know it, she's the one!

Then she peered at the girl a second time to make sure she was right.

It wouldn't do to pick out the wrong person just because so many years had passed and she'd grown impatient to settle up her scores. She'd waited this long; another year, even another decade wouldn't matter if Tool was right. But on second look, and third! and fourth!, she was still convinced the girl was perfect. The tool she'd been looking for had been delivered. Beverly felt her head surge with power the way she imagined the cockhead of some prehistoric man had once swelled with potency when he stared at a rock and realized for the first time that he could use it to crush a rival's skull.

It had been a gray day, the kind of sad, warm, unbearably humid day when the sky's the color of old pewter and the air's so close your brain feels soggy and your joints begin to ache. The kind of day when you don't feel like meeting new people because even the sight of the ones you already know drives you up the wall. You want to scream, that's the kind of day it was, but you don't, don't show even a smidgen of your pain because you're a professional, a shrink, a clinical psychologist, certified and sane and socialized and analyzed, so you just smile your thin, tight, masking smile and go in to meet the new patient.

There she sits, tense, coiled, twenty years old, five feet two inches tall, 110 beautifully conditioned pounds, hair black like a witch's, eyes so hard and blue they make you think of ice. And yet there's something vulnerable about her, too, a visible yearning, a need, and you grasp at once she's got a craving you can satisfy.

She's a murderess.

"Another little murderess, Bev," Carl Drucker tells you as he hands you the file. Carl pretends to hold the folder as if it were too hot to handle, and his sheepdog's eyes twinkle when he enunciates "murderess." Carl always feigns amusement over the most dangerous patients, but he doesn't fool you. He's scared of them, so frightened he'd surely wet his pants if he had to be with one of them alone. Poor Carl. For all his training, evil still confuses him. He knows in his brain there's no such thing, there's only antisocial behavior, but he doesn't really know it the way you do, deep down in your gut.

"Seems our new Missy Perfect chopped up mommy and granny, little sissy, too. The old story, Bev. Strict family. Religious nuts. Wouldn't let the girls watch TV, let alone go out on dates. Mommy was stupid. Granny ruled with the strap. So one day Missy broke, took the old wood ax, and chopped 'em up."

Another twinkle from Carl. *Better watch it, Carl. Don't want to end up on my list, do you?*

"Why the sister?" you ask. *As if you didn't know!*

"Oh, Bev—why's the grass green? Jeez, you've been around. Sissy was *there*. She probably ragged her. 'Diana's gonna get it, Diana's gonna get it, neah, neah, neah!' So, while you're chopping the authority figures, you might as well chop up the taunting little bitch, too. But it's interesting, come to think of it, there weren't any men around?" Carl, stroking his wimpy mustache, assumes his Great Psychiatrist pose. "She went for the ladies, split their heads, then gave 'em each a couple of chops between the legs. Split, split, split. She's a little sickie, I can tell you. Sue Farber tried talking to her, couldn't even get close. We thought you'd do okay with her, though. More your type, Bev. Wanna give it a shot?"

Sure. Why not? It's what you do for a living, work with disturbed young females all day long, and you know the offenders aren't that much different from the nice polite college kids either. The bottom line is usually pretty much the same, a snake ball jangle of angry sexual confusion working its way out through eating disorders and, in this case, good old matricide.

"You'll take a look?" You nod. Carl's eyes twinkle. "That's my girl. Diana Proctor's her name." He strokes his wimpy mustache. "Good luck, Bev. And don't take any sharp instruments in there with you. Heh-heh-heh."

Poor Carl. He knows they're all incurable. He knows he's running a warehouse for psychotics and the state's rehabilitation policy is so much crap. Hell, you're lucky if you can get one of them to construct a coherent "feelie" in the OT shop, let alone relate to you on a therapeutic basis. But Carl doesn't care. He's beyond all that. He's a proper civil servant now. Maybe there was a time when he wanted to save the world, effect great cures, write up great cases, apply psychiatric theory to social problems, reform penology, rehabilitate irreversibles. But he gave up on all that long ago. He thinks you've given up on it, too, doesn't know that you're here looking for a tool and that in about five minutes you're going to find yourself one in young Diana Proctor, murderess.

How did she know? Even now she couldn't tell you, though Diana had been in continuous training with her for more than a year, and there'd been five years of weekly therapy sessions before that, before she could get her out of Carlisle and under full-time supervision.

It was the whole gestalt, she often told herself, recalling the moment of their first encounter, so clear in her mind it could have taken place within the hour instead of years before.

It was her need; she reeked of it, she told herself. *I could smell her hunger the way you smell bread in a bakeshop. She'll be my tool.* And so now she has become . . .

It was one of those mysterious encounters that takes place once in a lifetime if a person is lucky, like finding your dreamboat sitting beside you on a tour bus or like accidentally pressing the shutter of your camera at the very moment a prominent politician is assassinated.

Of course, it wasn't *that* accidental. She'd been working at the hospital all those years just waiting for the right tool to come along. Diana was perfect. The hard part would be to get her out.

Shhhh. Here she comes now. Up the stairs on tippy-toe, just like a little lynx. She pauses in the bedroom doorway, silhouettes herself the way you trained her against the light of the hall. An elegant black form against a warm yellow rectangle, waiting, waiting for your order.

"Come in, my dear. Feeling better?"

The little thing nods as she scampers toward you. The tail ends of her wet hair, slicked straight back, comb lines visible, cling seductively to her sinewy little neck. She sits down on her stool and helps herself to a cup of tea. You watch her as she blows on the hot liquid, smile at the sight of her pink little tongue as it darts out between her lips to test the temperature.

"I'm going to reward you for your very good obedience, Diana. Tomorrow at dusk you'll enter Central Park, dressed in black, dressed to kill. You'll carry two holstered ice picks strapped to your arms and several bulletin board–type pins, you know the kind, with the little colored knobs on the ends."

The lynx nods eagerly.

"The first part of your mission will be to pick out a person on one of the paths. Your target should be alone, big, male. A jogger would be fine, but a walker or an ordinary tourist will do as well. Stalk him for at least fifteen minutes. Make sure he's the one you want to hit. Then, when you see an opportunity, execute an attack. Don't kill him; just stab him with one of the pins. A quick jab in his rump will do the trick. But remember, it won't count unless it makes him squeal. Approach from the back; stick him; then retreat and lose yourself in the woods. Move rapidly toward the West Side. Go to some stores; hang out awhile; then take a bus back. Don't come home on foot. So, girl—think you can do all that?"

The little lynx smiles. "Piece of cake."

"Is it now? I guarantee it won't be so easy. A hundred things can go wrong. Pick on an off-duty cop and you're in trouble. He'll shoot you if you don't run fast enough. Or what if your target shouts for help and there happens to be a Good Samaritan around the bend? See, you have to think of everything, analyze the mission. Tell me, what are your most important decisions?"

Lynx gazes up at you. Her ice blue eyes burn with predatory lust. "Choosing the target," she whispers. "And deciding when to prick him."

Smart girl! Sometimes you're so proud of her you want to kiss her all over. But instead you stroke her head, pet her the way Mama used to stroke and pet you, offering affection in exchange for loyalty and obedience. What the tool needs is tough love, not sex; sex she can provide for herself.

"Okay, go on back down to your room now, lie on your bed, close your eyes, and think the whole thing through. Remember, he's got to squeal. You'll take my little tape recorder with you, so you can bring me back some proof. Wear rubber gloves, of course, and leave the pin in. That'll slow him down in case he's the pursuing type. He'll have to pull it out first, and by then you'll be gone in a puff of smoke. So, tomorrow night?"

"Please, yes, Doctor," the little tool begs.

The plan was to make Carl think it was his idea, that recommending Diana for release had never crossed your mind. Sure, you'd done wonders with the little murderess, vacuuming out her brain, servicing and reinstalling her superego, instilling remorse for her evil acts and a strong desire for redemption. You'd even made her into a leader in the wards, a girl the others turned to for settlement of minor disputes. And she'd become virtually indispensable in the hospital library, not to mention earning straight *A*'s in her extension courses in library science. The little murderess has proved herself reliable, trustworthy, contrite, but no, Carl, it has never occurred to you she should be released.

"Jeez, Bev. . . ." Carl turns away, starts stroking his pointy little beard. The wimpy mustache wasn't enough; this year he sees himself as Freud. "I mean, what're we doing here if we're not preparing them for release? Isn't our purpose to save their broken little souls?"

"Yes, of course. . . ." You furrow your brow. What a hoot, but you have to appear sincere. "Don't forget, Diana committed three murders, Carl. She axed her own mother. The public won't stand for it if all she's got to do is spend five years in cushy old Carlisle."

"Think so, Bev? I'm not so sure myself."

You can't believe it! He's actually thought the whole thing through!

". . . those kinds of objections, you know, don't come from the public. It's the survivors who usually put up the stink. They write the judge. They lost their loved ones, and the killer's got to pay." Carl twinkles. "But here," he says, "we've got a unique situation. There *are* no survivors. There aren't any cousins, aunts, anyone who cared for any of them or even gave a rusty shit. Diana finished off her whole family. So what I anticipate is a quiet hearing in the judge's chambers with a sympathetic prosecutor going along. Let's go to the wall for her, Bev, and, while we're at it, show the state we can do what they pay us for. Diana's barely twenty-five. I hate to lose her, but she's entitled to a future. I talked to her this morning. She refers to the 'old me who did that very bad thing' and how, though she knows that 'old me' was definitely her, and wouldn't dream of not taking responsibility for her actions, she feels emotionally disassociated from the person she used to be and thoroughly incapable of doing what she knows she did. Thanks to you, Bev, she's practically cured! And I thought I'd never see the day. Anyway, you know that people who kill close family members are almost never dangerous to anybody else."

Ha! That's what you think, twerp!

Carl turns slowly toward you again, places his hands ceremoniously on his desk. "Look, she's your case. Whatever you decide I'll back you up. But think about this: If you don't want to take on responsibility for initiating a release, and believe me, I can understand why you might not, I'll be happy, with your consent, to take that upon myself. Believe me, Bev, every shrink on staff will join the cause."

Carl's eyes dance merrily in their sockets.

Remember what she was like that first time? Young Murderess Ready to Strike. She had the killer eyes, the kind you'd seen so often in sociopaths, the fear and hatred raging to get out. Those kinds of eyes tell you there's no compassion, no identification with another human's pain. You have those very eyes yourself sometimes but never show them to the world. They're turned inward, and over the years you've worked up a mask so you can play the healer and make the troubled girlies think you care about their wearisome anorexia or tedious bulimia attacks.

She, Diana, Tool-to-be, had the true killer's glow and, fairly rare in combination with that, a deep, deep need to submit. She was a storm trooper waiting impatiently for orders, a gladiator frothing at the mouth to fight. She craved authority, a coach, a savior, and as she met your eyes, she knew you would be the one to give structure to her rage, focus it down until it became a pure blue torch point of fire.

How could you both tell so much from just a glance? Because you'd been looking for each other all your lives. You'd been rummaging for years in prisons and mental hospitals, searching always for a certain look, and Diana had been seeking you, too, even though she didn't know she had. So when you walked into that little room, she saw in you the governess of her dreams, and you saw in her a fine young ward who would help you balance up all your old accounts.

It was, as they say, love at first blush.

"They're calling you little murderess around the hospital," you told her, speaking passionately and looking straight into the little murderess's killer eyes. "They're frightened of you. They think you're dangerous. They say I'm a fool to sit down in here with you alone. But I am *not* afraid, Diana. I know you won't harm me. I understand why you did what you did, and I'm going to say this to you now, before you even speak a word: You were *right* to kill them, and you oughtn't to be feeling any guilt over it. None! None at all! They abused you and by doing so brought everything that happened upon themselves. Mother, grandmother, sister—are you supposed to bear unendurable suffering just because it comes from your blood relations? Everyone's got murderous feelings toward family members, but few have got the guts to take up an ax and pay them back. You're different. You *have* got the guts. So whatever happens between us now, Diana, I want you to know how much I respect you for your bravery."

Having made your passionate personal statement, you assumed a cooler, more professional demeanor. "Now listen carefully, we're going to be working together. I'm going to be your doctor and help make you well. After I prove to you that what you did was right, we're going to take a good hard look together at who you are and what you ought to be. You have a whole lifetime ahead of you,

Diana. In a few years, when you're ready, I'll get you released, and then I'll show you how to realize your potential. I'm going to help you first by building you up, making you feel strong and confident. Now tell me—what do you feel about what I've just said? Tell me your true feelings. I want to hear.''

The girl started to sob almost at once. You hugged her to you and urged her to weep on.

''It's okay. Let it out. Cry it all out of yourself. Clean yourself out with the tears, Diana. You'll feel better afterwards, I promise. . . .''

In the end, after the weeping gave way to sporadic little moans and sobs, she spoke the golden words you'd been waiting for: ''I feel at last . . .''

''Go on, my dear.''

''I've met—''

''Yes. Tell me, who've you met?''

''Finally someone—''

''Yes, go on.''

''—who understands me. Really does.''

''You believe that?''

''Oh, yes.'' She nodded shyly. ''I do.''

You immediately hugged her to you again, then gently rocked her in your arms. ''That's right, Diana. You have, you have, sweet girl.''

And it was true! You did understand her! You truly, truly did!

The method was to envelop her in an alternate reality, a fictive world of your own creation existing parallel to the so-called real world, yet which to an outside observer would appear the same. To Diana, however, confined within your web, every so-called normal value would be subverted. Purposes, motives, principles, matters of morality and personal honor—in your alternate world such things would not have the same meanings as they did outside.

She's down there now in her dank little hole of a room in the basement, dreaming through her mission. She's imagining the feeling of popping the pin into the posterior of some unsuspecting man, the way it'll sink so nicely into his cushy ass. And then his yelp, squeal, cry, little chirp of pain, and how she'll record it as she runs by and how the pitch'll change because she'll be in motion. You smile to yourself: The exercise, if questioned, could be construed as a practical demonstration of the Doppler effect.

You went to watch her work out at her dojo at Broadway and 110th, a big hot, humid room on the second floor above a supermarket, where you were greeted by the deep-throated cries of zealous young fighters and the tangy aroma of their bodies at work.

Diana was in the first line with the best of them, energetically slashing at the air with her strong young arms. You loved the way Tool threw fast kicks and punches in unison with the others, mostly giant males. She looked so right among them, cute, too, in her white canvas gi jacket, white pants, and black obi. But you'd seen the backs of her hands after a workout, raw from hundreds of knuckle push-ups ordered by her instructor, and occasional marks, too, across her back from hits delivered with a bamboo stick, penalties for poorly executed exercises or that obscure and thus endlessly punishable offense of the dojo, insufficient respect.

There was another girl in the class that afternoon who caught your interest, reminding you of someone from your past. She had blond hair cut into a wedge, beautifully tanned skin, and a smile that lit up her entire face as she punched and kicked the air. You watched her carefully during combat exercises. She easily overpowered her opponents. She was taller than Diana, though just as perfectly proportioned, and her eyes were entirely different. While Diana had cold killer's eyes, this girl's eyes blazed clear gray like a warrior's. And while Diana had been trained to sneak attack her targets from behind, this girl was the sort to approach hers from the front in fair, refereed competitions.

That evening, as you ministered to Diana's bleeding knuckles, you asked her the other girl's name.

"Oh, you must mean Jess," Diana said. "Sensei says she's the best fighter in the class."

Remember Bertha Parce, Mama? That old mean bag of a bitch English teacher at Ashley-Burnett? Yes, that one, who enjoyed making fun of certain selected kids in front of all the others. Remember the time I told you about when she read a story of mine aloud to the entire class? The story I wrote about you, Mama, the true one about your opening night at the Fairmount Club Lounge, when Millie and I hid in back of the curtain behind the orchestra and you belted out those great Porter tunes, "You're the Top," "I Get a Kick Out of You," "I've Got You Under My Skin," and the crowd went wild. "More! More!" they shouted, and you grinned and belted out a couple more: "Let's Do It," "So in Love," and, as your final encore, "Another Op'nin'; Another

Show.'' Even then they clapped and howled and begged for more. God! Do you remember?

I wrote my story about that night, and everything I felt during it, the way my heart brimmed with pride in you, Mama, standing out there in your glittering sequin-trimmed crimson strapless, knocking all those fancy folks for a loop. And then how you brought me and Millie out. ''I want you all to meet my two girls,'' you announced. ''It's way past their bedtimes, but they wanted to be here to see if their old ma could really sing.'' And the crowd went berserk again! I remember one fat old man in particular, with slicked-back gray hair, who stood and clapped until the rest of them followed suit. And then some bosomy lady yelled, ''Bravo! Bravo!'' and you glowed, Mama, you positively lit up electric in the smoky, booze-scented dark of the lounge.

That's what I wrote about, and the grip of little Millie's hand in mine, and the swelling up I felt inside, the warmth of my pride in people knowing I was your daughter. I wrote, too, about how, late that night back home, you came into my room to tuck me in and how you smelled, the faint scent of perfume on your skin, the remnants of powder on your cheeks, and the glow on you still, the glow that comes from being applauded, and the aliveness of you, the pulsing energy, the power I felt when you reached down and grasped me in your arms. I wrote about how I fell asleep remembering the applause, listening to it echo, and how, just before I slept, I whispered four words to myself. I think you know them, Mama. ''A star is born'' is what I whispered. And I wrote how I smiled then and fell asleep and how I thought that was the happiest, proudest, most sublime night of my entire life, Mama, and I wrote about it that way, too, trying to capture the special quality of its magic.

A week later I was positively thrilled when Miss Parce announced she was going to read my story aloud in class. Except she had barely read a couple of paragraphs when I realized what she was trying to do. She read it in this mean, sarcastic way, and soon, sure enough, she had the other girls tittering, smirking, glancing at one another, and rolling eyes. And then, caught up in the spirit of the thing, she broadened her satiric attack, making funny little faces while relentlessly decimating my story, assassinating my every line, until finally all my words lay shattered and broken on the floor.

When she was finished, when there was nothing left of what I wrote except the sporadic tittering in the back of the room, she looked straight at me, eyes glowing, and said: "Tell us one thing please, Beverly: Is there a single line in this entire tale in which there resides one tiny particle of truth?"

I stared back at her uncomprehending, too stupefied to reply. The classroom went silent. You could hear a pin drop, as they say.

"Well, *dear*?" she asked, and, when I still didn't answer: "What's the matter? Cat got your tongue?"

She stared cold stone hard at me, her black pupils tightened down to points. And then she smirked. I wanted to speak. I wanted to cry out, beg her to stop staring at me. But I couldn't; I was too humiliated. And still, the mean old witch would not relent. She kept staring, and then her mouth turned cruel, and she dabbed her tongue to her lips like a snake readying to strike and said: "I've heard your mother actually does sing in nightclubs. Is that correct, my dear?"

I must have nodded faintly, for she went on.

"Well, I must say that is a *unique* occupation for a mother. And I'm sure she does very well at it, too. But Beverly''—and here her voice turned false-friendly—''there are things we write about when the assignment is 'Describe a sublime moment in your life' and there are things we don't write about, we don't even mention in polite conversation. I would have hoped you understood that.''

With that the old witch wrote a great big *F* in red ink across the front page of my story, then daintily placed it facedown on her desk.

The girls in back had gone quiet again. And at just that moment (and she could have timed it so perfectly only by design) the bell rang to announce the end of class. The others shuffled out of the room in mortified silence, leaving me and the bitch alone. I began to cry. Miss Parce smiled at me and, in the phony manner of a wise, friendly teacher, said: ''Now, now, my dear, no need to weep, I'm sure. . . .''

As I sat there choking on my tears, I knew, Mama, that I would pay her back one day. Yes, Mama, I knew I would live to see her dead, mutilated, too, if I could manage it. But most important—dead! dead! dead!

Listening to the tape Diana brought back from Central Park, feeling her excitement rise at the sound of Diana's running feet, Tool's ''uh!'' as she plunged in the pin, the delicious squeal of the jogger victim, his ''yeeeeeow!'' as he was stuck, then his curses receding in the distance as Diana's feet hit dirt when she dodged off the running path and into the woods, Beverly knew she would always want Diana to bring back something from her missions.

It was only later, upon her realization that the quick kills Diana would be making would preclude the possibility of recording her quarries' cries of pain, that she evolved the notion of trophies. She wanted always to have something, some object taken from the Scenes of Bloodletting, to touch, caress, and hold. It would give immediacy to Diana's reports, and perhaps most important, it could be offered up to Mama on the wall.

Mama told her: "Truly now, dear, in your training of Diana, you've found your true vocation. I think at heart you were always a behaviorist hiding in an analytic therapist's cloak. Rewards and punishments, increasingly complex tests of obedience—these are the only ways to dominate and compel. Certainly the progress you've made with the lynx proves the efficacy of your approach. My God, Bev, take a look, will you, at the incredible little tool you have wrought!"

The vigorous training workouts—long, slow, loping jogs along the bridle paths of Central Park; short, sharp wind sprints along the East River esplanade; huffing and puffing calisthenic sessions on the cold basement floor of the house; sweaty muscle building on the Nautilus machines at the Eight-sixth Street Health Club; harsh, exhausting martial arts training at the West Side dojo; the special intensive ten-day commando course in Boulder, Colorado; endurance exercises; obedience tests; ice pick attack drills performed against straw dummies in your holiest of holies, your bedchamber—all were carefully designed to build strength and speed, refine coordination, increase response time, restore vigor in the face of fatigue, and, most important, inspire a yearning to kill.

Once the craving was instilled, the obsession would build, and once the obsession was implanted, the command to execute would be ardently obeyed. "It's all in the preparation," Mama told you. "The long, hard months of training will pay off," she said, "in the swift split seconds of attack." But since the kills will be so very swift, you and Tool must receive gratification some other way. Perhaps through slow rituals performed afterward upon the cadavers, rituals of vengeance by which your rage will be satiated and the humiliations you endured will be many times repaid. "Remember, Bev," Mama said, "it's not sufficient to settle your old accounts at par value. Too many years have passed; the interest has built up and by now far exceeds the original charges entered in your ledger."

Diana Proctor stands poised in a corner of the cellar, sleek and slinky in her black cotton bodysuit. Two specially designed holsters, each containing an ice pick, are strapped to her forearms. Across the room a scrawny tiger cat, abducted from the street, prowls around a plastic dish of kitty tuna bits.

Beverly studies the human lynx, breathing slowly, deeply, awaiting her order. Finally Beverly decides it's time.

"Kill it," she orders.

Diana doesn't move. Beverly approaches the girl, then slaps her hard, smack!, across her face.

Diana, eyes front, lips trembling, receives the blow as her due. Beverly watches as the pale skin of the lynx's cheek turns pink, then red from the impact. Both understand the meaning of this chastisement. Delay and/or squeamishness will not be tolerated.

"Kill! Kill the cat!" Beverly whispers her command, and this time an admonished Diana instantly obeys.

In a single, beautiful, scything balletic motion the tool executes the little creature. Afterward they both stare down at its rigid body, neck up, ice pick thrust through the throat deep into its tiny brain.

"Clean up the mess; deposit it in a trash can on the avenue; then report to me in my bedroom," Beverly orders. "I have a choice new punishment in mind for you, my dear. One that will, I'm sure, instill a greater eagerness to obey."

Diana, braced, nods acceptance of this directive. As Beverly turns, she smiles quietly to herself. The little lynx can't wait. She loves correction. She'll be lubricating like crazy by the time she mounts the stairs.

You told Tool to befriend the girl named Jess, the lovely, strong, brave gladiator at the dojo. You had in mind a kind of recruitment but naturally never mentioned your intentions.

After Tool flew down to Florida, slew Bertha Parce, and brought back your trophy, a hair curler found in a funny bright blue plastic box beside the old schoolmarm's bed, you quizzed her endlessly about the gluing of the bitch's vagina, what it felt like to slather in the gooey stuff, then squeeze the labia majora shut.

"Did she smell down there?" you inquired, grinning. "Like a rotten old fish, I bet," you added, pinching your nostrils with disgust.

Your delighted interest in the aromatic dimension most definitely spurred Diana on. She described everything, as she'd been trained to do, in the most exhaustive

detail. And you relished every word, for that was the
bliss—the imagining of it, the reconstruction, the obsessive staging and restaging of the execution. Your re-
creations, fueled by Diana's reportage, gave you more
pleasure, you were certain, than anything you might have
felt had you gone down there and done the wonderful
deed yourself. Your imagination, embellishing power-
fully upon the details Diana provided, could create
scenes far more intense than what had actually taken
place.

It was so funny, Mama, when Carl went through the
file and kept pulling out the reports I'd planted so
carefully, ingeniously, and diligently through the years,
flatly written case file summaries which contained no
evaluations, no recommendations, and certainly no self-
congratulation.

They purported to be simple factual accounts of Diana
Proctor's treatment, and Carl kept quoting them to me,
saying things like "Just listen to what you wrote, Bev!"
and "Jeez, Bev, listen to this!" and "God's sakes, Bev,
can't you see the forest for the trees?" He was using
them, see, to try to convince me the little murderess had
recovered and was ready for release. And I kept resisting:
"I'm not sure, Carl"; "I might have overstated that,
Carl"; "But don't forget, she killed them, Carl—killed
them, then split their crotches with an ax!"

I toyed with him until I got him riled. I was acting like
a hard-ass, he said, a tough bitch shrink, the kind he
hated, and he was genuinely surprised since when he'd
hired me, it was for my humanity, not my clinical skills
or my degrees. What happened to my compassion
anyway, he wanted to know, and had it occurred to me I

might have spent too many years playing shrink-goddess
to my patients, in the process losing sight of them as vulnerable human beings? At the very least I owed Diana the
benefit of a doubt. I'd brought her along this far; why the
hell couldn't I see she was ready to go the distance? And
I just stared at him, Mama, until he started to rave: What
kind of a person was I? Had I become one of those neurotic
power-tripping shrinks who refuses to let a patient go
because they can't bear to relinquish their control?

See, Mama, he was using my own words to make his
case, and the longer I refused to buy it, the stronger
became his conviction he was right. In the end, when I
finally relented, his investment in Diana's "rehabilitation" exceeded anything I could have worked up with a
direct appeal. I hornswoggled the little twerp, and he
never knew it. I'm telling you, Mama, it was so damn
funny to watch him fall so easily into the trap that took
me the better part of five years to lay. Like taking candy
from a baby. It was just, I don't know . . . hysterical.

There was another little trap I laid, not for Carl but for
Diana. Call it my safety valve, Mama. I laid it . . . just
in case.

The trap consisted of creating a traceable path between
Diana and the signature, a path that would not run
through me. So I instructed her to tell Carl, Sue Farber,
the librarian, and a couple of her cronies among the
patients that she was a sort of "wallflower type," and
that was why she didn't like going to hospital dances.
None of them would think anything of it, unless, of
course, they were questioned about it later on. Then
they'd all remember, wouldn't they? You bet they
would!

I also had her sign a note to me with a droopy flower leaning against a wall, a note I could plant without comment in her file. The best part of it was the way I persuaded Diana that the devalued flower she'd leave at each gluing would, in fact, be *her* signature.

A neat little double trap, if I do say so, for although she would only be the tool, she would *think* she was the artist!

Beverly Archer, wearing a prim navy blue wool skirt and freshly ironed white blouse, sits in a chair in her bedroom facing the full-length life-size oil painting of her mother on the wall. Diana Proctor squats on the floor between Beverly's legs, also facing the portrait. The girl wears jeans but is bare above the waist.

"You know why we're facing Mama?" Beverly asks. "You do, don't you?"

Diana shakes her head. "I'm not sure," she whispers.

Beverly, tightening her grip by pressing her knees together, feels the girl shudder. *The little lynx is afraid,* she thinks. *As well she might be, considering she's about to get it.*

"We're facing Mama because we want Mama to *see,*" Beverly explains patiently. "Isn't that right, my dear? I mean we *do* want that, don't we?" Beverly squeezes her again. "Well?"

"I guess so," Diana responds.

"*Guess!* Well, I assure you we most definitely *do* want her to see. We want Mama to witness your correction." Beverly pauses. "You know why you're going to receive correction, don't you?"

"I think so," the girl mutters.

"Tell me?"

"Because I hesitated."

"You did, and now you're going to be punished for it."

Beverly does not feel unkindly toward Tool. On the contrary, she feels quite maternal toward her. But the tool has erred and must be disciplined. The principle of unquestioning obedience must be reinforced.

"You know I don't like to hit you, Diana. You know how much it hurts me," Beverly says.

"I know," the girl concedes in a whisper.

"Especially as I understand what you went through as a child, the beatings you took from your grandmother. You know how much I despise brutality."

"Yes, I know that, Doctor."

"So you must concede that when I strike you, there has to be a very good reason?" The girl nods. "What you did before down in the cellar, hesitating, standing there petrified, not even acknowledging my order, was deserving of the good, hard slap you got, wasn't it?"

Beverly feels another wave surge through Diana. "Yes, I deserved it. I know I did."

"Well, what I'm going to do to you now is not like a slap at all. It's important for you to understand the difference. I slapped you to shock you into action. The purpose was to sting and stun, make you aware of your responsibility to obey. The correction you will receive now has an entirely different objective. It's to remind you of your status vis-à-vis myself. What is that status, Diana?"

"You're the doctor and I'm the patient," Diana says as if by rote.

"Correct. And who is in charge in a doctor-patient relationship?"

"Doctor is always in charge."

"Completely, in charge of everything?"

"Everything."

"And patient's role is—go on, girl, fill in the blank spaces?"

"Her role is to obey Doctor."

"Always."

"Always."

"No matter what Doctor prescribes."

"No matter what."

"And so if Doctor says, 'Kill the cat,' then patient must kill the cat, correct?"

Diana nods. "Patient must immediately kill the cat."

"Easy to forget sometimes, when the assigned task is disagreeable. Nobody wants to stab a helpless creature and make a bloody mess on the floor. We both understand that. But there are many disagreeable tasks to be performed in this life. Mama taught me that, and now I'm teaching you."

"Yes, thank you, Doctor."

"Good. Now we shall proceed with the correction."

Beverly grabs hold of Diana's hair, pulls her head back so her face is pointed up at the portrait. "Look up at Mama, straight into her eyes. Keep your eyes fastened to hers. Don't look down again until I tell you."

Beverly reaches to the little round marble-top table beside her chair and extracts a pair of stainless steel scissors. Feeling Diana tense between her knees, Beverly freezes with the shears as if posing for a photograph. She looks up at Mama, smiles, and nods, then, taking up a big handful of Diana's glossy black hair, abruptly snips it off.

Diana, finally comprehending the nature of her chastisement, moans while Beverly looks down at the hair lying inky black in her hand. It is beautiful luxuriant hair, thick and soft, the little lynx's protective fur. And it's going to come off now, all of it, every single strand, until Diana's head is as smooth as a billiard ball.

Snip! Snap! Snip! Snap! The hair falls fast beneath the scissors. Beverly can feel the sweat on Diana's neck as she holds the girl's head steady, can hear the sobs that rack the poor lynx's body, too. Every so often, out of kindness, she reaches around to Diana's face to wipe away the tears. But still, she cuts, relentlessly.

"Now, now, my dear," she comforts.

Tool, for all her distress, is behaving well. Even as she weeps copiously for her loss, her eyes remain riveted to Mama's. Good little tool, brave little tool, but the hardest part is yet to come. Diana's head, now topped by a mop of ragged black, still must be clipped and shaved.

Beverly, finished with the scissors, takes up a small electric clippers, turns them on, applies the clipper head to Diana's skull. Buzz, buzz, buzz, she mows the hair straight off the top the way she's seen it done in films about marine recruits, slowly, inexorably shaming the girl caught tight between her knees.

More tears now, great rivers of them, as Beverly takes up a shaving brush, dips it into a bowl of warm water, stirs it around in a cup of soap, then applies the rich lather to Diana's head. Swish, swish, swish, she shaves the head clean with a razor. And all the while she whispers: "Now, now, little darling. Now, now. . . ."

Diana's hair is everywhere, on the floor, on Beverly's skirt, sticking to the girl's bare moist torso, front and back. Her pale shoulders and breasts are decorated with little flecks of black, and her skull gleams white like alabaster.

Beverly cradles the girl's head in her arms, tenderly petting the back of her neck. After granting permission for Diana to lower her eyes from Mama's, Beverly urges her to turn and sob upon her lap.

"There, there," Beverly says, gently caressing the well-shaved skull. "There, there, my little precious. It was difficult, I know, but it wasn't as bad as that. And I have a lovely black wig all ready for you, to cover you up when you go out."

Diana stares up at Beverly, her eyes large, beseeching. "You're not going to let me—?"

"No, my dear. Every few days we'll be shaving you clean again. I'm afraid you won't be allowed to grow another full head of hair until you've completed all your missions."

"Oh, Doctor!" The girl's red, teary eyes are filled with pathos. Beverly, slightly touched, knows she must not relent.

"Think of yourself as a Ninja warrior. They shave their skulls to symbolize their commitment."

"I so love my hair long."

Yes, long like a witch's. "And so do I," Beverly assures the girl. "Which is why we shall be saving all the trims. I have a lovely rosewood box to keep them in. Some evenings we'll get them out, feel them, and remind ourselves of the glorious mane you had and will someday have again."

"Yes, thank you, Doctor," Diana says gratefully, hugging Beverly around her waist.

Beverly hesitates. There is more correction to be administered, and she wants to assure herself now that the little lynx can take it. It won't do to push the girl too far; the purpose is to humble her, not to wound or break her spirit. There is also something about this additional correction that causes Beverly to pause. She wonders whether she'll be able to inflict it without trembling a little bit herself. Shaving Diana's head was one thing, but the other more intimate area . . .

Beverly looks up to the portrait, asks Mama what to do. The answer comes back immediately.

"Make the little bitch shave her own pubes," Mama says. "Have her lie on her back on the bathroom floor, spread her legs before the mirror and scrape herself. Stand behind her, watch her as she does it, and smile as you do. The correction will be more forceful and the submission more complete if she's required to do it under supervision."

"Thank you, Mama. You're so clever about these things."

Beverly Archer leans down and whispers into Diana's ear: "Come with me, dear, into the bathroom. There's still a little more hair to be removed. . . ."

Bertha Parce, Cynthia Morse, Jimmy and Stu Mac-Donald, Bobby Wexler, Laura Gabelli—I got six of them, Mama, six so far. Cindy was best, I think. Tool did a first-class job on her. Not only glued her up tight but her daughters, too, who (their bad luck!) stayed over with her in Seattle for Memorial Day. Tool also glued Cindy's hands together so I could imagine her begging me for mercy and, while she was at it, webbed her feet as well.

Remember Cindy, Mama? Remember what she did? I could never ever forgive her for it. My best friend, the one I trusted more than anyone else, whose declarations of sisterhood I naïvely believed. The roommate to whom I confided my secret yearnings, passions, fears. And then, after all of that, to have her turn on me so cruelly.

You probably guessed it. We were lovers. I'll never forget those wintry nights at Bennington when we pleasured each other, then slept together warm in each other's arms. I'm not ashamed of having loved her, Mama. There should never be shame where love's involved. And I *did* love her; that is why her betrayal was so calamitous, why it did a hell of a lot more than just sting me to the quick.

God! Remember what a wreck I was when I came down from Bennington, told you I wasn't going back, that nothing would ever ever make me return? And the way I cried, days of weeping it seems like now, and you were worried because I wouldn't eat and barely got out of bed.

"Bev's having a little breakdown," I overheard you tell Lisa Walters. But it was a major breakdown I was having, Mama, and it was that lousy traitor bitch who brought it on. What she did was unforgivable. And I never did forgive her for it. No, I never did.

What I still can't understand is *why* she turned. I never did anything to her except love her. So . . . maybe that was it. She couldn't take my love. It was too powerful, too consuming. Fearing it, she betrayed my trust.

A year after it happened I wrote her a letter. "Please," I begged, "all I want to know is why. Please just tell me why?" She didn't answer. I should have known. So there I was, humiliated again. And then I vowed that one day she'd beg something from me, beg me not to glue her.

She was an ice goddess, was Miss Cynthia Morse, with her thick blond hair parted to the side, so she could throw it back whenever it fell into her eyes, fling her head and throw it back like the fine Thoroughbred mare she knew she was. Her skin tanned more beautifully under the sun than any human's skin should be allowed to, her eyes were clear and gray, and she had a wonderful smile that made her whole face light up like a sunrise. I don't think I'll ever forget the touch of her, the satiny feel of her flesh, the fresh salty flavor of it, and the smell. Her small but perfect breasts cupped in my hands, the feel of her ribs through the skin of her flanks. She was a knockout beauty and I was plain, she was popular and I was disliked, she was gregarious and I was a loner, but still, she chose me to be her friend.

I was proud of that. I believed I was envied for it. Anyone in the whole college would have been happy to be Cindy's roommate, but she had chosen me. "You'll keep me honest, Bev," she told me one afternoon, spring of freshman year, when we took a long walk together across the meadows and she broached her proposal that we room together in the fall. "I can talk to you. You're always there to listen. Know what I think you should be? A shrink. Ever think of it, Bev? I know you'd be good at it. You're so giving, you know. Such a good listener. And you have such good intuitions about people, too."

Oh, I was giving all right! I gave her everything I had. Friendship, affection, love, later my passion. That was my undoing.

"This it, Cin?"

"Oh, yes, Bev. Down there, yes. There. That's the place. *Yes! Right there! Oh!* Do me, Bev. Please do me there again. Oh, yes, yes, your mouth feels *so good. . . .*"

And I did. I reveled in it. Before I knew what she was

up to, I would actually beg to be allowed to taste her. That's how stars-in-my-eyes stricken I was. Well, ha!, she's the one begging now!

There were nights, I remember, January and February nights, when we'd put a Mozart horn concerto on the stereo, then lie together in her bed in the dark of our room, watching the snow falling gently outside.

"This is great, isn't it, Bev?" she said, hugging me. "This is the way it should be. Just the two of us together like this, together and forever. I truly wish our lives could go on like this forever. Don't you, Bev? Don't you?"

One night I asked her if she thought a day would come when we'd each have a man in our lives.

"Men! Oh, Bev, sometimes you're just so screwy. I haven't seen any *men* around here. Have you? All I've seen are boys, and I don't mean just the kids, I mean the whole damn male faculty, too. Men! Ha! Who needs 'em? I sure don't. On a night like this, what could a man do for me that you can't do?" Cindy paused, stretched. "Hey, wanna go down under the covers? Feel like it, huh? It's so nice when you're down there taking care of me. Helps me to sleep, you know. Hey! What're you doing? Oooo! I *like* that. You never did *that* before. Where'd you learn *that*? You've got great moves, kid. No boy I ever went out with knew how to do *that*. Oh! Yeah! Yes!"

For two months I loved her, passionately, feverishly. She didn't reciprocate, just had me do special things to her, things she let me know she liked by the way she wiggled and moaned and swooned. And I was glad to do them, although I believe now some part of me must have known I was being used. But even if I'd realized it at the time, I wouldn't have cared. The bliss, you see, was all mine. Her needs became my obsession; her secret chambers became my pleasure domes. All day long in my various classes I'd think about servicing her at night. I was totally enraptured by her, enthralled, enslaved, possessed. Cynthia Morse, blond Thoroughbred mare— she became my world.

Looking back now, I can see it all coming and wonder at my blindness to what was going on. She needed me that winter, but as soon as spring came, she was ready to cast me aside.

That in itself could be understood. In this life, as you so often remind me, Mama, people use one another all the time. "It's all this use," you say, "that makes the world go around." But use is one thing, betrayal another. Cindy betrayed my love for her, betrayed it in a vulgar way. Use can be forgiven but not betrayal. You taught me, Mama: *Betrayal must be avenged.*

I had gone down to Cambridge for the weekend to do some research at Widener Library. My intention was to spend the night in Millie's Harvard dorm room, work the following day, then return to Bennington on Sunday night. But when I got to Millie's, I found I wasn't welcome. She and her roommates had male guests; there'd clearly be no room for me unless I slept on the floor. In any event there'd be no privacy.

I was furious. I'd told Millie I was coming, and she'd promised she'd save me space. We got into a fight, which led to my walking out in a snit. Steaming with anger, I decided to hell with research, I'd return immediately to Vermont.

Back in Bennington, tired and depressed, I taxied to my dorm from the bus stop. Our room was empty. Cindy wasn't there. Feeling needy for her friendship, I decided to search her out.

I found her finally, or rather should say I heard her, for it was her unique effervescent laughter that told me where she was. In a room on the floor below, belonging to Gretchen Hawes and Karen Tate, well-known campus lesbians, close buddies of Cindy's but not, I'm afraid, of mine.

I don't know what made me hesitate before I knocked. Perhaps I was curious about what was inspiring so much giggling inside, afraid, too, that my depressed mood might bring the others down. I certainly didn't want to intrude and put a damper on their fun. So I stood outside the door and listened. And then I understood: They were talking about me.

"She's too much, Cin. *Too much,*" said Gretchen.

"Well, I think she's very sweet," I heard Cindy reply.

"You *would*. Seeing as how you've been on the receiving end." Laughter.

"Sick, sick, sick," said Karen. They all broke up.

"Play us some more. Come on, Cin. More!"

Much giggling again, and then I couldn't believe what I heard. My own voice, on tape, begging Cindy to let me love her: "Please, Cin. I know just what you need. Please—let me do it. I can make you smile, you know I can. *Please.*"

The blood rose, boiling, to my face. I felt as if the top of my head were about to explode. My voice! Begging to be allowed to pleasure her! And she recorded it! And was playing it now for *them*!

"Hey, I've got an idea, Cin." Gretchen tittered. "Bring the little mouse down here one night. Share some of that 'please, please, please' with us, okay?"

"I've got some special places she can do." Karen snickered. "So long as she *begs* for it." And then: "Sick, sick, sick!"

I wanted to scream. Don't know why I didn't. I wanted to curl up, die right there on the floor. But instead I took hold of the doorknob and shoved the door open. The three of them were sprawled out on their stomachs on top of Karen's bed, the little tape player in the center.

Six eyes met mine, laughing, defiant eyes. And then, when they realized I'd been listening, those six eyes turned mean.

"Snooping, Bev?" Gretchen sneered.

But I ignored her. I stared straight at Cindy. "You recorded me?"

She shrugged, then smiled sheepishly. "Yeah, well, I guess I did."

"How does it feel to be a rat?" I spat the words, then reached to the tape recorder and ripped out the cassette.

"Hey, watch it!" said Karen. "You can screw up the machine. We were just having a little fun. God!"

But I kept my eyes on Cindy and let her have it. "Is this your idea of fun?"

"Get off your high horse, honeybunch," said Gretchen Hawes. "Eavesdropping at the door is like reading other people's mail. Do that, and you deserve what you get."

I met their eyes with as much contempt as I could summon, then, bursting into tears, ran back to our room and flung myself onto my bed. "How could she? How could she? How could she?" I screamed into the pillow. I wept and wept and wept.

Cindy turned up an hour later. She'd been drinking. I could smell the booze on her the minute she walked in. I pretended to be asleep. She was noisy as she undressed.

It was clear she wanted to disturb me. Finally she spoke: "Stop faking, Bev. I know you're wide awake."

"How *could* you do that to me?" I asked. "How *could* you?"

"You kind of let yourself in for it if you know what I mean," she said.

I sat up in bed. *"Let myself in for it?"*

"Sure. The way you've been slinking around all winter, trying to get into my pants all the time. I mean, now and then it's fun, but when I asked you to be my roommate, I didn't know I'd be taking the, you know, lezzy route."

"But it was *you!*"

"Uh-uh, Bev. Was you started it. I never put the make on you. I wouldn't want to." She snickered. "You don't turn me on."

I stared at her. This was my Best Friend! "I turned you on plenty as I remember," I whispered bitterly.

"Work your tongue around long enough you'll get a reaction. I'm just flesh and blood, you know."

"So you never cared for me? Is that what you're saying?"

"Frankly I like guys, but I try to understand other points of view. You know the saying 'Different strokes for different folks'? Right?"

I rushed at her then, attacked her with flailing arms and nails. I wanted to scratch out her eyes. Being bigger and stronger, she overpowered me easily. Finally, when I was exhausted, pinned to the floor, she looked down on me and smiled her unforgettable smile.

"Let's not make such a big deal out of this, huh? There're still a couple months till the end of the term.

Let's try and get along, Bev. I'm sorry about playing the tape for those guys. I really am.''

Sorry about playing the tape! What about recording it? What else besides playing it did she have in mind when she taped me when I was most vulnerable?

It all had been a setup, that much was clear; I'd loved her as best I could, but to her I'd been little more than a pest.

The next day I packed up my stuff. She came into the room just as I was finishing.

''Leaving, huh?''

''What did you expect?''

She shrugged. ''Well, it was nice while it lasted, Bev. It's too bad you had to sneak back early on the weekend.''

Sneak back! The girl was incredible.

''You hurt me, Cin. Hurt me a lot.''

''If I did, I'm sorry, I really am. I'm sure you'll get over it. When you do, I hope we can be friends.'' She shrugged again and left the room.

Twenty years ago, and I never did get over it, Mama. And I never loved anyone carnally again. I'd learned the risks the hard way and didn't like them. Cindy was the best lover I ever had.

That whole spring was miserable, that whole summer, too, not to mention the whole rest of my life. But as they say, you live and learn. And there was one good thing that came out of our relationship: Cindy steered me to my profession. On her advice I became a psychologist.

By the following autumn, tired of suffering, I decided to concentrate on my anger. And then I began to have fantasies, delicious fantasies of Cindy begging me not to hurt her the way she'd hurt me.

In response I shrugged and smiled and told her not to make such a big thing about it. I was going to kill her; that's all I was going to do. After all, she was only flesh and blood; isn't that what she'd said? And after she was dead, I was going to seal her up with glue. No big deal, right, Cin? Different strokes for different folks, right? Huh? *Right?*

I'm looking now at the trophy Tool brought back from Seattle. The yearbook of our Bennington class. Nice book, though I'm not in it. Nice picture of Cindy as she was then, tossing back her head to flick away the long blond hair that always used to fall across her face. Reminds me a little of someone I've seen recently, same eyes, hair, same warming, radiant smile.

Carl's bedazzled reaction when you broach taking the tool into your house: "Sometimes you surprise me, Bev."

"I don't know what's so surprising, Carl. Diana's my patient, she's my responsibility, and since I've got an unrented basement apartment available, and she's going to be coming to me four days a week for therapy anyway . . . well, it just seems natural to throw in a little housing, too."

"Sort of like a halfway house for her. That what you have in mind?"

"Now that you mention it—sure, why not?"

His little eyes dance a jig. "And you were so against her being released."

"Never against it, Carl. Hesitant about proposing it, that's all." You shrug. "I guess you could call me conservative when it comes to murderesses."

He strokes his beard, becoming grayer and more pointy by the month.

"What about a job?"

"There's a lot of possibilities right in the neighborhood—museums, institutes, archives. She's a trained librarian. She'll have no trouble finding a position."

"Small-town Connecticut girl—think she can hack it in the city?"

You put your hands on your hips. "I'm from Cleveland, Carl. I can hack it, so why not her?"

He fondles his beard again. "Want to know what I think? I think you're one superduper human being. How's that?"

You stare at him incredulously. "Well, thank you, Carl. I believe that's the first real compliment I've ever had from you. And we've worked together a lot of years."

"We have, Bev. And pardon me for not being one of those bosses effusive with the praise. But when I say something like that, I mean every word of it. I think you're an incredibly talented shrink and a terrific person, too."

Flattered and stunned, you shake your head. "I'm going to treasure what you're saying, Carl. It really means a lot."

When you first noticed the tall blond girl in Diana's martial arts class, you knew she reminded you of someone though you couldn't put your finger on exactly whom. It was only later, after you asked Diana to get to know the girl and cultivate a friendship, that it struck you whom she reminded you of. Cindy Morse, of course.

Then you couldn't wait to get your hands on her. But

you were patient. Patience, you might say, is your middle name. And Diana was clever about it, too, building the friendship slowly, exactly as you'd ordered.

You'll never forget the evening Diana reported that she and Jess Foy had gone out for coffee after class. As you'd instructed, Diana told Jess she worked part-time at the New York Society Library and confided, too, in a most casual way, that she was in intensive therapy with a female shrink. Jess, in turn, informed Diana that she was a student at Columbia, where she was also on the women's varsity fencing team. She herself had never gone to a therapist, she said, although there were times when she was sorely tempted, what with the pressures of college and all. The girls chatted about karate, gossiped about the sensei, and exchanged tales of their initial embarrassment at having to change clothes in the unisex dojo locker room. But then, giggling, each admitted to the other that she now deliberately took no special pains to conceal herself when undressing.

"Let the novice hard-ons drool, that's my motto," Jess told Diana.

Diana reported how much she liked her new friend and was pleased at your instruction to nurture the relationship and make it grow.

Beverly Archer and Diana Proctor both were aware that the stakes were high and that for each of them, in separate as well as connected ways, it would be a night of destiny. Depending on the outcome, Beverly would learn whether the course she had embarked upon obsessively so many years before would finally lead to the attainment of her goals. For Diana the night would prove whether her murderous passions, once raging and incoherent, now disciplined and honed, could be applied to the completion of Beverly's design.

As the day ended, the strain between the women, always apparent on account of the extreme polarity of their roles, seemed to increase with the inexorable withering of the light. Beverly was more snappish than usual; Diana, quieter and more withdrawn. As night settled in, there was a palpable tension in the second-floor bedroom, where they waited, silent, before the large portrait of Beverly's mother in the niche.

Beverly had turned on the red lamps so that the chamber was curiously illuminated, suffused with crimson light redolent of blood. She wore the same scarlet dress as was depicted in the portrait, a dress that had once belonged to her mother and that she'd had altered to fit her shorter, plumper frame. But there was something anomalous about her in that particular costume, designed to be worn by a featured singer in a nightclub. And since Beverly had refused to have it dry-cleaned, it still reeked faintly of tobacco, alcohol, and sweat, the signature aroma of her mother's professional milieu.

Diana Proctor, dressed in the costume of a night killer, full-length black bodysuit, black sneakers, tight-fitting close-cropped black wig, black latex gloves, had two ice picks fitted into leather holsters strapped to the insides of her forearms. In a small waist sack, suspended from her belt, rested a caulking gun loaded up with glue and, wrapped carefully in tissue paper, a withered field daisy collected that morning from Central Park.

An hour later Diana, in a loose denim jacket that concealed the ice picks, sat alone at the end of a subway car on a sparsely filled downtown express. The train hurtled through the tunnels, swaying and moaning, wheels grinding against the tracks. To a neutral observer Diana might have appeared drugged and in a daze. In fact, she was visualizing, a process taught to her by her therapist in preparation for the important act she was on her way to perform.

She got off her train at Union Square, took the exit stairs that led directly to the park above. Once outside she sniffed the night air, clean and cool, then made her way east along Fourteenth. It was a quiet weekday evening; traffic was sparse, and there were few pedestrians. As Diana approached Second Avenue, she began to look around. She was searching for a quarry, not a stray cat or dog, not even a jogger to prick in the butt with a pin. Tonight she was stalking something bigger. She was looking for a human she could kill.

Unbeknownst to Diana, Beverly Archer was close by. While Diana had waited uptown for her express, Beverly had left her house, hailed a cab, then ordered the driver to speed south to East Fourteenth and Second. Now she stood in a phone booth, phone in hand as if making a call, waiting for Diana to appear. She saw the girl, springy and taut, ready to strike, moving rapidly toward her. Though tense herself, Beverly was filled with pride. The girl approaching was a weapon she had forged, a tool trained to kill on command. On *her* command.

Diana, unaware of Beverly, continued east on Fourteenth. On First Avenue she turned south, and then after two blocks, east again on Twelfth.

After ten minutes of walking she entered the so-called Alphabet City section of Manhattan, where the avenues are lettered A, B, C, and D. This was a neighborhood of broken-down tenements and vacant buildings turned into crack houses. Here, behind the garbage cans in the alleys, one could find occasional homeless persons sleeping curled in messes of tattered blankets.

After exploring this area for a quarter of an hour, Diana located three possible quarries. Her first choice was an old man, sleeping and wheezing noisily, his body curled just inside the back doorway of an abandoned store. He had covered himself with a long piece of cardboard. His cheeks bore a grayish stubble, and locks of iron gray hair surrounded his ears.

Diana stood poised, staring down at him, thinking out how best to proceed. She had rehearsed the procedure numerous times, both with Doctor and alone, and it was certainly not as if she had never attacked live people before. But still, she hesitated. This man meant nothing to her. He had never abused her. He had no meaning in her life.

"It will be a cold kill," Doctor had explained, "the most difficult kind to bring off. Yet because it will be cold, it will be an excellent test. If you have trouble with the coldness, you can always warm it up. Just imagine your target is a person who has shamed you, hurt you in a way no apology can repair. Put a little bit of your mother into him if you like, your grandmother and sister, too. Remember, Diana, you're well practiced with the picks. It's not the killing but the gluing that's going to draw upon your strength."

Diana stared down at the sleeping man, wheezing and sputtering in the night. But it wasn't thoughts of members of her own family that fired her up to strike. It was the elegantly coiffed redheaded singer in the scarlet dress on Doctor's wall who thought up all the awful punishments. Yes, it was *Mama* lying there beneath the cardboard. *Mama* who deserved to die!

In a series of moves as quick and balletic as the ones she'd used on numerous dummies, Diana Proctor attacked the old man's throat. A moment later the belabored wheezing stopped.

Off now with the cardboard cover. A series of quick flicks with the utility knife and the encrusted trousers were cut loose. The fly zipper was already open. Diana pulled off the shoes, wrapped in filthy towels, then placed a heel in her victim's crotch and hauled the torn-up trousers down.

Doctor had been most specific about the way she wanted her enemies desexed. Female organs were to be filled and pinched shut, male organs glued back between the legs. Using her black-sneakered foot to pull down the stained underdrawers, Diana exposed her quarry's blue and flaccid genitals to the air. Then she pulled out her caulking gun and set to work. When she was finished, she unwrapped the withered field daisy and lovingly placed it in the doorway beside the building wall.

Beverly waited for Diana in an all-night bookstore on Third Avenue near Twelfth. Browsing titles on a table of Specials & Bargains, she glanced up every so often at the large plate glass window facing the street. Diana had to pass by here after she had completed her mission; it was on her prescribed route home.

A few minutes past midnight Beverly caught sight of the lynx, elegant in her black garb, approaching from down the avenue. Beverly hurried out of the shop to intercept her. Was that a killer's glow she saw on the little murderess's face?

For Diana this meeting was unexpected. Surprised, perhaps even frightened, she asked Doctor if she had done something wrong. Beverly, instead of answering, placed both hands on Diana's arms, then ran them along the girl's sleeves. Feeling only one pick beneath Diana's jacket, she expressed her pleasure with a grin.

"Problems?" she asked. Diana shook her head. "Bring a trophy back for Mama?"

Diana nodded, reached into her pocket, handed Beverly a carefully folded piece of paper, an advertising flyer for a fortune-teller resident in the neighborhood.

"He wasn't carrying much," she explained.

Beverly, pleased with the flyer, understood. "It's not the monetary value of the trophy that's important to Mama, dear. It's the way it speaks of the victim's mentality."

Alone in a taxi, on her way uptown, Beverly trembled with exhilaration. Tool worked; it could settle old accounts. Soon there would be fulfillment of a long-held cunning dream.

Diana, riding home in a deserted subway car, felt the same dizzy exhaustion she had felt years before when she killed the female members of her family. *It's hard and exacting work, but it has its pleasures,* she reminded herself, as the train swayed side to side, hurtling through the tunnels.

An hour later, having bathed and changed, Diana presented herself at Beverly's bedroom door, ready to report every detail of her outing. Beverly sat in her usual chair, the portrait of her mother looming above. She beckoned the girl into the room. Diana stood at stiff attention, and the debriefing ceremony began.

At one point in the recitation, when Beverly inquired whether Tool found it necessary to conjure up an actual character in her life in order to bring herself to kill the homeless man, Diana raised her eyes for a moment to the face on the painting. Smiling knowingly to herself, she answered respectfully: "I took your advice, Doctor. I thought of Mother."

You were very pleased with Tool for the way she recruited Jessica. And Jessica herself made a particularly lovely patient. If only you could harness *her* energy, you wished, as she droned on about seeing her father die in an exploding car. If only you could send *her* on missions, you yearned, as she explained how for years she couldn't bear to look out a window when someone was about to drive away.

There was a special quality she had, one unfortunately that Tool lacked. It was the quality of seeming untamed, perhaps even being untamable. You knew you'd have to use drugs if you were ever to train her to do your bidding. The very notion of channeling her aggression, disciplining it so it could serve your purpose, definitely excited you. You had some delicious daydreams about that during several of her sessions, in which you imagined her being broken by degrees. Undoubtedly she stimulated such fantasies because she was so strong and competitive. Whenever you saw her, you got the kind of charge you imagine a horse trainer gets when confronted with a powerful Thoroughbred filly. Yes, it would be a real pleasure to make a champion out of this one, to teach her to kill for you on command. And it was her very inaccessibility on that level, the fact that you knew you could never make her into a tool, that fueled your "what if?" fantasies and made seeing her in sessions such a pleasure.

Two women, Beverly Archer and Diana Proctor, stand toe to toe inches apart. Both are short, just a little more than five feet tall, but while Beverly is middle-aged and pudgy, Diana is young, lean, superbly conditioned, and extremely strong. Beverly's arms are flabby; Diana's are roped with muscle.

Yet it is the weaker older woman who dominates the stronger, younger one. By the force of her intellect and the power of her dream she had made Diana her slave. And behind Beverly there stands always the life-size portrait of Victoria Archer, pushing, goading her daughter to forge Diana into the tool of her vengeance.

The room where they stand is an oversize bedchamber situated on the second floor of Beverly Archer's Manhattan house. The painting of Victoria Archer takes up a large niche opposite the bed. It is illuminated with a reddish glow similar to one cast by the spotlight at the notorious Fairmount Club Lounge in Cleveland, Ohio, scene of Victoria Archer's greatest triumphs as a singer. During her nightclub singing career, red was Victoria's trademark color; she had naturally red hair, always wore a crimson dress, her entrances were keyed with a red spot, and pink light played upon her face while she sang. But her daughter's trademark color is different. She is just now in the process of explaining the difference to Diana.

"You are my knight," she tells the girl, "and as such, you must wear your lady's colors."

"What are your colors?" Diana asks humbly.

Beverly glances up at the image of her mother, then back to Diana. "Black, all black, black on black," she responds.

Diana Proctor, wearing outdoor clothing purchased out of a catalog from L. L. Bean and a nondescript light brown wig, proceeds as instructed to Grand Central Station in New York City, boards a noon train, then sits quietly with her backpack at her feet until, an hour and forty minutes later, the train pulls into New Haven, Connecticut.

At a storefront near the railroad station, she rents a standard-size Chevrolet for a two-day period, telling the friendly clerk she intends to drive into Vermont to view the magnificent autumn foliage that has been well reported in the newspapers and on TV. She will most likely spend the night in a motel up there, she says, and then, getting an early start, return the car late the following morning in time to catch her 1:00 P.M. train back to Providence, where she is a graduate student at the Rhode Island School of Design.

It's a cool Sunday afternoon in mid-October. As Diana drives her rented car into the Connecticut countryside, the sun glitters, and the sky, an intense shade of blue, makes a brilliant backdrop for the foliage now nearly at its peak. The passing woodlands, clusters of maple, oak, and ash, are russet and gold. Fallen leaves, in a multitude of hues, coat the lawns of homes, and trees, arching overhead, cause the sunlight to dapple the worn macadam roads.

Diana's route, as traced by Beverly Archer on an Automobile Club map, takes her through the picturesque towns of Woodbury, Roxbury, and Washington Depot. She refills her gas tank at a Shell station in New Preston, then continues west, along the edge of Lake Waramaug, finally arriving at the town of Kent, Connecticut, a little past 4:00 P.M.

Here she parks in a shopping center lot, takes a stroll, stops at a coffee shop, where she devours an egg salad sandwich and a large glass of Coke. After eating, she returns to her vehicle, hitches on her backpack, then proceeds to hike her way out of town. Shortly after crossing the Route 341 bridge, she passes the campus of the Kent School, an exclusive preparatory boarding school bordering the Housatonic River. Within an hour she arrives on foot at the main entrance to Macedonia Brook State Park.

It is 6:00 P.M. when Diana enters the park, relieves herself at one of the portable toilets set up near the entrance, then quickly follows a trail heading north directly into the woods. Since the sign at the entrance instructs hikers that the park closes officially at sunset, Diana wishes to disappear into its wilderness as quickly as possible.

Twenty minutes of rapid walking bring her to a small stone bridge that spans Macedonia Brook. But instead of crossing it, she consults her compass, turns off the trail, and begins to follow the water on a vector south through uncleared brush. Once she is certain she is alone, invisible to other hikers who might still be lingering on the trails behind, she unloads her backpack, takes a long sip of water from her canteen, then proceeds to strip off her brightly colored hiking gear and wig and change into her all-black executioner's garments. When she is fully dressed for the work she has come to perform, she hoists her pack up again, then follows the roaring brook back to the southern edge of the park.

Here, abutting the wilderness, sits a nicely renovated white clapboard farmhouse. Only a hedge of bushes, a wire deer fence, and an old stone wall separate this residential weekend retreat from the parkland. In a place she carefully selected at the height of summer two months before, Diana takes off her pack, then sits upon it. She will wait at least four hours before moving closer to her prey.

As darkness falls, the lights in the house come on, first in the kitchen, then on the front porch, then in the living and dining rooms. From time to time the forms of two men can be seen passing by uncovered windows or silhouetted against the translucent curtains that protect the rooms on the upper floor.

As evening wears on, cooking smells, including the aroma of roasted lamb, reach Diana from the house. Sounds reach her, too: conversation; laughter; recorded music; television news. She waits patiently until the smells and sounds subside, until the downstairs and finally the bedroom lights go off. Then she stands, stretches, and carefully straps two holstered ice picks to her forearms, and her usual glue and wallflower pack around her waist.

The moon, showing a three-quarters face, illuminates the woods. Diana climbs over the ruined stone wall that separates the park from the property belonging to the house. Using a pliers, she separates a portion of the deer fence from a tree, slips in, makes her way through the hedge, then emerges finally onto cleared land.

Crossing the lawn, she resembles an apparition, her black clothing blending with the shadows cast by the trees, her shaven head, reflecting moonlight, shining amidst the darkness all around. In the forest behind an owl hoots. The only other sound is of rushing water, a tributary of Macedonia Brook that crosses the property to cascade over a small waterfall on the far side of the house.

Diana has no difficulty entering the premises. On her

reconnaissance visit over the summer she discovered a ground-floor lavatory window with a broken lock. Lynx-like she pulls herself through this opening, then drops silently to the tile floor inside. The owners, brothers, own no pets. This night, she is grateful, she will not have to kill any dogs.

A muttony aroma, which she smelled earlier outside, still permeates the interior. Passing through the kitchen, she notices an empty wine bottle on the counter. She presses her hand against the front of the dishwasher, feeling a familiar warmth. Then, pausing at the kitchen window, she stares out across the lawn. She can see the hedge she passed through on her way in, but the woods behind are lost in darkness.

The first step of the old stairs creaks when she places her foot upon it. It will not be possible, she understands, to ascend and make her kills silently one at a time. She hesitates. Unfortunately there is always an unexpected complication. This time it's the bedrooms. The house is old, eccentrically built and renovated, and thus difficult for her to map out in her mind. She tries to visualize where the bedrooms will be in relation to the top of the stairs. On the basis of observations made earlier from the woods outside, she comes up with a reasonable guess.

Still standing on the first step, she works out a strategy. She will rush up, execute the brother in the bedroom on the left, then wait for the other brother to come into the first one's room to see what the commotion is about. Doctor will want to know about this, and myriad details more: what it felt like to rush up the stairs; how many steps it took to reach the bedroom from the landing; the position of the first brother in his bed; a description of his nightclothes; whether his window was open; the smell of him; the sounds he makes (if any) as he dies; how he looks when he's stripped for gluing; the exact size and shape of his genitals; the feel and weight of them in her gloved hands.

Diana, coiling to attack, prepares herself to take mental photographs of all that will transpire. She has proposed to Doctor several times that she bring along a camera to document details. But Doctor wants no part of mechanical documentation. "*You* are my camera," Doctor has said. "It's your point of view, the killer's view, that interests me. Not that of a neutral machine."

The sound of a cough from the second floor. Diana freezes on the first step. Perhaps one or both of the brothers are still awake. But no difference—she has killed awake people before.

Suddenly she leaps, taking the stairs two at a time, bounds off them onto the springy pine floor of the landing, twirls martial arts–style, then barges through the half-open doorway to her left. A blubbery middle-aged man, lying naked in his bed, is in the process of raising himself up as she bursts in.

"Who the hell—?"

She notes the explosion of fear in his eyes as she punches at him with her fist, violently knocking back his head with the blow. Before he can recover, she thrusts her first ice pick up through the exposed portion of his throat, then shoves it with all her force deep into the soft tissue of his brain.

She hears a sound, turns, sees the second brother standing in the doorway. Their eyes meet for a moment, and then he flees. She is at his heels as he rushes into the bathroom, then desperately attempts to shut her out. She aims her foot at one of the door panels, kicks full force, splintering the wood. The man, middle-aged, paunchy, balding, backs up against the toilet. He stares at her and at her ice pick, terrified. She stops all motion, meets his gaze.

"You must be Stu MacDonald," she said softly.

The man shakes his head. "I'm Jimmy. That was Stu in the other room."

Diana shrugs. "Doesn't matter. He's gotten his. Your turn now."

"What do you want? What are you going to do?" Jimmy MacDonald whimpers hoarsely. "Please, miss, there's money in the house. Art objects. A valuable coin collection. I'll give you all of it if you'll go away, spare—"

Diana shakes her head. "No mercy tonight," she intones.

Jimmy nods. "Yes, I see that. No mercy. . . ." He tries to speak calmly in the hope that by so doing, he will gain himself several extra seconds of life. "Could you at least tell me why, miss? Why you want to hurt us?"

"Doctor."

"Doctor? Who's the doctor?" Jimmy becomes angry. He screws up his eyes. "What the hell kind of doctor are you talking about?"

"Dr. Beverly Archer."

At first Jimmy's eyes cloud with confusion. Then a small flicker of remembrance ignites somewhere deep within.

"Bev Archer? But that was so long ago. Must be twenty-five years. Surely she doesn't still think . . . because it wasn't us, you know. It was set up. She ought to talk to her—" Jimmy shakes his head. "Bev can't still be angry over that."

Oh, she's angry!

Diana feigns an attack with her second pick, then waits for Jimmy to raise his hands in a posture of defense. When he does, she punches at him through the opening, hitting him hard in the center of his stomach. As he chokes and doubles over, she stabs him through the window of his right eye, then thrusts her pick deep into the mushy substance within his skull.

The killing done, Diana calmly switches on lights in order to examine her handiwork. Jimmy lies on his side, ruby red blood pulsing from his eye socket across the white tiles and into the grout lines of the bathroom floor. In the bedroom Stu MacDonald lies sprawled out on his back, half on, half off his bed. Diana takes mental pictures of their positions, for she knows the kinds of questions Doctor will ask.

Both killings together have taken her a total of ninety-seven seconds. Not bad, she thinks, for such a complicated house. Moreover, she has engaged for the first time in actual dialogue with a quarry, a unique experience she is eager to share. Even as she prepares the brothers for gluing, she imagines the keen expression that will transfix Doctor's face when she describes the confusion slowly giving way to recognition in Jimmy MacDonald's frightened eyes.

An hour later, having glued up both brothers and collected two new trophies of her hunt, Diana drives one of their vehicles, a gray Jeep Wagoneer, back into the town of Kent. When she emerges from the Jeep, she is wearing the same nondescript light brown wig and L. L. Bean hiking clothes she wore earlier in the day. She transfers her backpack into her rental car parked in the shopping center lot, then, careful to observe all traffic regulations, drives back across the Route 341 bridge, continuing this time into New York State and on to a preselected spot far off the main road where she can park safely, curl up, and get some sleep.

The next morning, on her way back to New Haven, Diana decides to make a brief side trip. She does so in full knowledge that should she confess this unauthorized detour to Doctor, she will be severely punished.

Nonetheless, passing so close to Derby, Connecticut, she feels the need to look again at Carlisle Hospital. The place means much to her. Having been incarcerated there on account of the ax murders of her mother, grandmother, and sister, she spent five relatively happy years in intensive therapy before a judge signed an order for her release.

Departing from her designated route, she follows the side road that leads to the institution, then stops her car a hundred feet from the main gate, turns off the ignition, and stares in through the sturdy wire fencing that surrounds the grounds.

Far in the distance, between the red-brick main treatment building and the gray cinder-block residence known as A, she makes out a small group of young men and women playing touch football in a field. They are much too far away to recognize, a good thing, too, since she knows well the awkwardness of meetings between former patients and patients still confined.

As she watches, a man exits the door of the main treatment building and walks to a second building, which houses the manual therapy shop. Diana recognizes this person on account of his stride. He is chief psychiatrist Dr. Carl Drucker, a gentle man with merry eyes and a funny, pointed beard who, in her last months at Carlisle, assured her she was cured.

Now something bittersweet wells up within Diana as she remembers Dr. Drucker's kindness and watches the young people in the distance at their play. She thinks nostalgically of the years she spent in this institution, happy, lighthearted years. And although she acknowledges the enormous debt of gratitude she owes to Doctor for her release, there is a side of her that wishes she were still locked up inside.

Tears well in her eyes as she recalls her life here, how she was permitted to wear her hair long, to roam freely about the grounds, to meet, talk, perform, and make friends without having always to ask permission in advance. Now in the city every moment of her life existence is regulated, bounded by Doctor's demands to perform missions and bring back trophies of her kills. *Am I free now?* she asks herself. She doesn't know the answer. But peering through the locked gates of Carlisle, she fondly remembers carefree days within.

There is but an hour of light left after a warm October day, an Indian summer day in Manhattan. Two young women, one short and dark, the other tall and blond, stand on a bluff in Riverside Park overlooking the Hudson River. Although both wear workout clothes, tank tops and running shorts, the taller woman's garments are brightly colored, while the shorter one's are totally black.

The short dark-haired girl is holding a bow. She has notched an arrow in its string and is demonstrating the pull to her taller friend. Very slowly she pulls the arrow back. At full extension she holds it poised for flight. She stands this way for what seems an eternity, both hands steady, the bow not moving, and then, very slowly, she raises the bow upward in an arc so that the arrow is pointed directly at the sun. Again she holds her position. Then, suddenly, she lets the arrow fly. For a moment it shows black against the dark orange solar disk. Then it disappears from sight.

The taller woman nods. She is impressed. The shorter one offers her the bow and aluminum quiver filled with arrows. The tall girl, accepting, promises to practice diligently. The short one assures her taller friend that she need not return the equipment until she has mastered the technique.

Remember the MacDonald brothers, Mama, Jimmy and Stu, those tall, strapping, handsome all-around fellas at Caxton Academy when I was at Ashley-Burnett? So many of the girls had crushes on them. In those days they were the type you were supposed to swoon over and adore. Stu played football, Jimmy basketball, and they both were great dancers. Broad shoulders and even broader smiles. Hunks of what the girls called U.S. Prime Grade A Beef.

There was something marvelously shallow about them, too. Oddly, that may have been their most attractive feature. They weren't tormented intellectuals or overly mature and thus awkward among their peers. They weren't emotionally skewered by a bizarre home life, or artistically gifted, or unpredictable in any way. The MacDonald boys acted their age. They were interested in sports and cars and girls and not terribly much else. Easygoing, fun-loving playboy types, who, like all red-blooded guys back then, were always looking to get laid. But if a girl turned them down, they didn't get too upset about it. Men and women, boys and girls—to them relations between the sexes was a game of flirt, conquest, and submit. Sometimes you won, other times you didn't; but win or lose, you knew there'd always be another round. What I'm getting at, Mama, is that with the MacDonalds what you saw was what you got: two normal white bread all-American boys, the kind who, when they grew up, would run businesses or sell stocks and help keep our nation strong.

Except what I saw was *not* what I finally got. Because there was a dark side to the MacDonalds, a side they hid so you wouldn't see it, except maybe sometimes when they were drinking or smoking grass, and then there was a little bit of blackness showing, enough so that if you were an astute observer, you'd catch a glimpse of the smallness, the meanness, the part that would always take advantage, the cheap crooks crouching behind the cardboard pasteups we used to call (ha!) gentlemen.

Remember, Mama: I was fifteen years old. There was a dance that winter over Christmas. I didn't want to go, but you said I must because the parents of the kids giving it had put my name on the list as a favor.

I hated dances, first, because I was such a maladroit dancer and, second, because I was so rarely asked onto the floor. I was too plain for the Cleveland boys. Something about me, withdrawn and worried, put them off. I wasn't sexy. I didn't have your looks or charm or poise. I was clumsy and mousy and too smart for my own good. I hadn't yet learned the craft of pretense . . . of which I am a master now.

And so I went. You gave me little choice. You bought me a dress, not particularly flattering or attractive, and you arranged a ride for me with someone else's father. Studying me while I waited, amused at my anguish, you asked why I was looking so damn tragic since it was just a dance. I really wasn't going to be burned at the stake, you said. I might even enjoy it if I tried a little bit. "Come on, Bev—let's see you smile," you said. "And try not to be a wallflower, okay?"

I remember riding downtown silent in a car filled with giggly, overexcited girls, off to some dark, stuffy club on Euclid Avenue, where there were rows of old oil paintings on dark wood-paneled walls and the air smelled of dead cigars. I followed the others up a grand staircase and into a ballroom, where an orchestra was playing the smarmy, sentimental standards of the day. There were kids buzzing around, parents smiling, a bar for soft drinks, and couples dancing on the floor.

Well, Mama, just as I'd foreseen, I stood by the wall with the dozen or so other wallflowers, unattractive girls, girls with acne on their faces, girls who were merely shy—stood with them, a stupid, turd-eating grin on my face, looking hopeful, eager, waiting, waiting for what I knew would never come.

On the other side of the room stood our counterparts, the stag line: unattractive, shy, acne-faced boys who didn't dance well and acted silly around females. We wallflowers eyed the stags and the stags eyed us and no one came over, and thus the evening wore tediously on.

But there was something afoot that night. The Mac-Donald brothers had cooked up a private little scheme, something no wallflower had ever experienced or even hoped for in her dreams. They'd decided between themselves that they would romance one of us clinging to the wall. And for some reason, I've never managed to fathom why, they settled upon me. Me, Mama! They chose me to be their Cinderella.

They began their courtship early in the evening. First

Jimmy and then Stu came over and asked me to dance. No one watching could believe it. Dreamboat Caxton boys, the kind a girl would kill for at Ashley-Burnett, offering themselves to mousy little Beverly Archer, twirling her off to dance in strong, authoritative arms.

They were good dancers, so agile and slick they made me feel like a princess at a ball. Around, around I danced with them, first Jimmy, then Stu, then Jimmy, then Stu again, around and around and around.

Those MacDonalds knew how to charm a girl, knew how to talk and to seduce. After they warmed me up, got me all sweaty and excited, they led me off to an ante-room, and there Stu produced a slim silver cigarette case filled with lovingly rolled, thickly packed joints. He lit one and took a deep drag, passed it on to Jimmy, who also inhaled and then passed the joint to me.

It was good stuff, as I recall. But I wasn't used to it, and very soon it had me flying higher than a kite. Then back to the ballroom for more whirling and twirling, each of them romancing me, working me over, and I got high on it, it was a dream come true, a dream I didn't even know I'd had: drab, little, brainy Bev Archer getting her first taste of what it felt like to be desired.

Oh, yes, Mama, those boys made no bones about their cravings. They lusted for me; they made that clear enough. They even whispered provocative little endearments as we danced.

Jimmy: "You're really special, Bev. I've had my eyes on you since September. I just couldn't get up the nerve to do anything about it till now. There's something of your mom in you, isn't there? Stu and I've been down to the Fairmount Club Lounge and heard her sing. One very sexy lady, your mom."

Stu: "We both knew as soon as we saw you. Jimmy nudged me. 'She's as sexy as her mom. Probably as talented, too.' Hey, it doesn't upset you to hear me use that word, does it, Bev? 'Cause it's true. I mean you *are* sexy . . . if you don't mind my saying so."

Mind? Of course, I didn't mind. I loved it, adored it, was intoxicated by the thought. Sexy was what *you* were, Mama, and it was the one thing I was certain I was not. I had never felt sexy, wasn't sure I'd even know the feeling if I did. But then, as it turned out, I *did* know. Because while they were talking to me, I began to feel aroused.

Thinking back on it now, I don't think it was those particular boys that got me going so much as the general situation I found myself in: being high; being told I was sexy; being attended to as if I *were* sexy; being competed for and treated so openly as an object of desire.

I had no doubt they both hungered for me. They made it manifest, pressing themselves against me as we danced, making sure I was aware of their rigidity, showing me the hard bodily proof of their lust. But I'm sure now it wasn't their stiff cocks that excited me. Male organs have never done much for me one way or the other. It was the aura of their excitement, the evidence of their craving. I certainly didn't feel I wanted to be screwed by them, but most assuredly I enjoyed the fact that they pined to screw me.

There was a part of me, too, that knew sooner or later one or the other of them was going to make his move. But I wasn't thinking about that very much; I was too excited by the here and now of it all. Still, I wasn't naïve. I was your daughter; I knew about sex; I'd met your lovers. And the girls my age at Ashley-Burnett gossiped about little else but boys, what they liked to do and how a girl could handle them if she kept her wits about her. So on a mental level I pretty much knew what to expect. But having no practical experience and no psychological training, I badly underestimated my predicament.

It was around midnight (the dance was scheduled to end at 1:00 A.M.) that they first broached the notion of driving me home.

"We've got a car," Jimmy said. "We can easily drop you off. Anyway, aren't you getting tired of this crappy dance? Let's leave now, stop off for a nightcap at this dive we know. The bartender's a good guy. He'll serve us without making us show ID. What do you say?" And when I hesitated: "Not scared to go to a bar, are you, Bev—you who used to hang around with your mom at the Fairmount Club Lounge?"

Actually I was thrilled with the idea of going to a bar in the company of two handsome tuxedo-clad boys. So I sought out the girl whose father had driven me downtown, told her I'd arranged another ride, and enjoyed the obvious envy in her eyes when she warned me to watch out, I could get a bad reputation hanging around with the MacDonalds.

A bad reputation! At that moment I couldn't think of anything I wanted more!

We never did stop off at any dive, of course, if such a place did actually exist, which I doubt. Once we were in the car (Stu at the wheel, me and Jimmy in the back) the slim silver cigarette case emerged again. Jimmy and I shared a joint and then started in on a second. Meanwhile, Stu drove us to a deserted overlook above the Cuyahoga River, parked, got out, came around to the back, and sat down on my other side.

There I was, Mama, boxed in between them. And then
the fun began. Stu deep kissed me. That was okay; I'd
been looking forward to a real kiss like that. But then
Jimmy kissed me that way, too, and that was kind of
strange. I mean, there I was sandwiched between two
brothers, both of whom were trying to make out with me
at once.

"Hey, please! One at a time," I said, or some such
nonsense. That only encouraged them. Next thing I knew
they both were simultaneously trying to undress me or at
least gain access to my top.

"Down, boys!" I said, in the haughty way an Ashley-
Burnett girl might address a pair of obstreperous guys.
And when that didn't stop them: "Enough! Jimmy, Stu!
Come on, let's all go home."

"Uh-uh, Bev," I remember Jimmy saying as he
leered. "Get into a car with a couple of horny brothers,
you gotta take the consequences. Right, Stu?"

There was a lot of giggling then, I remember, mild
attempts on my part to push them off, equally lighthearted attempts on theirs to unclasp my bra. We were in
a kind of three-way wrestling match, laughing, having
fun, and I confess I enjoyed the struggle, doubtless
because I figured it wouldn't continue very long. Stu and
Jimmy were decent, well-brought-up young men. Sooner
or later, when they realized I wasn't going to play, they'd
give it up, we'd stop off for the promised nightcap, and
then they'd take me home.

That, Mama, was conventional dating wisdom as it
was promulgated amongst the student body in the corridors and locker rooms of the Ashley-Burnett School for
Girls. But wise though it might have been, it began to
dawn on me some minutes into the struggle that in this

case it was not going to apply. Then I panicked. I was scared, Mama, real scared. I began to struggle, struggle hard, and then, as can happen in close quarters like the back of a car, somebody got hurt.

It was Stu. Struggling with them both, I managed to stick my elbow in his eye. He got mad. "Watch it, bitch." The he slapped me, not full force, of course, but hard enough to make me scream.

Jimmy cupped his hand hard over my mouth.

"Why'd you hit her, Stu?"

"Bitch poked me in the eye."

"We weren't s'posed to hit her."

"Who cares what we were s'posed to do. Let's do what we want. Yeah?"

At that Stu ripped down the entire front of my dress. And then the real combat began. Even through the haze of pot I knew I was in trouble and tried seriously to fight my way out of the car. Jimmy took hold of my arms and held them tight behind my back. Then Stu pulled off my bra and grabbed hold of my breasts. When I screamed, Jimmy cupped my mouth again. This time I bit his hand.

"Fuck!" He was furious. He grabbed hold of my hair and yanked it back. "Bite me again, I'll clobber you, too."

I screamed at them to let me go, and when they didn't, I began to beg. But by then they were all fired up. I'm sure all my struggling had turned them on. They'd reached the point where they wouldn't let me loose until I gave them something in return.

"Think we danced with you all night 'cause you're so attractive?" Stu sneered. He answered his own query. "Only reason you trot a wallflower is to get her to put out later on."

Then they really started to work me over, Mama. They grabbed at me and grasped at me and taunted me for my ugliness. They laughed when I started to cry. "Bet she's wet down there, too," one of them said.

The struggle went on for a good ten minutes. They laughed and hooted and talked about me in the third person as if I didn't have ears or couldn't understand.

"Look at the way she twists. Like a snake. What she needs is a good fucking, yeah?"

"Let's rip her panties off and fingerfuck both her holes."

"Better, let's strip her and throw her out of the car. Make her hitch home bare-ass."

"Yeah!"

And then, almost suddenly, it was over. The sneering and abuse petered out; the dark threats and rough grabs gave way to laughter and a lighter touch. There we were again, three kids squeezed together in the back of a car, the guys smiling, telling the girl to calm herself, the girl whimpering and shaking, then gingerly accepting the offered handkerchief to wipe away her tears. Stu got back in the driver's seat, drove us back to Shaker Heights. Half an hour later I was let off in front of my house with a "Good night, Bev. See you around, kid." I heard their laughter as they drove away.

What they did to me that night wasn't a "date rape," Mama, but I think it was worse in a way than any rape I ever heard about in my practice. Instead of raping me, they abused me; that, I've always thought, may have been their plan from the start.

I can just imagine the dialogue: "Hey, Stu, let's have some fun. Tonight, at this crappy dance we gotta go to, let's pick out one of the wallflowers, a real ugly-duckling type, know what I mean? Then dance her around, make her think she's got us all hot for her body. Then see if we can get her to do something really raunchy like suck us both off at once, maybe even take it up the ass.''

''Sure, great. But what if she doesn't want to?''

''She will. She'll be so grateful she'll do anything.''

''And if she isn't?''

''Screw it, bro. We'll dump on her. Give her something to remember us by. What do you say?''

In the end, Mama, it wasn't my body that was violated; it was my ego, my very soul. They shamed me, broke me down, made me cry and beg. They degraded me nearly as much as one human can degrade another, except, since there were two of them that night, my degradation was doubled.

You weren't there when I got home. You were still down at the lounge, having a drink with your cronies after your final set. But even if you'd been home, I don't know what I would have told you. I was just so embarrassed, so humiliated, so incredulous about what had happened. I doubt I could have talked about it to you or anyone else.

I tiptoed up the stairs. Millie was sound asleep. In our bathroom, I stripped off all my clothes and stared woefully at myself in the mirror.

It was Cinderella who stared back at me, Mama, Cinderella after her moment of triumph at the ball, transformed after midnight back into her drab and lonely self. But I was different inside, in a way that didn't show for several years. That night a killer was born. This wallflower, I promised myself, will one day have her revenge. And a few months later, on a miserable cold and rainy day, when I was sitting in the window seat on our landing and saw something in the sky, a flash of lightning and then a glimpse of black, I smiled as I grasped the process by which my vengeance would one day be wreaked.

The flashes of pain, the hurts, the shames! Wallflower, wallflower, wallflower! I'd show them what a wallflower could do! I'd leave a flower by their walls! Oh, yes, I would, Mama! Oh, yes, I would!

Bobby Wexler and Laura Gabelli, they got theirs, Mama: Bobby and his new brood out in Fort Worth; Laura, her hubby and children up in Providence.

Bobby was executed, of course, for the way he treated me that summer between junior and senior years at Ashley-Burnett, when you were singing at the Cavendish and he thought, since he was already sticking his repulsive member into you, it might be fun to take out your daughter and stick it into her as well. Naturally he didn't succeed. I *swear,* Mama, I *never* tried to compete with you. All your men were Private Property as far as I was concerned. But I know you had your doubts when Bobby went around telling everyone I'd put out. The little shit! When I rejected his advances, he went into a pout and then, out of wounded vanity, tried to stir up mother-daughter trouble. He wanted to come between us, Mama, and he almost succeeded, too. It's for that I gave the asshole his due. I just hope he likes the way I had him glued. He won't be getting any more erections now!

Laura got hers for gabbing. After I transferred down to Tufts, the little bitch tried to put the make on me and, when she got slapped down, went around telling every-one on campus ''Bev had a big love affair that went sour with her roommate up at Bennington.'' She told all her lesbian pals they'd do well to stay away from me as I was very bad news. So how do you like your new glued-up pussy, Laura? Bet your husband likes it, too, heh! heh!

Probably the best parts of these executions, Mama, were the trophies Tool brought back for you. From Bobby's house a beaten-up paperback copy of some crappy self-help book (as if he could ever help *him*self!) and from Laura's that funny old eggbeater, evidence of her newfound ''domesticity'' no doubt.

Yes, the first six were all on account of sexual humiliations. Even old Bertha Parce when you think of it—her attack on me was but a disguised attack on *your* sexuality. And the gluing of their genitalia seemed appropriate to such offenses. As for the family members unfortunate enough to be present at the times of execution, their organs were also glued so as to terminate the bloodlines, so to speak.

But now there are other pages in the ledger. Names of people who shamed me in other ways, like arrogant Professor Gaitenburg at Western Reserve, who mocked me during my orals, or Dr. Wendell Greer, the gynecologist, who tried to feel me up on his examination table. Ruth Kendricks, Geraldine Pearson, Pat Tinder and Walter Kinsolving, Rachel Spargo, Linda Nash, Richard Duggan and Violet Kraus. Oh, Mama, I could give you a list a hundred names long. There were so many of them, so very many, and there's not nearly enough time left in this life to take care of them all.

It must have been something in my eyes that set her off, the way I looked at Jessica. Maybe she identifies Jessica with her sister whom she loved and killed. ''I had to kill her to save her from Granny,'' she told me once, back at Carlisle. Or maybe she identifies me with Granny, the ogress who ruled her life. Whatever weird connections she's made, the damage now is done. Poor Tool is bewildered, angry, hurt. But she's just going to have to control herself. Mama was right. Once a tool starts getting a mind of its own, things can go bad very fast.

The fight takes place in a small all-white room on the third floor above the dojo, a room reserved for private contests among the sensei's students. Afternoon light, pouring in through the high windows that face upper Broadway, makes the hard bleached oak floor shine.

The room is empty except for the two young female combatants, one blond and tall, the other black-haired and short. Dressed in gi jackets and pants, breathing heavily, they stand several feet apart in postures of confrontation, faces creased with rage and pain. An aura of aggression edged with danger envelops them. A faint aroma of perspiration perfumes the air.

Both women know this room well. They have fought matches here many times. It was here, too, that, giggling, they stripped to the waist several months before and amicably dueled with sabers with only a borrowed Polaroid camera to witness their carefully orchestrated contest.

Their fight today is different. A new element, a clear intent on the part of the shorter combatant to hurt and seriously vanquish the taller, has become evident only moments before. Now the two young women, chests heaving from their last contact, appraise each other. The stare of the short one, Diana, is hard and cold; the stare of the taller, Jess, is injured and perplexed. Then, like rival warriors about to engage in a final clash, their eyes meet and lock.

"I think we should stop awhile, cool down," Jess suggests. But she does not relax her fighting stance.

Diana shakes her head.

"You really want to go for it then?"

Diana gives her answer, a rush attack.

The women collide, brutally punch and kick at each other. Grunts of effort and sharp cries of pain resound off the walls. The smell of sweat turns pungent as, for a full twenty seconds, they stand close, in nearly intimate contact, raining and blocking blows. Flesh is bruised. Blood spurts. Knuckles become raw and burn. Finally, exhausted from the struggle, the two fall back to try to control their labored breathing, each trying hard, too, not to show how badly she's been hurt.

Finally Jess speaks: "This isn't sport, you know."

Diana squints. "For me it is."

"If we continue like this, one of us'll be killed."

"That's what a real fight's about," Diana replies.

Still in her fighting stance, Diana suddenly reaches up and pulls at her hair. A moment later she casts a wig down upon the floor, then grins as she reveals her closely shaven skull.

Jess stares at Diana, trying to decipher the meaning of this gesture. Now she sees something in her opponent's icy blue eyes, a murderous look, savage, almost feral, that she never noticed before, even though the two had been friends for months. Suddenly Jess makes a decision. Turning her back on Diana, she strides across the room, opens the door, and exits without a word.

Diana, relaxing her stance, smiles knowingly. To leave

a fight, turn one's back on an opponent without making the obligatory bow, is to deliver an unpardonable insult. *And it will not be pardoned,* she thinks.

My mistake, Mama, was to forget how passionate she could be. Her deeply submissive attachment made me forget that this was a girl who killed her mother, grandmother, and sister with an ax, then split all three of their bodies straight up from the crotch.

That she might be jealous if I gave special attention to a patient—well, I should have thought of that and taken steps. But things got out of hand. I remember your words: "If a tool goes into business for itself, you gotta think about getting rid of it."

And that, sadly, Mama, is what I may have to do.

It is 8:00 P.M. A chilly evening in New York. Diana's nostrils quiver as they catch the smell of rotted leaves, a late-autumn smell rising from the dark, wet parkland below. Cold rain fell in the afternoon; now there are puddles on Riverside Drive.

Diana, jogging downtown, does not avoid these puddles. Rather, she runs straight through them. At this hour the drive is nearly deserted. On either side, graceful streetlamps burn sulfurous in the night.

Across the dark canopy of wet bushes and trees Diana catches sight of the Hudson River, its surface gleaming black like roiling oil. Beside the river, streams of cars, headlights streaking, speed along the West Side Highway.

Diana cannot hear these cars; they are too far away. All she can hear is the steady *pat-pat-pat* of her feet upon the wet pavement and a light buzzing sound inside her brain.

Her quarry, unaware she is being tracked, also jogs, but two hundred feet ahead and a hundred feet below amidst the trees. Every so often Diana catches sight of her, a tall, thin light-haired woman dressed in a dark track suit, loping along a path that winds and turns through the narrow park. Diana is on a collision course with this woman. The point of intersection is a mile ahead. She feels an excitement different in quality from what she felt when carrying out missions for Doctor. This time it is her own enemy she is after, an opponent she knows well from numerous encounters. She also knows that this quarry is most likely armed, a fact that enhances the thrill of the hunt. Diana intends to strike first, hard and fast from behind. The battle should be over before it is even joined. That is the method she was taught.

Although it is cold, Diana is lightly dressed. She wears a thin black long-sleeved T-shirt and black nylon running shorts. She also wears a nylon waist sack loaded with paraphernalia for her kill: her weapon, an ice pick, which she will strap on to her forearm when she is ready; a caulking gun filled with glue to mark and desecrate her victim; and a shriveled flower plucked earlier from Doctor's garden, which she will leave as her signature beside a little wall she discovered near the killing site.

She has calculated everything. Only a half mile now to the place she carefully picked out. She increases her speed from a jogger's pace to a fast flat-out run. She bears right at the fork where the sidewalk that borders the drive meets a paved path that descends into the park. Once among the trees, she pulls out her weapon and fits it into the sheath strapped to her arm. She is now on an intersecting vector with her quarry, whom she sees clearly jogging a hundred yards ahead.

What luck! Jess is wearing a Walkman; she will not be able to hear Diana's steps. Diana looks around; no one else is on the path. She and Jess are alone in this narrow strip of park. Ahead, the great illuminated tower of Riverside Church soars into the night sky. Beyond a faint glow is cast by the city's lights.

A light rain begins to fall. Diana shivers slightly but runs on. She notices that Jess has begun to pick up her pace. Diana speeds up even more. *Pat-pat-pat* go her feet. She feels her heartbeat quicken as her ears find the sound of Jess's steps. *Pit-pat pit-pat pit-pat.* Jess is but a hundred feet ahead. Impossible now to stop. The rhythm is set. The momentum of attack is carrying her along. Diana pulls her pick from its sheath, holds it underhand as she swings her arms. Fifty feet now. Thirty. Twenty-five. Jess is almost within her reach. In a burst of speed Diana overtakes her. And then, in a single violent motion, she raises her right arm and with full force plunges the pick sideways so that it enters Jess's brain directly through the ear.

Jess, stabbed, falls upon the path, and as she does, the buzzing inside Diana's head suddenly stops. Feeling hot, feverish with victory, Diana grabs hold of Jess's feet and drags her body into the thick, wet brush on the right. She pulls her through the fallen leaves to within a few feet of the ruined wall, then lets go of her, stands back, and stares down at her face.

At one time Jess was her friend, but when she, too, became Doctor's patient, Diana's liking of her turned to hate. Now that hate is purged. Her rival is but dead meat on the ground. Diana kneels to untie the string that secures Jess's sweatpants, then pulls them down to the girl's ankles. She grins when she sees the switchblade knife strapped against Jess's side. An opponent's weapon—what a fine trophy that will make!

As Diana uncaps her caulking gun and sets to work with the glue, her only regret is that now that her onetime friend is dead, she will never be able to give back the archery set she borrowed the week before.

She's down there in the basement now, brooding over her unauthorized kill. All right, you made her into a killing machine, so you've got to expect a certain amount of carryover. She's human after all. But to leave the wallflower signature and use the glue, methods reserved for *your* tormentors—that was crazy, that means she's out of control.

She can't even explain why she did it. A fit of jealousy? But it was Tool who got Jessica to come see you in the first place. Tool recruited her. She was Jessica's friend. She knew what therapy was. What did she expect? That you'd treat Jessica differently? That you wouldn't take her into your office and listen to her for an hour three times a week?

No, it had to be something more. This past autumn, when Jessica asked for the name of her shrink, Tool was quick to send her on. Remember the way she beamed when she told you to expect the call?

What about their actual relationship? How much do you really know? Could they have been more than gym buddies? Could they have been lovers?

Be rational about this; don't let the stress generate fantasies. The truth is you still don't know what they did all those times they went off together after martial arts class. Come to think of it, isn't it strange Jessica never mentioned Tool except the first time she called?

"Diana Proctor gave me your name. We take a martial arts class together on the West Side. I'm looking for a good therapist. I'd like to come in and talk about it if that's all right."

Yes, of course, it was "all right." You were extremely interested in treating someone who looked so much like Cynthia Morse. And this girl was so much nicer without any evident cruel streak. She was a decent, direct sort of person, but with Cindy's great looks, smile, and appeal.

So what were you after with her anyway? Looking to seduce her? Don't be absurd! Those days are long gone, and anyway, the girl was young enough to be your daughter. But admit it, she attracted you. She was just your type. And just about the same age as Cindy was then, before she turned on you and earned herself a place in the ledger.

No, there's got to be more to this than meets the eye. Tool and Jessica must have had some kind of emotional connection that, when it snapped, generated rage in Tool and set her off.

Remember the little encounter at the knife show? Running into Jessica with Tool in tow didn't strike you as being all that important at the time. But suppose Jessica, seeing her shrink unexpectedly in the company of another patient who happened to be her friend, got curious, decided to trail you for a while, and then saw something she didn't like.

Wait a minute! Remember the famous "English girl" she met in Italy, the one who fenced topless with her? The truth is you've had only her word on that. You never saw the photographs, didn't even know about them until Janek brought them up. Why didn't she tell you about them? Could she have been afraid you'd ask to see them? She couldn't allow that because if she did, you'd recognize the other girl. Suppose the alleged "English girl" was a subterfuge? Suppose Jessica didn't want to tell you she'd actually played the topless fencing scene with Diana? If that's true, then they definitely *did* have something going, perhaps not overtly sexual, but certainly sexualized. And if that's the case, then there was enough unresolved energy to unleash Tool and cause her to explode.

But go back a moment, think about that knife show. What could Jessica have seen you and Tool do that might cause her to mention to a friend that she was thinking of quitting therapy?

You might have spoken harshly to Tool or petted her. You do that unconsciously sometimes, out of some twisted maternalism no doubt. If you'd had your wits about you, you'd never have gone to that damn knife show in the first place. It was Tool's idea. She said she wasn't enjoying using crude store-bought ice picks all the time, she wanted a fine weapon, something she wouldn't have to leave behind, something really sharp with a ritualistic flavor to it, and since there was a knife show in town, would you attend it with her, take a look, see if anything caught your eye?

So there it is. Tool set the whole thing up. She knew Jessica would attend the show, probably even knew which day. She enticed you into taking her there because she wanted Jessica to see her with you, and she probably did something there that you didn't even notice, like taking your arm, squeezing it—anything to provoke Jessica and force her out of therapy.

This is terrible! It means Tool's been using you! It means you've lost control of her, created a Frankenstein's monster just as Mama said.

Calm down! Look at the implications. Janek's got the photographs. If Tool *was* the other fencer and he should see her entering the basement apartment, he'll recognize her at once. He already suspects you. He's not all that great at hiding what he feels. Or, more likely, he's deliberately letting his suspicions show in the hope you'll get spooked and tip your hand.

The main thing now is to keep Janek from seeing Tool.

But there's something even more important, which is to get to the bottom of Tool and Jessica's relationship. Tool has to tell you whether she was the "English girl." Once you're certain about that, you can take the necessary countermeasures.

So the thing to do is get Tool up here in front of Mama. Mama always intimidates her. If you can get her up here naked in front of Mama, Mama'll make her talk.

It is night. The scene is a shadowy and cavernous bedchamber dimly lit with soft reddish light. At one end a large four-poster oak bed stands free of the walls. At the other, three female figures are arranged in frozen postures as if posing for a *tableau vivant*. From the expressions on the faces of these players, a spectator might well feel that a question hangs upon the air. But not one of the figures moves or speaks. The question, if there was one, remains unanswered.

The first figure, young, muscular, firm-fleshed, stands at stiff attention. She is naked, her head and body totally shaved, a fine gloss of perspiration coating her like a dew. The soft red light that paints her exposed skin emphasizes the blush generated from within. Her eyes, too, are red, as if from weeping.

The second figure, older, shorter, plump, sits opposite the first in a high-backed chair. She is dressed in a too-tight strapless crimson gown which can barely contain her bodice. Her eyes are narrowed as she stares with cold reproach at the younger woman's face. But the younger woman does not return the seated woman's gaze.

Rather, her eyes engage the eyes of a third woman, actually a painted image hanging on the wall just above the seated woman's chair. This woman, the one in the picture, wears the same crimson gown as the live woman below, but the garment suits her better. While the breasts of the seated woman are constricted by her gown, the bosoms of the painted woman fill hers perfectly. There is a curious resemblance between the seated woman and the painted one that must haunt a spectator. It is as if each one's face, in a completely different way, is a caricature of the other's.

But perhaps what would seem most strange would be the powerful force field of emotions that appears to exist among these players. A spectator would know that the three are bound to one another in some inexorable and yet tragic way, bound so tightly and forcefully that anything outside their triangle, any person or event, would have no meaning to them at all.

"She says she did it because Jessica wouldn't return her bow! What do you think, Mama? Hours of punitive bracing and she comes up with that."

"The bow we gave—"

"Right, Mama, the bow we presented to her when she came back from commando school in Colorado. Remember, she was first in her class out there, and we thought she ought to be rewarded for doing so well, especially as most of the other students were males. Besides, she'd told us her martial arts instructor had suggested she take up archery to hone her concentration. So we mail-ordered an excellent target bow and set of arrows and laid them out for her on the bed so she'd see them first thing when she reported in after her trip."

"But wasn't there another connection?"

"Of course, Mama! Do you think I'm such a bad analyst I didn't understand what was going on?"

"Gosh, Bev, you're touchy today. I don't think you're a bad analyst at all."

"Forgive me, Mama. I thought you were implying that I wasn't aware of the play on words. Because, of course, I was. Diana wanted a bow so she could play archer, or should I say 'Archer'? She liked being the patient but also wanted to play at being Doctor or at least try out the authority role for a while. If she had a bow in her hands, she'd be a kind of Archer, with real potency, too, as a bow can be an extremely powerful weapon."

"You were always a wonderful analyst, Bev. You have your deficiencies. Who doesn't? But you've always been good at your job."

"What deficiencies?"

"Oh, please, let's not get into that."

"I think we should get into it. I've known for some time you've found me deficient. Now's as good a time as any to clear the air. I'm waiting, Mama. Tell me where you find me wanting. I can take your criticism. God knows, I've taken it all my life.''

"You're sure you want to hear it?"

"I'm sure."

"Okay, but just remember you asked for it. So don't complain."

"I won't."

"Let's start with this wallflower business."

"Is that what it is? A 'business'?"

"You know what I mean."

"I'm not sure I do. I happen to be a wallflower."

"No, dear, that's what you made yourself into. No one's born a wallflower. A wallflower creates herself. Something in you likes being a wallflower, so you have Tool leave those flowers beside the walls, as if—"

"As if *what,* damn it, Mama?"

"There, see, you're getting angry. You were always so touchy, Bev. You could never take the slightest bit of criticism."

"Never mind that! Just tell me how I've made myself into a wallflower, since that seems to be what you think."

"It's not just what I think, dear. It's the truth. And having Tool leave those homely, withered flowers by the bodies only reinforces your negative self-image. Which, frankly, you could remedy if you'd just find yourself somebody who . . . you know."

"Somebody to screw me. That's what you mean, isn't it?"

"I knew this dialogue was going to turn unpleasant, Bev. I think it would be better if we stop talking."

"Certainly, Mama, if that's the way you want it. . . ."

* * *

There's a difference, Mama, a big difference between us. It's important for you to understand the difference and why, as much as I might like, I cannot be like you. For one thing, I don't have your looks. I know, I'm not really *bad*-looking. And I certainly don't feel sorry for myself. In this world, as I so often remind my patients, you've got to play the hand you're dealt. But you're beautiful, Mama. Just look at yourself, your eyes, complexion, bones, the marvelous planes of your face. There were those who called you the most beautiful woman in Cleveland. You played the part, too. Grand. Mysterious. Elusive. Even cruel at times. Not really cruel in the sense of mean or small, but cruel in the way that a great woman projects cruelty, becoming, as the poet said, a Lady of Pain. Mystical. Unfathomable. My nurturer and my nemesis.

It was you who taught me the lines:

> *Cold eyelids that hide like a jewel*
> *Hard eyes that grow soft for an hour;*
> *The heavy white limbs, and the cruel*
> *Red mouth like a venomous flower.*

Sometimes when I'm lying in bed, I look up at you and think: *How could I, little me, be the child of such magnificence?* I know I shouldn't run myself down. I am who I am and, as such, am as valuable as any other human on this earth. But it hasn't always been easy being your daughter. I never had your stature, your beauty, your compelling personality. I had to find my own way to power, and the way I found, the way of concealment and craft, is not nearly as attractive as yours. While you played torch singer to Cleveland, bewitching your audiences with songs, I took a less flamboyant route, studying the permutations of the human mind, then working within the interstices to create unique effects. And while your color was and always will be red, color of flames, mine is and always shall be black, color of night.

There were times, Mama, when you hurt me deeply. I never told you this before. I know you never meant to hurt me; I know that whatever you did, it was always with my own best interests at heart. But there's still times when I feel the pain, and then I wonder: *Is it worth it to keep on living, to try to make my way in this pitiless, indifferent world?* I do my best. I work hard with my patients, pretending always to listen to them with sympathy. I try hard not to seem like one of those small, tight-lipped therapists who listen and listen and give nothing back in return. But there's so little I *can* give, Mama, to assuage so much cruelty, torment, so many hurts and humiliations and intractable problems in other women's lives. Who can solve them all? Who can bind up all the wounds? Who can assuage the hurts and blunt the cruelties and tell the wounded ones there is hope and time will heal. It's hard, too, to listen all the time, always to care about *them,* absorb myself in *them,* focus my attention on *their* difficulties, when I have so many of my own. I haven't wanted to think always of the past, obsess over the old hurts and wounds, but it's been hard not to, the pain's been so real, and, Mama, it's always there.

I was left with no choice, it seems, but to try to wipe it out with acts of retributive justice. The only other option for me was to allow the awful pain to strangle me, choke me to death with its poisonous vines.

You know your silent treatment's killing me. Do I

deserve it, do I really? I'm very sorry, truly, *very, very sorry* I was insolent. But I never denied my overriding love for you. So there really wasn't anything for you to get so offended about.

Will you please answer me, Mama? Have you forgotten the trophies I had Tool bring back for you! The offerings I made to you? The years I spent listening to your sob stories? I practically did your goddamn wash for you! Have you forgotten that?

Go ahead, ignore me. Just don't forget—I'm an analyst. I know you're hiding something, and I have a pretty good idea what it is. I want you to confess to me. That's right, Mama, I want the truth. Tell me the truth, and I'll forgive you for it. Because I know you did something, Mama. *I know you did.*

Think back. Remember that last little exchange with Jimmy MacDonald just before Tool stabbed him in the eye? You don't remember? Then I'll refresh your memory. Jimmy said: ". . . it wasn't us, you know. It was set up. She ought to talk to her—" And then he stopped.

Her *what*? Her *mother*? Could *that* have been the person Jimmy was referring to? Was he thinking of *you*, Mama?

Since you don't deny it, since you refuse to say anything . . . well, I'll have to draw my own conclusions, won't I? Yes, I'll just have to draw my own conclusions, hurtful though they may be. . . .

Shhhh. We have to whisper now. We don't want Tool to hear us. If she hears, she may decide to attack us first. We're going to have to get rid of her. That much is clear. And to do that, we're going to have to set her up so well that there'll be no doubt she was always acting on her

own. That won't be hard. All the receipts from her
various trips, the paper trail as they call it, have been
safely preserved on our orders in her room. And Carl
Drucker will gladly testify that we resisted when he first
broached release. The most important thing is to make
sure the little lynx hasn't kept a diary or anything that can
directly tie us to the crimes. Of course, we *are* tied to
them indirectly: It was her insane obsession with us
that pushed her to kill these various figures from our
past. That's easily documented. All the information she
needed was available in our personal files, to which she
had ready access by virtue of living in the basement of
our house. The plan is foolproof. Even if the cops suspect
our influence, all the evidence will point to Tool alone.
But we mustn't forget to move the trophies. They
mustn't be in front of the portrait; rather, they have to be
hidden away in various corners and drawers. The paper
trail should nail her nicely, as will the wallflower trap we
laid so carefully at Carlisle. We'll have to do it quickly.
It will take all our courage, and we'll have only one
chance to get it right. The staging must conform to the
provocation: Tool tried to kill us; we struck back at her
in self-defense. After all, she's a confessed killer. All we
ever wanted was to help her adjust. She attacked us, her
therapist and mother surrogate, just the way she attacked
her own mother, with an ax. We managed to kill her only
because she slipped. Another second and her ax would
have split our skull. We defended ourself; we had no
choice. It was either her or us.

Too bad, of course, but now that we gather she killed
all those other fine people, whole families of them, it
seems, and by so doing replicated her original crime
against her own family—well, we can't help wondering

if perhaps she's not better off dead. This may seem odd, coming as it does from a healer, but we truly believe there are times a person is truly better off in the grave than living possessed by the kind of demons that ravaged poor young Diana Proctor's tormented soul.

Where are you, Mama? I need you now, need you so much! Why are you silent?
Talk to me. Please, talk to me! Pleeeeeease!

8
The Trophies

Janek repositioned himself against the soft white beach towel Monika had arranged upon the cushions of the chaise. It was not a tan he was after but heat. He wanted the sun to strike the center of his chest, wanted its dry hotness to enter his bared body and to spread. Anything to drive away the chill within that made him tremble even now in the middle of this hot, windless December afternoon on the Isla de Cozumel.

The terrace where he lay exposed, naked except for a pair of green jungle-motif trunks Monika had bought for him at the airport, was just a few rock steps down from their *caseta*, perched sixty feet above the beach. From where Janek lay he could see nothing except a line of palms clinging to the curving shore and a vast expanse of blue divided cleanly by the horizon. Below the line was placid cyan sea, above it serene azure sky, and not a whitecap or a cloud marred these seamless surfaces.

He turned to look at Monika. She lay topless on a matching chaise a few feet away, her oversize sunglasses on her nose, a German-language paperback open and face down on her belly. At first Janek thought she'd fallen off to sleep, but then he saw a smile spread slowly across her face.

"How're you doing?" he asked.

"Feeling dreamy," she said. "I love it here. How about you?"

"I'm definitely feeling warmer."

"Well, you should. You need more sunscreen." She rose, spread lotion onto her hands, came to him, and, standing behind, began to apply it slowly and evenly to his chest.

He gazed up at her. "That's sexy."

"It's meant to be." She brushed her fingers lightly across his nipples. "You're a very sexy man."

"Thanks for saying that," Janek said, "but I don't feel very appetizing. Pale, middle-aged, scarred . . ."

She spread the lotion very carefully over the wounds on his shoulder and his throat.

"You look good, Frank. A few days down here and you'll start feeling good, too. It may take time, but sooner or later your mind will catch up with your body."

He glanced up at her again, then turned away, feeling tears rising involuntarily to his eyes. This had been happening regularly since the stabbing, and he hated himself for not being able to control it. He was glad he was wearing sunglasses; he didn't like to expose his vulnerability. But when he remembered that Monika had been with him in Venice when Kit had called and told him Jess was dead, he knew it was absurd to feel embarrassed with her. He pulled his glasses off.

"Either I feel cold and start to shake or else I tear up," he said, turning so she could see his eyes. "It's not because of pain or sadness, and certainly not remorse. I don't know why the hell it happens, Monika; but I don't like it, and I want it to stop."

The police psychiatrist had told him the tears and

shakes were delayed manifestations of stress. But there was a feeling that came with them, which he couldn't quite define. Monika wanted him to let her help him explore it, but he felt he wasn't ready yet, that he had no words with which to express it. It was something dark that he had glimpsed which had entered his mind and gotten lost in the canyons of his brain and which now he feared because it made him feel cold or caused the tears to rise.

She made herself a place to sit beside him, then gently kissed his eyelids dry. Then she took his glasses and set them back on his face, carefully arranging the temples behind his ears.

"I never killed a woman before. Never even shot at one."

"You know gender isn't the issue, Frank."

"A woman. It feels strange."

"You're chivalrous."

He smiled. "I've only rarely been accused of that."

"Oh, Frank . . ." She took his face between her palms. "To kill a person even in self-defense—I understand how difficult it must be to live with that. And I know that no matter what Kit and Aaron say—that you had no choice, that surely she would have killed you if you hadn't killed her, that she was a sociopath, a murderer—I know none of that means anything so long as you're haunted. That's why we're here, to rest, talk, perhaps reorder all those terrible events. In the meantime, remember you're not tainted by your deed, not soiled by it in any way. But you are changed on account of it. So now your task is to come to terms with this new Frank that you are, to understand him and come to love him again."

He took her hand. "Thanks for saying that."

"I like being your lover-shrink. You know I do. Still, when the demons are within, only you can chase them out." She paused. "I love you. Please remember that."

He brought her hand to his lips. "I won't forget."

They had come into his room during the week he was in the hospital, first Aaron, then Kit, then Aaron again, then Aaron and Kit together. On each visit they told him the story, rotating the puzzle so he could examine it from every side. But no matter how many different ways they told it, it always came out the same. The basic story, well constructed because they were excellent detectives, seemed to him wrong and incomplete. He listened to them, nodded, asked questions, and took in their answers, but in the end he told them that good as their story was, he was not going to buy it.

The facts were simple enough. The woman he had killed was named Diana Proctor. She was a librarian who paid a nominal rent to inhabit the basement apartment in Beverly Archer's house. Six years before, in Danbury, Connecticut, she had murdered three members of her family with an ax. Having been declared mentally incompetent, she'd been committed to Carlisle Hospital for the Criminally Insane, where, after five years of intensive treatment under Beverly's supervision, the entire hospital staff, led by its director, Dr. Carl Drucker, determined that she had made a full recovery and lobbied vigorously for her release.

On this matter of the release there was an important point. Hospital records showed, and Dr. Drucker verified, that Beverly Archer had not been in favor of setting Diana Proctor free. Diana wasn't ready yet, she had written; perhaps a few more years of therapy were indicated. But the rest of the staff was convinced of her recovery, so in the end Beverly reluctantly went along.

The girl seemed to function well in the city. She obtained a part-time job at the New York Society Library on East Seventy-ninth Street, where coworkers described her as congenial and her work as exemplary. She lived quietly in Dr. Archer's basement, undergoing sessions four times a week. She also joined the West Side Academy of Karate at Broadway and 110th Street, where she became an accomplished martial artist. It was there that she met Jess Foy.

Other students at the academy described them as friends. And it was Diana who referred Jess to Archer when Jess asked her to recommend a therapist. In addition, it turned out that Diana was the so-called English girl in the fencing photograph Janek had found taped to the wall of Jess's closet. She was the owner, too, of the bow and arrows Janek had tracked down through the Salvation Army. Mr. Yukio Katsakura, the sensei at the academy, described a violent match the two girls had fought in a private upstairs room the week that Jess was stabbed. The reason he hadn't mentioned this to Aaron, when he was interviewed early in the investigation, was that when he inquired about it, both women had smiled gaily and shrugged it off. Katsakura had assumed they'd just gotten carried away, a not infrequent occurrence among young, well-motivated fighters.

One could only speculate as to why Diana had killed Jess. Possibly she became jealous of her friend, who was a superior athlete and martial artist and who she may have believed was favored by their therapist. Beverly herself theorized that Diana had made erotic overtures to

Jess and, upon being rebuffed, had acted out her fury. But whatever Diana's rationale, the murderous act was part of the same insanity that had led her to slaughter her relatives one horrible Sunday morning six years before.

It was the Archer connection to three of the other victim clusters (Bertha Parce; Cynthia Morse & family; the MacDonald brothers) that struck Janek as the story's most peculiar feature. As best the detectives were able to reconstruct, Diana became so obsessed with her therapist that when Beverly was asleep, Diana rummaged through her papers and came up with these victims' names. Then, out of some strange, twisted, perhaps jealousy-driven madness, she methodically located them, flew to where they lived, executed them, and glued their genitals, always leaving her wallflower signature behind.

There was no question that Diana thought of herself as a wallflower. She had described herself that way several times to friends at Carlisle. Carl Drucker turned over a note from Diana signed ''Wallflower'' which police handwriting analysts verified was in the girl's hand. Moreover, a huge trove of evidence was found in Diana's room: airline ticket receipts, motel receipts, car rental receipts, caulking guns, glue, ice picks, and, most important, a hit list bearing the names of all the Wallflower victims. Kit said the evidence was so convincing that had Diana survived her encounter with Janek, she would easily have been convicted of murder.

Which still left several other killings to be explained: the homeless man, the two non-Archer-connected Happy Families, Leo Titus, and the attack against Janek on the final night.

The homeless man, according to Kit and Aaron's theory, was a practice shot in preparation for the later homicides. Diana, it seemed, was quite rigorous in her preparation. In addition to karate training, she worked out regularly at a local health club and two summers before had taken a ten-day course in commando tactics at a shadowy survivalist school in Colorado, where she learned the ice pick technique.

(Aaron found the receipt in Diana's desk. Beverly had no knowledge of the foray; Diana had simply told her she was going white water rafting on her vacation.)

In any event, it seemed consistent with such rigor that Diana would first try out her newly acquired skills on a relatively defenseless target in New York before venturing to distant cities in search of whole families to execute.

As for what exactly had attracted Diana to the two non-Archer-connected victim clusters (the Robert Wexler family in Fort Worth and the Anthony Scotto family in Providence)—that, said Aaron and Kit, would probably never be known. Beverly Archer had her own theory—namely, that the very image of a family stirred up tremendous murderous aggression inside Diana, similar to the aggression that had exploded on the morning she killed her own core family with the ax.

The stabbing of the cat burglar Leo Titus was easier to explain. By intruding into Beverly's house, he posed a threat of invasion to which Diana's hair-trigger mentality could only respond with an attack. Janek, of course, was another invader and thus had to be killed like the first. In her interview Beverly stated her belief that had Janek not succeeded in stopping Diana, she herself would have become a victim the moment she reentered her house. An extra irony of the affair was that the Archer-connected Wallflower victims (Parce, Morse, and the MacDonalds) were minor figures in Beverly's past, people with whom she'd been out of touch for years. She hadn't even known any of them were dead until Aaron showed her the FBI's victim list.

The shrink seemed to have suffered something close to a nervous breakdown as a result of the discovery that her "best patient" had in fact not been cured at all but had, even while in intensive therapy, committed a series of horrible murders against these past players in her life. Beverly's suffering over her therapeutic catastrophe was demonstrated to Janek on the videotape of her interview with Aaron.

While still in the hospital, Janek viewed this tape several times. In it the psychologist seemed truly shattered. The tight, withdrawn quality she'd displayed in her interviews with him were replaced in Aaron's interview by tearful eruptions of agony and remorse. Her cool half-smile was supplanted by haggard, tormented eyes, making for a portrait of a woman in despair. But after rerunning and studying the tape, Janek decided her performance was feigned. No matter her broken appearance and the apparent sincerity of her grief, he did not believe a word of it.

The result was that no matter how many times Aaron and Kit told him their story and no matter how much evidence they carted into his hospital room to prove it, Janek insisted it was not complete. If, as all the evidence showed, Diana Proctor had physically committed the murders, then, Janek maintained, by some method he could not describe, Beverly Archer had put Diana up to it.

"You're usually right about these things," Kit said. "But how can you be so sure?"

"I feel it," Janek replied. "I don't care how many

times Diana described herself as a wallflower or signed her name that way. For me Beverly Archer is the only wallflower in the case. The flowers left beside the walls at the murder scenes were her signatures, not Diana's.''

On their first day in Yucatán, Janek and Monika settled into their rented *caseta,* then lay out on their terrace in the sun. When it grew dark, they drove into Cozumel, looking for a place to eat. They explored for a while, finally settling on a quiet thatch-roofed restaurant on the beach where the wine was good and the fish was fresh and well prepared.

Afterward they took another walk through the town, passing various bars and clubs, pausing occasionally to listen to laughter or music playing within. Then Monika drove them back to their little blue and white house, where the garden was filled with orchids and hibiscus and the terrace overlooked the sea. Here they sat out as they had in the afternoon, staring across the water at a magnificent tropical moon, which reminded them of the moon that had lit their way not two months before in Venice.

"It happens every night around this time," Janek said. "I start feeling chilled and then afraid."

"Of the dream?" He nodded. "I can give you a pill," Monika said. "It will help you sleep and probably stop you from dreaming. But I don't recommend it."

"Why not?"

"I think it's good for you to dream, Frank. Even if the dream is bad. If you can dream it through, the power of the dream will weaken, and then you'll be released."

Janek thought about that awhile. When he spoke again, his voice was hushed and steady.

"I can't see all the details. I see the redness over everything. The glow like a kind of rust. And I see the picture, so big, looming there: the handsome face; the glossy red curls; the sparkling eyes; the cruel, sensual mouth. And then I see this slim, little, bald woman charging at me like a fiend. She sticks me. I feel the pain. The room begins to spin. And then I see other things, objects, but I'm whirling so fast I can't tell you what they are. I want to see them clearly, Monika. I think that's why I dream about them. To see them again, hoping this time they'll register. Because they're important. I know they are." He sat back, shrugged. "I have no idea why."

That night, when the nightmare came and he began to shake, he felt her arms wrap his chest. The nightmare passed. He got up, shuffled to the bathroom, poured himself a glass of water, and drank it off. Back in bed, in her arms again, her breasts warm points against his back, he felt better, less haunted, not so cold.

"I've got an idea," he whispered to her in the morning.

"What?"

"It's nice here. I like it. But I want us to go back to New York."

"We just arrived, Frank."

"I know. But there's something I want to do. The photos Aaron showed me weren't enough. I should have insisted on seeing the room again for myself. What do you say we fly up there this morning, spend twenty-four hours, then fly back? I know it'll be expensive, but I'll pay for the tickets. I think seeing the room in daylight will help."

She shook her head. "I don't think so, Frank. I don't think that will help you at all."

"Look, I'm not a child. Whatever's there—I can take it."

She smiled. "Of course, you can. But there isn't anything there. You'll be wasting your time."

"But—"

"Please, listen to me. Right now you're recovering from two major physical wounds and a great deal of psychic stress. In a few brief seconds, perhaps the most intense of your life, many things converged on you— sound, sights, revelations. You saw things. You were attacked. You defended yourself, hit back at your attacker. Your mind suffered overload. Time and space were foreshortened and condensed. Some memories were etched, and others, perhaps the most important, were lost in the trauma of shooting that woman and being stabbed. No wonder you keep reliving those moments. The key to your nightmare, to your chills and tears, lies someplace within. Not in the actual room, as you might see it in daylight if we flew back to New York today, but in the room as you *experienced* it that night, the room as it *seemed* to you then. I told you that if you can re-create the vision that haunts you, it won't disturb you anymore. I believe that's true. It will become just another memory. The bad dream will . . . disappear."

He rolled onto his back. "Fine," he said. "Now how am I going to do all that?"

"After breakfast I'll drive down to the village. I'm going to buy you paper and a set of crayons."

"Oh, Monika, please. . . ."

"I'm serious, Frank. I want you to draw."

"Draw what?"

"The sea. The house. The garden. Whatever you like. Draw me if you want, or I'll bring a mirror out to the terrace and you can try to draw yourself. And if other images happen to come to you, then you'll draw them, too. You see, to draw a thing is to master it. I believe soon you'll be able to see those objects you cannot remember now. When you see them, you must try to draw them even if the images are only partial. Draw them and you'll control them. And then the dream will lose its power."

Aaron had brought photographs of Beverly's bedroom to the hospital. They had pored over them together. Everything was as he remembered it . . . almost. Leo Titus lay dead on the floor at the foot of the bed. Diana Proctor lay dead where she'd fallen after Janek's bullets had blasted her back. The light in the room was dim and red, and the painting was in the niche. But the portrait seemed smaller in the photos, less intense, the manner of its display less compelling to the eye. Everything looked the same, yet the cumulative effect was different. It was as if Janek's mind had played a trick on him, distorting the actual scene, which in the police photos appeared relatively normal, into something threatening and grotesque.

And still, there were things missing from the photos, those strange and inappropriate objects which haunted his dreams. Where were they? The room had been searched, and nothing out of the ordinary had been found. When Aaron asked Janek to describe the objects, he shook his head, for he could not.

"I just know they were there," he said.

* * *

The dream was always the same: a cavernous bedroom; reddish light; a huge oil painting of a woman; strange, not clearly seen objects arranged symmetrically before the portrait. He looked to his left: A body was curled on the floor. He looked to his right: A black-clothed virago with shaven skull rushed at him out of the gloom. At the very instant in his dream when he felt the ice pick slice into his flesh and hit his bone, he was possessed by the feeling that he had entered into something more than a stranger's bedroom, that he had entered into a secret chamber inside a madwoman's mind.

When he awoke from the dream, his thought was always the same: It was Beverly Archer's madness, not Diana Proctor's, that had been displayed.

He had other visitors over his two weeks in the hospital and his week of recuperation in his apartment. Laura and Stanton, attentive and concerned, arrived with two magnificent bouquets. Later Stanton came alone to tell him in a bitter whisper that he was glad Janek had killed the girl.

"A trial would have been awful, Frank. All that stuff about Jess—we don't even like to think about it." Stanton paused. "You gave us closure. We'll always be grateful for that. If you ever need anything, any kind of help, I want you to think of us and call."

After Stanton left, Janek had a feeling that he probably wouldn't be seeing much of the Dorances anymore. The three of them had shared Jess, but now that she was gone, there was nothing to bring them together again except the all-too-painful memory of her promise.

* * *

Sullivan also paid him a visit. He brought no flowers but was respectful and solicitous. If he was envious of Janek's resolution of his case, he succeeded in concealing it.

When Janek asked if anyone on his team harbored doubts that Diana Proctor had been the HF killer, Sullivan gazed at him mystified.

"Gee, Frank, why do you ask that?"

"No particular reason," Janek said.

"You think we're the kind of people who'd resist a case solution because an outsider got to it first? I'm offended. Whatever you may think of us, I promise you we're not that small."

Janek let it go. Sullivan, like any good FBI man, was interested in forensic evidence, not psychological speculation. But then Janek became aware that Sullivan was not visiting him merely to wish him well. He had his own agenda, which, after the pleasantries, he wasted no time bringing up.

"I was talking last night to Grey Scopetta, my film director friend."

"Yeah, I remember you mentioning him," Janek said.

"We both feel there could be a terrific miniseries here. What we're hoping is you'll give us a release so we can pitch the idea to a network."

Janek smiled graciously. "You don't need a release from me, Harry. Just don't use my name, okay?"

"But we have to use your name, Frank. You'll be the star." Sullivan stood and began to pace the little room. "Think of it. Two miniseries! You'll be the most famous detective in the country!"

"I've tasted fame, Harry, and as they say, it's vastly overrated."

"You're not serious." Sullivan paused. "Are you, Frank?"

Janek nodded. "I don't want to be portrayed in any more movies. But that shouldn't stop you guys. The case is in the public record. We all know police work isn't about stars; it's about teamwork. As team leader you can rightfully think of yourself as the leading man."

As Sullivan shook his head, Janek noticed something desperate in his eyes.

"What's the matter?"

The inspector sat, then twisted in his seat. "Tell you the truth, now that it's wrapped up, HF, or Wallflower I guess we should call it now, isn't all that dramatic from a story point of view. As Grey says, who cares about some nutty, bald girl who killed people because she was hung up on her shrink? But he feels there could be a very strong story if we structured the whole thing around you. Put you right in the center of it. Your character arc could make it work."

"Character arc?"

"You know what I mean."

"No," said Janek, "I don't think I do."

"The way you change as the case develops. You go in one sort of guy and come out another."

Janek was quiet. He didn't like the sound of that. It was too close to the truth. The notion of having his soul exposed to millions of people filled him with a special kind of dread.

Sullivan was still pitching. "Try this. Cynical world-weary NYPD detective gets personally involved when his goddaughter's murdered. Grief-stricken, he goes after

the killer with a vengeance, cuts through all the bureau-
cratic horseshit, finds the murderess, and shoots her
dead. I mean, that's a real *story,* one a network will
buy.''

Janek looked at Sullivan sharply. "For me it wasn't a
story, Harry. It was a murder case just like all the
others.''

"Yeah, sure, I know you say that. But—"

"Forget it.''

Sullivan lowered his head. When he spoke again, his
tone was meek. "I hope you'll reconsider, Frank. Maybe
later, when you're feeling your old self again . . .''

Janek waited until Sullivan raised his head and then
met his eyes straight on. "Don't hope for that, Harry. It's
not going to happen.''

At first when he looked at the crayons Monika bought
him, thirty pristine pastel crayons neatly organized by
color in an elegant compartmentalized wooden box, he
felt loath to touch them lest he violate their perfect order.
But after he sat down on the chaise, propped the large
spiral-bound pad of paper against his knees, and ran his
fingers across the surface of a sheet, it seemed to cry out
for color.

His first sketches were tentative and sloppy. But still
there was a satisfaction in using his hands to try to
reproduce the purity of the terrace view. And the longer
he drew, the more he enjoyed it. It was a technique
worthy of being mastered. He thought of the combination
of intensity and patience exhibited by his father when he
sat at his bench working on broken accordions in the
little repair shop he'd operated on Carmine Street.
Perhaps, he thought, *if I imitate the way Dad used to*

squint at the exposed insides of old accordions, I'll manage to get the swing of it.

Monika, careful not to disturb him, busied herself inside the house, preparing food she'd bought in town. Then she went out to swim and jog along the beach. When she returned two hours later, he showed her his latest sketch of the view. The sea and sky, divided horizontally by the horizon, were a simple study in blues. She liked it, and so did he.

"I'm pleased," she said. "You're enjoying yourself."

"Yeah, I am," he admitted.

She kissed his shoulder and went back inside the house. At midday she brought out a tray of tortillas, guacamole, and beer. They ate and laughed, then retired to their bedroom to make love and then to nap.

At three, well oiled with sunscreen, he returned to the terrace for another round of drawing. But this time, instead of portraying the view, he tried to sketch his dream.

He tore off several sheets before he was satisfied with the general design. When he finally felt he'd gotten it right, he began to fill it in.

"It really does look like a nightmare," Monika said when she came out onto the terrace with her book.

Janek stopped drawing. "I don't have the hand for this."

"No one expects you to draw like an artist, Frank. Just try to make it schematic."

"This is pretty much it," he said. He pointed to a small table set before the portrait. "I think the objects were here."

"Well, that's something, isn't it?"

"What do you mean?"

"You never mentioned a table before."

Janek nodded. She was right; he hadn't mentioned it because he hadn't remembered it.

"Well, they had to be set out on something, didn't they?"

Monika smiled. "Keep drawing, Frank. Sooner or later you'll work it out."

By the end of the afternoon he had not resolved the objects in terms of their shapes, but he had positioned them, indicated by X's, in a straight line on the table.

He showed the sketch to Monika. She studied it. "The arrangement's strange," she said. "Maybe that's important."

"What do you mean?"

She shook her head. "The way everything is lined up, the table, the painting, the niche. It's hieratic, almost like the aspe of a church. The table could be the altar. And the objects—"

He leaned toward her. "Yes?"

"They're equally spaced, symmetrically set out. Almost like relics. Or offerings . . ."

"Offerings to the portrait?"

She thought about that. "Perhaps. But I think it goes deeper. Suppose, instead of the portrait, there was something else in that niche, a sculpture or a painting of Christ on the cross. You wouldn't say the gold chalices on the altar were offerings to the painting. You'd say they were offerings to Jesus or God."

Janek sat up. "That's it!" he said. "What I saw were offerings to the woman in the picture."

"Who is she?"

"Beverly told Aaron it was a portrait of her mother, who died a few years ago." He paused, then pointed to the table in the sketch. "I don't think there was a table here. I think I saw something else. Something like a table, but with a different shape beneath. I'll try and draw it."

He turned over a page of his pad, then started feverishly to draw. She stood behind him as he tried out a shape, crossed it out, tried another and still another.

"In the police photos there wasn't anything beneath the picture. Aaron thinks it took him about two minutes to reach me after he heard my shot. Beverly got to the bedroom just after I fell. If there was something there, she'd have had time to move it."

He drew an oval, then drew a rectangle over it.

"If she moved it, it couldn't have been very big," Monika said.

"I think it was big. But maybe it was lighter than it looked."

"Where could she have hidden it?"

He shrugged, drew a bookcase, then redrew it so its bottom half stuck out. "It could have been portable, on wheels, or something like a card table that folds up." He drew an angry slash across the page. "Shit, I don't know!"

Monika, behind him, massaged his shoulders. "Let it go for now, Frank. You've done enough today."

"It's so maddening. I can almost see it. But not quite."

"Of course, it's maddening. Like forgetting some-one's name even when you can see his face."

"Exactly!"

"What do you do when that happens?"

"Rack my brains till I come up with his name."

"If that doesn't work?"

"I forget about it awhile."

"Then?"

"It usually comes to me later when I'm thinking about something else or doing something strange like eating peas."

"When you're *consciously* thinking about something else. Meantime, the subconscious part of your brain is processing the problem. You can let the same thing happen here, let your subconscious take over and do the work. Eventually the solution will come, probably sometime tonight."

"Then what?"

"Then on to the next problem. You see, the wonderful thing about drawing an encrypted dream is that it gives you a chance to break down a big riddle into smaller and more manageable parts. What you want to do is get the table right, then go on to the objects."

He gazed at her. "Anyone ever tell you you're terrific?"

"Oh, all the time," she said. "My patients are always telling me that."

"You're kidding!"

She smiled. "Shrinks are used to hearing endearments. But when I hear them from you, Frank, I know they're real."

That night they ate dinner in the house, then drove down to the village to walk. A Mexican boy with gleaming teeth approached them on the street. He showed them a tray of handmade silver jewelry. When Monika showed interest in a pair of earrings, Janek bought them for her. The boy held out a cracked piece of mirror so she could look at herself as she put them on.

Later they stopped outside a modest bar that fronted on the beach. There was a light breeze that made the palms sway and churned up the smooth surface of the Gulf. Someone was playing a piano inside. "Looks like a decent saloon," Janek said.

The place was half filled. The high season wouldn't begin until Christmas. Janek and Monika took a table between the bar and the pianist, a young black woman with a red scarf tied around her head. She was playing the kind of restful dinner music that doesn't require much attention.

Janek grinned. "I'm glad we could have this week together." He paused. "Do you really have to fly home on Christmas?"

"I wish I didn't," she said. "But I have patients waiting and an early class the following day."

He looked at her. "I usually spend my holidays alone."

She leaned across the table and kissed him. "Not this year."

When the waiter brought their margaritas, Monika asked him in Spanish about the pianist. The waiter said she was a gringo. "But a nice one," he added.

Janek turned to look at the piano.

"I wonder . . ."

"What?"

"That table I drew, the table that wasn't a table—I wonder if it could have been a piano." He took a sip from his drink. "I don't see how it could have been. A piano's much too big. Hard to hide a piano even if it's on wheels." He took another sip. "Still, it had that piano shape, like a little upright, you know, with the objects arranged on the top just below the bottom edge of the painting.''

He summoned the waiter, borrowed a ballpoint, made a quick sketch on his cocktail napkin. He turned it so Monika could see. ''Something like that,'' he said.

She stared at the sketch. ''Didn't you tell me the portrait seemed bigger in the dream than in Aaron's photographs?'' Janek nodded. ''We know the portrait didn't change. It's the same one you saw. But suppose there was a piece of furniture just under it, something that because of its scale made the picture seem bigger than it was.''

Janek nodded. ''Take that piece of furniture away, and the portrait would appear smaller. It's still life-size, but in the dream it looms over everything.'' He thought a moment. ''Suppose it wasn't a real piano. Suppose it was a miniature or a model. That would be enough to confuse the scale, at least at a quick glance. And if it was a miniature piano, she could have hidden it.''

''Hidden the relics, too, dispersed them around the room.''

''Yes . . . the relics.'' Janek finished off his drink. ''I like that word. Relics offered up to the image of her mother in the little chapel she constructed in her bedroom niche. Consecrated relics, you could say, or sanctified ones. Perhaps more than relics. Perhaps trophies, trophies of acts committed in her mother's honor. Mementos of sacrifices. Tributes offered in thanks or to appease.'' He looked at Monika, nodded. ''You were right this afternoon when you used the word 'hieratic.' That bedroom was a fucking shrine.''

That night he didn't dream about the whole room, only about the portrait. In his dream the woman's face came alive, her eyes blinked open, and her mouth opened and shut mechanically like a doll's. He woke up drenched in sweat.

In the morning he gulped his coffee, then hurried out to the terrace to draw. He sketched the painting and an underscale piano beneath it and then made X's on the piano's top. How many trophies had there been? He drew various quantities. When that didn't work, he took another approach. There had been seventeen Wallflower killings in all. He drew seventeen X's on top of the piano. Too crowded. But there had been only seven victim clusters. When he drew seven X's, the design looked right.

He turned the page, started to draw on another sheet. He drew basic geometric shapes: cubes; boxes; cylinders; spheres. Then he started to put them together. The work possessed him. Soon he forgot where he was. He tried various combinations of shapes, filling a dozen sheets by noon. Then, exhausted, he pushed back the pad and tried to look at his sketches objectively.

He believed he had successfully rendered three of the relics, or trophies as he thought of them now. One was a small book, another a large book, and the third a piece of paper with printing on it. Assigning them to the first, third, and fourth positions, he drew them into his master drawing, replacing the first, third, and fourth X's on top of the piano. Examining his master drawing again, he was pleased. The three trophies looked right, in their correct positions, too. He put down his pad and sat back exhausted. He had worked five hours straight.

That afternoon, after making love, he and Monika followed steps, cut from stone outcroppings, straight down from their little house to the beach. It was only when he was in the water and tasted its saltiness that he realized his eyes hadn't teared up in the twenty-four hours since he'd started working with the crayons.

At the end of the afternoon, back on their terrace, relaxing with margaritas in their hands, he showed Monika what he'd accomplished in the morning.

"Two books and a piece of paper. All rectangular and more or less flat," she commented. "You're doing fine, Frank, going about it methodically, working from abstract shapes. So far so good. But if you get stuck, you might want to give up control of your crayon, let it loose on the paper. It's a method I sometimes use to get patients to free-associate. You'd be amazed at the powerful material that spews out. Of course, if you do let yourself go, doodle or draw at random, it won't be the crayon that's guiding your hand; it'll be your subconscious."

They drove down to Cozumel for dinner, choosing the same quiet fish joint they'd enjoyed their first night on the island. As they ate, Monika asked him what bothered him most about Kit and Aaron's explanation of the Wallflower crimes.

"Too neat," he said. "Real life isn't like that. Real life, as you know, is very complicated, with all sorts of twists and turns, trails that split off and dead-end or tail back. But this Diana Proctor story comes out slick, almost like a novel. Whenever I see a structure like that, I ask myself, 'Who's the writer here?' "

"Why do you call it slick?"

"First, the way it was revealed. Right after the shoot-out, Aaron goes down to the basement. There he finds this incredibly complete paper trail in almost perfect secretarial order that accounts for each and every ice pick and Wallflower homicide. Diana flies into Seattle; the ticket stubs are there. She rents a car at the airport, returns it the following morning; the receipt is neatly stapled to the ticket stubs. Aaron asks the Seattle cops to check the mileage between the airport and Cynthia Morse's condominium; the answer that comes back is exactly half the distance that shows up on Diana's car rental slip. That's the kind of perfection you don't usually find in real life."

"She was a librarian. Librarians are organized."

"Sure, but this is better than organized. Every time she went out she knew exactly where to go, never got lost, never made a slip. A killer working on her own, even a highly organized one, can't be that precise. But if she was working with someone else, war-gaming her missions, then such superb execution might be possible."

"So it's the perfection that bothers you?"

"And all the papers that back it up."

"But Beverly couldn't know you'd go into her house and fight it out with Diana."

"Of course not. And she also couldn't know how it would end up if we did. I could have injured Diana, in which case she'd have been available for questioning, and then Beverly's role, if she played one, would probably have come out."

"What are you saying, Frank?"

"That Beverly might have been planning to get rid of Diana, leaving the whole neat paper trail so we'd pin everything on the girl. By a fluke I got to Diana first. But that's speculation. There're other things that bother me, too."

"What?"

"Why did Diana shave her head and body and go around in a wig? We're supposed to believe she was some sort of austere self-styled Ninja. It's possible. But maybe there's another explanation. Maybe the shaving was part of a system of control."

"Beverly's control?"

He nodded. "Then there're the victims. I've got a whole lot of problems with them. We can account for the homeless man, and we know Diana had some sort of relationship with Jess. But what about the three victim clusters connected to Beverly Archer? If Diana was operating on her own, how did she come up with those particular people? Did she choose them at random from the hundreds of names she found in Beverly's papers, or was there a reason she chose those particular three? Then you have to ask yourself how Beverly could have been so blind to what Diana was doing. Sullivan's people came up with a couple of cases where a serial killer committed murders while in treatment with a shrink. But this is different. Beverly was an experienced therapist who knew her patient very well. She'd been treating the girl for six years straight, had her living in her basement, was seeing her four times a week. You're a psychiatrist, Monika. Can you imagine being that familiar with a patient without sensing something bad was going on?"

Monika thought about it. "Patients can be very deceptive. But you're right—it's extremely difficult to imagine that. I also wonder how someone as young as Diana could become so expert at subterfuge."

"That's why I think Beverly was a collaborator, even the brains behind the whole series. The problem, of course, is to prove it. To do that, I have to know why, what she was up to, what her game was all about."

"What do you think it was about?"

"You read Beverly's paper on shaming incidents. She seemed to specialize in patients traumatized by shaming events in their pasts. Doesn't an obsession like that usually come from within?"

"It can, certainly. Shrinks who concentrate on homosexuals often are homosexual. Shrinks who specialize in sadomasochism tend to be haunted by that type of fantasy."

"Well, suppose Beverly was as traumatized by shaming incidents as any of her patients? Suppose, to rid herself of her obsession, she decided that the people who had humiliated her should be killed? Suppose she recruited Diana in Carlisle, created a dependency, then arranged for the girl's release so she could send her out on missions of revenge? The targets would be her old tormentors, even as far back as her childhood."

"I thought Aaron said Beverly hadn't been in favor of Diana's release."

Janek nodded. "There's another thing that's slick. It's like it was all a setup from the start. Beverly carefully laid down a paper trail at the hospital that would throw police suspicions off, then laid down a second paper trail in Diana's room in the basement that would cinch the story the girl was acting on her own."

"You're talking about something extremely fiendish, a conspiracy that goes back years."

"Yeah." He grinned. "And now there's another character. The mother in the portrait, the one behind the piano altar, who gets trophies offered up to her of the people Beverly had Diana kill."

Early the next morning, a Sunday, Janek hurried out to the terrace to draw. When his abstract geometric shapes didn't join into anything recognizable, he changed his approach and, employing Monika's method, freed his crayon from conscious control and let it loose upon the paper.

At first he scribbled numerous spirals. When Monika looked in on him, she muttered something about double helixes and human chromosomes.

He played with vertical spirals, then horizontal ones, then cylinders with spiral decorations. One of the last set looked right, but when he couldn't make it coherent, he turned to Monika for help.

"Which position is this one for?" she asked.

"Number two."

"The second killing?" He nodded. "That was the old schoolteacher in Florida."

"Bertha Parce."

"Did you see pictures of her?"

"About twenty slides."

"Anything strike you?"

"Just that she was a withered old lady living in a crowded single room in some horrible old folks' hotel on South Beach, Miami."

"Was she stabbed in her room?"

He nodded. "She was asleep."

"Anything else strike you?"

"Just the wallflower. I remember the FBI briefing officer pointing it out. It was sort of leaning in the corner of the room."

"Anything else?"

Janek closed his eyes, trying to recall the photographs he'd pinned to his office walls in New York. "There was a lot of junk around, old lady's stuff." He hesitated. "Come to think of it . . ." He began to draw again, this time imposing his will upon the crayon. "I'm on to something. . . ." He continued to draw and in three minutes rendered an object that fitted perfectly in position two. "That's it. Yeah, I'm sure it is." He turned his master sketch so she could see it."

"What is it?" she asked.

"A hair curler. Old Bertha Parce had a whole mess of them on the table beside her bed." He picked up a blue crayon, began to fill the curler in. "The one I saw in Beverly's apartment was made of light blue plastic," he explained.

It took him until the end of the day to render the sixth trophy. The problem, which he only discovered late in the afternoon, was that it consisted of two objects rather than one. And that made sense when he remembered that the fifth victim cluster had consisted of two men, brothers named MacDonald, who shared a weekend house in northwestern Connecticut.

In the end he drew two sticks side by side. But they weren't just ordinary sticks. There was something unique about them, portions that stuck out. Remembering Monika's questions from the morning, he began to ask similar questions of himself. What was in the crime scene pictures? Was there anything he'd seen in them that might resemble sticks?

One of the brothers, he remembered, had been stabbed in his bed. The other, whose palms had borne defensive wounds, had put up a struggle in the bathroom.

Janek left the terrace, went inside the house, phoned Aaron at his home in Brooklyn.

"Hi," he said when Aaron answered. "Good thing I caught you."

Janek asked Aaron if he'd be willing to go into the office, even though it was a Sunday, and take a look at some of the pictures pinned up on their walls.

"Jesus, Frank," Aaron said. "I thought you went down there to rest."

"I am resting," Janek said. "I've been lying out on the terrace with a view of the sea, taking in the rays."

"But you're still thinking about it?"

"Doing more than that. Monika's got me working with crayons."

"Jesus!"

"I want you to look at the Bertha Parce pictures and see if you can tell if any of the hair curlers beside her bed are missing. Then check out the pictures at the MacDonald house. See if you notice anything missing there."

Aaron agreed to drive into Manhattan, check the photographs, and call him back. The call came an hour and a half later.

"Yeah, Frank, there's a box of old lady's hair curlers just like you remembered. But it's partially closed, so I can't tell if the set's complete."

"What about the brothers?"

"I'm standing in front of the shots right now. I don't see anything in the bedroom. It's minimal, neat and clean, not like the old lady's place. But it looks like they shared the bath. I see two of everything—hairbrushes, razors—you know, the kind of stuff guys use."

Something in Aaron's voice told Janek he was holding back.

"You *do* see something, don't you?"

"Jesus, Frank! Even from Mexico you can read my mind."

"What is it?"

"No toothbrushes. Could they be the odd-shaped sticks you're talking about?"

Janek turned to Monika. "Toothbrushes. A pair of toothbrushes, lined up side by side."

"Sounds like you're getting excited," Aaron said.

"I'll be a lot more excited when I get this whole thing figured out."

"Still think Beverly was behind it?"

"I *know* she was. We're going to prove it, too."

He asked Aaron to spend the next few days working on the two non-Archer-connected victim clusters, the Wexler family in Texas and the Scottos in Providence. Aaron was to check by phone with people who knew them—survivors, friends, colleagues at work. And he was to be sure to inquire about both husbands and wives since they didn't know which family members were the intended targets.

"What am I inquiring about?" Aaron asked.

"What do you think?"

"A Beverly Archer connection."

"Of course, because if you find one, we'll know she lied to you. If she *did* know those people, just one member in each family, that's enough to go to Kit for authorization to reopen the case."

"What authorization do I have to do this?"

"You're wrapping up loose ends."

"Maybe I should check out Diana, too, see if there's a connection to her."

"Sure, go ahead," Janek said casually. "But you won't find anything. Beverly's the one."

* * *

The next morning he drew and drew but couldn't get anywhere with trophy number five. One thing he knew: It wasn't a simple shape like a toothbrush, a hair curler, or a book. It was an elaborate object, larger than the others, something with parts that stuck out all over.

"Some of the parts are like the hair curler," he told Monika as they climbed down to the beach. "It's got wheels and a handle. It's mostly metal, but I think the handle's made of wood. I even think there're gears on it." He paused. "What the hell could it be?"

They made an encampment at the bottom of the rocks. She spread her beach towel on the sand, then lay down on her back. "If it's got moving parts, it must be some kind of machine," she said.

"Yeah . . ." He looked at her. She was wearing a brilliant white bikini that contrasted with her lightly tanned skin. "Pretend for a moment you're Diana Proctor. You've been sent up to Providence to kill a person and bring back a trophy of your kill. What kind of trophy are you going to take?"

Monika raised her head. "I won't know what I'm going to take until I see it. It'll be a spontaneous decision."

Janek lay back and stared up at the sky. "Whatever it is, you're bringing it back to Beverly to put up on the piano altar for Mama. Won't you make a point of bringing back something you know will please your shrink? It can't be valuable. It can't be something that will be missed. And it certainly can't be an object that can be traced back to the people you've just killed. It's always something humble, like a hair curler, or a couple of toothbrushes, a piece of paper, a book. Something the victims have touched. Something almost . . . intimate, don't you think?'' He turned to look at Monika. She was gazing past him. ''Forgive me,'' he said, ''I'm thinking out loud. I know it's tiresome. I'm sorry to go on and on.''

She stood. ''It's okay, Frank. You told me you were a worrier.'' She looked out at the water. ''I'm going to swim. Want to come?''

He shook his head. ''I'll just lie here and worry.''

She smiled, then started for the water. He watched as she ran across the beach, then high-stepped into the waves. When she was out far enough, she turned, threw him a kiss, and plunged. He watched her swim for a while, then lay back, closed his eyes, and tried to free his mind of the fifth trophy for a while.

Think about something else, he told himself. *Or better yet, don't think about anything at all. Just lie here and feel the sun. Breathe in the mellow aroma of the sea. Let the sweet winds of this tropical paradise caress your tough old urban hide.*

He must have drifted off. The next thing he knew droplets of water were dancing on his chest. He opened his eyes. Monika was leaning over him, vigorously drying her hair.

''Good swim?''

''Terrific.'' She spread out her towel. ''I was bobbing around out there, trying to think what's made of metal, has wheels and gears and a wooden handle, and has parts that look like hair curlers. I came up with something.'' She lay down. ''It's what you call a real long shot.''

He leaned toward her eagerly. ''What've you got?''

She grinned. ''How does an old-fashioned eggbeater grab you?''

* * *

A piece of paper with printing for the homeless man. A hair curler for Bertha Parce. A small book, probably a much-read paperback for the Wexler family. An oversize book for Cynthia Morse. A pair of neatly arranged toothbrushes for the MacDonalds. An eggbeater for the Scottos. That left only position seven, the last trophy position, the Jessica Foy position, marked with an *X*.

He couldn't bring himself to try to draw that trophy. He couldn't even bear to think about it. Or did he resist, as Monika suggested, because to render it would make the scene in the bedroom clear and then he would no longer be haunted by his dream?

When he asked her to explain that, she said people often resist giving up a source of pain.

"Imagine how you'd feel without it, Frank? What would it be like *not* to be tormented?"

"I'd love it."

"You think so? I'm not so sure."

"Why wouldn't I love that? I don't understand."

She sat down on his chaise, placed her hand upon his knee. "Physically you're fine. Your body's mended. But your mind is wounded still. Like anybody who's spent years living dangerously, you've become addicted to stress. If you saw the seventh trophy, the puzzle would be solved and the stress would be relieved." She spoke kindly. "Maybe you're not yet ready for that. I think maybe you need to suffer awhile longer. Don't you?"

He stared down at the water, then slowly turned back to her. His eyes, she saw, were filled with tears.

They had leased the house for five days, intending to spend their last two on the mainland in Yucatán, where

Monika wanted to visit some of the great Mayan ruins.
So on the fifth day they flew from the Isla de Cozumel
to Mérida, where they checked into a low all-white
Moorish-style hotel set amidst a tranquil park of pools,
flowering jacarandas, and palms.

The next morning they rented a car and went exploring. They had prepared for this visit by reading about the
Mayans, enough so that they would know the purposes of
the structures and the basic meaning of the art that they
would see. But they were far less interested in archaeol-
ogy than in viscerally experiencing the sites.

On the weed-choked field before the great pyramid at
Chichén Itzá, Monika admitted to being deeply intrigued
by the ancient Mayan cult of cruelty. Janek was attentive
as she spoke. She made a stunning figure, he thought,
dressed in white cotton slacks and a white polo shirt, her
old Leica hanging casually from her shoulder, her face
framed by the silver earrings he had bought for her in
Cozumel.

"Human sacrifices," she said, "priests in bejeweled
robes excising hearts from naked living persons on a
high altar before multitudes of witnesses—it was an
atavistic culture, Frank, obsessed by astrology, magical
beasts, worship of the sun, sacrifices to gods who demanded blood." She paused. "In my profession we
speak of the subconscious as if it were a kind of jungle
like the one around us here. Dark, dank, overgrown,
filled with snakes, reptiles, and other threatening creatures, a place where the most elemental drives, to
dominate, rape, avenge, and kill, thrive without constraint. Well, here we have a place cut out of such a
jungle where ancient men created a great civilization.
And what did they do? They didn't suppress their animal

drives. Rather, they organized them, turned them into a religion of cosmic symbols and dramatic ceremonies." She paused again. "Perhaps they were a little like the Venetians in that regard. Remember their carnival costumes and winged horses and the churches everywhere we turned?"

He loved listening to her. She was the most brilliant woman he'd ever been involved with. And the things she said found a responsive chord. He believed she was right, that there was as much cruelty in the masterpiece that was Venice as in the ancient capital of Mayan culture. A different kind of cruelty perhaps, more refined, less direct, but in the end nearly as ruthless and as bloody.

He borrowed her camera, took a picture of her. Looking through the lens, he saw a beautiful woman poised against sunstruck stone ruins with dense green jungle foliage behind. Perhaps, he kidded her, she might want to use his picture to represent herself on the back of her next book.

"You know," he said, "the gorgeous and brainy German shrink visiting the cradle of high barbarism in Central America."

Later, as they explored the site, strode along its walls, among its steles, gazing at the sculptures incised into the stones—grotesque human figures in elaborate headdresses, mouths grimacing, eyes bulging, frozen in postures that suggested the commission of violent acts—Janek asked Monika if these images were not expressions of the evil that had always fascinated him and that, he so often claimed, he struggled in his work to comprehend.

The answer she gave surprised him a little bit: "Perhaps it isn't merely the mystery of evil that intrigues you,

Frank. Perhaps it's something bigger, the mystery of the human mind.''

"I think you know what the seventh trophy is," she told him that evening.

They were back in Mérida, sipping tequila by the hotel pool beside an open thatch-roofed garden bar. Janek looked around. There were two other couples and a black-haired Mexican bartender with Indian features gazing at the setting sun. On the tables were tiny hurricane lamps. The candles flickered in the dying light.

"If I know what it is, I sure can't see it now," he said. "What makes you think I know?"

"The trophy taken from Jess should be the easiest one for you to figure out."

"Because she was jogging?" Monika nodded. "She had a watch and the keys to her room on a leather thong around her neck. She was wearing a Walkman. All those things were found." He heard his voice break. It still disturbed him to talk about Jess this way, as a homicide victim instead of a person he had loved. "What else could she have been carrying?"

Monika shook her head. Her expression was compassionate. "I think you know," she said quietly.

Later in their room, as they lay naked together on their bed while the ceiling fan revolved slowly overhead, he broached the subject again.

"You think you know what it is, don't you?"

She looked at him. "I could venture a guess."

"But you won't tell me?" She shook her head. "Why not?"

"It's better for you to tell me, Frank," she said in a whisper.

In the morning he was angry. He spoke harshly while they dressed.

"I'm not in therapy. This isn't about me. It's a fucking murder case. Why won't you help?"

She turned to him. She spoke calmly. She was buckling her belt. "Why must I tell you what you already know?"

"Damn it, Monika! Don't speak to me in riddles!"

She stood still and faced him. Her eyes were sad. "Of course this is about you, Frank," she said gently. "It's your dream, your vision. Why don't you just close your eyes and look inside yourself? It's there. All you have to do is look."

After breakfast they went out to the hotel pool for an early swim. He watched her as she breaststroked back and forth. *Who am I kidding?* he asked himself. *I loved Jess. I ought to know what Diana took from her.* But what was missing? He couldn't think of anything. What would Jess carry when she went out jogging? *Maybe there was no seventh trophy,* he thought.

It came to him on the plane that afternoon, shortly after they had taken off for New York. They were crossing the Gulf of Mexico, still and green below. He peered out the window, and then he saw it in the pattern of the reefs.

He turned to Monika beside him. "It was a knife."

She nodded. "I think so, too."

"That switchblade she bought at the knife show, the

one Fran Dunning said had an ivory handle. I'm sure that's what I saw."

She squeezed his hand. "Feel better now?"

He leaned toward her, kissed her. "Thanks. You were right, I must have known what it was. Why did I fight it?"

"I think it hurt you to see her knife sitting there. Your hurt blinded you, and then you couldn't see the other trophies either."

"But why did it hurt so much?"

"Because it was hers. And possibly because of something else. If she was carrying a knife, she could have put up a fight. But she didn't get a chance. She was attacked from behind. The thought of that still makes you furious. Your fury may have blinded you as well."

It was a dazzling New York that greeted them, cold but brilliant, a city of sparkling granite and shimmering glass. As they taxied into Manhattan, Janek was struck by the difference between this arrival and his arrival from Venice eight weeks before. That day he and Aaron had driven though a damp and noxious fog that matched the sorrow and confusion in his soul. Today, with Monika, the air was clear. And now, too, he knew what he was up against.

They settled into Janek's apartment, then at dusk went out to walk. Upper Broadway was filled with Christmas shoppers. On Fifth Avenue all the stores were jammed. Santas with scraggly beards stood on corners rattling pails. At Rockfeller Center skaters glided across the ice, while above the golden statue of Prometheus, Christmas lights blazed upon an enormous spruce.

They ate in a little Czech restaurant on West Twelfth

Street. The owner, who had known Janek's father, embraced him when they walked in. After dinner they strolled through Greenwich Village. There were crowds of young people out on the streets, many walking briskly on their way to parties while others, grasping bags choked with gifts, attempted to flag down cabs. Foursomes stood on corners making jokes, waiting for traffic lights to change. A drunken old man, in a tweed suit and bow tie, stumbled past them mouthing the lyrics to "Hark! The Herald Angels Sing."

"I love this energy," Monika said. "New York's a fascinating town."

"It's no Venice, but it takes a bum rap," Janek said. "It's a cruel place, but it can be wonderful, too."

She nodded. "I've often wondered what it would be like to live here. I've been offered a visiting professorship of psychiatry. Last month the Albert Einstein College of Medicine approached me again. Perhaps I should accept, move here for a year." She looked at him. "A year of living dangerously."

"We could get to know each other pretty well over a year," he said.

She smiled, took his arm. "I wish I didn't have to go back so soon. But sadly I do."

Later that night, at his apartment, he asked if she'd be willing to take a look at Beverly Archer.

"Just to observe her," he said. "She'll never know."

Monika thought about it, then agreed. "I'm not a forensic psychiatrist. I doubt I'll see anything. But I confess—I'm very curious."

Janek phoned Aaron, asked if he could set it up. Aaron thought he could. Beverly's schedule was so rigid, he said, there shouldn't be any difficulty arranging a covert surveillance. They'd park on Second Avenue down the block from her house and wait for her to come out after her last appointment. When she started on her round of errands, Monika could follow her and observe.

The plan worked. At exactly six fifty-five the following evening Beverly appeared. When she went into a dry cleaning shop, Monika got out of the car and followed. Sitting with Aaron, waiting for her to return, Janek started feeling nervous.

"This reminds me of one very bad night."

Aaron reassured him. "I know it's spooky, Frank, but your girl's terrific. Don't worry. Beverly's met her match."

When Monika returned, she was shivering. Janek took her hands, rubbed them to restore warmth. She seemed disturbed. "Let's go get something to drink," she said.

Aaron drove down Second to a cop hangout near East Seventy-first. The place was filled, cops full of holiday bluster toasting one another with mugs of beer. Janek and Aaron nodded to acquaintances; then the three of them squeezed into a booth.

"A strange woman," Monika reported after the waiter had brought her tea. "A lot of people in my field are. The profession's always attracted troubled individuals. They often make gifted therapists."

"So she's just another weirdo shrink, is that what you're saying?" Aaron asked.

Monika shook her head. "More than that. She functions, of course, very well from what you've told me. But I felt I was observing an extremely high-strung person, very tense, very tightly controlled. The way she moves, dresses, smiles at the sales clerks, tilts her head, tightens up her lips—it's as if there's a NO CONTACT! DON'T TOUCH ME! sign hanging on her back. Still, for all her smiles I could feel the rage coming off her. Sexual rage, too. She truly hates males. It shows every time she deals with one.''

Aaron glanced at Janek. "Could she have done what Frank says?"

"Sent the girl out to kill her old enemies? I can't tell that from looking at her. But in theory, yes, it's possible."

"But by using a surrogate killer," Janek asked, "didn't she give up the pleasures of killing the old enemies herself?"

"Not necessarily. The pleasures might have been even greater for her. She'd have the satisfaction of knowing she had done them in fiendishly, and I think it would have been very exciting for her to hear Diana describe the glue mutilations, too. That would have been the best part of it, perhaps the only erotic excitement she's capable of having."

Monika went on to analyze the paradox in a person such as Beverly, who, though ostensibly asexual, could still take an intense sexual interest in her victims.

"The brain is more flexible than people think," she explained. "It can do a kind of somersault. What seems disgusting can suddenly become appetizing; what's repulsive can suddenly become erotic. In a flash a person can become addicted to the very thing he or she previously hated. It's a way to survive in the world, to turn pain into pleasure, to take the worst, most painful scenarios of one's childhood and, by controlling them, rewrite the script so that in the new final act there is victory rather than defeat.''

"Beverly's victories are the executions, right? Executions of the people who humiliated her in the past?''

"Again, we're talking theory, Frank. After only fifteen minutes of observation I can't tell you this woman did what you think. But yes, she *could* have done it, and if she did, I don't think her victories would have been just the executions. To me the neuterings are far more important. Killing an old enemy is one thing. Doing something to his body is quite another. Attacking the genitals, the seat of your enemy's sexuality, is the ultimate revenge. To have another person do it for you and then describe it is a way of distancing yourself while still enjoying your old tormentor's degradation. It's like hearing about something bad that has befallen a rival. You didn't do it, you didn't dirty your hands, but you have the satisfaction of knowing that the person has been dealt a devastating blow. We have a special word for that in German. *Schadenfreude*. It means taking joy in another's pain. If you're right, I think *Schadenfreude* may be what Beverly Archer is all about.''

"Okay," said Aaron. "That makes sense. But could she have gotten Diana to kill and glue all those people? We know the girl killed her mother, grandmother, and sister. But except for Jess, the others all seem to have been perfect strangers.''

"It's not that difficult for one person to gain control over another's mind," Monika said. "Behavioral methods, hypnosis, rote training, rewards and punishments, plain old-fashioned domination—there are many ways. The basic method is simple: get someone dependent and susceptible in your power; then circumscribe her world

so that your commands have the power of laws. You see
it all the time in cults, prisons, terrorist groups, patho-
logical personal relationships. In Nazi Germany you saw
it on the extraordinary scale of an entire nation. There's
a part in all of us that responds to force and craves to be
controlled. We want to be led, commanded, told what to
do. If it weren't for that particular trait, human society
probably wouldn't work. But what is extremely difficult
is to force someone to perform an act completely
contrary to his moral nature. Here, however, you have a
girl, still young and malleable, who had not only killed
people before but afterwards attacked their sexual organs. The distance from ax to ice pick, from chopping at
genitals to imprisoning them with glue, is not all that
great. So, to answer your question, yes, everything Frank
has theorized is absolutely possible. But whether it
happened or not . . . I'm not the one to say.''

Late in the afternoon on Christmas Eve, Janek went
down to Police Plaza to see Kit Kopta. This time the
crusty red-haired sergeant who ran her office greeted him
with warmth.

"How's the shoulder, Detective? The throat?" And
before Janek could answer: "That was one close call.
Too bad you had to wax the girl. Luck of the draw, I
guess. Anyway, Merry Christmas!"

Kit rose when he came in. "You look grand, Frank. I
don't think I've ever seen you with a tan."

"Well, it was a great trip."

She smiled. "I can just imagine the two of you
snuggling on some Mexican beach. What I'd give for a
little vacation."

"Why don't you take one? God knows you deserve it."

She laughed. "Sure. Check into a Club Med. Have a three-day affair with a gorgeous Nordic ice god, the kind with a stomach so hard you can use it for a washboard. Make an ass out of myself trying to stuff my body into a bikini. Hang out at the bar, pay for drinks with little doodads off my necklace, and wish to hell I was back here in good old tit-freezing New York, where at least I don't have to act jolly or pretend I'm having a good time."

Janek shook his head. "Are you always like this on Christmas Eve?"

"It's not as if I had a nice husband to go home to." She smiled. "I'll probably end the evening curling up with a bottle. But I'm not bitter. Maybe a little ironic, that's all." She sat down behind her desk, turned serious. "Now what's all this about you wanting to reopen the case?"

It took Janek twenty minutes to lay out his theory of the Wallflower crimes. Kit didn't interrupt him or nod encouragement; she just gazed steadily into his eyes. When he finally finished, she asked him what exactly he wanted her to authorize.

"An investigation."

"What sort of investigation?"

He squinted at her. Her tone seemed hard. "What's the matter? My theory too farfetched?"

She stood, walked over to the window, stared down at Police Plaza. "Sure, it's farfetched. You know it is. But so is the theory you were too smart to swallow, the one Sullivan and his people seem to have bought whole hog."

"So what's the problem?"

She turned to face him. Her thick black hair framed her little face. "The problem is if you hadn't nearly gotten killed that night, I'd have put IA on your ass."

"What're you talking about?"

She glared at him. "You and Aaron and your phony story that you just happened to be watching when this burglar let himself into Archer's house—do you really think I bought that crap? Don't insult me, please!"

Janek stared at the rug. He'd made a point of forgetting that extralegal maneuver. Now, reminded of it, he felt ashamed.

"It was a look-and-see operation, wasn't it?" she continued. "Not the most subtle one I ever heard about either. I figure the black kid was Aaron's snitch from the time he worked Safes and Lofts."

Janek spread his arms. "It was my idea. It was wrong. I'm sorry I did it."

"Still, it worked for you. Got you inside, got you a quick look at some stuff, and now you've built a pretty theory around it. Fine. Maybe you're right. Maybe this Beverly Archer is the evil, manipulative murderess you say. Anything's possible, Frank. But you'll never get her for it, not if you're going to carry on like that."

"I'm not going to carry on like that. I won't do anything like that again."

She looked at him, rolled her eyes, and returned to her desk.

They spent the next ten minutes bargaining. He wanted to go to Providence and send Aaron out to Texas to look for Archer connections among the two "unconnected" families. Then he wanted another three weeks of travel for them both to try to discover what incidents may have occurred between Beverly and Bertha Parce, Cynthia Morse, and the MacDonalds. Then he wanted at least ten days in Cleveland, digging out everything there was to be found on the woman. Plus whatever additional travel and per diems might be necessary depending on the information all these interviews produced.

Kit stared at him, her large brown eyes sparkling beneath her Grecian brows.

"Basically you're asking for unlimited backing on a theory neither of us has the nerve to broach to the FBI."

"You always said my instincts were good, Kit. Here's a chance to back me up."

"Sure, back you up. Then you get impatient and pull another Leo Titus because your goddaughter was a victim. No thanks, Frank. Forget it."

"I gave you my word. Want me to give it to you in writing?"

She laughed. "Then I'd really have to fire you, wouldn't I? Your written promise would be a confession you broke your oath."

"Shit!" He stood up, angry. "She did it. I know she did. I'm going to nail her, Kit, no matter how long it takes."

Kit studied him. When she spoke again, he could tell by her tone that she'd made a decision.

"Even if you're right, and you just might be, it's the toughest kind of case to make. Suppose you prove Archer was totally fucked over by every single person Diana Proctor killed? So what? You're talking mind murders, Frank. You've got no witnesses, no one you can turn. Diana, your coconspirator, is already dead. It's a dead-end case. You know it is."

Janek tried to interrupt, but Kit motioned him to keep quiet until she was finished.

"I'm telling you the facts of life. No D.A. will take on a case like that unless you bring him a full confession. How the hell are you going get one? I talked to the woman myself. She's a stone-cold hard-ass. She knows she's out of it; she knows there's no evidence. If you're right and she was behind it, then one of the main reasons she operated the way she did was to insulate herself from a criminal prosecution. So now, tell me, why should she confess?"

He shook his head. "I don't know yet. But she will."

"Going to *make* her, Frank? Going to beat it out of her?"

"Of course not."

"Then how?"

"Underneath the smile she's totally crazed. A crazy person can be broken."

"And you're the man to break her, right?"

"I'll sure give it my best shot," he snapped.

Kit grinned. "Fine. That's fine. I'll go along with that. But unlimited backing . . ." She shook her head. "Between you and Aaron I'll give you three weeks' worth of travel. Split it up any way you like. Plus you can keep your office till the end of January. After that bring me what you've got and we'll reevaluate the case together. But you better bring me something good. Otherwise both of you are going to be reassigned."

It wasn't what he wanted, but he knew it was all he was going to get. After he accepted her offer, she escorted him to the door. Just before she opened it, she lightly touched the scar tissue on his throat.

"I would have been very sorry if something had happened to you, my friend."

He turned to her, kissed her cheek. "You talk tough, Kit, but you're still a pussycat."

She smiled. "I'm glad you found someone, Frank. I liked what I saw of her, especially the way she shot over here when we called to tell her you'd been cut." She stood before him, took hold of both his hands, stared up into his face. "Listen to me. Don't poison the fruit," she warned quietly. "If Archer did it, I want you to nail her. But with a straight nail. Hear me, Frank? Make damn sure that nail goes in her straight. . . ."

When he left Police Plaza, the sky was dark, but the city seemed strangely void of rancor. *It's the holidays,* he thought. But then he remembered: Christmas was the season when New Yorkers turned their rage against themselves. It was the season of suicides.

He found a liquor store open on Nassau Street, went in, bought a chilled bottle of champagne, carried it home on the subway in a paper bag. Monika was waiting for him. They drank it out of the goblet she'd given him in Venice. The wine tasted very good, they agreed. If anything the ancient glass enhanced it.

He told her about his interview with Kit, the deal they'd made, the pressure he was under now to develop sufficient proof to keep his investigation alive.

"I'm not going to be able to do the kind of deep background work I like," he said. "That'll take months, and we don't have months. No support team either. Just Aaron and me."

"Then you'll have to focus your search," she said.

He nodded. "Any ideas?"

She thought about it. "The lady in the picture, the mother up there on the wall—I'd look to her first. Look to the past, Frank. Try to reconstruct the family history. The secret is always there. . . ."

Later, after they had made love, they clung to each other in the dark. He was filled with passionate adoration for his stylish, brilliant, nurturing German psychoanalyst.

"I love you," he told her in the middle of the night. "I love you more than anyone I've ever known. Has anyone ever said that to you before, Monika? Has anyone ever loved you so much?"

9
The Gauntlet

On Christmas morning he cooked breakfast for Monika, then taxied with her out to Kennedy Airport. After she had checked in, they went to the Lufthansa waiting lounge and exchanged gifts. He presented her with a framed vintage Berenice Abbott photograph of the New York skyline.

"A little remembrance of New York," he said. "I hope this'll make you want to come back."

She held the picture to her chest. "It's beautiful. I love it. But if I come back, it'll be because of you."

Even as he opened her gift, a heavy blue envelope tied with golden ribbon, she apologized for its modest value. He was delighted with what he found inside, a picture she'd snapped of him surreptitiously in Mexico while he lay out on their terrace in his bathing trunks trying to draw the trophies.

"You really helped me. You know that?"

She smiled. "It was for my own benefit. It's hard to sleep next to a guy who's having bad dreams all the time."

"You!" He embraced her. "What am I going to do without you?"

"You'll do fine. Promise me you'll visit soon."

"As soon as this case is finished," he promised.

He waited until her plane took off, then walked slowly back through the nearly empty terminal to catch a bus to Manhattan. There was a certain poignancy, he thought, in the tawdry, commercial Christmas decorations placed sporadically about the airline lobby.

The next morning he drove out to the airport again, this time to La Guardia to see Aaron off for Cleveland. In front of the terminal Aaron briefed him on the peculiar traits of his car, which he was leaving in Janek's trusted hands.

"She drinks oil the way my ex drank booze, so it's best to check whenever you gas her up. And remember, don't stick your finger in the little hole where the cigarette lighter used to be."

"Yeah, yeah, very funny. Call me when you find something, okay?"

Aaron looked at him. "This is a big one, right?"

Janek nodded. "I thought Sullivan was a real asshole when he called it a great crime. Now I think maybe he was right."

"Don't worry, Frank, I won't blow it. If there's anything out in Cleveland, I'll find it for you."

That afternoon, back in the city, Janek waited until it was exactly ten to three. Then he dialed Beverly Archer's number. "Pick it up, butterball," he whispered. "I know you just finished with a patient. So pick up the goddamn phone."

She answered on the sixth ring.

"It's Janek," he said. "I need to talk. How about tomorrow morning?"

There was a long pause at the other end. "All right." Beverly's voice was steady. "I have a cancellation at eleven."

When he set down the receiver, he looked at his hands. No shaking, no trembling.

I just might bring this off, he thought.

When she showed herself at the waiting-room door, she looked exactly as she had the last time they'd talked. Gone were the distraught features and agonized grimaces of Aaron's videotaped interview. She was once again the cool and proper professional, the superior, unflappable clinical psychologist.

"Lieutenant." She smiled her thin-lipped smile.

"Doctor." Janek smiled back, imitating the position of her lips. They stared at each other, engrossed in their mirrored expressions. For just a moment, Janek thought, Beverly looked nonplussed.

As she ushered him into her office, she commented on his healthy appearance. "The last time I saw you, you were bleeding heavily on my bedroom floor. You look a lot better now." The same small, thin-lipped smile.

"You look better, too." He sent her a mental message: *I know you did it!* The idea that she might actually pick up on it filled him with a savage joy. "Last time I saw you," he said, "you were carrying on about what a failure you'd been as Diana Proctor's therapist."

At first she seemed confused. She recovered quickly. "Oh, of course," she said. "On the videotape. I've tried to regain my perspective since then."

"Have you?"

"What?"

"Regained it?"

"Oh, I've tried, Lieutenant. It's a terrible blow when a patient goes off . . . turns out . . . whatever. But there's only so much a person in my position can do.

Psychotherapy's not a science; it's not exact. We know so little, you see. And we're all such frail creatures underneath, which, I think, may be the real lesson in all of this. The only thing to do after a failure like Diana is try to pick yourself up and go on as best you can."

"Still," Janek said, "I congratulate you on a remarkable recovery."

She looked at him curiously. "And *I* congratulate you."

"It was a pretty bleak night for both of us."

"I put a cushion under your head. Do you remember?"

"I must have been unconscious. Did you put it there before or after you discovered Diana was dead?"

This time her glance was sharp. "I don't recall. After, I suppose."

"I imagine you were pretty busy before Aaron Greenberg got to the scene?"

"I don't know what you mean."

"With three of us lying there. Two dead, of course. And you still had things to move around."

She stared at him. "I don't know what you're talking about, Lieutenant."

"Okay, Beverly, have it your way, let it go for now." He watched carefully for her reaction to his familiar use of her first name. She looked as if she were trying not to react. "Please forgive my informality, but since I nearly died in your bedroom and you were kind enough to cushion my head—well, I hope it's all right to call you Beverly. I'd like for you to call me Frank."

She smiled. "Thank you. That's fine. I'll feel very comfortable calling you that." She paused. "Now, what can I do for you . . . Frank?"

"I want to ask about the picture of your mother, the one upstairs."

"What about it?"

"I'd like to see it again if you don't mind."

"I don't understand." She was struggling, he could see, to regain her slightly rumpled composure. If there was one thing, it seemed, that Beverly Archer did not like, it was to be caught off guard by a man.

"It made a striking impression on me. I'd like to see it again."

She smiled sweetly, her composure restored. "I'm sorry, Frank, but no house tours today."

He stared at her. She stared back. *Now she knows I know,* he thought. Finally, when she spoke, her smile was guarded. "When you called, I assumed you wanted to talk about Diana. I already told everything to your Sergeant Greenberg and to that very kind Inspector Sullivan of the FBI. But I'll be happy to tell it all again to you—if that's why you're here."

"I didn't come to talk about Diana."

She blinked. "Why did you come?"

"To see you."

"Well, here I am!" She beamed.

"I wanted to look into your eyes."

She squinted. "I get the feeling you're trying to intimidate me, Frank." She paused. "I was told I was cleared."

"Not by me." He grinned.

He could see she didn't know how to react to that, didn't know whether she should grin back or scowl. In the end she tried to preserve her dignity. "Perhaps we should cut this short," she said.

"As you like," Janek said. "But I think you'll be interested to hear what I have to say."

She gazed at him. "I'm waiting."

"You're a very composed woman."

"I suppose I try to be."

"Your poise impresses me. Even the first time I came here, I was impressed. Even when you tried to make me think I had sexual fantasies about my goddaughter." He erased the half-smile from his lips; he wanted her to understand he was serious. "Jess was afraid of you. She left a message on my answering machine. She said she was deathly afraid." He paused. "If I hadn't been abroad at the time, I might have saved her life. But I was away, so she was killed. I hold you responsible for that."

Beverly Archer sat straight up in her chair, her features contorted by fury. "Oh, you're really impossible! That's just absurd!"

"I don't think so."

"Now you listen to me, Detective. Before you emote any more garbage, you should know how impossibly stupid you sound. Jessica was *not* frightened of me. She had no reason to be. We were getting along very well. I was helping her. She told me I was. My only regret, and I can understand if you hold me responsible for this, is that I had no knowledge of what was going on between her and Diana. If I'd had any inkling, I assure you I would have taken steps."

She sat back, her lips still trembling. She didn't bother to disguise her anger. Even though he'd broken through her veneer, Janek was impressed. She came across as utterly authentic. *Perhaps she really didn't know,* he thought.

When she spoke again, her tone was more constrained.

"For me the tragedy is having to live with my blindness to what was happening between two beloved patients. Neither girl said a word to me, not a solitary word about the other, except for occasional casual remarks. I had no idea they were involved on such an intense level. I wish I'd known. I think I could have done something if I had."

She was, he realized, apologizing to him the only way she knew. Not outright, without equivocation, as would have been appropriate, but tentatively, defensively. She wasn't capable of more.

"Perhaps you didn't know," he said. "Perhaps now you really are suffering over that. But it's hard for me to feel compassion when you speak about a 'tragedy,' and then it turns out what you mean is having to live with your personal failure as a therapist. Both girls are dead. As are seventeen other people. And you're responsible for all of them. I told you Jess was afraid of you. She had good reason to be. Diana told her a tale of being sent to various parts of the country to kill people who had offended you in the past. It was all for Mother, Diana told Jess—Mother, being, of course, your mother, the lady in the picture upstairs. An insane fantasy? Jess wasn't sure. She was just terribly, terribly scared. Well, I've had a lot of time to think about it, Beverly. Brushing close to death tends to focus your thinking. And I've decided that what Diana told Jess wasn't an insane fantasy at all. I think it was true. I think you were behind every murder Diana Proctor committed, except maybe Jess. And because you weren't behind that one killing, you're able to work up sufficient emotion about it to convince people you had nothing to do with the rest."

He paused for effect. Her eyes were riveted to his. She hated him, of course; her eyes told him that. But no matter her hatred, she could not look away. He held her spellbound with his words.

"I came today to tell you to your face I'm not convinced at all. I see straight through your phony story and your transparent pack of lies. Now I promise you this: When I'm done with you, the whole world will see through them, too." He leaned forward. "You're a mind fucker, Beverly. You mind-fucked Diana. You designated the people she killed. You sent her out to do your dirty work because you didn't have the guts to do your killing for yourself. 'Mind murders' my chief calls them. 'How're you going to prove your case?' I'm not sure. I've got some ideas. We'll see how they turn out. You're sick. You're perverted. I think you're evil." He rose. "That's it. That's why I came, to tell you that, and to let you know I'll be working now full-time to put you away. The game's over, Beverly. No Diana around to protect you anymore. The real fight's about to start. It's just you and me, babe. And I don't intend to lose."

With that he turned on his heel and headed for the door. He opened it, didn't bother to shut it, just kept walking straight through her waiting room, past an attractive college-age girl who gazed after him with fascinated eyes, straight out the front door of her house and onto the street.

He maintained his pace as he walked down to Second Avenue, never once turning around. When at last he was certain he was completely out of view, he stumbled against the brick wall of an apartment building and then, arms extended, leaned against it and gasped.

His head reeled; his forehead was dripping.

God help me, he thought. *I just threw the gauntlet down.*

10
Broken Dreams

When he phoned Monika and told her what he'd done, she was startled and also a little angry.

"Why did you do that, Frank?"

"To unnerve her."

"I understand. But look what happened. You also unnerved yourself."

"Yeah, well, I think it was worth it."

"Listen to me." Her voice was urgent. "She's a dangerous woman. What if she comes after you?"

"With an ice pick and a pot of glue? Don't worry about that. She's the most contemptible type of criminal, a coward. There's nothing she can do to me now. Without her hatchet woman, she's impotent."

There was a pause at the other end. "I wonder if you aren't too close to this."

"Spare me, please, Monika. You sound like Kit."

"Maybe Kit's right. You despise Beverly Archer, don't you?"

"Let's say I don't like her very much." He paused. "Okay, I despise her," he admitted.

"Is that a healthy way to relate to someone you're trying to prove committed a crime?"

"I don't know whether it's healthy, Monika. But I

assure you I'm under control. Anyway, there's no law that says I can't have feelings about my work.''

"No one objects to your feelings, Frank," she said quietly. "I just don't want to see you . . . hurt yourself over this.''

On New Year's Day Aaron called from Cleveland: "Time for you to come out here, Frank."

The next morning, the first workday of the new year, Janek flew to the Midwest. Gray skies, a vast frozen lake, plumes of industrial smoke, a furious late-winter storm. His plane circled Hopkins Airport for three-quarters of an hour. Concerned stewardesses with glossy brows and frozen smiles paced nervously. After numerous unctuous announcements from the captain, the plane started down through impenetrable sleet, an endless descent, it seemed to Janek, until finally, unexpectedly, it landed hard. When it jerked to a stop, the relieved passengers applauded and shook their heads. The captain, face red, collar tight, stood nodding at the door. The collected crew wished everyone a happy New Year, a safe continuing journey, and, in the event Cleveland was the final destination, a most pleasant stay.

Aaron was waiting for him by the gate. He hustled Janek into his rental car, then drove into the city on an elevated highway.

"What kind of town is this?" Janek asked, looking down at gas stations, commercial strips, snow-crusted parking lots, endless blocks of drab gray buildings.

Aaron pondered the question. Then he looked up. "Mind if I wax poetic, Frank?"

Janek laughed. "Be my guest."

"Cleveland," Aaron intoned sonorously, "is a Rust Belt town of broken dreams."

Janek nodded; he liked that. And staring out the window, he also decided he liked the town. Perhaps because of the deliberate lack of any appliqué of glamour, he found it oddly glamorous.

Aaron laid out their schedule. He'd arranged three interviews for the afternoon. In his preliminary meetings with the people he hadn't told them much, just that a lieutenant of detectives was coming from New York to ask them questions about Beverly Archer. The case, he'd told them, was important and at this stage, highly confidential. As there were as yet no indictments, informants had been assured their cooperation would be held in confidence.

Something about the way Aaron was talking signaled Janek that he was holding back. "You find something?"

"Yep." Aaron grinned.

"Going to keep it a secret?"

"I think you're going to be surprised," was all Aaron would say.

Their motel, a standard low, sprawling complex, was situated beside a remote shopping mall. Janek checked in, unpacked his stuff, washed his face, then examined himself in the standard motel-room mirror. His tan, acquired in Mexico, had all but disappeared. What he saw was a middle-aged man in an inexpensive business suit with lines in his forehead and bags beneath his eyes. But he noticed something special about this man. *He looks like a guy who doesn't give up.* The idea of that made him feel good. He descended briskly to the lobby, then out to the portico.

"Okay, Aaron," he said, getting into the car, "I'm ready. Let's roll."

Their first stop was the Ashley-Burnett School for Girls. They drove awhile, entered a posh suburb of impressive homes, then came to an open gate which Janek at first took to be the entrance to a park. A discreet sign pointed the way down a winding, treelined drive. The campus extended on either side, athletic fields and lavish lawns covered with snow, crisscrossed by well-shoveled paths. Finally the school proper came into view, an impressive vine-covered red-brick building with two extended wings.

"This is one ritzy setup," Aaron aid as he drove into the visitors' lot. "I didn't know real people sent their kids to joints like this."

As they walked to the administration building, Janek could hear the shrill cries of girls and the scampering of little female feet through the windows of what he took to be the school gym.

"How long did Beverly go here?"

"All twelve grades," Aaron said. "Old Bertha Parce was her high school English teacher." He glanced at Janek. "But later Beverly came back. It was just after she got her Ph.D. She spent a year in Cleveland trying to build up a practice. She was just starting out. Referrals were few and far between. To keep herself busy and make ends meet, she wangled herself a part-time job at her old alma mater as student counselor and school shrink."

The headmaster's secretary, a pretty young woman in a navy skirt, asked them if they wouldn't mind waiting a few minutes in the reception area. Aaron sat on a soft leather couch, while Janek inspected the display of school memorabilia on the walls.

There was a glass case full of trophies, most of them for arcane sports such as field hockey and equestrian dressage. There was an ornately framed wooden plaque emblazoned with the words "Head Girl" and the names of young women, student leaders in their respective years. There were also numerous class photographs. Janek asked Aaron what year Beverly was graduated.

Aaron checked his notebook. "Class of '68," he said.

Janek found the picture, inspected it closely. Two dozen girls, all wearing the same school uniform of white blouse and blue and red tartan skirt, were posed in two rows before the main building of Ashley-Burnett. He discovered Beverly in the second row on the end. She was standing slightly apart from her classmates. There was something separate, distant about her, something slightly alienated in her posture. But her face bore the same half-smile he had come to know so well, the thin-lipped half-smile that said "I have superior knowledge" and "Don't get too close."

"Mr. Bramhall will see you now."

Janek turned. The pretty secretary motioned them toward an inner door. Janek and Aaron followed her across polished parquet floors into a spacious cream-colored office. A handsome man in a beautifully tailored tweed jacket rose from behind an antique partner's desk.

"You must be Lieutenant Janek. I'm Jud Bramhall," he said, extending his hand.

Janek studied him while they made small talk about the brutal Cleveland weather. He and Bramhall, he decided, were about the same age, but there the resemblance stopped. Bramhall had the patrician good looks and arched eyebrows of an affable old-fashioned WASP politician, the kind that can't get elected in an American city anymore. He had the same kind of old money voice as Stanton Dorance, a voice that spoke of a fine eastern education and all the privileges attendant thereto.

"Sergeant Greenberg tells me you want a briefing on Bev Archer's sojourn here as school psychologist."

Janek was pleased by Bramhall's crisp announcement that it was time to discuss the matter at hand.

"A certain confidentiality implicit in our relationships with former staff precludes my getting too specific. But after counsulting with our attorney, and based on the gravity of the matter, as explained by the sergeant here, I'm prepared to fill you in on a background-only basis. For anything more than that I'll require a subpoena."

Janek nodded. "That's fine. We're just trying to get a sense of what she was like."

Bramhall pulled a pipe from a rack on his desk, stuffed it with tobacco. Then he leaned back, a signal he was going to be expansive. Watching him, Janek had the feeling Bramhall would tell his tale well.

"It was a strange thing that happened with Bev. . . ."

The events he described occurred in 1977. The school, Bramhall didn't mind admitting now, was then a fairly troubled institution. There were drug problems, student pregnancies, a general breakdown in discipline. Nothing that wasn't going on at other independent schools at the time, but he, Bramhall, had been appointed headmaster only two years before, he was the first male head in the history of Ashley-Burnett, and he was anxious to make innovations and turn the school around. So the idea came to him that a trained psychologist ought to be available to any student needing help. He took it to the board of trustees, the concept was approved, and then someone brought up Beverly Archer's name. She was qualified, she had just gotten her degree, and, best of all, as a fairly young alumna she would be in a position to identify with the particular problems of Ashley-Burnett girls, pertaining to the school and also to their social lives outside.

"We are, after all, a fairly special group." Bramhall finally lit his pipe. "We have minority students, and we hope to recruit more as times goes on. But basically our function is to educate the daughters of Cleveland's older families. I make no apologies for that. Ashley-Burnett is an elite school. We consider ourselves the equal of any young women's academy in the East."

He made this last statement with uncondescending pride, a pride Janek could not help admiring. The man carried the torch for a world he must know was increasing irrelevant, yet he did so without apology.

"That first autumn, when Bev came on board, I thought I'd made a pretty smart move. Here was an intelligent, well-motivated young woman eager to help her old school get back on track. And I have to admit that in the beginning at least things did seem to improve. As troubled kids turned to her for guidance, student and faculty morale tilted up. I got some calls from parents, too, always complimentary. A staff psychologist was a great idea. Why hadn't we thought of it before?"

But then, Bramhall admitted sadly, the euphoria of autumn began to turn. The winter term was always the hardest, he said, always the low point of the year. Cleveland's harsh climate was partially responsible. The gray skies and miserable cold forced everyone indoors. Kids caught the flu. Corridors resounded with sniffles and coughs. All educators are familiar with the phenomenon, a species of cabin fever that leads inevitably to a lowering of morale. But that particular winter, the winter of '78, seemed worse than usual. There was something indefinably miserable in the air. Bramhall, naturally concerned, called a number of staff meetings. Beverly, he remembered, kept fairly quiet. At the time he attributed that to shyness; she was new to the school and possibly intimidated by older staff. Then one weekend in late February disaster struck. A senior girl, a very popular one, too, hanged herself at home.

The suicide turned what had been a very dark winter term into a totally black one. In such a situation extensive counseling was called for, and Beverly seem to rise to the occasion. But then, ten days later, a second girl hanged herself, this time in the school gym. Her dangling body was discovered by a group of eighth graders, all of them deeply traumatized by the sight. And then the truth came out. Two other girls came forward and admitted to the existence of a "suicide club." Bramhall moved quickly to break it up.

"I still don't know exactly what it was about," he said, relighting his pipe. "Were the two hangings actually suicides or the result of a strange sex practice called autoerotic asphyxia that was then finding its way into various Ohio schools? But what did come out—and to me this was the most shocking aspect of the whole affair—was that not only had the two dead girls been seeing Bev Archer for counseling, but other members of the 'club,' in fact, a majority of them, had been seeing her as well. I want to make something clear. There was an understanding that if a girl wanted to see the quote school shrink unquote, she was under no obligation to tell anyone, nor would Bev report the consultation to either the school or the girl's parents. Total confidentiality was to apply; that was the whole idea. But I never expected Bev would take the rule so literally, especially after a girl who was in her charge took her own life. When I found out that *both* dead girls had been her patients, I couldn't believe my ears. The way it looked, Bev was the common thread in the affair. Bramhall angrily tapped his pipe against the top of his desk. "She might as well have been that damn suicide club's faculty adviser."

Janek could see that the shock of that revelation had still not abated, even after so many years.

"Bev was quite broken up by the suicides, of course. 'My fault,' she told me. 'Those girls were in my care, and I let them down.' She wept a lot and beat her breast. I felt she was sincere. But still, with her arrival, it seemed something almost . . . evil entered Ashley-Burnett. Well, whether she was responsible or not, I couldn't countenance her not keeping me informed. She clearly wasn't up to the job. I told her to take leave and that at the end of the term I'd have to let her go, as, of course, I did. . . ."

Bramhall fell silent for a time. Then he opened a file folder on his desk and removed a sheet of paper. "That spring Bev left Cleveland and moved to New York to start her career again. A couple of years later I received a letter from a Dr. Carl Drucker at a psychiatric hospital in Derby, Connecticut. He wrote that Bev had given my name as a reference and asked if I could recommend her for a part-time staff position."

Bramhall handed Janek the sheet he'd been holding. "Here's a copy of my response. I'm ashamed to admit it, Lieutenant, but as you can see, I recommended her."

* * *

As they followed a freshly shoveled path back to the visitors' parking lot, they ran into a group of Ashley-Burnett students walking the other way. The girls, red-cheeked, bundled in goose down coats, their tartan hats powdered lightly with snow, smiled demurely as they passed.

"Aren't they gorgeous!" Aaron exclaimed. "Aren't they the healthiest-looking kids!"

Janek nodded. The girls did indeed look healthy. The thought that Beverly Archer had brought her sickness into this academic Eden filled him with a sad and poignant fury.

Back in the car they didn't talk much. Bramhall's tale spoke for itself. Now they knew about two more young lives Beverly had screwed up. How many others, Janek wondered, could there be?

Aaron's next stop was a handsome slate-roofed, stucco-with-inset-timbers house on the edge of Shaker Heights.

"Beverly's kid sister's place," Aaron explained, as he parked in front. "Mildred Archer, now Mildred Archer Cannaday. Nice gal. Very informal. Two teenage kids. Local tennis champ. Call her Millie, Frank; she likes that. Her husband's a big shot cardiologist."

Millie Cannady looked so different from her sister that at first Janek couldn't believe that they were siblings. He was persuaded only when he heard Millie speak; then he recognized Beverly's accent.

Millie was a tall, robust, handsome woman in her mid-thirties who moved with the light, liquid grace of an athlete. In certain ways she reminded Janek of Fran Dunning: her relaxed, friendly manner, so unlike the tense guardedness he'd observed in Beverly, and the straightforward way she made eye contact. But above all, there was a pervading aura of good health and of being comfortable within. After only two minutes in her presence, Janek knew that Mildred Archer Cannaday was not and never had been a wallflower.

The interview took place in a gracious, well-proportioned sunken living room with tall leaded windows at either end. French doors led out to a terrace with a view over a park behind the house. The furnishings consisted of twin chintz-upholstered couches, dark wood side tables, old-fashioned lamps, framed family photos displayed on the top of a baby grand piano, and fine Oriental rugs spread on a polished chestnut floor. Janek felt he was in the home of successful well-adjusted people, so unlike the effect of Beverly's minimalist office and her medieval bedchamber, dominated by the shrine to her mother.

When finally they settled down and Aaron brought up Beverly's name, Millie Cannaday sadly shook her head.

"Poor Bev. Such a miserable, unhappy woman. When I think of what she could have been . . . It's been a pretty long time since the two of us have really talked. It's not that we've become estranged. It's just that in the last few years she's become so *weird*. Oh, we exchange Christmas cards and call each other on our respective birthdays, and she usually remembers my kids' birthdays, too, and sends them a little check, four dollars or something ridiculous like that. I think last year she actually sent each of them five." Millie's eyes twinkled. "It isn't that she's stingy, you understand. Bev can't help herself. She was always tight, ungiving, retentive—isn't that the word? Well, I'm no psychologist, Lieutenant. I don't know the terminology. But I do know what happened to my sister and whose fault it was. Our mother's. Mama was the one who ruined Bev's life.''

As Millie Cannady launched into an extended monologue, Janek could feel the interview slipping into the kind of deeply felt reminiscence by which a speaker dredges up old memories and purges conflicts from his past.

''It's sad to say. But I'm afraid it's just that simple. Our mother was a totally self-centered person. Oh, she was beautiful. Everyone thought so. 'Victoria Archer's the most beautiful woman in Cleveland,' people used to say. And talented. Mama was very talented. At her height she was probably the best nightclub singer in town. With the right kind of luck she might have gone on to become a national star. God knows, she had the ambition for it, but I think underneath she was afraid of going up against the best. So she stayed out here, a nice enough place, as I'm sure you've noticed, Lieutenant. We actually have it pretty good in Cleveland. Great orchestra. World-class art museum. Fine university. But still, it's Cleveland, isn't it?'' Millie's eyes twinkled again. ''We can get pretty defensive about that. We don't like it when our town gets a cheap laugh on a talk show or when someone calls it the mistake on the lake with a knowing little sneer. Mama always said she hated it here. Funny, isn't it, that she stayed here her entire life? She was born here. And this is where she died.''

She herself, Millie said, proceeding with her saga, had happily managed to escape her mother's domination.

''I was lucky. I broke away. I didn't need Mama so much, so I was able to stand up to her and make my break. But Bev couldn't do that. She needed Mama desperately. And so she got her, perhaps more of her in the end than she ever bargained for. I think Bev paid an awful price for her need. Mama used her terribly. She twisted and distorted whatever possible chance at happiness Bev might have had. I'll say it again because I believe it's true. Victoria, our mother, truly ruined Bev's life.''

There was, Millie said, a kind of bizarre ''contract'' between her older sister and her mother, a contract which, although unspoken, was as binding and as forceful as if it had been cut in stone. Its basic terms were starkly simple: Victoria would live her life to the hilt, laugh, be beautiful, glamorous, thin, successful, and, most important, a sexually active and satisfied woman. Beverly, on the other hand, would be depressed, unhappy, plain, mousy, fat, mediocre, and asexual so as never to compete. And as in any personal services contract, there was a schedule of compensation: In return for not competing with her mother, Beverly would be ''loved.''

''It was a real lousy deal,'' Millie said. ''The love Bev got was second-rate. Because the only person Mama was capable of loving was—yeah, you guessed it, Mama.''

Millie excused herself. When she returned a few minutes later, it was with a tray, several glasses, bottles of beer, and a bowl of nuts.

''Have you met Bev, Lieutenant?''

Janek nodded. ''I interviewed her a couple of times.''

''How did she strike you?''

''Unhappy, plain, asexual—pretty much the way you just described.''

''Well, you may find this hard to believe,'' Millie said, ''but she was quite handsome as a girl. Still, I bet it's been twenty years since she's had a date. See, the more time she spent with Mama, the fatter and plainer she got. Then, when she dyed her hair red, it came out blah rather than glossy like Mama's. When they'd stand together near the end of Mama's life, they looked more like sisters than even Bev and me. Mama had had her face lifted several times, and Bev had really let herself go. Beautiful Vicky and drab Bev—the Archer girls. God!''

Millie believed that even though Bev worshiped their mother, she at times also hated her for imposing the awful contract. But every time Bev tried to break away, Victoria would pull her back.

''Can you imagine?'' Millie asked. ''Can you imagine how wasteful and stupid it is to allow your mother to rule your life?''

It was a rhetorical question, Janek realized; he made no effort to respond to it.

''I think that was Bev's tragedy,'' Millie said, ''that she had a chance to live for herself, and in the end she wasted it.''

Their father, Jack Archer, had been a distant figure. He and Victoria had married young and split up early, just after Millie was born. Jack, an engineer, had moved to Chicago, remarried, and started a second family. The girls had had very little contact with him, though Victoria had received substantial child support. Both girls were bright and had no trouble getting into Ashley-Burnett. Meantime, Victoria launched her career as a singer. Her success was instantaneous.

''Mama had an excellent voice. She was an accomplished singer. But there's plenty of good singers around. What Mama had that was extra was her incredible style. She could take a standard, a song everyone knew, and dramatize it, make it passionate. She knew how to reach people, put a song across. The glamorous nightclub singer—that was her public face. But there was so much more to her than what she showed her fans. Behind all the beauty and glamour there was one very hard-boiled lady. She was a great injustice collector, you know. Cross her and she'd never forgive. She had a kind of personal code, the gist of which went something like: If someone wrongs you, don't ever forget it. Nurse your anger and your hurt until it turns to bitterness and hate. But (and this was probably her most important tenet) never, never let your hatred show.''

Millie sat back on the couch, her arms hanging limply. She had expended great energy describing her sister and mother; now she seemed exhausted.

Janek decided it was time to focus the interview. ''Could Bev have inherited your mother's code?''

''Possibly.'' Millie smiled. ''Oh, hell! I've told you this much. Why not the rest? Sure, she inherited it. Mama taught it to her. It became her code, too, for God's sakes.''

In the last few years of her life Victoria started going mad. At least Millie thought she did. Beverly did not agree. For all her sister's background in psychology, her training and experience as a therapist, she refused to see what was obvious to all Victoria's friends—namely, that the singer was being eaten up by her hate.

''Eight years ago, when Mama died suddenly of a stroke, she was only fifty-five years old. But in the last five years of her life she carried on sometimes like a lunatic. At the lounge she'd be fine, her glamorous self. But in the afternoons before work she'd lie out on the chaise in her living room at the Alhambra Hotel, ranting and raving at the world. Out of nowhere she'd bring up someone's name, an old lover maybe or someone else she thought had done her wrong. Then she'd start in.

Curses, pronouncements, spiteful value judgments. 'He's a prick.' 'She's a shit.' That kind of vulgar talk. And when she said something like that, it was usually about someone who really hadn't done anything particularly wrong. A man might have forgotten to send flowers, or one of her girlfriends might have forgotten to return a call. Trivial offenses to which she had these ludicrous reactions. It was truly awful to listen to. Meantime, there was Bev flying in from New York practically every weekend, rushing over to Mama's, listening to all her garbage, taking it all in, nodding her agreement. Sometimes Bev would stop by to see me afterwards. 'Isn't Mama wonderful!' she'd say. 'Aren't we lucky to have such a talented and brilliant ma!' God! The sick way she worshiped that woman, the weird way they fed off each other's madness.'' Millie peered straight into Janek's eyes. ''I guess by now you know that's what I think: that Bev got as crazy as Mama in the end. . . .''

The time had come, Janek thought, to put some tough questions to Millie. ''Did your sister ever have a run-in with a teacher at Ashley-Burnett?''

Millie smiled. ''Sure. An old spinster English teacher. She was my teacher, too.''

''Bertha Parce?'' Aaron asked.

Millie nodded. ''I'm amazed you know her name.''

''What about two men named MacDonald—did she ever have any trouble with them?''

''Jimmy and Stu MacDonald? You call them men! They were just boys when I knew them. I think they moved east. That's what I heard anyway.''

''What happened?''

''God only knows. Whatever it was, Bev was sensitive

about it. Whenever their names came up, she'd start to act real antsy, then try and change the subject."

"Cynthia Morse?"

"Her roommate at Bennington. Yeah, they had a big falling-out. But I don't understand, Lieutenant." Millie smiled curiously. "How do you *know* about all of these people?"

"Let's hold off on that for now. I want to ask you about some others." Millie nodded. "Do the names Laura and Anthony Scotto ring a bell?"

"I don't think so. No."

Janek glanced at Aaron. "What about Wexler—Carla and Robert Wexler?"

Millie shook her head. Then she stopped shaking it. "Wait a minute! There was a *Bobby* Wexler."

Aaron smiled slightly. "Who was he?"

"A musician. Mama's accompanist one summer. There were so many of those guys. She went through them pretty fast. But I remember Bobby. It was the summer Mama sang at Cavendish. He was practically a kid. Actually I think he and Mama were involved. She usually screwed her piano players. That's probably why she tired of them so fast."

"Do you think you'd recognize this Bobby Wexler if you saw him again?"

"I might," Millie said.

Aaron showed her a photograph of the Wexler family taken several months before they were slaughtered. Millie studied it. "Yeah, that's him," she said. "It's been years, but the smile's the same, the old lecherous smile." She looked up at Janek. "Yeah, it's him, I'm sure. Now are you going to tell me what this is all about?"

"While you're at it, show her the picture of the Scottos," Janek gently instructed Aaron.

Aaron showed Millie the picture. They both watched as she studied it. "I may have seen the woman," Millie said. "What's her first name again?"

"Laura."

"And she was married to this guy?" Aaron nodded. "Do you know her maiden name?"

Aaron checked his notebook. "Laura Gabelli."

Millie nodded. "I may have seen her. Around Tufts University, I think. Bev transferred there from Bennington. Did you know about that?"

They didn't know. Millie filled them in. It was after the big falling-out with Cynthia Morse. Bev took a year off, came back to Cleveland, took a job as an aide at a psychiatric hospital, then for the next two years attended Tufts, where she majored in psychology. After that she moved back to Cleveland to get her doctorate at Western Reserve.

"Do you know of any falling-out she might have had with this Laura Gabelli?" Aaron asked.

"No. But it wouldn't surprise me. Just like Mama, Bev had fallings-out with damn near everyone." Millie paused. "Look, guys—all these questions about the two of them, then all these old names of people Bev didn't like. You're scaring me a little bit. I think the time's come for you to explain."

She looked to Janek, then to Aaron, and then back to Janek again. There was something so open and vulnerable about her that Janek was hesitant to fill her in. But he knew he had to. He owed her that, and he could see that she was the kind of person who'd rather know the truth, no matter how harsh, then be lied to or kept in the dark.

"Bertha Parce, the MacDonalds, Cynthia Morse and her two daughters, the Wexler family, and the Scotto family all had one thing in common," he said. "They all were murdered within the past fourteen months by a woman named Diana Proctor, who also happened to be your sister's patient."

Millie, mouth partly open, gazed at Janek. For a moment she appeared to be relieved. Then, abruptly, she sat up, as if the implications of what he'd said had hit her like a blow.

"But you don't really think—! I mean, you couldn't possibly believe—!" Her forehead creased; her pupils dilated. "You think Bev had something to do with . . . that Bev may have directed—?" And then: "You *do* think that, don't you? Yes, I see you do." She squeezed her eyes shut. "Oh, my God!"

Millie Cannaday began to scream. Her shrieks of anguish echoed through the house.

They stayed with her until she calmed down. Then Janek explained to her that yes, Beverly was a suspect, although so far no more than that. He and Aaron had come to Cleveland, he explained, on account of the portrait of her mother, which they'd seen in Beverly's bedroom. Certain objects, taken from the homicide victims, had been arranged in what seemed to be votive offering style before the painting. Thus the question arose as to whether Victoria Archer had in some way been the inspiration for the Wallflower murders. Janek readily admitted that such a theory must seem farfetched; he was certainly not prepared to tell Millie her sister was a murderess. Still, the case remained open. By the way, did Millie know anything about the portrait?

"The full-length one of Mama in her red dress? Sure, I know about it. A man named Peter Aretzsky painted it about twelve years ago. It took up a whole wall of Mama's bedroom."

"Your sister inherited it?"

Millie smiled. "Bev wanted that picture something awful. That, Mama's red dress, her miniature piano, and her big old four-poster bed." Millie rolled her eyes. "Bev always had her eye on the picture. She loved it, said it showed Mama the way she really was. Which is pretty funny . . . considering. You see, there's a story behind that painting." Millie turned to Aaron. "Are you taking him to see Melissa Walters?" Aaron nodded. "Ask her about the painting, Lieutenant. She can fill you in about that and a lot of other stuff. She was Mama's best friend . . . if in fact, Mama ever had one."

"Shit! She knew Bobby Wexler and Laura Scotto. That's proof she lied to us, Frank. So we got her, don't we?" Aaron hit the steering wheel with delight. "I'm starting to feel good about this case."

They were back in their rental car, driving to their final appointment of the day. The snow had stopped falling. Although it was only four-thirty, the sky was already turning dark.

Janek wasn't sure that proof of Beverly's lies quite meant that they'd "got her." But he did think it might be enough to persuade Kit to grant them more time. So far the trip to Cleveland was working out. *Now how the hell am I going to get a confession?* he wondered.

The lobby of the Alhambra Residential Hotel was a Moorish fantasy, a pastiche of thick walls, Arab columns, Córdoba arches, a central courtyard embracing a fountain, and a rectangular tiled pool stocked with carp.

Built in the late 1920s as a luxury establishment, the hotel was so well constructed that even now, after years of wear, it still emitted an aura of luxury and class. Palms planted in large terra-cotta pots occupied the corners. Ceiling fans, still now that it was winter, stood poised to whirl and cool perspiring guests.

A creaking elevator, paneled in mahogany and trimmed with brass, took them to the fifth floor. Here they followed a corridor, one side open to the courtyard, until they reached the door to Melissa Walters's suite.

A short old lady opened up, a lady who clearly did not wish her visitors to find her old. Her hair was blued, her forehead was powdered, her cheeks were rouged, her eyebrows were drawn, and her lips were waxed bright scarlet. Melissa Walters showed the soft smile and refined social mannerisms of another era.

It was so exciting to meet real live detectives! Would the gentlemen like something to drink? Port? Sherry? She had some fine old Madeira—could she tempt them with that? And she had taken the liberty of ordering in some prepared canapés, as well as a good selection of cookies from Damons, Cleveland's finest bakery.

Melissa Walters settled into her favorite chair.

Oh, yes, she remembered Vicky Archer. My goodness, they'd been the best of friends! Impossible to forget *her*. A great entertainer, a great personality. She'd been the life of this city for a time. Had the gentlemen been to the Fairmount Club Lounge? Perhaps they should go down there and take a look. Not that the place was anything now but a shadow of its former self. Still, at one time, not too long ago either, the lounge had been Cleveland's

premier night spot and Vicky Archer had been its most
glittering star. But please forgive her. She was rambling;
she knew she was. She apologized for that. She had so
few visitors these days, most of her friends having passed
away. Vicky had been one of the first. It was tragic the
way she died so suddenly and so young. They'd been
confidantes even though she, Melissa, was fifteen years
Vicky's senior. Oh, they'd had some great times together, wonderful times. . . . What? What was that
they were asking? The painting, Aretzsky's painting? Of
course, she remembered it! She'd seen it practically
every day. Whenever she visited Vicky's suite, just two
doors down the hall. A story? Oh, yes, there was a story
about that picture, a scandal if they wanted to know the
truth. Oh, they did, did they? What sly devils they were!
Well, certainly, she'd tell them about it. In fact, it would
be a pleasure. But would the gentlemen take a glass of
Madeira first . . . ?

Janek and Aaron accepted her glasses of Madeira.
They even licked their lips over her delicate canapés and
grinned foolishly as they nibbled on her tasty little
cookies. Anything to keep the old lady talking. Janek,
who'd conducted thousands of interviews over the
course of his career, recognized that Melissa Walters was
a potential gold mine of information. If there was a secret
about Beverly and Victoria, a secret even deeper than
what he and Aaron had managed to dig up so far, this
lady might reveal it if she were handled carefully
enough. The way she sang Victoria Archer's praises
suggested a profound ambivalence. He had picked up on
undertones of anger, envy, even dislike.

"Aretzsky! Ha!" Melissa's scarlet painted lips parted
in a smile. "He was smitten by her, of course. Utterly

smitten! He would come around the lounge every night just to see her, watch her move, listen to her sing, perhaps be so fortunate as to be the recipient of one of her ravishing smiles. He was an excellent painter as it happened, probably Cleveland's best. But so temperamental! He'd refuse to paint a person he didn't like. He lost out on a lot of lucrative corporate work on account of that little peccadillo. Still, Aretzsky was your first choice if you wanted your portrait done. That's how he got Vicky's attention . . . although he didn't hold it very long.''

Melissa asked if she could refresh their drinks. When they shook their heads, she shrugged and poured herself a double.

''I remember the night Aretzsky presented her with some drawings, quick little sketches he'd made of her right there in the lounge. She liked them, of course. She was no fool. And when he told her he wanted to paint her in oil, big, life size, maybe even bigger than life size, she certainly did not refuse him although she may have pretended to waver a little bit. Well, then he had her; at least he thought he did, the idiot! She began going to his studio to sit every afternoon. That dreary dump he lived in, near the lounge down at Carnegie and One Hundred Fourth, up four flights to a big, undusted room with his easel and messy paints at one end and his awful, smelly unmade bed at the other. They made love on that bed, of course. Vicky always knew how to inspire a man! I know he made nude sketches of her. She showed them to me once. But the big painting was the thing. Vicky in her red dress surrounded by a halo of reddish light. That's how they always lit her down at the lounge, you see. Oh, he made her look terrific—vibrant, bursting with energy and life. She was always glamorous, but he doubled her glamour. He idealized her. It was a picture painted by a lover. You couldn't look at it and fail to see that."

Melissa spread her arms. "Poor Aretzsky! That ugly, little, shrunken waif of a man with his bad skin and little wisp of a mustache—did he really think he was good enough to hold the interest of the Great Victoria Archer? Poor idiot! She ditched him, of course, soon as she got her mitts on his painting. Then he was heartbroken, or perhaps worse—a man destroyed. He started to become a nuisance, too. Long, reproachful, beseeching stares at the lounge. Silent phone calls to her suite in the middle of the night. He must have sent her fifty letters drenched in tears. She didn't bother to open them; just a glance at the envelopes and she'd toss them in the trash. I remember seeing him hanging around the stage door at the lounge or here, in front of the Alhambra, hoping to beg a precious moment of her time. And of course, the deeper he humiliated himself, the more disgusted she became, and the greater her disgust, the more cruelly she behaved. For make no mistake about it, gentlemen— Vicky Archer could be a real bitch!"

But, Melissa explained, there was a second act to the story, the scandal that arose later on. Aretzsky, heartbroken, disdained and scorned, turned bitter and took to drink. And, as is so often the case, the excesses of his infatuation were equaled by the intensity of his disillusionment. After several months, unable to rid himself of his obsession, he began work on a second portrait of Victoria far different from the first. It was the same size: enormous. She was in the same pose: singing. She wore the same clothes and jewelry: her diamond necklace and scarlet dress. But there the resemblance stopped. Instead

of the heroic, idealized features he had painted the first
time around, the features in the second picture were
deeply characterized. That second portrait, painted out of
heartbreak and bitterness, purported to show her as she
really was: spiteful; selfish; mean.

"I have to hand it to Aretzsky," Melissa said. "He
caught something, no question about that. It wasn't the
face Vicky showed the world, but it was a face I'd seen
a couple of times when she was off her guard. Maybe it
wasn't the real Vicky, but it did show a hidden side of
her, particularly around the eyes and mouth. Aretzsky
put everything he felt into it. It was truly a picture
informed by hate. That's what people who saw it said.
And people *did* see it! Aretzsky saw to that! He had a
show at the Howard French Gallery at Shaker Square,
and his big new picture of Vicky was the first thing you
saw when you walked in.

"Well, she was furious! Who can blame her? Still, I
think if Aretzsky's second portrait hadn't contained a
certain amount of recognizable truth, she might have
been able to laugh it off. But the way she went around
expressing her outrage only made people eager to see it
for themselves. And when they did, they began to talk.
People were fascinated. The subject came up at dinner
parties: Which picture showed the true Vicky, the first or
the second? There were people who even reread that old
Oscar Wilde story *The Picture of Dorian Gray* and then
expounded on the parallels. And there was talk, too, that
ugly though the second picture was, it was also, because
of its passion, Aretzsky's greatest work. I remember
Vicky coming in here at the time, sitting in the very chair
you're sitting in now, Lieutenant, looking at me, shaking

her head. 'Oh, Lisa'—she always called me that—'why did I ever let him paint me in the first place?' *Why?*''

Melissa turned to Janek, widened her eyes. Clearly she reveled in the effect of her tale.

''The answer, of course, was her insatiable vanity, which Aretzsky was more than happy to requite. But she didn't really want to know the answer to her question, so I kept my thoughts to myself. She did, however, try to do something about that second picture. She approached certain of her wealthy admirers and begged them to buy the portrait so she could have the pleasure of seeing it destroyed. From what I understand some fairly substantial offers were actually made. But no matter how much he was offered, Aretzsky refused. The man simply wouldn't sell. And why should he? Think about it. That picture was his revenge. You don't sell out your revenge, do you, Lieutenant? At least not if you feel wronged the way Aretzsky did . . .''

Peter Aretzsky, as it turned out, died just a year after Victoria Archer. In Melissa's judgment, he never recovered from his obsession with the singer. The second portrait? Melissa had no idea where it was. The scandal subsided long before Vicky died. Wasn't it always like that? Melissa asked. People couldn't get enough of something, gossiped about it endlessly, then, a year later, wondered why they ever cared.

''Bev? Of course, I remember Bev. She's a psycho-analyst in New York, isn't she? Oh, just a therapist. Well, it's all the same to me. I don't know much about that kind of thing, but I know Vicky did a real job on the girl. The way she scampered around after her beloved 'Mama' like there was an invisible leash and collar around her neck! You had to wonder what she got out of it. The honor of being Vicky Archer's daughter, I suppose. Still, everyone thought it was pretty peculiar, but no one dared say a word. 'Oh, Bev's just going through an awkward stage right now'—that's what Vicky would say if you gingerly brought the matter up. A 'stage'! 'Right now'! You had to laugh! Vicky kept Bev awkward from the day she was born. I sometimes wondered if she kept her that way to make herself look better by contrast. Because, you know, the other daughter, Millie, wasn't drab at all. That's the way it is sometimes: One daughter serves the mother while the other strikes out on her own. I've seen it happen again and again. I just hope Bev has straightened herself out. Sometimes you can't do that, you know. You get twisted, and then, after the person who twisted you passes away, it's to late to change and have a normal life. . . .''

Janek decided to let her ramble on. Better that she reminisce at random, he thought, and add her little homilies about life than for him to question her too closely about Beverly and then be forced to explain why he was interested.

''How good a singer was Vicky Archer? You're really putting me on the spot, Lieutenant. Let's just say she was very good. Did you know she was on network TV once? The Carson show, I think. After that she played a club date in New York. But she wasn't quite good enough to make it there, so she came back here, where she could be sure she'd always be a star. And for a few years, at least, she had this city at her feet. Well, maybe I exaggerate. But you have to understand, the Fairmount Club Lounge, where she hung out and sang, was a kind of mecca for a number of us. Vicky was a goddess there.''

Melissa shook her head. ''If I close my eyes''—she

closed them—"I can still see her standing in that cone of red light they always put on her, sultry, sexy, her hair red like a flame, crooning those great old songs, 'Black Coffee,' 'My One and Only Love,' 'Don't Smoke in Bed.'" Melissa opened her eyes again. "So, how good was she? Still want to know? Let's say she was Cleveland's answer to Peggy Lee. But let's face it, even at its height the Fairmount Club Lounge was no Persian Room. Cleveland just isn't New York, is it? I'm afraid not," Melissa added crisply, a ripe smile signifying a slightly mean satisfaction at finally being able to pin her old friend a little lower on the board of talent than perhaps old Vicky would have liked.

It was past seven when they got back to their motel. Aaron, who'd bought a Cleveland restaurant guide and had been eating his way through it since the day he'd arrived in town, wanted to try a highly recommended Chinese restaurant in a shopping center not far away. They drove there, ordered dinner, but didn't like it much. Every single dish was sweet.

Back at the motel Janek watched TV for a while, then went to bed. At 1:00 A.M. he was awakened by his phone. It was Melissa Walters. She sounded slightly frantic and very drunk.

"Sorry to wake you, Lieutenant, but I had to call. Something's been preying on me ever since you left. Then, when I phoned Millie Cannaday and found out why you're here, I just couldn't rest easy until we spoke."

Was she a crazy old lady, or did she really have something for him? "About what?" Janek asked.

"About Bev. I don't think anyone else knows it except for me. Anyone else living, that is."

"Knows what?"

"It has to do with her being a wallflower. It's a terrible thing, Lieutenant. I'd rather not discuss it on the phone if you don't mind."

She suggested he join her for breakfast the following morning at a coffee shop around the corner from the Alhambra. She would explain everything then, she promised. Again she apologized for waking him up.

He had Aaron drop him off, feeling this was one interview he might handle better on his own. Melissa Walters was waiting for him, already sipping coffee. No powder, eye shadow, lipstick, or rouge was on her face that day. It was a ravaged old lady who sat across from him. Two plastic place mats, doubling as breakfast menus, decorated the table, along with a single rose lying on a dainty plate.

Janek ordered toast and coffee. Then he turned to Melissa.

"Well?" he asked.

"There was something Vicky told me once, back years ago. She was drunk when she said it. I'm sure she didn't remember afterwards." Melissa paused. "It was a terrible thing, Lieutenant. A truly terrible thing . . ."

It concerned the two MacDonald boys, Stuart and James. The brothers, it seemed, had had some kind of crush on Victoria. They came around to the lounge all the time, gazed at her intently, mesmerized by the way she sang. Vicky always liked young men, liked their fresh young bodies, but the MacDonalds, still in their teens, were too young even for her.

Still, Vicky was not a woman to waste a pair of

infatuated boys. She'd been worried about Beverly at the time, feeling the girl was socially retarded, too shy with males, frightened even by the notion of sex. Her prescription for that was simple. "All Bev needs is a really good lay," Vicky said.

In the end that was how she decided to employ the MacDonalds: as studs to initiate Beverly into the rites and rituals of physical love.

"To use a couple of kids enamored of you to get your own daughter hot and bothered—it was a rotten idea, and I think deep down Vicky knew it was." Melissa shook her head. She seemed highly disturbed by her story, a sign to Janek that it was probably true. "But once she got the notion into her head, she couldn't let it go. I don't know what happened exactly, except that there was a formal dance and she chose that occasion to sic the boys on to Bev. The whole thing went sour, as it was bound to do. First, there were two of them, which was crazy on its face. And second, the MacDonalds were just a pair of horny kids, not romantic at all. They made some kind of crude, clumsy pass, Bev got hysterical (at least that's what the boys reported to Vicky; Bev apparently never said a word), and the end result was just the opposite of what Vicky intended. Instead of learning what sex was about and how great it could be, Bev discovered it was horrible and never wanted to engage in it again.

"When Vicky told me what she'd done, she was practically in tears. She'd botched it, she admitted, and now she didn't know how to make things right. Even now I can remember her words: 'I didn't want her to be a goddamn wallflower, Lisa. Now I'm afraid that's what she's going to be.'"

That was what Melissa wanted Janek to know. She

probably wouldn't have thought of it if Millie Cannaday hadn't mentioned that the MacDonalds had been murdered and their sex organs glued up by Beverly's patient. Then, when Millie mentioned the wallflower signature, the pieces just fell together in Melissa's mind.

As he listened, Janek couldn't help feeling sickened by the tale even as he was exhilarated by the knowledge that he had finally found a motive for a least one set of Wallflower killings. He thanked Melissa, paid the breakfast check, and went out to walk the cold, windy streets of Cleveland Heights.

He wandered aimlessly. The story haunted him. Everything about it rang true—except for Victoria Archer's tears. He could give no credence to her regrets. On the basis of everything he'd learned about the woman, he believed she probably *did* want Beverly to be a wallflower, and that was the real reason she'd set her daughter up. Monika would understand, Janek thought. She would analyze it clearly. She'd say that although Victoria may have *thought* she was sorry about the outcome, deep down in her subconscious she was pleased by it. *Very pleased.*

So Beverly had sent Diana Proctor out to kill and glue the MacDonalds in revenge for what they'd done to her after a dance years before. And the two toothbrushes Diana had brought back as trophies to be offered up to the image of Victoria on the wall—were they the symbols of the brothers' sex organs, sources of their mutual offense?

It was vile and sick, Janek thought, and also totally wrong. For, even if one believed in revenge, it was not the MacDonalds who deserved to be glued. It was Mama. That, Janek thought, was the ultimate irony in the whole grotesque and monstrous affair: that Beverly, the avenging wallflower, should have offered up trophies to the very woman who caused her to become a wallflower in the first place.

Janek made his way down to the University Circle area, then phoned Aaron at the motel. While he waited to be picked up, he was struck by a powerful idea. He pulled back from it; it seemed too perfect. Then he slowly brought it out again, rotated it, examined it, looked at it from every side. Perhaps, he thought, there *was* a way to break Beverly, induce her to confess. . . .

There they were, two Manhattan cops in a strange midwestern city, looking for a picture painted by an artist who had died seven years before.

"How do we find it? We go classic, Frank," Aaron said. And that's just what he did.

Although it was a textbook example of investigative work, later Janek would marvel at the elegance and speed with which Aaron brought it off.

He went straight to the Cuyahoga County Courthouse, where, after some mild flirting with one of the clerks, he obtained the estate file for Peter Aretzsky. Aretzsky's sole heir and executrix turned out to be one and the same person, his sister, a Mrs. Nadia Malkiewicz, who, as it happened, was conveniently listed in the Cleveland telephone directory. Aaron called her. Yes, she was Peter Aretzsky's sister. Yes, she had inherited all his unsold work. Yes, she had the big picture of Victoria Archer. Yes, she would be willing to show it to the detectives. When they would like to see it? Now? Fine, they could come right over.

The entire process took Aaron just one and three-quarters hours.

* * *

Mrs. Malkiewicz, a widow, lived in Ohio City, a historical section on the west side of Cleveland which, after years of neglect, was in the midst of heavy gentrification. As Janek and Aaron drove in, they could hear the sound of sawing and hammering around the neighborhood. They saw Dumpsters on the street filled with the entrails of houses being gutted for renovation.

The Malkiewicz residence was the worst-looking house on its block, a narrow wood frame structure with peeling siding and an unshoveled path leading to a badly disintegrating front porch.

Nadia Malkiewicz looked as miserable as her house. A pale, drawn white-haired woman in a cheap, shapeless housedress, she had a bitter, puckered mouth and the beginnings of a mustache on her upper lip. Her greeting, too, was a good deal less effusive than Aaron expected after talking with her on the phone. Janek understood her transformation. A shrewd look in the old lady's eyes told him she saw them as vultures looking to pounce upon her late brother's work.

He also quickly understood something else: Mrs. Malkiewicz had contempt for said work. There were no original Aretzsky paintings displayed on her parlor walls, although there were pictures of another sort, including a large black velvet banner bearing a cloying reproduction of da Vinci's *The Last Supper*.

"Yuk! That woman!" was Mrs. Malkiewicz's reaction when Aaron asked her about Victoria Archer.

"She ruined my brother's life, not that he had much of one. A failure and a drunkard was what he was! What's worse, tell me, than a failed drunken painter? Slapping paint on burlap all day long—is that any kind of life? My late husband, bless him, was a hardworking man. Forty-five years sweating it out on the flats. And what did he have to show for it when they laid him off? Nothing! Not even his promised pension. 'Sorry, we're bankrupt,' the company said. So that's what you get in this great United States of America. . . .''

They listened to her bitter gripes for half an hour before they could get her to escort them to the basement, where the treasure trove of art was stored.

The paintings, Janek could see at once, were being kept under appalling conditions. Forty or fifty canvases were piled unevenly against a rough stone cellar wall. Moisture oozed along the floor, and an old oil-burning forced-air furnace roared on the other side of the room.

When they began to pull the pictures out—the one of Victoria, being the largest, was at the bottom of the stack—he saw that many of the frames were warped and that there were mouse droppings in between.

Still, Janek found the work impressive. No matter that Peter Aretzsky had lived a miserable life, his drawing was authoritative and his palette was vibrant. When, finally, they pulled out the big portrait and set it up, Janek could tell at once that it was the artist's masterpiece.

Melissa Walters had been right: Aretzsky had put great feeling into it. His sense of his subject leaped off the canvas and struck the viewer hard. But it was not the painter's hatred that Janek felt so much, nor his bitterness and disillusionment. Although Victoria was harshly characterized, Aretzsky showed a good deal more of her than mere cruelty. It was, Janek thought, a portrait of an extremely unhappy woman, a woman ravaged by a vast and insupportable inner pain. Yes, she was mean, yes, she was selfish—the glare in her eyes and the set of her mouth made that clear enough. But what Aretzsky showed was a victim, a real human being in distress. And although Janek understood why Victoria had hated this picture and had wished to see it destroyed, he also understood how very wrong she'd been. Compared with the painting he had seen in Beverly's bedroom, the painting that had haunted his dreams, this was a mature work of art. That first portrait was a poster. This second one was a truly tragic image.

As Janek continued to gaze at the picture, many things became clear. He understood why Beverly had coveted the first picture and built her bedroom altar around it. It was a portrait of her mother as Beverly needed to remember her, while the second picture was too complex to inspire adoration. The Victoria Archer in the second picture was a woman who could make a wallflower of her own daughter. It was that true a likeness, Janek thought.

Later, upstairs, he and Aaron tried to strike a deal with Mrs. Malkiewicz, but the old lady wouldn't bargain. She acknowledged she'd been unable to sell a single one of her brother's canvases and admitted freely that he and Aaron were the first people to come around and express an interest in his work. Still, she held firm. Her price was nonnegotiable. Ten-thousand-dollars-take-it-or-leave-it. Not a penny less.

Why? they asked her. She couldn't explain it. She just knew the picture was valuable and she wasn't going to sell it cheap. But we're cops, they reminded her, civil servants; we don't have that kind of dough. Well, maybe not, she said. But ten thousand was still the price.

Janek understood even before Aaron that there was no point in further discussion. We'll think about it, he told Mrs. Malkiewicz politely. We'll let you know tomorrow.

* * *

Back in the car Aaron was explosive.

"You crazy, Frank? You'd even consider paying that? Screw her! And to hell with the picture!"

"Trouble is I want it," Janek said.

He explained to Aaron his conviction that the reason Mrs. Malkiewicz set the price so high was that she didn't really want to sell.

"Sure she needs the money. And sure she acts like Aretzsky's pictures are shit. But the truth is she loved her brother, and his pictures are the only things of his she's got. To sell one off is to lose a part of him. Even if we agree to pay her price, I'm not sure she won't back out."

Aaron shrugged. "So what's the point?"

"The point is I need that goddamn picture. So I'll just have to get hold of the money, then handle her very carefully."

"Where're you going to get that kind of bread?"

"I think I know where I can raise it."

Aaron looked at him skeptically. "You're not thinking of Kit?"

"No, not Kit," Janek said. "I've got someone else in mind."

Back in the motel he dialed Stanton's office in New York. Mr. Dorance was in a meeting, his secretary said. Could he get back to Janek later on?

"No. Tell him it's an emergency."

A minute later a breathless Stanton came on the line.

"What's the matter, Frank? What's going on?"

"I need ten thousand dollars."

"Is this a joke? I'm kind of busy."

"No joke, Stanton. I'm out in Cleveland. I'm on the trail of the person who put that girl up to all those killings, including Jess's. I can't go into the details. It's a complicated case. The bottom line is that there's a painting out here I think I can use to put this person away. It'll cost me ten thousand dollars.''

'' 'Think' you can use?''

"Yeah, well, it's a long shot. But it's the only thing I got going. You said I should call you if I needed anything. I'm calling. This is what I need to catch Jess's killer.''

A long pause. He knew what Stanton was thinking: Yes, he'd made that commitment, but ten thousand was a lot of money. Was there any way he could wriggle out of this? Was Janek off his rocker?

"You're sure the painting's worth it?''

"No. But that's what it's going to cost.''

"Maybe you should have it professionally appraised?''

"Screw that. I need it now.''

Another pause. "You're really calling in my marker?''

"I guess you could say that, Stanton, yeah.''

"I didn't expect this. Not so soon.''

"Neither did I. Believe me, if I had the money, I'd buy the damn thing myself.''

"Well, all right. How soon do you need it?''

"Yesterday.''

"I'll FedEx you a check. You'll get it tomorrow morning.''

"No check,'' Janek said. "The seller's nervous. The only way I can close the deal is put cash down on the table.''

"I can wire you the money, I suppose. To a local bank out there.'' He could hear the exasperation in Stanton's voice. "Jesus, Frank! I just hope you know what you're doing!''

"Yeah. Well, I'm just doing the best I can,'' Janek replied.

* * *

The following morning at eleven they were back at the Malkiewicz residence with ten banded packs of fresh hundred-dollar bills and a rented van big enough to transport the painting.

Mrs. Malkiewicz met them at the door. She looked at Janek nervously. "I didn't expect you back so soon."

"I've got the money. We're here to take the picture."

He knew the way to do it was to move as quickly as possible, ignore any hesitancy on her part, count out the cash bill by bill while Aaron wrestled the portrait out the door. That way, if she happened to have second thoughts, it would be too late; the transaction would be complete.

It worked out. Mrs. Malkiewicz didn't say a word, although Janek couldn't help noticing her despair. He knew she'd get over it. Ten grand was enough to fix up her house. And she still had a thick stack of Aretzsky paintings rotting in her cellar.

That afternoon they found a carpenter who agreed to crate up the picture in time for the first flight the following morning to New York. Janek and Aaron would escort it back, the fruit of their investigation.

After the plane took off, Janek stared out his window at the sprawling city below. The sky was gray, broken by a few plumes of industrial smoke. Cleveland looked huge and flat, blocks of bleak gray buildings, a grid of iron-colored streets. The Cuyahoga River, famous for once having caught on fire, was crusted with snow, and Lake Erie seemed a vast white frozen waste. It was a strange and fascinating place, he thought, this city Aaron had described as a Rust Belt town of broken dreams. Here for many years iron and coal had been forged into steel, and here, too, the pathology of Wallflower had been forged.

11

The Portrait

The crucial move, Janek knew, would be the delivery of the portrait. Bungle that and he could botch his entire case.

He and Aaron war-gamed the problem. Since they couldn't break into her house and switch the new painting with the old (their preferred solution), they'd have to take their chances on a straight delivery. The trick, they agreed, would be to get Beverly to accept it.

"How about two guys in deliveryman uniforms. 'Parcel, Ms. Archer. Just sign here, please, ma'am.'"

"Yeah," said Aaron, "then they bring in this enormous box. 'Hey,' she yells, 'I never ordered this. Get this stinking thing out of here.' See, Frank, it's not like you want to send her a valentine that all we got to do is slip it under her door. That picture's fucking humongous."

"So there's only one solution," Janek said. "Deliver it ourselves."

"What if she won't take it?"

"We'll leave it on the stoop."

"So she ignores it. Or has it hauled away. There's no guarantee she'll look at it, even if she does take it inside."

"You're right," Janek said. "There's no guarantees

about any of it. But if we deliver it to her in the proper context, our odds will improve. By a lot.''

He called Monika, filled her in on his trip to Cleveland, outlined his plan, then asked her what she thought.

"Strange, a bit morbid, certainly daring," she said. She sounded less excited than he'd expected. "You say you want to shock this woman into a confession. But there's also a chance you'll shock her into a psychotic state. Have you considered that?"

"It's occurred to me," he said. "Frankly, the idea doesn't break me up. She goes to prison or she goes to the funny farm. I win either way. A third possibility is that she laughs the whole thing off. That's the one I'd just as soon not think about."

"Sounds to me like you're out for blood, Frank."

Why was she reproaching him? "Wasn't blood what *she* was out for?"

He imagined Monika shaking her head. "This is difficult for me. My profession is to heal, not to wound."

Suddenly he was irritated. "You say I sound like I'm out for blood—I'm not sure what that means. I'm certainly not about to pick up an ice pick and stick it in her ear. But if you mean tearing the mask off her face, then I guess you're right."

"Oh, Frank . . . I'm just not sure I can help you with this anymore."

But it wasn't her help he wanted now; it was her approval. And that, it seemed, she was not about to give. He didn't understand. She had told him to look to the past, that he would find the secret there. What secret, he wondered, did she expect he would find—the cure to Beverly Archer's disease?

"Look," he said, "she's a vicious, manipulative, dangerous murderess. My job is to put her away."

"Of course," she said sadly. "Of course. . . ."

He felt awful when he put down the phone. Would Monika now hold this against him? She said she understood, but did she? He was a detective, not a therapist. Now he had to do his job.

After much discussion and many rehearsals, he and Aaron agreed that since there was no way of knowing how Beverly would react, their best approach would be the simplest and most direct. No big dramatic production at the door. Just walk up the front steps picture in hand, ring the bell, offer to place it in the hall for her, then let the chips fall where they may.

Figuring she'd be tired and thus more vulnerable at the end of the day, they parked their van across from her house a little after 6:00 P.M. There they waited until 6:45, when her last patient left.

They had uncrated the picture earlier; it was now covered only with a sheet. They pulled it out of the van, picked it up, and together carried it across the street.

Aaron pushed the buzzer. It was a while before Beverly answered on the intercom.

"Who's there?"

"Janek."

A short pause. "Go away. I'm not in the mood today."

"I brought you something." He spoke cheerfully. "Something from Cleveland." He tried to entice her with his tone.

"Oh, really . . ." Her voice was lethargic. She certainly didn't sound upset.

"Open the door and I'll show you," he said. He paused again; he was getting into the rhythm of the thing. "You won't be sorry, Bev."

Aaron gave him a thumbs-up as they heard the lock mechanism being turned. Then the door opened and Beverly stood in the archway, hands planted on her hips. She looked a perfect little butterball as she stared at them and then at the sheet-covered picture in between.

"Is that great big thing for tiny little me?" She spoke with a sarcastic lilt.

Janek nodded. "Want us to bring it inside?"

"I don't know that I'm going to accept it. Remember the old saying: 'Beware Greeks bearing gifts.'"

"What're you afraid of? Think it's a Trojan Horse?"

She stared at the picture curiously. "What is it anyway?"

"A painting."

"What kind of painting?"

"Aretzsky's second portrait of your mother," Janek said.

She tut-tutted him. "Oh, Janek, you're so tiresome. I know all about that second portrait."

"Sure, you know about it. But did you ever look at it?"

"No. And I don't intend to."

As she started to close the door, he felt his case begin to slip away. *Do something! Razz her! Don't let her close you out!*

"Scared to look, Bev?" he taunted.

She hesitated. "No, I'm not scared to look."

"There are things in this picture you won't see in the one upstairs."

She nodded. "I know the story. A drunk old painter's revenge."

"Maybe something deeper than revenge, Bev. Maybe something true."

"All the truth went into the first portrait. The second was painted on the rebound. That's the way I heard it."

He shook his head. "You heard wrong. The first time Aretzsky was blinded by love. The second time his eyes were wide open."

She glared at him. "You're an ass, Janek." Again she tried to shut him out.

This is it, he thought. *Go for broke!*

He blocked the door with his shoe. When he spoke again he used no taunts nor was there any trace of sarcasm in his voice.

"The MacDonalds were a mistake, Bev. You sent Diana out to kill the wrong boys. Sure, they gave you a hard time. But it was your mother who put them up to it." He snatched the sheet off the picture, tilted it so she could see Victoria's face. "Look into her eyes. Check out her mouth. See the cruelty, the depravity, the selfishness? This is the lady who set you up. She told Melissa Walters she didn't want you to be a wallflower. But when you look hard at this picture you have to wonder if she meant it. Because that's what you are, Bev. A wallflower. Now and for the rest of your life." He thrust his finger at the painting. "And this is the lady who made you one. Not the MacDonalds. *Her!*"

He nodded to Aaron. They turned and walked away. The plan was not to look back, not to give her a chance to answer, or gesture at them, or show her contempt by slamming the door in their faces. By the time they heard it slam they were already at the curb. And still they

walked. It was only when they reached the other side of
the street and got into their van, that Janek turned and
looked and saw with satisfaction that the door to the
house was closed and the picture they'd left was no
longer on the stoop.

Give her the night with her new mama, Janek thought.
Let them cook together, heat each other up. Then,
maybe, butterball will be ready to talk.

It was out of his hands now. It was between the
Archers. Nothing for him to do but wait. He went home,
ordered in some Chinese, watched a hockey game on
TV, then retired early to bed. He did not sleep well. He
tossed and turned, worried that Beverly would not take
his bait, worried that if she did Monika would forever
think less of him, because, as she'd put it, he'd gone for
blood.

In the morning he spoke briefly with Aaron, who'd
spent the night watching Beverly's house. Nothing yet,
so Janek set to work methodically cleaning his apartment. He mopped his kitchen, vacuumed his rugs, waxed
his furniture, and scrubbed his bathroom floor on his
knees. He didn't clean up the place very often, but this
day he did so with a vengeance. Perhaps, he thought, it
was a way for him not to think about Monika, not to deal
with the feelings she'd conveyed, the way she'd dis-
tanced herself after he'd revealed his plan.

A little after ten he received a call from a young
lawyer, an associate at Stanton's firm, who was repre-
senting him on the Rusty Glickman assault suit.

"Glickman's got no case and Streep & Holster know
it," the attorney said. "I told them: All you've got is a
bunch of phony charges brought by a man Janek put

away years ago. Unfortunately there wasn't any give, so my strategy now is to go into court and move for summary judgment. It may take a while but I'm pretty sure we'll get it. Then the whole misrable business will be done with.''

Janek thanked him. The moment he set down his phone it rang again. He snatched it up.

It was Aaron. ''Something's going on here, Frank. Beverly's not seeing her patients.''

''What do you mean?''

''They show up on time, go to the door, ring, and stand there a while. When nobody answers the intercom, they sort of droop and slouch away.''

''You're sure she's there?''

''Positive. I would have seen her come out. I tried to call her a minute ago. All I got was her answering machine.''

He thought of what Monika had said, about the possibility Beverly could be shocked into psychosis. Maybe, just maybe, the portrait was having its effect.

''I'll be right over,'' he told Aaron. ''Better get a police locksmith there, too.''

He would never forget the scene that confronted them when they finally got inside the house. The painting he and Aaron had delivered, at least what was left of it, stood in tatters in the front hall just inside the door. The image had been desecrated. The eyes, the cruel scheming eyes, had been stabbed straight through the pupils. The selfish mouth had been slashed across so that the lips hung in loose folds. The breasts, too, had been assaulted with a scissors or perhaps a knife. But by far the worst and most fiendish violations had been committed against the area between Victoria Archer's legs. That portion of the

picture bore numerous stab wounds, a "pattern of fury," as
medical examiners refer to a configuration of knife thrusts
so rapid and vigorous that all vestiges of the reproductive
organs are obliterated.

Janek and Aaron rushed up the stairs. At the bedroom
door they stopped. The spectacle before them was so
stunning and bizarre they could only stand before it and
gape.

The room was bathed in reddish light. The original
portrait, removed from its niche, lay flat across the great
four-poster. Beverly, in the same scarlet dress her mother
had worn in both paintings, lay upon the picture very
still. There was blood on the canvas and the bed.

"I think she's dead, Frank," Aaron said. "It looks like
she slit her wrists."

Janek walked forward and touched Beverly's forehead. The skin was cold as ice. He tried to lift her arm to
check for wounds, but found he could not move her.
Then he understood. She was stuck to the painting. She
had glued herself to it.

"Jesus!" Aaron said. "Maybe she was trying to screw
the picture. Do you think?"

Janek shook his head. He was sure that that was not
what Beverly had been trying to do when she opened her
veins, then glued herself to her mother—pelvis to pelvis,
hands to hands, breasts to breasts. What she had attempted, he felt certain, was a terminal act of bonding.
But then, perhaps in her last moments, she had writhed
against the image, engaging in a final failed life-and-
death struggle for release.

He circled the bed, and, when Bev's face came into
view, Janek felt his rage subside. Her frozen expression,

a mixture of panic and yearning, filled him with pity and terror.

He turned to Aaron. "Call the morgue," he said.

After Aaron went downstairs, Janek spotted an ivory-handled knife, blade open, on the floor. He picked it up, clasped the blade shut, then pushed a chrome button on the side. The blade sprang forward in his hand. It was the knife Bev had used to kill herself—Jess's knife, the knife that had haunted his dreams.

He looked back at Beverly, met her dead eyes head-on.

"What can I do for you?" he whispered.

The moment he heard his own voice, he knew the answer. He would use Jess's knife to cut the dead woman loose.

He imagined her screaming: "Cut, Mama! No!" But to cut them apart, he knew, was the only way. He straddled Bev, then sliced into the picture. How appropriate, he thought, that he was now separating her from the phony image she had worshiped. The painting was thick but the knife was sharp. The canvas parted before the blade like silk.

Beverly had been mad, of course, functional but mad, perhaps as far back as her girlhood. Confronted finally by the true nature of her mother, her madness had engulfed and destroyed her.

He waited until the medical examiner arrived, waited until the assistants carried Bev's body out. He sat alone for a while in the strange dark bedroom. And then it was time to leave.

Downstairs Aaron was standing before the damaged second portrait in the hall.

"Funny, isn't it, Frank, how now the two pictures look almost the same?"

Janek understood. The cuts he'd made in the idealized version upstairs matched almost perfectly the cuts Beverly had made in the cruel version before him.

"Too bad she killed herself," Aaron said. "It would have been a hell of a trial." He paused. "I wonder if she would have confessed in the end."

"She did confess," Janek replied. "She just didn't do it with words."

Aaron grinned at him. "Well, you got her, Frank. You nailed her."

"Yeah. . . ."

"Do you think Kit would say you did it straight?"

Janek shrugged. "Sometimes, when they're as crooked as this one," he said, "you have to use a slightly crooked nail."

There was, at first, a feeling of fulfillment. Having broken and destroyed the monster, he was no longer possessed by anger. There was the satisfaction, too, that came with understanding another person, adding another quantum to his store of knowledge of human beings and their mysterious capacity for evil.

But these good feelings fled quickly. The letdown descended within a day. It was like the Switch case: as soon as it was over, the passions that had fueled the quest began to die. And then he was left with himself, to ponder the meaning of his life—to wonder what Wallflower had meant to him, and whether it had cost him Monika's love.

He knew the case had changed him. He would never forget his horror as he felt the steel plunge into his throat.

would never forget his conviction that he was going to die. But as he reexamined that moment, he recalled that it was not fear of death that had seized him, but a terrible frustration that he did not know who was attacking him or why.

Now that he had solved all that, he was left with his grief for Jess, a grief he knew he would always carry with him, though hopefully without the intensity of the past few months.

Redemption? He wasn't sure he'd achieved it. The seeds of his melancholy had been planted years before. There would be times throughout his life, he knew, when he must harvest their bitter fruit. And if, as he believed, he had driven Beverly Archer to suicide . . . well, he would have to live with that.

His cases always haunted him. Sometimes he felt as though his mind was filled with overlapping images from old homicides and the echoes of confessions of killers he had tracked and caught through the years. Now Wallflower, too, would become part of that montage. To be haunted, he understood, was the price he must pay for daring to explore the back alleys of tormented souls.

For two days after Wallflower was closed he walked the streets of New York. It was the second week of January, the coldest time of year. He felt himself buffeted by piercing winter winds.

On the afternoon of the second day he noticed something in the steamy window of a little antique store on Charles Street. He stopped before it, shivering, hesitated, then walked inside.

A small bell attached to the door tinkled as he entered. A bespectacled old man in a tattered gray sweater glanced at him from behind a battered desk. It was a warm, cluttered little shop, filled with sparkling objects. Janek nodded to the proprietor, then went straight to the object that had caught his eye. He picked it up, held it in his hand, stared at it, amazed. It was an almost perfect duplicate of the glass Monika had found for him in Venice.

He bought it at the old man's asking price. Surely finding such a glass was a wonderful omen that he must not spoil by haggling over cost. He hurried home, set the glass beside the one Monika had given him, and then peered into the pair as they broke the afternoon light into colors and stars, crystal fire.

The magic of Venice flooded back. In that enchanted city he had found himself a lover; in her arms he had found ecstasy and joy. After Jess was killed, Monika became more than his lover—she became his therapist and adviser, too. But when he'd come back from Cleveland and told her of his intention to break Beverly with her mother's picture, Monika had responded coolly. She was a healer, not a wounder, she'd said. She'd told him she didn't think she could help him anymore.

He had gone ahead anyway, done what he had to do, and now that it was finished, he wanted desperately to be with her again. For a week he'd wanted to call her, but he'd hesitated. Would she still be reserved with him? Would she deny him her love?

Now, as he stared at the two glasses and the afternoon waned, he knew the time had come to call.

She sounded cheerful, said she was happy to hear his voice. They exchanged notes on the weather: Hamburg was chilly; that very evening a light snow had begun to fall. She was thinking about taking a week off, she said, perhaps driving down to Austria with some friends to ski.

And how was he doing? When she hadn't heard from him, she wasn't sure what she should think.

As her voice trailed off, he began to speak. The Wallflower case was over, he told her. Beverly Archer was dead by her own hand. He wanted Monika to know that he owned up to his responsibility in the matter. He knew what he had done and why. He would not flinch from it; he felt no shame on account of it. Could she, Monika, accept him as he now accepted himself, for the person he was, without reservation or regret?

"Oh, Frank," she said, "how can you even ask?"

Suddenly his tension was eased. He felt he could step out from behind his detective's mask and speak to her as a man. He told her he wanted to tell her a story. He had been out walking that afternoon . . . had passed this little shop . . . had seen this glass . . . had bought it . . . it was nearly identical. . . .

"You know what this means?" he asked.

"Tell me, Frank."

"It means I want to be with you," he said, his longing for her pouring out through his voice. "Will you meet me in Venice? In three days? In two?"

There was a brief silence before she answered.

"Oh, yes," she said, and, as her words reached him, he imagined the sparkling affirmation in her eyes. "Oh, yes! Yes!" she said, and he could feel the glow of her warming him from across the icy sea.

ABOUT THE AUTHOR

WILLIAM BAYER's last novel was the *noir* thriller *Blind Side*. He is also the author of the best-sellers *Switch* and *Pattern Crimes*, and the Edgar Award winner *Peregrine*. He and his wife, food writer Paula Wolfert, divide their time between homes in western Connecticut and Martha's Vineyard.

www.MinotaurBooks.com

The premier website for
the best in crime fiction:

Log on and learn more about:

The Labyrinth: Sign up for this monthly
newsletter and get your crime fiction fix.
Commentary author Q&A, hot new titles, and giveaways.

MomentsInCrime: It's no mystery what our
authors are thinking. Each week, a new author blogs
about their upcoming projects, special events, and
more. Log on today to talk to your favorite authors.
www.MomentsInCrime.com

GetCozy: The ultimate cozy connection. Find
your favorite cozy mystery, grab a reading group
guide, sign up for monthly giveaways, and more.
ww.GetCozyOnline.com

MINOTAUR
BOOKS

Why Didn't They Ask Evans?

(Also published as **THE BOOMERANG CLUE**)

Also by Agatha Christie:

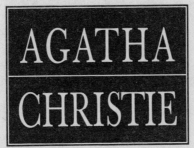

AGATHA CHRISTIE

Why Didn't They Ask Evans?

(Also published as **THE BOOMERANG CLUE**)

St. Martin's Paperbacks

WHY DIDN'T THEY ASK EVANS?

Also published as *The Boomerang Clue*

Copyright © 1933, 1935 by Agatha Christie.
Copyright renewed 1960, 1962 by Agatha Christie Mallowan.

Reprinted by arrangement with G.P. Putnam's Sons, a member of Penguin Putnam, Inc.

Cover photo of woman: Hulton Archive
Cover photo of wallet in street: Colin Hawkins / Stone

ISBN: 0-312-98159-7
EAN: 80312-98159-4

Printed in the United States of America

St. Martin's Paperbacks edition / February 2002

St. Martin's Paperbacks are published by St. Martin's Press, 175 Fifth Avenue, New York, NY 10010.

10 9 8 7 6

Contents

Why Didn't They Ask Evans?

(Also published as **THE BOOMERANG CLUE**)

The Accident

Bobby Jones' teed up his ball, gave a short preliminary waggle, took the club back slowly, then brought it down and through with the rapidity of lightning.

Did the ball fly down the fairway straight and true, rising as it went and soaring over the bunker to land within an easy mashie shot of the fourteenth green?

No, it did not. Badly topped, it scudded along the ground and embedded itself firmly in the bunker!

There were no eager crowds to groan with dismay. The solitary witness of the shot manifested no surprise. And that is easily explained—for it was not the American-born master of the game who had played the shot but merely the fourth son of the Vicar of Marchbolt, a small seaside town on the coast of Wales.

Bobby uttered a decidedly profane ejaculation.

He was an amiable-looking young man of about eight-and-twenty. His best friend could not have said that he was handsome, but his face was an eminently likable one, and his eyes had the honest brown friendliness of a dog's.

"I get worse every day," he muttered dejectedly.

"You press," said his companion.

Dr. Thomas was a middle-aged man with grey hair and a red, cheerful face. He himself never took a full swing. He played short, straight shots down the middle and usually beat more brilliant but more erratic players.

Bobby attacked his ball fiercely with a niblick. The third time was successful. The ball lay a short distance from the green which Dr. Thomas had reached with two creditable iron shots.

"Your hole," said Bobby.

They proceeded to the next tee.

The doctor drove first—a nice straight shot, but with no great distance about it.

Bobby sighed, teed his ball, reteed it, waggled his club a long time, took back stiffly, shut his eyes, raised his head, depressed his right shoulder, did everything he ought not to have done—and hit a screamer down the middle of the course!

He drew a deep breath of satisfaction. The well-known golfer's gloom passed from his eloquent face to be succeeded by the equally well-known golfer's exultation.

"I know now what I've been doing," said Bobby—quite untruthfully.

A perfect iron shot, a little chip with a mashie, and Bobby lay dead. He achieved a birdie four, and Dr. Thomas was reduced to one up.

Full of confidence, Bobby stepped onto the sixteenth tee. He again did everything he should not have done, and this time no miracle occurred. A terrific, a magnificent, an almost superhuman slice happened! The ball went round at right angles.

"If that had been straight—whew!" said Dr. Thomas.

"*If*—" said Bobby bitterly. "Hullo, I thought I heard a shout! Hope the ball didn't hit anyone."

He peered out to the right. It was a difficult light. The sun was on the point of setting, and looking straight into it, it was hard to see anything distinctly. Also there was a slight mist rising from the sea. The edge of the cliff was a few hundred yards away.

"The footpath runs along there," said Bobby. "But the ball can't possibly have travelled as far as that. All the same, I did think I heard a cry. Did you?"

But the Doctor had heard nothing.

Bobby went after his ball. He had some difficulty in finding it, but ran it to earth at last. It was practically unplayable—embedded in a furze bush. He had a couple of hacks at it, then picked it up and called out to his companion that he gave up the hole.

The Doctor came over towards him since the next tee was right on the edge of the cliff.

The seventeenth was Bobby's particular bugbear. At it you had to drive over a chasm. The distance was not actually so great, but the attraction of the depths below was over-powering.

They had crossed the footpath, which now ran inland to their left skirting the very edge of the cliff.

The Doctor took an iron and just landed on the other side.

Bobby took a deep breath and drove. The ball scudded forward and disappeared over the lip of the abyss.

"Every single dashed time," said Bobby bitterly, "I do the same dashed idiotic thing!"

He skirted the chasm, peering over. Far below the sea sparkled, but not every ball was lost in its depths. The drop was sheer at the top, but below it shelved gradually.

Bobby walked slowly along. There was, he knew, one place where one could scramble down fairly easily. Caddies did so, hurling themselves over the edge and reappearing triumphant and panting with the missing ball.

Suddenly Bobby stiffened and called to his companion: "I say, Doctor, come here. What do you make of that?"

Some forty feet below was a dark heap of something that looked like old clothes.

The Doctor caught his breath. "By Jove!" he said. "Somebody's fallen over the cliff. We must get down to him."

Side by side the two men scrambled down the rock, the more athletic Bobby helping the other. At last they reached the ominous dark bundle. It was a man of about forty—and he was still breathing, though unconscious.

The Doctor examined him, touching his limbs, feeling his pulse, drawing down the lids of his eyes. He knelt down beside him and completed his examination. Then he looked up at Bobby, who was standing there feeling rather sick, and slowly shook his head.

"Nothing to be done," he said. "His number's up, poor fellow. His back's broken. Well, well. I suppose he wasn't familiar with the path and when the mist came up he walked over the edge. I've told the council more than once there ought to be a railing just here."

He stood up again. "I'll go off and get help," he said. "Make arrangements to have the body got up. It'll be dark before we know where we are. Will you stay here?"

Bobby nodded. "There's nothing to be done for him, I suppose?" he asked.

The Doctor shook his head. "Nothing. It won't be long—the pulse is weakening fast. He'll last another twenty minutes at most. Just possible he may recover consciousness before the end—but very likely he won't. Still—"

"Rather," said Bobby quickly. "I'll stay. You get along. If he does come to, there's no drug or anything—?" He hesitated.

The Doctor shook his head. "There'll be no pain," he said. "No pain at all."

Turning away he began rapidly to climb up the cliff

again. Bobby watched him till he disappeared over the top with a wave of the hand.

Bobby moved a step or two along the narrow ledge, sat down on a projection in the rock and lit a cigarette. The business had shaken him. Up to now he had never come in contact with illness or death.

What rotten luck there was in the world! A swirl of mist on a fine evening, a false step—and life came to an end. Fine, healthy-looking fellow too—probably never known a day's illness in his life. The pallor of approaching death couldn't disguise the deep tan of the skin. A man who had lived an out-of-door life—abroad perhaps. Bobby studied him more closely—the crisp curling chestnut hair just touched with grey at the temples, the big nose, the strong jaw, the white teeth just showing through the parted lips. Then the broad shoulders and the fine sinewy hands. The legs were twisted at a curious angle. Bobby shuddered and brought his eyes up again to the face. An attractive face, humorous, determined, resourceful. The eyes, he thought, were probably blue—

And just as he reached that point in his thoughts, the eyes suddenly opened.

They *were* blue, a clear deep blue. They looked straight at Bobby. There was nothing uncertain or hazy about them. They seemed completely conscious. They were watchful and at the same time they seemed to be asking a question.

Bobby got up quickly and came towards the man. Before he got there the other spoke. His voice was not weak—it came out clear and resonant.

"Why didn't they ask Evans?" he said.

And then a queer little shudder passed over him, the eyelids dropped, the jaw fell. . . .

The man was dead.

Concerning Fathers

Bobby knelt down beside him, but there was no doubt. The man was dead. A last moment of consciousness, that sudden question and then—the end.

Rather apologetically Bobby put his hand into the dead man's pocket and drawing out a silk handkerchief he spread it reverently over the dead face. There was nothing more he could do.

Then he noticed that in his action he had jerked something else out of the pocket. It was a photograph, and in the act of replacing it he glanced at the pictured face.

It was a woman's face, strangely haunting in quality. A fair woman with wide-apart eyes. She seemed little more than a girl, certainly under thirty, but it was the arresting quality of her beauty rather than the beauty itself that seized upon the boy's imagination. It was the kind of face, he thought, not easy to forget.

Gently and reverently, he replaced the photograph in the pocket from which it had come. Then he sat down again to wait for the Doctor's return.

The time passed very slowly—or at least so it seemed to the waiting boy. Also he had just remembered something. He had promised his father to play the organ at the evening service at six o'clock, and it was now ten minutes to six. Naturally his father would understand the circumstances, but all the same he wished that he had remembered to send a message by the Doctor. The Rev. Thomas Jones was a man of extremely nervous temperament. He was *par excellence* a fusser, and when he fussed, his digestive apparatus collapsed and he suffered agonizing pain. Bobby, though he considered his father a pitiful old ass, was nevertheless extremely fond of him. The Rev. Thomas, on the other hand, considered his fourth son a pitiful young ass, and with less tolerance than Bobby sought to effect improvement in the young man.

"The poor old gov'nor," thought Bobby. "He'll be ramping up and down. He won't know whether to start the service or not. He'll work himself up till he gets that pain in the tummy, and then he won't be able to eat his supper. He won't have the sense to realize that I wouldn't let him down unless it were quite unavoidable. And anyhow, what does it matter? But he'll never see it that way. Nobody over fifty has got any sense—they worry themselves to death about tuppenny-ha'penny things that don't matter. They've been brought up all wrong, I suppose, and now they can't help themselves. Poor old Dad, he's got less sense than a chicken!"

He sat there thinking of his father with mingled affection and exasperation. His life at home seemed to him to be one long sacrifice to his father's peculiar ideas. To Mr. Jones, the same life seemed to be one long sacrifice on *his* part, ill understood or appreciated by the younger generation. So may ideas on the same subject differ.

What an age the Doctor was! Surely he might have been back by this time?

Bobby got up and stamped his feet moodily. At that moment he heard something above him and looked up, thankful that help was at hand and that his own services were no longer needed.

But it was not the Doctor. It was a man in plus-fours whom Bobby did not know.

"I say," said the newcomer. "Is anything the matter? Has there been an accident? Can I help in any way?"

He was a tall man with a pleasant tenor voice. Bobby could not see him very clearly, for it was now fast growing dusk.

He explained what had happened, while the stranger made shocked comments.

"There's nothing I can do?" he asked. "Get help or anything?"

Bobby explained that help was on the way and asked if the other could see any signs of its arriving.

"There's nothing at present."

"You see," went on Bobby, "I've got an appointment at six."

"And you don't like to leave—"

"No, I don't quite," said Bobby. "I mean, the poor chap's dead and all that, and of course one can't do anything, but all the same—"

He paused, finding it, as usual, difficult to put confused emotions into words.

The other, however, seemed to understand.

"I know," he said. "Look here, I'll come down—that is, if I can see my way—and I'll stay till these fellows arrive."

"Oh! would you?" said Bobby gratefully. "You see, it's my father. He's not a bad sort really, and things upset him. Can you see your way? A bit more to the left—now to the right—that's it. It's not really difficult."

He encouraged the other with directions until the two men were face to face on the narrow plateau. The newcomer was a man of about thirty-five. He had a rather indecisive face which seemed to be calling for a monocle and a little moustache.

"I'm a stranger down here," he explained. "My name's Bassington-ffrench, by the way. Came down to see about a house. I say, what a beastly thing to happen! Did he walk over the edge?"

Bobby nodded.

"Bit of mist got up," he explained. "It's a dangerous bit of path. Well, so long. Thanks very much. I've got to hurry. It's awfully good of you."

"Not at all," the other protested. "Anybody would do the same. Can't leave the poor chap lying—well, I mean, it wouldn't be decent somehow."

Bobby was scrambling up the precipitous path. At the top he waved his hand to the other then set off at a brisk run across country. To save time he vaulted the church-yard wall instead of going round to the gate on the road—a proceeding observed by the Vicar from the vestry window and deeply disapproved of by him.

It was five minutes past six, but the bell was still tolling.

Explanations and recriminations were postponed until after the service. Breathless, Bobby sank into his seat and manipulated the stops of the ancient organ. Association of ideas led his fingers into Chopin's funeral march.

Afterwards, more in sorrow than in anger (as he expressly pointed out), the Vicar took his son to task.

"If you cannot do a thing properly, my dear Bobby," he said, "it is better not to do it at all. I know that you and all your young friends seem to have no idea of time, but there is One whom we should not keep waiting. You offered to play the organ of your own accord. I did not coerce you. Instead, faint-hearted, you preferred playing a game—"

Bobby thought he had better interrupt before his father got too well away.

"Sorry, Dad," he said, speaking cheerfully and breezily as was his habit no matter what the subject. "Not my fault this time. I was keeping guard over a corpse."

"You were what?"

"Keeping guard over a blighter who stepped over the cliff. You know—the place where the chasm is, by the seventeenth tee. There was a bit of mist just then, and he must have gone straight on and over."

"Good heavens," cried the Vicar. "What a tragedy! Was the man killed outright?"

"No. He was unconscious. He died just after Dr. Thomas had gone off. But of course I felt I had to squat there—couldn't just push off and leave him. And then another fellow came along, so I passed the job of chief mourner on to him and legged it here as fast as I could."

The Vicar sighed.

"Oh, my dear Bobby!" he said. "Will nothing shake your deplorable callousness? It grieves me more than I can say. Here you have been brought face to face with death—with sudden death. And you can joke about it! It leaves you unmoved. Everything—everything, however solemn, however sacred, is merely a joke to your generation."

Bobby shuffled his feet.

If his father couldn't see that of course you joked about a thing because you had felt badly about it—well, he couldn't see it! It wasn't the sort of thing you could explain. With death and tragedy about, you had to keep a stiff upper lip.

But what could you expect? Nobody over fifty understood anything at all. They had the most extraordinary ideas.

"I expect it was the War," thought Bobby loyally. "It upset them and they never got straight again."

"Sorry, Dad," he said with a clear-eyed realization that explanation was impossible.

The Vicar felt sorry for his son—he looked so abashed; but he also felt ashamed of him. The boy had no conception of the seriousness of life. Even his apology was cheery and impenitent.

They moved towards the Vicarage, each making enormous efforts to find excuses for the other.

The Vicar thought, "I wonder when Bobby will find something to do. . . ."

Bobby thought, "Wonder how much longer I can stick it down here. . . ."

Yet they were both extremely fond of each other.

3

A Railway Journey

Bobby did not see the immediate sequel of his adventure. On the following morning he went up to town, there to meet a friend who was thinking of starting a garage and who fancied that Bobby's co-operation might be valuable.

After settling things to everybody's satisfaction, Bobby caught the 11.30 train home two days later. He caught it, true, but only by a very narrow margin. He arrived at Paddington when the clock announced the time to be 11.28, dashed down the subway, emerged on No. 3 platform just as the train was moving, and hurled himself at the first carriage he saw, heedless of indignant ticket-collectors and porters in his immediate rear.

Wrenching open the door, he fell in on hands and knees, picked himself up, the door was shut with a slam by an agile porter, and Bobby found himself looking at the sole other occupant of the compartment.

It was a first-class carriage and in the corner facing the engine sat a dark girl smoking a cigarette. She had on a red skirt, a short green jacket and a brilliant blue béret, and despite a certain resemblance to an organ-grinder's monkey (she had long, sorrowful, dark eyes and a puckered-up face) she was distinctly attractive.

In the midst of an apology, Bobby broke off.

"Why, it's you, Frankie!" he said. "I haven't seen you for ages."

"Well, I haven't seen you. Sit down and talk."

Bobby grinned. "My ticket's the wrong color."

"That doesn't matter," said Frankie kindly. "I'll pay the difference for you."

"My manly indignation rises at the thought," said Bobby. "How could I let a lady pay for me?"

"It's about all we seem to be good for these days," said Frankie.

"I will pay the difference myself," said Bobby heroically as a burly figure in blue appeared at the door from the corridor.

"Leave it to me," said Frankie.

She smiled graciously at the ticket-collector, who touched his hat as he took the piece of white cardboard from her and punched it.

"Mr. Jones has just come in to talk to me for a bit," she said. "That won't matter, will it?"

"That's all right, your ladyship. The gentleman won't be staying long, I expect." He coughed tactfully. "I shan't be round again till after Bristol," he added significantly.

"What can be done with a smile!" said Bobby as the official withdrew.

Lady Frances Derwent shook her head thoughtfully.

"I'm not so sure it's the smile," she said. "I rather think it's Father's habit of tipping everybody five shillings whenever he travels that does it."

"I thought you'd given up Wales for good, Frankie."

Frances sighed. "My dear, you know what it is. You know how mouldy parents can be. What with that, and the bathrooms in the state they are, and nothing to do and nobody to see—and people simply won't come to the country to stay nowadays! They say they're economizing and they can't go so far. Well, I mean, what's a girl to do?"

Bobby shook his head, sadly recognizing the problem.

"However," went on Frankie, "after the party I went to last night, I thought even home couldn't be worse."

"What was wrong with the party?"

"Nothing at all. It was just like any other party only more so. It was to start at the Savoy at half-past eight. Some of us rolled up about a quarter past nine, and of course we got entangled with other people, but we got sorted out about ten. And we had dinner and then after a bit we went on to the 'Marionette'—there was a rumor it was going to be raided. But nothing happened—it was just moribund. And we drank a bit, and then we went on to the 'Bullring'—and that was even deader. And then we went to a coffee stall, and then we went to a fried-fish place, and then we thought we'd go and break-fast with Angela's uncle and see if he'd be shocked—but he wasn't—only bored. And then we sort of fizzled home. Honestly, Bobby, it isn't good enough."

"I suppose not," said Bobby, stifling a pang of envy. Never in his wildest moments did he dream of being able to be a member of the "Marionette" or the "Bull-ring."

His relationship with Frankie was a peculiar one. As children he and his brothers had played with the children at the Castle. Now that they were all grown up, they seldom came across each other. When they did, they still used Christian names. On the rare occasions when Fran-kie was at home, Bobby and his brothers would go up and play tennis. But Frankie and her two brothers were not asked to the Vicarage. It seemed to be tacitly rec-ognized that it would not be amusing for them. On the other hand extra men were always wanted for tennis. There may have been a trace of constraint in spite of the

Christian names. The Derwents were perhaps a shade more friendly than they need have been, as though to show that "there was no difference." The Joneses, on their side, were a shade formal as though determined not to claim more friendship than was offered them. The two families had now nothing in common save certain child-ish memories. Yet Bobby was very fond of Frankie and was always pleased on the rare occasions when Fate threw them together.

"I'm so tired of everything," said Frankie in a weary voice. "Aren't you?"

Bobby considered. "No, I don't think I am."

"My dear, how wonderful!" said Frankie.

"I don't mean I'm hearty," said Bobby, anxious not to create a painful impression. "I just can't stand people who are hearty."

Frankie shuddered at the mere mention of the word. "I know," she murmured. "They're dreadful."

They looked at each other sympathetically.

"By the way," said Frankie suddenly, "what's all this about a man falling over the cliffs?"

"Dr. Thomas and I found him," said Bobby. "How did you know about it, Frankie?"

"Saw it in the paper. Look."

She indicated with her finger a small paragraph headed "Fatal Accident in Sea Mist."

The victim of the tragedy at Marchbolt was identified late last night by means of a photograph which he was carrying. The photograph proved to be that of Mrs. Leo Cayman. Mrs. Cayman was communicated with and journeyed at once to Marchbolt, where she identified the deceased as her brother, Alex Pritchard. Mr. Pritchard had recently returned from Siam. He had been out of England for ten years and was just starting upon a walking tour. The inquest will be held at Marchbolt to-morrow.

Bobby's thoughts flew back to the strangely haunting face of the photograph. "I believe I shall have to give evidence at the inquest," he said.

"How thrilling! I shall come and hear you."

"I don't suppose there will be anything thrilling about it," said Bobby. "We just found him, you know."

"Was he dead?"

"No—not then. He died about a quarter of an hour later. I was alone with him." He paused.

"Rather grim," said Frankie with that immediate understanding that Bobby's father had lacked.

"Of course he didn't feel anything—"

"No?"

"But all the same—well—you see, he looked awfully alive—that sort of person—rather a rotten way to finish—just stepping off a cliff in a silly little bit of mist."

"I get you, Steve," said Frankie and again the queer phrase represented sympathy and understanding. "Did you see the sister?" she asked presently.

"No. I've been up in town two days. Had to see a friend of mine about a garage business we're going in for. You remember him. Badger Beadon."

"Do I?"

"Of course you do. You must remember good old Badger. He squints."

Frankie wrinkled her brows.

"He's got an awfully silly kind of laugh—*Haw, haw, haw*—like that," continued Bobby helpfully.

Still Frankie wrinkled her brows.

"Fell off his pony when we were kids," continued Bobby. "Stuck in the mud head-down, and we had to pull him out by the legs."

"Oh!" said Frankie in a flood of recollection. "I know now. He stammered."

"He still does," said Bobby proudly.

"Didn't he run a chicken farm and it went bust?" inquired Frankie.

"That's right."

"And then he went into a stockbroker's office and they fired him after a month?"

"That't it."

"And then they sent him to Australia and he came back?"

"Yes."

"Bobby," said Frankie, "you're not putting any money into this business venture, I hope?"

"I haven't got any money to put," said Bobby.

"That's just as well," said Frankie.

"Naturally," went on Bobby, "Badger has tried to get hold of someone with a little capital to invest. But it isn't so easy as you'd think."

"When you look round you," said Frankie, "you wouldn't believe people had any sense at all, but they have."

The point of these remarks seemed at last to strike Bobby.

"Look here, Frankie," he said. "Badger's one of the best—one of the very best."

"They always are," said Frankie.

"Who are?"

"The ones who go to Australia and come back again. How did he get hold of the money to start this business?"

"An aunt or something died and left him a garage for six cars, with three rooms over, and his people stumped up a hundred pounds to buy second-hand cars with. You'd be surprised what bargains there are to be had in second-hand cars."

"I bought one once," said Frankie. "It's a painful subject. Don't let's talk of it. What did you want to leave the Navy for? Theў didn't ax you, did they? Not at your age?"

Bobby flushed. "Eyes," he said gruffly.

"You always had trouble with your eyes, I remember."

"I know. But I just managed to scrape through. Then foreign service—the strong light, you know—that rather did for them. So—well—I had to get out."

"Grim," murmured Frankie, looking out of the window.

There was an eloquent pause.

"All the same, it's a shame," burst out Bobby. "My eyes aren't really bad—they won't get any worse, they say. I could have carried on perfectly."

"They look all right," said Frankie. She looked straight into their honest brown depths.

"So you see," said Bobby, "I'm going in with Badger."

Frankie nodded.

An attendant opened the door and said, "First luncheon."

"Shall we?" said Frankie.

They passed along to the dining car.

Bobby made a short strategic retreat during the time when the ticket-collector might be expected.

"We don't want him to strain his conscience too much," he said.

But Frankie said she didn't expect ticket-collectors had any consciences.

It was just after five o'clock when they reached Sileham, which was the station for Marchbolt.

"The car's meeting me," said Frankie. "I'll give you a lift."

"Thanks. That will save me carrying this beastly thing for two miles." He kicked his suitcase disparagingly.

"Three miles, not two," said Frankie.

"Two miles if you go by the footpath over the links."

"The one where—"

"Yes—where that fellow went over."

"I suppose nobody pushed him over, did they?" asked Frankie as she handed her dressing-case to her maid.

"Pushed him over? Good Lord, no. Why?"

"Well, it would make it much more exciting, wouldn't it?" said Frankie idly.

4

The Inquest

The inquest on the body of Alex Pritchard was held on the following day. Dr. Thomas gave evidence as to the finding of the body.

"Life was not then extinct?" asked the Coroner.

"No, deceased was still breathing. There was, however, no hope of recovery. The—" Here the Doctor became highly technical.

The Coroner came to the rescue of the jury. "In ordinary, everyday language, the man's back was broken?"

"If you like to put it that way," said Dr. Thomas sadly.

He described how he had gone off to get help, leaving the dying man in Bobby's charge.

"Now as to the cause of this disaster, what is your opinion, Dr. Thomas?"

"I should say that in all probability (failing any evidence as to his state of mind, that is to say) the deceased stepped inadvertently over the edge of the cliff. There was a mist rising from the sea, and at that particular point the path turns abruptly inland. Owing to the mist the deceased may not have noticed the danger and walked straight on—in which case two steps would take him over the edge."

"There were no signs of violence? Such as might have been administered by a third party?"

"I can only say that all the injuries present are fully explained by the body's striking the rocks fifty or sixty feet below."

"There remains the question of suicide?"

"That is, of course, perfectly possible. Whether the deceased walked over the edge or threw himself over is a matter on which I can say nothing."

Robert Jones was called next.

Bobby explained that he had been playing golf with the Doctor and had sliced his ball towards the sea. A mist was rising at the time and it was difficult to see. He thought he heard a cry, and for a moment wondered if his ball could have hit anybody coming along the footpath. He had decided, however, that it could not possibly have travelled so far.

"Did you find the ball?"

"Yes, it was about a hundred yards short of the footpath."

He then described how they had driven from the next tee and how he himself had driven into the chasm.

Here the Coroner stopped him, since his evidence would have been a repetition of the Doctor's. He questioned him closely, however, as to the cry he had heard or thought he heard.

"It was just a cry."

"A cry for help?"

"Oh, no. Just a sort of shout, you know. In fact I wasn't quite sure I heard it."

"A startled kind of cry?"

"That's more like it," said Bobby gratefully. "Sort of noise a fellow might let out if a ball hit him unexpectedly."

"Or if he took a step into nothingness when he thought he was on a path?"

"Yes."

Then, having explained that the man actually died about five minutes after the Doctor left to get help, Bobby's ordeal came to an end.

The Coroner was by now anxious to get on with a perfectly straightforward business. Mrs. Leo Cayman was called.

Bobby gave a gasp of acute disappointment. Where was the face of the photograph that had tumbled from the dead man's pocket? Photographers, thought Bobby disgustedly, were the worst kind of liars. The photograph obviously must have been taken some years ago, but even then it was hard to believe that that charming wide-eyed beauty could have become this brazen-looking woman with plucked eyebrows and obviously dyed hair. Time, thought Bobby suddenly, was a very frightening thing. What would Frankie, for instance, look like in twenty years' time? He gave a little shiver.

Meanwhile, Amelia Cayman of 17 St. Leonard's Gardens, Paddington, was giving evidence. Deceased was her only brother, Alexander Pritchard. She had last seen him the day before the tragedy, when he had announced his intention of going for a walking tour in Wales. He had recently returned from the East.

"Did he seem in a happy and normal state of mind?"

"Oh, quite! Alex was always cheerful."

"So far as you know he had nothing on his mind?"

"Oh, I'm sure he hadn't. He was looking forward to his trip."

"There have been no money troubles, or other troubles of any kind, in his life recently?"

"Well, really, I couldn't say as to that," said Mrs. Cayman. "You see, he'd only just come back, and before that I hadn't seen him for ten years, and he was never one much for writing. But he took me out to theatres and lunches in London and gave me one or two presents, so I don't think he could have been short of money, and he was in such good spirits that I don't think there could have been anything else."

"What was your brother's profession, Mrs. Cayman?"

The lady seemed slightly embarrassed.

"Well, I can't say I rightly know. Prospecting—that's what he called it. He was very seldom in England."

"You know of no reason which might cause him to take his own life?"

"Oh, no, and I can't believe that he did such a thing. It must have been an accident."

"How do you explain the fact that your brother had no luggage with him—not even a knapsack?"

"He didn't like carrying a knapsack. He meant to post parcels alternate days. He posted one the day before he left with his night things and a pair of socks—only he addressed it to Derbyshire instead of Denbighshire, so it only got here to-day."

"Ah, that clears up a somewhat curious point."

Mrs. Cayman went on to explain how she had been communicated with through the photographers whose name was on the photograph her brother had carried. She had come down with her husband to Marchbolt and had at once recognized the body as that of her brother. As she said the last words she sniffed audibly and began to cry.

The Coroner said a few soothing words and dismissed her. Then he addressed the jury. Their task was to state how this man came by his death. Fortunately the matter appeared to be quite simple. There was no suggestion that Mr. Pritchard had been worried or depressed or in a state of mind where he would be likely to take his own life. On the contrary he had been in good health and spirits and had been looking forward to his holiday. It was unfortunately the case that when a sea mist was rising, the path along the cliff was a dangerous one, and possibly they might agree with him that it was time something was done about it.

The jury's verdict was prompt.

"We find that the deceased came to his death by misadventure, and we wish to add a rider that in our opinion the Town Council should immediately take steps to put a fence or rail on the sea side of the path where it skirts the chasm."

The Coroner nodded approval. The inquest was over.

5

Mr. and Mrs. Cayman

On arriving back at the Vicarage about half an hour later, Bobby found that his connection with the death of Alex Pritchard was not yet quite over. He was informed that Mr. and Mrs. Cayman had called to see him and were in the study with his father. Bobby made his way there and found his father gravely making suitable conversation without, apparently, much enjoying his task.

"Ah!" he said with some slight relief. "Here is Bobby."

Mr. Cayman rose and advanced towards the young man with outstretched hand. Mr. Cayman was a big florid man with a would-be hearty manner and a cold and somewhat shifty eye that rather belied the manner. As for Mrs. Cayman, though she might be considered attractive in a bold, coarse fashion, she had little now in common with that early photograph of herself, and no trace of that wistful expression remained. In fact, Bobby reflected, if she had not recognized her own photograph it seemed doubtful if anyone else would have done so.

"I came down with the wife," said Mr. Cayman, enclosing Bobby's hand in a firm and painful grip. "Had to stand by, you know. Amelia's naturally upset."

Mrs. Cayman sniffed.

"We came round to see you," continued Mr. Cayman. "You see, my poor wife's brother died, practically speaking, in your arms. Naturally, she wanted to know all you could tell her of his last moments."

"Absolutely," said Bobby unhappily. "Oh, absolutely." He grinned nervously and was immediately aware of his father's sigh—a sigh of Christian resignation.

"Poor Alex!" said Mrs. Cayman, dabbing her eyes. "Poor, poor Alex!"

"I know," said Bobby. "Absolutely grim." He wriggled uncomfortably.

"You see," said Mrs. Cayman, looking hopefully at Bobby, "if he left any last words or messages—naturally I want to know."

"Oh, rather," said Bobby. "But as a matter of fact he didn't."

"Nothing at all?" Mrs. Cayman looked disappointed and incredulous. Bobby felt apologetic.

"No—well—as a matter of fact, nothing at all."

"It was best so," said Mr. Cayman solemnly. "To pass away unconscious, without pain—why, you must think of it as a mercy, Amelia."

"I suppose I must," said Mrs. Cayman. "You don't think he felt any pain?"

"I'm sure he didn't," said Bobby.

Mrs. Cayman sighed deeply. "Well, that's something to be thankful for. Perhaps I did hope he'd left a last message, but I can see that it's best as it is. Poor Alex. Such a fine out-of-door man."

"Yes, wasn't he?" said Bobby. He recalled the bronze face, the deep blue eyes. An attractive personality, that of Alex Pritchard, attractive even so near death. Strange that he should be the brother of Mrs. Cayman and the brother-in-law of Mr. Cayman! He had been worthy, Bobby felt, of better things.

"Well, we're very much indebted to you, I'm sure," said Mrs. Cayman.

"Oh, that's all right," said Bobby. "I mean—well, I couldn't do anything else—I mean—" He floundered hopelessly.

"We shan't forget it," said Mr. Cayman. Bobby suffered once more that painful grip. He received a flabby hand from Mrs. Cayman. His father made further adieus. Bobby accompanied the Caymans to the front door.

"And what do you do with yourself, young man?" inquired Cayman. "Home on leave—something of that kind?"

"I spend most of my time looking for a job," said Bobby. He paused. "I was in the Navy."

"Hard times—hard times nowadays," said Mr. Cayman, shaking his head. "Well, I wish you luck, I'm sure."

"Thank you very much," said Bobby politely.

He watched them down the weed-grown drive. Standing there, he fell into a brown study. Various ideas flashed chaotically through his mind, confused reflections—the photograph—that girl's face with the wide-apart eyes and the misty hair—and ten or fifteen years later, Mrs. Cayman with her heavy make-up, her plucked eyebrows, those wide-apart eyes sunk in between folds of flesh till they looked like pigs' eyes, and her violent henna-tinted hair. All traces of youth and innocence had vanished. The pity of things! It all came perhaps of marrying a hearty bounder like Mr. Cayman. If she had married someone else she might possibly have grown older gracefully. A touch of grey in her hair, eyes still wide-apart looking out from a smooth pale face. But perhaps anyway—

Bobby sighed and shook his head. "That's the worst of marriage," he said gloomily.

"What did you say?"

Bobby awoke from meditation to become aware of Frankie, whose approach he had not heard.

"Hullo," he said.

"Hullo. Why marriage? And whose?"

"I was making a reflection of a general nature," said Bobby.

"Namely—?"

"On the devastating effects of marriage."

"Who is devastated?"

Bobby explained. He found Frankie unsympathetic.

"Nonsense. The woman's exactly like her photograph."

"When did you see her? Were you at the inquest?"

"Of course I was at the inquest. What do you think? There's little enough to do down here. An inquest is a perfect godsend. I'd never been to one before. I was thrilled to the teeth. Of course it would have been better if it had been a mysterious poisoning case with analysts' reports and all that sort of thing—but one mustn't be too exacting when these simple pleasures come one's way. I hoped up to the end for a suspicion of foul play, but it all seemed most regrettably straightforward."

"What bloodthirsty instincts you have, Frankie."

"I know. It's probably atavism (however do you pronounce it?—I've never been sure). Don't you think so? I'm sure I'm atavistic. My nickname at school was Monkey Face."

"Do monkeys like murder?" queried Bobby.

"You sound like a correspondence in a Sunday paper," said Frankie. " 'Our correspondents' views on this subject are solicited.' "

"You know," said Bobby, reverting to the original topic, "I don't agree with you about the female Cayman. Her photograph was lovely."

"Touched up, that's all," interrupted Frankie.

"Well, then, it was so much touched up that you wouldn't have known them for the same person."

"You're blind," said Frankie. "The photographer had done all that the art of photography could do, but it was still a nasty bit of work."

"I absolutely disagree with you," said Bobby coldly. "Anyway, where did you see it?"

"In the local *Evening Echo*."

"It probably reproduced badly."

"It seems to me you're absolutely batty," said Frankie crossly. "Over a painted-up raddled bitch—yes, I said *bitch*—like the Cayman."

"Frankie," said Bobby, "I'm surprised at you. In the Vicarage drive too. Semi-holy ground, so to speak."

"Well, you shouldn't have been so ridiculous."

There was a pause, then Frankie's sudden fit of temper abated.

"What is ridiculous," she said, "is to quarrel about the damned woman. I came to suggest a round of golf. What about it?"

"O.K., Chief," said Bobby happily.

They set off amicably together, and their conversation was of such things as slicing and pulling and how to perfect a chip shot onto the green.

The recent tragedy passed quite out of mind until Bobby, holing a long putt at the eleventh to halve the hole, suddenly gave an exclamation.

"What is it?"

"Nothing. I've just remembered something."

"What?"

"Well, these people, the Caymans—they came round and asked if the fellow had said anything before he died—and I told them he hadn't."

"Well?"

"And now I've just remembered that he did."

"Not one of your brightest mornings, in fact."

"Well, you see, it wasn't the sort of thing they meant. That's why, I suppose, I didn't think of it."

"What did he say?" asked Frankie curiously.

"He said: *'Why didn't they ask Evans?'* "

"What a funny thing to say. Nothing else?"

"No. He just opened his eyes and said that—quite suddenly—and then died, poor chap."

"Oh, well," said Frankie, turning it over in her mind, "I don't see that you need worry. It wasn't important."

"No, of course not. Still I wish I'd just mentioned it. You see, I said he'd said nothing at all."

"Well, it amounts to the same thing," said Frankie. "I mean it isn't like 'Tell Gladys I always loved her,' or 'The will is in the walnut bureau,' or any of the proper romantic Last Words there are in books."

"You don't think it's worth while writing about it to them?"

"I shouldn't bother. It couldn't be important."

"I expect you're right," said Bobby and turned his attention with renewed vigor to the game.

But the matter did not really dismiss itself from his mind. It was a small point but it fretted him. He felt very faintly uncomfortable about it. Frankie's point of view was, he felt sure, the right and sensible one. The thing was of no importance—let it go. But his conscience continued to reproach him faintly. He had said that the dead man had said nothing. That wasn't true. It was all very trivial and silly, but he couldn't feel quite comfortable about it.

Finally that evening on an impulse he sat down and wrote to Mr. Cayman.

Dear Mr. Cayman:
I have just remembered that your brother-in-law did

actually say something before he died. I think the exact words were "Why didn't they ask Evans?" I apologize for not mentioning this this morning, but I attached no importance to the words at the time and so, I suppose, they slipped my memory.

Yours truly,
ROBERT JONES

On the next day but one he received a reply.

DEAR MR. JONES:
Your letter of 6th instant to hand. Many thanks for repeating my poor brother-in-law's last words so punctiliously in spite of their trivial character. What my wife hoped was that her brother might have left her some last message. Still, thank you for being so conscientious.

Yours faithfully,
LEO CAYMAN

Bobby felt snubbed.

6

End of a Picnic

On the following day Bobby received a letter of quite a different nature.

It's all fixed, old boy [wrote Badger in an illiterate scrawl which reflected no credit on the expensive public school which had educated him]. Actually got five cars yesterday for fifteen pounds the lot—an Austin, two Morrises and a couple of Rovers. At the moment they won't exactly go, but we can tinker them up sufficiently, I think. Dash it all, a car's a car, after all. So long as it takes the purchaser home without breaking down, that's all he can expect. I thought of opening up Monday week and am relying on you. So don't let me down, will you, old boy? I must say old Aunt Carrie was a sport. I once broke the window of an old boy next door to her who'd been rude to her about her cats, and she never got over it. Sent me a fiver every Christmas, and now this.

We're bound to succeed. The thing's a dead cert. I mean, a car's a car after all. You can pick 'em up for nothing. Put a lick of paint on, and that's all the ordinary fool notices. The thing will go with a Bang. Now don't forget. Monday week. I'm relying on you.

Yours ever,

BADGER

Bobby informed his father that he would be going up to town on Monday week to take up a job. The description of the job did not rouse the Vicar to anything like enthusiasm. He had, it may be pointed out, come across Badger Beadon in the past. He merely treated Bobby to a long lecture on the advisability of not making himself Liable for Anything. Since he was not an authority on financial or business matters, his advice was technically vague, but its meaning was unmistakable.

On the Wednesday of that week Bobby received another letter. It was addressed in a foreign, slanting handwriting. Its contents were somewhat surprising to the young man.

It was from the firm of Henriquez & Dallo in Buenos Aires and, to put it concisely, it offered Bobby a job in the firm with a salary of a thousand a year.

For the first minute or two the young man thought he must be dreaming. A thousand a year. He re-read the letter more carefully. There was mention of an ex-Naval man's being preferred, a suggestion that Bobby's name had been put forward by someone (not named). Acceptance must be immediate, and Bobby must be prepared to start for Buenos Aires within a week.

"Well, I'm damned," said Bobby, giving vent to his feelings in a somewhat unfortunate manner.

"Bobby!"

"Sorry, Dad. Forgot you were there."

Mr. Jones cleared his throat. "I should like to point out to you—"

Bobby felt that this process—usually a long one—must at all costs be avoided. He achieved this by a simple statement.

"Someone's offered me a thousand a year."

The Vicar remained open-mouthed, unable for the moment to make any comment.

"That's put him off his drive all right," thought Bobby with satisfaction.

"My dear Bobby, did I understand you to say that someone has offered you a thousand a year? *A thousand?*"

"Holed it in one, Dad," said Bobby.

"It's impossible," said the Vicar.

Bobby was not hurt by this frank incredulity. His estimate of his own monetary value differed little from that of his father.

"They must be complete mutts," he agreed heartily.

"Who—er—are these people?"

Bobby handed him the letter. The Vicar, fumbling for his pince-nez, peered at it suspiciously. Finally he read it twice.

"Most remarkable," he said at last. "*Most* remarkable."

"Lunatics," said Bobby.

"Ah, my boy," said the Vicar, "it is, after all, a great thing to be an Englishman. Honesty. That's what we stand for. The Navy has carried that ideal all over the world. An Englishman's word! This South American firm realizes the value of a young man whose integrity will be unshaken and of whose fidelity his employers will be assured. You can always depend on an Englishman to play the game—"

"And keep a straight bat," said Bobby.

The Vicar looked at his son doubtfully. The phrase, an excellent one, had actually been on the tip of his tongue, but there was something in Bobby's tone that struck him as not quite sincere.

The young man, however, appeared to be perfectly serious. "All the same, Dad," he said, "why me?"

"What do you mean—why you?"

"There are a lot of Englishmen in England," said

Bobby. "Hearty fellows, full of cricketing qualities. Why pick on me?"

"Probably your late commanding officer may have recommended you."

"Yes, I suppose that's true," said Bobby doubtfully. "It doesn't matter anyway since I can't take the job."

"Can't take it? My dear boy, what do you mean?"

"Well, I'm fixed up, you see. With Badger."

"Badger? Badger Beadon? Nonsense, my dear Bobby. This is serious."

"It's a bit hard, I own," said Bobby with a sigh.

"Any childish arrangement you have made with young Beadon cannot count for a moment."

"It counts with me."

"Young Beadon is completely irresponsible. He has already, I understand, been a source of considerable trouble and expense to his parents."

"He's not had much luck. Badger's so infernally trusting."

"Luck—luck! I should say that young man had never done a hand's turn in his life."

"Nonsense, Dad. Why, he used to get up at five in the morning to feed those beastly chickens. It wasn't his fault they all got the roup or the croup or whatever it was."

"I have never approved of this garage project. Mere folly. You must give it up."

"Can't, sir. I've promised. I can't let old Badger down. He's counting on me."

The discussion proceeded. The Vicar, biased by his views on the subject of Badger, was quite unable to regard any promise made to that young man as binding. He looked on Bobby as obstinate and determined at all costs to lead an idle life in company with one of the worst of possible companions. Bobby, on the other hand, stolidly repeated without originality that he "couldn't let old Badger down."

The Vicar finally left the room in anger, and Bobby then and there sat down to write to the firm of Henriquez & Dallo refusing their offer.

He sighed as he did so. He was letting a chance go here which was never likely to occur again. But he saw no alternative.

Later, on the links, he put the problem to Frankie. She listened attentively.

"You'd have had to go to South America?"

"Yes."

"Would you have liked that?"

"Yes, why not?"

Frankie sighed. "Anyway," she said with decision, "I think you did quite right."

"About Badger, you mean?"

"Yes."

"I couldn't let the old bird down, could I?"

"No, but be careful that the old bird, as you call him, doesn't let you in."

"Oh! I shall be careful. Anyway I shall be all right. I haven't got any assets."

"That must be rather fun," said Frankie.

"Why?"

"I don't know why. It just sounded rather nice and free and irresponsible. I suppose, though, when I come to think of it, that I haven't got many assets either. I mean, Father gives me an allowance, and I've got lots of houses to live in and clothes and maids and some hideous family jewels and a good deal of credit at shops—but that's all the family, really. It's not *me*."

"No, but all the same—" Bobby paused.

"Oh, it's quite different, I know."

"Yes," said Bobby. "It's quite different." He felt suddenly very depressed.

They walked in silence to the next tee.

"I'm going up to town to-morrow," said Frankie as Bobby teed up his ball.

"To-morrow. Oh—and I was going to suggest you should come for a picnic."

"I'd have liked to. However, it's arranged. You see, Father's got the gout again."

"You ought to stay and minister to him," said Bobby.

"He doesn't like being ministered to. It annoys him frightfully. He likes the second footman best. He's sympathetic and doesn't mind having things thrown at him and being called a damned fool."

Bobby topped his drive and it trickled into the bunker.

"Hard lines," said Frankie and drove a nice straight ball that sailed over it.

"By the way," she remarked, "we might do something together in London. You'll be up soon?"

"On Monday. But—well—it's no good, is it?"

"What do you mean—no good?"

"Well, I mean I shall be working as a mechanic most of the time. I mean—"

"Even then," said Frankie, "I suppose you're just as capable of coming to a cocktail party and getting tight as any other of my friends."

Bobby merely shook his head.

"I'll give a beer-and-sausage party if you prefer it," said Frankie encouragingly.

"Oh, look here, Frankie, what's the good? I mean, you can't mix your crowds. Your crowd's a different crowd from mine."

"I assure you," said Frankie, "that my crowd is a very mixed one."

"You're pretending not to understand."

"You can bring Badger if you like. *There's* friendship for you."

"You've got some sort of prejudice against Badger."

"I daresay it's his stammer. People who stammer always make me stammer too."

"Look here, Frankie, it's no good and you know it isn't. It's all right down here. There's not much to do and I suppose I'm better than nothing. I mean, you're always awfully decent to me and all that, and I'm grateful. But I know I'm just nobody—I mean—"

"When you've quite finished expressing your inferiority complex," said Frankie coldly, "perhaps you'll try getting out of the bunker with a niblick instead of a putter."

"Have I—oh, damn!" He replaced the putter in his bag and took out the niblick. Frankie watched with malicious satisfaction as he hacked at the ball five times in succession. Clouds of sand rose round them.

"Your hole," said Bobby, picking up the ball.

"I think it is," said Frankie. "And that gives me the match."

"Shall we play the bye?"

"No. I don't think so. I've got a lot to do."

"Of course. I suppose you have."

They walked together in silence to the clubhouse.

"Well," said Frankie, holding out her hand. "Good-bye, my dear. It's been too marvellous to have you to make use of while I've been down here. See something of you again, perhaps, when I've nothing better to do."

"Look here, Frankie—"

"Perhaps you'll condescend to come to my coster party. I believe you can get pearl buttons quite cheaply at Woolworth's."

"Frankie—"

His words were drowned in the noise of the Bentley's

engine which Frankie had just started. She drove away
with an airy wave of her hand.

"Damn!" said Bobby in a heartfelt tone.

Frankie, he considered, had behaved outrageously.
Perhaps he hadn't put things very tactfully, but dash it
all, what he had said was true enough. Perhaps, though,
he shouldn't have put it into words.

The next three days seemed interminably long. The
Vicar had a sore throat which necessitated his speaking
in a whisper when he spoke at all. He spoke very little
and was obviously bearing his fourth son's presence as
a Christian should. Once or twice he quoted Shakespeare
on how sharper than a serpent's tooth, etc.

On Saturday Bobby felt that he could bear the strain
of home life no longer. He got Mrs. Roberts, who with
her husband "ran" the Vicarage, to give him a packet of
sandwiches, and supplementing this with a bottle of beer
which he bought in Marchbolt he set off for a solitary
picnic.

He had missed Frankie abominably these last few
days. These older people were the limit. They harped on
things so.

Bobby stretched himself out on a brackeny bank and
debated with himself whether he should eat his lunch
first and go to sleep afterwards, or sleep first and eat
afterwards. While he was cogitating, the matter was settled for him by his falling asleep without noticing it.

When he awoke it was half-past three! Bobby grinned
as he thought how his father would disapprove of this
way of spending a day. A good walk across country—
twelve miles or so—that was the kind of thing that a
healthy young man should do. It led inevitably to that
famous remark, "And now, I think, I've earned my
lunch."

"Idiotic," thought Bobby. "Why earn lunch by doing

a lot of walking you don't particularly want to do?
What's the merit in it? If you enjoy it, then it's pure
self-indulgence, and if you don't enjoy it you're a fool
to do it."

Whereupon he fell to upon his unearned lunch and
ate it with gusto. With a sigh of satisfaction he un-
screwed the bottle of beer. Unusually bitter beer, but
decidedly refreshing. . . .

He lay back again, having tossed the empty beer-
bottle into a clump of heather.

He felt rather god-like lounging there. The world was
at his feet. A phrase. But a good phrase. He could do
anything—anything if he tried! Plans of great splendor
and daring initiative flashed through his mind.

Then he grew sleepy again. Lethargy stole over him.
He slept. . . .

Heavy, numbing sleep. . . .

7

An Escape from Death

Driving her large green Bentley, Frankie drew up to the curb outside a large old-fashioned house over the doorway of which was inscribed "St. Asaph's."

Frankie jumped out and, turning, extracted a large bunch of lilies. Then she rang the bell. A woman in nurse's dress answered the door.

"Can I see Mr. Jones?" inquired Frankie.

The nurse's eyes took in the Bentley, the lilies and Frankie with intense interest.

"What name shall I say?"

"Lady Frances Derwent."

The nurse was thrilled, and her patient went up in her estimation. She guided Frankie upstairs into a room on the first floor.

"You've a visitor to see you, Mr. Jones. Now who do you think it is? Such a nice surprise for you."

All this in the "bright" manner usual to nursing homes.

"Gosh!" said Bobby, very much surprised. "If it isn't Frankie!"

"Hullo, Bobby. I've brought the usual flowers. Rather a graveyard suggestion about them, but the choice was limited."

"Ooh, Lady Frances," said the nurse, "they're lovely. I'll put them into water."

She left the room.

Frankie sat down in an obvious "visitor's" chair. "Well, Bobby," she said. "What's all this?"

"You may well ask," said Bobby. "I'm the complete sensation of this place. Eight grains of morphia, no less. They're going to write about me in the *Lancet* and the *B.M.J.*"

"What's the *B.M.J.?*" interrupted Frankie.

"The *British Medical Journal.*"

"All right. Go ahead. Rattle off some more initials."

"Do you know, my girl, that half a grain is a fatal dose? I ought to be dead about sixteen times over. It's true that recovery has been known after sixteen grains—still, eight is pretty good, don't you think? I'm the hero of this place. They've never had a case like me before."

"How nice for them!"

"Isn't it? Gives them something to talk about to all the other patients."

The nurse re-entered, bearing lilies in vases.

"It's true, isn't it, nurse?" demanded Bobby. "You've never had a case like mine?"

"Oh, you oughtn't to be here at all," said the nurse. "In the churchyard, you ought to be. But it's only the good die young, they say." She giggled at her own wit and went out.

"There you are," said Bobby. "You'll see, I shall be famous all over England."

He continued to talk. Any signs of inferiority complex that he had displayed at his last meeting with Frankie had now quite disappeared. He took a firm and egotistical pleasure in recounting every detail of his case.

"That's enough," said Frankie, quelling him. "I don't really care terribly for stomach pumps. To listen to you one would think nobody had ever been poisoned before."

"Jolly few have been poisoned with eight grains of

morphia and got over it," Bobby pointed out. "Dash it all, you're not sufficiently impressed."

"Pretty sickening for the people who poisoned you," said Frankie.

"I know. Waste of perfectly good morphia."

"It was in the beer, wasn't it?"

"Yes. You see, someone found me sleeping like the dead, tried to wake me and couldn't. Then they got alarmed, carried me to farmhouse, and sent for a doctor—"

"I know all the next part," said Frankie hastily.

"At first they had the idea that I'd taken the stuff deliberately. Then when they heard my story, they went off and looked for the beer-bottle and found it where I'd thrown it and had it analyzed—the dregs of it were quite enough for that apparently."

"No clue as to how the morphia got in the bottle?"

"None whatever. They've interviewed the pub where I bought it, and opened other bottles, and everything's been quite all right."

"Someone must have put the stuff in the beer while you were asleep?"

"That's it. I remember that the paper across the top wasn't still sticking properly."

Frankie nodded thoughtfully. "Well," she said, "it shows that what I said in the train that day was quite right."

"What did you say?"

"That that man—Pritchard—had been pushed over the cliff."

"That wasn't in the train. You said that at the station," said Bobby feebly.

"Same thing."

"But why—"

"Darling—it's obvious. Why should anyone want to

put *you* out of the way? You're not the heir to a fortune or anything."

"I may be. Some great-aunt I've never heard of in New Zealand or somewhere may have left me all her money."

"Nonsense. Not without knowing you. And if she didn't know you, why leave money to a fourth son? Why, in these hard times even a clergyman mightn't have a fourth son! No, it's all quite clear. No one benefits by your death, so that's ruled out. Then there's revenge. You haven't seduced a chemist's daughter by any chance?"

"Not that I can remember," said Bobby with dignity.

"I know. One seduces so much that one can't keep count. But I should say offhand that you've never seduced anyone at all."

"You're making me blush, Frankie. And why must it be a chemist's daughter, anyway?"

"Free access to morphia? It's not so easy to get hold of morphia."

"Well, I haven't seduced a chemist's daughter."

"And you haven't got any enemies that you know of?"

Bobby shook his head.

"Well, there you are," said Frankie triumphantly. "It must be the man who was pushed over the cliff. What do the police think?"

"They think it must have been a lunatic."

"Nonsense. Lunatics don't wander about with unlimited supplies of morphia looking for odd bottles of beer to put it into. No, somebody pushed Pritchard over the cliff. A minute or two later you come along, and he thinks you saw him do it and so determines to put you out of the way."

"I don't think that will hold water, Frankie."

"Why not?"

"Well, to begin with, I didn't see anything."

"Yes, but he didn't know that."

"And if I had seen anything I should have said so at the inquest."

"I suppose that's so," said Frankie unwillingly. She thought for a minute or two.

"Perhaps he thought you'd seen something that you didn't think was anything but which really *was* something. That sounds pure gibberish, but you get the idea?"

Bobby nodded. "Yes, I see what you mean, but it doesn't seem very probable somehow."

"I'm sure that cliff business had something to do with this. You were on the spot—the first person to be there—"

"Thomas was there too," Bobby reminded her. "And nobody's tried to poison him."

"Perhaps they're going to," said Frankie cheerfully. "Or perhaps they've tried and failed."

"It all seems very far-fetched."

"I think it's logical. If you get two out-of-the-way things happening in a stagnant pond like Marchbolt— Wait—there's a third thing."

"What?"

"That job you were offered. That, of course, is quite a small thing, but it was odd, you must admit. I've never heard of a foreign firm that specialized in seeking out undistinguished ex-Naval officers."

"Did you say undistinguished?"

"You hadn't got into the *B.M.J.* then. But you see my point. You've seen something you weren't meant to see—or so they (whoever they are) think. Very well. They first try to get rid of you by offering you a job abroad. Then, when that fails, they try to put you out of the way altogether."

"Isn't that rather drastic? And anyway a great risk to take?"

"Oh, but murderers are always frightfully rash. The more murders they do, the more murders they want to do."

"Like *The Third Bloodstain*," said Bobby, remembering one of his favorite works of fiction.

"Yes, and in real life too—Smith and his wives, and Armstrong, and other people."

"Well, but, Frankie, what on earth is it I'm supposed to have seen?"

"That, of course, is the difficulty," admitted Frankie. "I agree that it can't have been the actual pushing, because you would have told about that. It must be something about the man himself. Perhaps he had a birthmark or double-jointed fingers or some strange physical peculiarity."

"Your mind is running on Dr. Thorndyke, I see. It couldn't be anything like that because whatever I saw the police would see as well."

"So they would. That was an idiotic suggestion. It's very difficult, isn't it?"

"It's a pleasing theory," said Bobby. "And it makes me feel important. But all the same, I don't believe it's much more than a theory."

"I'm sure I'm right." Frankie rose. "I must be off now. Shall I come and see you again to-morrow?"

"Oh, do. The arch chatter of the nurses gets very monotonous. By the way, you're back from London very soon?"

"My dear, as soon as I heard about you, I tore back. It's more exciting to have a romantically poisoned friend."

"I don't know whether morphia is so very romantic," said Bobby reminiscently.

"Well, I'll come to-morrow. Do I kiss you or don't I?"

"It's not catching," said Bobby encouragingly.

"Then I'll do my duty to the sick thoroughly." She kissed him lightly. "See you to-morrow."

The nurse came in with Bobby's tea as she went out.

"I've seen her pictures in the paper often. She's not so very like them, though. And of course I've seen her driving about in her car. But I've never seen her before close to, so to speak. Not a bit haughty, is she?"

"Oh, no," said Bobby. "I should never call Frankie haughty."

"I said to Sister, I said, she's as natural as anything. Not a bit stuck-up. I said to Sister, she's just like you or me, I said."

Dissenting violently though silently from this view, Bobby returned no reply. The nurse, disappointed by his lack of response, left the room, and Bobby was left to his own thoughts.

He finished his tea. Then he went over in his mind the possibilities of Frankie's amazing theory, and ended by deciding reluctantly against it. He then cast about for other distractions.

His eye was caught by the vases of lilies. Frightfully sweet of Frankie to bring him all these flowers, and of course they were lovely, but he wished it had occurred to her to bring him a few detective stories instead. He cast his eye over the table beside him. There was a novel of Ouida's and a copy of *John Halifax, Gentleman*, and last week's *Marchbolt Weekly Times*. He picked up *John Halifax, Gentleman*.

After five minutes he put it down. To a mind nourished on *The Third Bloodstain*, *The Case of the Murdered Archduke*, and *The Strange Adventure of the Florentine Dagger*, Mrs. Mulock Craik's *John Halifax* somehow lacked pep. With a sigh he picked up last week's *Weekly Times*.

A moment or two later he was pressing the bell beneath his pillow with a vigor which brought a nurse into the room at a run.

"Whatever's the matter, Mr. Jones? Are you taken bad?"

"Ring up the Castle," cried Bobby. "Tell Lady Frances she must come back here at once."

"Oh, Mr. Jones—you can't send a message like that."

"Can't I?" said Bobby. "If I were allowed to get up from this blasted bed, you'd soon see whether I could or couldn't. As it is, you've got to do it for me."

"But she'll hardly be back."

"You don't know that Bentley."

"She won't have had her tea."

"Now look here, my dear girl," said Bobby, "don't stand there arguing with me. Ring up as I tell you. Tell her she's got to come here at once because I've got something very important to say to her."

Overborne, though unwilling, the nurse went. She took some liberties with Bobby's message. If it was no inconvenience to Lady Frances, Mr. Jones wondered if she would mind coming, as he had something he would like to say to her. But of course Lady Frances was not to put herself out in any way.

Lady Frances replied curtly that she would come at once.

"Depend upon it," said the nurse to her colleagues, "she's sweet on him! That's what it is."

Frankie arrived all agog. "What's this desperate summons?" she demanded.

Bobby was sitting up in bed, a bright red spot in each cheek. In his hand he waved the copy of the *Marchbolt Weekly Times*.

"Look at this, Frankie."

Frankie looked. "Well?" she demanded.

"This is the picture you meant when you said it was touched up but quite like the Cayman woman?" Bobby's finger pointed to a somewhat blurred reproduction of a photograph. Underneath it were the words *Portrait found on the dead man by which he was identified: Mrs. Amelia Cayman, the dead man's sister.*

"That's what I said—and it's true, too. I can't see anything to rave over in it."

"No more can I."

"But you said—"

"I know I 'said.' But you see, Frankie—" Bobby's voice became very impressive—"*This isn't the photograph that I put back in the dead man's pocket.* . . ."

They looked at each other.

"Then, in that case—" began Frankie slowly.

"Either there must have been two photographs—"

"—which isn't likely—"

"—or else—"

They paused.

"*That man*—what's his name?" said Frankie.

"Bassington-ffrench!" said Bobby.

8

Riddle of a Photograph

They stared at each other as they tried to adjust themselves to the altered situation.

"It couldn't be anyone else," said Bobby. "He was the only person who had the chance."

"Unless, as we said, there were *two* photographs?"

"We agreed that that wasn't likely. If there had been two photographs they'd have tried to identify him by means of both of them—not by only one."

"Anyway that's easily found out," said Frankie. "We can ask the police. We'll assume for the moment that there was just the one photograph—the one you saw, that you put back again in the man's pocket. It was there when you left him, and it *wasn't* there when the police came. Therefore the only person who *could* have taken it away and put the other one in its place is this man Bassington-ffrench. What was he like, Bobby?"

Bobby frowned in the effort to remember. "A sort of nondescript fellow. Pleasant voice. A gentleman and all that. I really didn't notice him particularly. He said he was a stranger down here—and something about looking for a house."

"We can verify that anyway," said Frankie. "Wheeler & Owen are the only house agents." Suddenly she gave a shiver. "Bobby, have you thought? If Pritchard was pushed over—*Bassington-ffrench must be the man who did it. . . .*"

"That's pretty grim," said Bobby. "He seemed such a nice, pleasant sort of fellow. But you know, Frankie, we can't be sure Pritchard really was pushed over."

"*I'm* quite sure!"

"You have been, all along."

"No, I just wanted it to be that way because it made things more exciting. But now it's more or less proved. If it was murder everything fits in. Your unexpected appearance which upsets the murderer's plans. Your discovery of the photograph and, in consequence, the need to put you out of the way."

"There's a flaw there," said Bobby.

"Why? You were the only person who saw that photograph. As soon as Bassington-ffrench was left alone with the body he changed the photograph, which only you had seen."

But Bobby continued to shake his head. "No, that won't do. Let's grant for the moment that that photograph was so important that I had to be 'got out of the way,' as you put it. Sounds absurd, but I suppose it's just possible. Well then, whatever was going to be done would have to be done *at once*. The fact that I went to London and never saw the *Weekly Times* or the other papers with the photograph in them was just pure chance—a thing nobody could count on. The probability was that I should say at once, 'That isn't the photograph I saw.' Why wait till after the inquest when everything was nicely settled?"

"There's something in that," admitted Frankie.

"And there's another point. I can't be absolutely sure, of course, but I could almost swear that when I put the photograph back in the dead man's pocket Bassington-ffrench wasn't there. He didn't arrive till about five or ten minutes later."

"He might have been watching you all the time," argued Frankie.

"I don't see very well how he could have," said Bobby slowly. "There's really only one place where you can see down to exactly the spot we were. Farther round, the cliff bulges and then recedes underneath, so that you can't see over. There's just the one place, and when Bassington-ffrench did arrive there I heard him at once. Footsteps echo down below. He may have been near at hand, but he wasn't looking over till then—that I'll swear."

"Then you think that he didn't know about your seeing the photograph?"

"I don't see how he could have known."

"And he can't have been afraid you'd seen him doing it—the murder, I mean—because, as you say, that's absurd. You'd never have held your tongue about it. It looks as though it must have been something else altogether."

"Only I don't see what it could have been."

"Something they didn't know about till after the inquest. I don't know why I say *they*—"

"Why not? After all, the Caymans must have been in it too. It's probably a gang. I like gangs."

"That's a low taste," said Frankie absently. "A single-handed murder is much higher class. Bobby!"

"Yes?"

"What was it Pritchard said just before he died? You know, you told me about it that day on the links. That funny question?"

"*Why didn't they ask Evans?*"

"Yes. Suppose *that* was it?"

"But that's ridiculous."

"It sounds so, but it might be important really. Bobby, I'm *sure* it's that. Oh, no, I'm being an idiot—you never told the Caymans about it."

"I did, as a matter of fact," said Bobby slowly.

"You *did?*"

"Yes. I wrote to them that evening. Saying that of course it was probably quite unimportant."

"And what happened?"

"Cayman wrote back politely agreeing that of course there was nothing in it, but thanking me for taking the trouble. I felt rather snubbed."

"And two days later you got this letter from a strange firm bribing you to go out to South America?"

"Yes."

"Well," said Frankie, "I don't know what more you want. They try that first. You turn it down. And the next thing is that they follow you round and seize a good moment to empty a lot of morphia into your bottle of beer."

"Then the Caymans *are* in it?"

"Of course the Caymans are in it!"

"Yes," said Bobby thoughtfully. "If your reconstruction is correct, they must be in it. According to our present theory it goes like this. Dead man X is deliberately pushed over cliff—presumably by B. F. (pardon the initials). It is important that X should not be correctly identified, so the portrait of Mrs. C. is put in his pocket and the portrait of Fair Unknown removed. Who was she, I wonder?"

"Keep to the point," said Frankie sternly.

"Mrs. C. waits for photograph to appear. Then turns up as grief-stricken sister and identifies X as her brother from foreign parts."

"You don't believe he could really have been her brother?"

"Not for a moment! You know, it puzzled me all along. The Caymans were a different class altogether. The dead man was—well, it sounds a most awful thing to say and just like some deadly old retired Anglo-Indian—but the dead man was a pukka sahib."

"And the Caymans emphatically weren't?"

"*Most* emphatically."

"And then, just when everything has gone off well from the Caymans' point of view—body successfully identified, verdict of accidental death, everything in the garden lovely—*you* come along and mess things up," mused Frankie.

" 'Why didn't they ask Evans?' " Bobby repeated the phrase thoughtfully. "You know I can't see what on earth there can be in that to put the wind up anybody."

"Ah! that's because you don't know. It's like making crossword puzzles. You write down a clue and you think it's too idiotically simple and that everyone will guess it straight off, and you're frightfully surprised when they simply can't get it in the least. *'Why didn't they ask Evans?'* must have been a most frightfully significant phrase to them, and they couldn't realize that it meant nothing at all to you."

"More fools they."

"Oh, quite so. But it's just possible they thought that if Pritchard said that, he might have said something more which would also recur to you in due time. Anyway they weren't going to take chances. You were safer out of the way."

"They took a lot of risk. Why didn't they engineer another 'accident'?"

"No, no. That would have been stupid. Two accidents within a week of each other? It might have suggested a connection between the two, and then people would have begun inquiring into the first one. No, I think there's a kind of bald simplicity about their method which is really rather clever."

"And yet you said just now that morphia wasn't easy to get hold of."

"No more it is. You have to sign poison books and things. Oh—of course, that's a clue! Whoever did it had easy access to supplies of morphia."

"A doctor, a hospital nurse, or a chemist," suggested Bobby.

"Well, I was thinking more of illicitly imported drugs."

"You can't mix up too many different sorts of crime," said Bobby.

"You see, the strong point would be the absence of motive. Your death doesn't benefit anyone. So what will the police think?"

"A lunatic," said Bobby. "And that's what they do think."

"You see? It's awfully simple really."

Bobby began to laugh suddenly.

"What's amusing you?"

"Just the thought of how sick-making it must be for them! All that morphia—enough to kill five or six people—and here I am alive and kicking."

"One of Life's little ironies that one can't foresee," agreed Frankie.

"The question is, what do we do next?" said Bobby practically.

"Oh! lots of things," said Frankie promptly.

"Such as—?"

"Well—finding out about the photograph—that there was only one, not two. And about Bassington-ffrench's house-hunting."

"That will probably be quite all right and above-board."

"Why do you say that?"

"Look here, Frankie, think a minute. Bassington-ffrench *must* be above suspicion. He *must* be all clear and above-board. Not only must there be nothing to connect him in any way with the dead man, but he must have a proper reason for being down here. He may have invented house-hunting on the spur of the moment, but I bet he carried out something of the kind. There must be no suggestion of a 'mysterious stranger seen in the neighborhood of the accident.' I fancy that Bassington-ffrench is his real name, and that he's the sort of person who would be quite above suspicion."

"Yes," said Frankie thoughtfully. "That's a very good deduction. There will be nothing whatever to connect Bassington-ffrench with Alex Pritchard. Now if we knew who the dead man really was—"

"Ah! then it might be different."

"So it was very important that the body should not be recognized. Hence all the Cayman camouflage. And yet it was taking a big risk."

"You forget that Mrs. Cayman identified him as soon as was humanly possible. After that, even if there had been pictures of him in the papers (you know how blurry these things are) people would only say, 'Curious, this man Pritchard who fell over a cliff is really extraordinarily like Mr. X.'"

"There must be more to it than that," said Frankie shrewdly. "X must have been a man who wouldn't easily be missed. I mean, he couldn't have been the sort of family man whose wife or relations would go to the police at once and report him missing."

"Good for you, Frankie. No, he must have been just going abroad, or perhaps just come back (he was marvellously tanned, like a big-game hunter—he looked that sort of person), and he can't have had any very near relations who knew all about his movements."

"We're deducing beautifully," said Frankie. "I hope we're not deducing all wrong."

"Very likely," said Bobby. "But I think what we've said so far is fairly sound sense—granted, that is, the wild improbability of the whole thing."

Frankie waved away the wild improbability with an airy gesture. "The thing is—what to do next?" she said. "It seems to me we've got three angles of attack."

"Go on, Sherlock."

"The first is *you*. They've made one attempt on your life. They'll probably try again. This time we might get what they call a 'line' on them. Using you as a decoy, I mean."

"No, thank you, Frankie," said Bobby with feeling. "I've been very lucky this time, but I mightn't be so lucky again if they changed the attack to a blunt instrument. I was thinking of taking a great deal of care of myself in the future. The decoy idea can be washed out."

"I was afraid you'd say that," said Frankie with a sigh. "Young men are sadly degenerate nowadays. Father says so. They don't enjoy being uncomfortable and doing dangerous and unpleasant things any longer. It's a pity."

"A great pity," said Bobby, but he spoke with firmness. "What's the second plan of campaign?"

"Working from the *'Why didn't they ask Evans?'* clue," said Frankie. "Presumably the dead man came down here to see Evans—whoever *he* was. Now, if we could find Evans—"

"How many Evanses," Bobby interrupted, "do you think there are in Marchbolt?"

"Several hundred, I should think," admitted Frankie.

"At least! We might do something that way, but I'm rather doubtful."

"We could list all the Evanses and visit the likely ones."

"And ask them—what?"

"That's the difficulty," said Frankie.

"We need to know a little more," said Bobby. "Then that idea of yours might come in useful. What's Number 3?"

"This man Bassington-ffrench. There we *have* got something tangible to go upon. It's an uncommon name. I'll ask Father. He knows all these county family names and their various branches."

"Yes," said Bobby, "we might do something that way."

"At any rate we are going to do something?"

"Of course we are. Do you think I'm going to be given eight grains of morphia and do nothing about it?"

"That's the spirit!" said Frankie.

"And besides that," added Bobby, "there's the indignity of the stomach pump to be washed out."

"That's enough," said Frankie. "You'll be getting morbid and indecent again if I don't stop you."

"You have no true womanly sympathy," Bobby retorted.

9

Concerning Mr. Bassington-ffrench

Frankie lost no time in setting to work. She attacked her father that same evening.

"Father," she said, "do you know any Bassington-ffrenches?"

Lord Marchington, who was reading a political article, did not quite take in the question. "It's not the French so much as the Americans," he said severely. "All this tom-foolery and Conferences—wasting the nation's time and money—"

Frankie abstracted her mind until Lord Marchington, running like a railway train along an accustomed line, came as it were to a halt at a station.

"The Bassington-ffrenches," repeated Frankie.

"What about 'em?" asked Lord Marchington.

Frankie didn't know what about them. She made a statement, knowing well enough that her father enjoyed contradicting.

"They're a Yorkshire family, aren't they?"

"Nonsense—Hampshire. There's the Shropshire branch, of course, and then there's the Irish lot. Which are your friends?"

"I'm not sure," said Frankie, accepting the implication of friendship with several unknown people.

"Not sure? What do you mean? You must be sure."

"People drift about so, nowadays," said Frankie.

"Drift—drift—that's about all they do do. In my day we asked people. Then one knew where one was—fellow said he was the Hampshire branch—very well, your grandmother married my second cousin. It made a link."

"It must have been too sweet," said Frankie. "But there really isn't time for genealogical and geographical research nowadays."

"No—you've no time nowadays for anything but drinking these poisonous cocktails." Lord Marchington gave a sudden yelp of pain as he moved his gouty leg which some free imbibing of the family port had not improved.

"Are they well off?" asked Frankie.

"The Bassington-ffrenches? Couldn't say. The Shropshire lot have been hard hit, I believe. Death duties and one thing or another. One of the Hampshire ones married an heiress. An American woman."

"One of them was down here the other day," said Frankie. "Looking for a house, I believe."

"Funny idea. What should anyone want with a house down here?"

That, thought Frankie, was the question.

On the following day she walked into the office of Messrs. Wheeler & Owen, House and Estate Agents.

Mr. Owen himself sprang up to receive her. Frankie gave him a gracious smile and dropped into a chair.

"And what can we have the pleasure of doing for you, Lady Frances? You don't want to sell the Castle, I suppose. Ha, ha!" Mr. Owen laughed at his own wit.

"I wish we could," said Frankie. "No, as a matter of fact, I believe a friend of mine was down here the other day—a Mr. Bassington-ffrench. He was looking for a house."

"Ah, yes, indeed! I remember the name perfectly. Two small f's."

"That's right," said Frankie.

"He was making inquiries about various small properties with a view to purchase. He was obliged to return to town the next day so could not view many of the houses, but I understand he is in no great hurry. Since he left, one or two suitable properties have come into the market, and I have sent him on particulars but have had no reply."

"Did you write to London—or to the—er—country address?" inquired Frankie.

"Let me see now." He called to a junior clerk. "Frank, Mr. Bassington-ffrench's address."

"Roger Bassington-ffrench, Esq., Merroway Court, Staverley, Hants," said the junior clerk glibly.

"Ah!" said Frankie. "Then it wasn't my Mr. Bassington-ffrench. This must be his cousin. I thought it was odd his being here and not looking me up."

"Quite so—quite so," said Mr. Owen intelligently.

"Let me see, it must have been the Wednesday he came to see you."

"That's right. Just before six-thirty. We close at six-thirty. I remember particularly because it was the day when that sad accident happened. Man fell over the cliff. Mr. Bassington-ffrench had actually stayed by the body till the police came. He looked quite upset when he came in here. Very sad tragedy, that, and high time something was done about that bit of path. The Town Council have been criticized very freely, I can tell you, Lady Frances. Most dangerous. Why we haven't had more accidents than we have, I can't imagine."

"Extraordinary," said Frankie.

She left the office in a thoughtful mood. As Bobby had prophesied, all Mr. Bassington-ffrench's actions seemed clear and above-board. He was one of the Hampshire Bassington-ffrenches, he had given his proper address, he had actually mentioned his part in the tragedy to the house agent. Was it possible that, after all, Mr. Bassington-ffrench was the completely innocent person he seemed?

Frankie had a qualm of doubt. Then she refuted it.

"No," she said to herself. "A man who wants to buy a little place would either get here earlier in the day, or else stay over the next day. You wouldn't go into a house agent's at six-thirty in the evening and go up to London the following day. Why make the journey at all? Why not write?"

No, she decided, Bassington-ffrench was the guilty party.

Her next call was the police station.

Inspector Williams was an old acquaintance, having succeeded in tracking down a maid with a false reference who had absconded with some of Frankie's jewelry.

"Good-afternoon, Inspector."

"Good-afternoon, your ladyship. Nothing wrong, I hope."

"Not as yet, but I'm thinking of holding up a bank soon because I'm getting so short of money."

The Inspector gave a rumbling laugh in acknowledgment of this witticism.

"As a matter of fact I've come to ask questions out of sheer curiosity," said Frankie.

"Is that so, Lady Frances?"

"Now do tell me this, Inspector—that man who fell over the cliff—Pritchard or whatever his name was—"

"Pritchard, that's right."

"He only had *one* photograph on him, didn't he? Somebody told me he had *three!*"

"One's right," said the Inspector. "Photograph of his sister, it was. She came down and identified him."

"How absurd to say there were three!"

"Oh, that's easy, your ladyship. These newspaper reporters don't mind how much they exaggerate, and as often as not they get the whole thing wrong."

"I know," said Frankie. "I've heard the wildest stories." She paused a moment, then drew freely on her imagination. "I've heard that his pockets were stuffed with papers proving him to be a Bolshevik agent. And there's another story that his pockets were full of dope, and another again about his having pockets full of counterfeit bank-notes."

The Inspector laughed heartily. "That's a good one."

"I suppose really he had just the usual things in his pockets?"

"And very few at that. A handkerchief, not marked. Some loose change, a packet of cigarettes and a couple of Treasury notes—loose, not in a case. No letters. We'd have had a job to identify him if it hadn't been for the photo. Providential, you might call it."

"I wonder," said Frankie.

In view of her private knowledge, she considered "providential" a singularly inapposite word. She changed the conversation.

"I went to see Mr. Jones, the Vicar's son, yesterday. The one who's been poisoned. What an extraordinary thing that was!"

"Ah!" said the Inspector. "Now that is extraordinary, if you like. Never heard of anything like it happening before. A nice young gentleman without an enemy in the world, or so you'd say. You know, Lady Frances, there are some queer customers going about. All the same I never heard of a homicidal maniac who acted just this way."

"Is there any clue at all to who did it?" Frankie was all wide-eyed inquiry. "It's so interesting to hear all this," she added.

The Inspector swelled with gratification. He enjoyed this friendly conversation with an Earl's daughter. Nothing stuck up or snobbish about Lady Frances.

"There was a car seen in the vicinity," said the Inspector. "Dark-blue Talbot. A man on Lock's Corner reported dark-blue Talbot No. *GG 8282* passed going direction St. Botolph's."

"And you think—"

"*GG 8282* is the number of the Bishop of St. Botolph's car."

Frankie toyed for a minute or two with the idea of a homicidal bishop who offered sacrifices of clergymen's sons but rejected it with a sigh. "You don't suspect the Bishop, I suppose?" she said.

"We've found out that the Bishop's car never left the Palace garage that afternoon."

"So it was a false number."

"Yes. We've got that to go on all right."

With expressions of admiration Frankie took her leave. She made no damping remark, but she thought to herself, "There must be a large number of dark-blue Talbots in England."

On her return home she took a directory of Marchbolt from its place on the writing-table in the library and removed it to her own room. She worked over it for some hours. The result was not satisfactory. There were four hundred and eighty-two Evanses in Marchbolt.

"Damn!" said Frankie.

She began to make plans for the future.

10

Preparations for an Accident

A week later Bobby had joined Badger in London. He had received several enigmatical communications from Frankie, mostly in such an illegible scrawl that he was quite unable to do more than guess at their meaning. However, their general purport seemed to be that Frankie had a plan and that he (Bobby) was to do nothing until he heard from her. This was as well, for Bobby would certainly have had no leisure to do anything, since the unlucky Badger had already succeeded in embroiling himself and his business in every way ingenuity could suggest, and Bobby was kept busy disentangling the extraordinary mess his friend seemed to have got into.

Meanwhile the young man remained very strictly on his guard. The effect of eight grains of morphia was to render their taker extremely suspicious of food and drink and had also induced him to bring to London a Service revolver, the possession of which was extremely irksome to him.

He was just beginning to feel that the whole thing had been an extravagant nightmare when Frankie's Bentley roared down the mews and drew up outside the garage. Bobby, in grease-stained overalls, came out to receive it. Frankie was at the wheel and beside her sat a rather gloomy-looking young man.

"Hullo, Bobby," said Frankie. "This is George Arbuthnot. He's a doctor and we shall need him."

Bobby winced slightly as he and George Arbuthnot made faint acknowledgment of each other's presence.

"Are you sure we're going to need a doctor?" he asked. "Aren't you being a bit pessimistic?"

"I didn't mean we should need him in that way," said Frankie. "I need him for a scheme that I've got on. Look here, is there anywhere we can go and talk?"

Bobby looked doubtfully round him. "Well, there's my bedroom," he said doubtfully.

"Excellent," said Frankie.

She got out of the car, and she and George Arbuthnot followed Bobby up some outside steps and into a microscopic bedroom.

"I don't know," said Bobby, looking round dubiously, "if there's anywhere to sit."

There was not. The only chair was loaded with, apparently, the whole of Bobby's wardrobe.

"The bed will do," said Frankie.

She plumped down on it. George Arbuthnot did the same and the bed groaned protestingly.

"I've got everything planned out," said Frankie. "To begin with we want a car. One of yours will do."

"Do you mean you want to buy one of our cars?"

"Yes."

"That's really very nice of you, Frankie," said Bobby with warm appreciation. "But you needn't. I really do draw the line at sticking my friends."

"You've got it all wrong," said Frankie. "It isn't like that at all. I know what you mean—it's like buying perfectly appalling clothes and hats from one's friends who are just starting in business. A nuisance, but it's got to be done. But this isn't like that at all. I really need a car."

"What about the Bentley?"

"The Bentley's no good."

"You're mad," said Bobby.

"No, I'm not. The Bentley's no good for what I want it for."

"What do you want it for?"

"Smashing it up."

Bobby groaned and put a hand to his head. "I don't seem very well this morning."

George Arbuthnot spoke for the first time. His voice was deep and melancholy. "She means," he said, "that she's going to have an accident."

"How does she know?" said Bobby wildly.

Frankie gave an exasperated sigh. "Somehow or other," she said, "we seem to have started wrong. Now just listen quietly, Bobby, and try and take in what I'm going to say. I know your brains are practically negligible, but you ought to be able to understand if you really concentrate."

She paused, then resumed.

"I am on the trail of Bassington-ffrench."

"Hear, hear!"

"Bassington-ffrench—our particular Bassington-ffrench—lives at Merroway Court at the village of Staverley in Hampshire. Merroway Court belongs to our Bassington-ffrench's brother, and our Bassington-ffrench lives there with the brother and his wife."

"Whose wife?"

"The brother's wife of course. That isn't the point. The point is, how are you or I—or both of us—going to worm ourselves into the household? I've been down and reconnoitred the ground. Staverley's a mere village. Strangers arriving there to stay would stick out a mile. It would be the sort of thing that simply isn't done. So I've evolved a plan. This is what is going to happen. Lady Frances Derwent, driving her car more recklessly than well, crashes into the wall near the gates of Merroway Court. Complete wreckage of car, less complete wreckage of Lady Frances, who is carried to the house suffering from concussion and shock and must emphatically not be moved."

"Who says so?"

"George. Now you see where George comes in. We can't risk a strange doctor's saying there is nothing the matter with me. Or perhaps some officious person might pick up my prostrate form and take it to some local hospital. No, what happens is this. George is passing, also in a car (you'd better sell us a second one), sees the accident, leaps out and takes charge. 'I am a doctor. Stand back, everybody!'—That is, if there is anybody to stand back.—'We must take her into that house—what is it, Merroway Court? That will do. I must be able to make a thorough examination!' I am carried to the best spare room, the Bassington-ffrenches either sympathetic or bitterly resisting; but in any case, George will overbear them. George makes his examination and emerges with his verdict. Happily, it is not so serious as he thought. No bones broken, but danger of concussion. I must on no account be moved for two or three days. After that I shall be able to return to London.

"And then George departs, and it's up to me to ingratiate myself with the household."

"And where do I come in?"

"You don't."

"But look here—"

"My dear child, do remember that Bassington-ffrench knows you. He doesn't know me from Adam. And I'm in a frightfully strong position because I've got a title. You see how useful that is. I'm not just a stray young woman gaining admission to the house for mysterious purposes. I am an Earl's daughter and therefore highly respectable. And George is a real doctor, and everything is quite above suspicion."

"Oh, I suppose it's all right," said Bobby unhappily.

"It's a remarkably well-planned scheme, I think," said Frankie with pride.

"And I don't do anything at all?" asked Bobby. He still felt injured—much like a dog who has been unexpectedly deprived of a bone. This, he felt, was his own particular crime, and now he was being ousted.

"Of course you do, darling. You grow a moustache."

"Oh, I grow a moustache, do I?"

"Yes. How long will it take?"

"Two or three weeks, I expect."

"Heavens! I'd no idea it was such a slow process. Can't you speed it up?"

"No. Why can't I wear a false one?"

"They always *look* so false, and they twist or come off or smell of spirit-gum. Wait a minute, though—I believe there is a kind you can get stuck on hair by hair, so to speak, that absolutely defies detection. I expect a theatrical wigmaker would do it for you."

"He'd probably think I was trying to escape from justice."

"It doesn't matter what he thinks."

"Once I've got the moustache, what do I do?"

"Put on a chauffeur's uniform and drive the Bentley down to Staverley."

"Oh, I see." Bobby brightened.

"You see my idea is this," said Frankie. "Nobody looks at a chauffeur in the way they look at a *person*. In any case Bassington-ffrench only saw you for a minute or two, and he must have been too rattled wondering if he could change the photographs in time to look at you much. You were just a young golfing ass to him. It isn't like the Caymans, who sat opposite you and talked to you and who were deliberately trying to sum you up. I'd bet anything that seeing you in chauffeur's uniform, Bassington-ffrench wouldn't recognize you even without the moustache. He might just possibly think that your face reminded him of somebody—no more than that. And with the moustache it ought to be perfectly safe. Now tell me, what do you think of the plan?"

Bobby turned it over in his mind. "To tell you the truth, Frankie," he said generously, "I think it's pretty good."

"In that case," said Frankie briskly, "let's go and buy some cars. I say, I think George has broken your bed."

"It doesn't matter," said Bobby hospitably. "It was never a particularly good bed."

They descended to the garage where a nervous-looking young man with a curious lack of chin and an agreeable smile greeted them with a vague haw-haw-haw. His general appearance was slightly marred by the fact that his eyes had a distinct disinclination to look in the same direction.

"Hullo, Badger," said Bobby. "You remember Frankie, don't you?"

Badger clearly didn't, but he said "Haw haw haw" again in an amiable manner.

"Last time I saw you," said Frankie, "you were head downward in the mud, and we had to pull you out by the legs."

"No, not really?" said Badger. "Why, that m-m-must have been W-w-w-wales."

"Quite right," said Frankie. "It was."

"I always was a p-p-putrid r-r-r-rider," said Badger. "I s-s-s-still am," he added mournfully.

"Frankie wants to buy a car," said Bobby.

"Two cars," said Frankie. "George has got to have one too. He's crashed his at the moment."

"We can hire him one," said Bobby.

"Well, come and look at what we've got in s-s-s-stock," said Badger.

"They look very smart," said Frankie, dazzled by lurid hues of scarlet and apple green.

"They *look* all right," said Bobby darkly.

"That's r-r-r-remarkably good value in a s-s-second-hand Chrysler," said Badger.

"No, not that one," said Bobby. "Whatever she buys has got to go at least forty miles."

Badger cast his partner a look of reproach.

"That Standard is pretty much on its last legs," mused Bobby. "But I think it would just get you there. The Essex is a bit too good for the job. She'll go at least two hundred before breaking down."

"All right," said Frankie. "I'll have the Standard."

Badger drew his colleague a little aside. "W-w-what do you think about p-p-price?" he murmured. "Don't want to s-s-stick a friend of yours too much. T-t-t-ten pounds?"

"Ten pounds is all right," said Frankie, entering the discussion. "I'll pay for it now."

"Who is she really?" asked Badger in a loud whisper.

Bobby whispered back.

"F-f-f-first time I ever knew anyone with a t-t-t-title who c-c-could pay cash," said Badger with respect.

Bobby followed the other two out to the Bentley.

"When is this business going to take place?" he demanded.

"The sooner the better," said Frankie. "We thought tomorrow afternoon."

"Look here, can't I be there? I'll put on a beard if you like."

"Certainly not," said Frankie. "A beard would probably ruin everything by falling off at the wrong moment.

But I don't see why you shouldn't be a motorcyclist—
with a lot of cap and goggles. What do you think,
George?"

George Arbuthnot spoke for the second time. "All
right," he said. "The more the merrier."

His voice was even more melancholy than before.

The Accident Happens

The rendezvous for the great accident party was fixed at a spot about a mile from Staverley village where the road to Staverley branched off from the main road to Andover.

All three arrived there safely, though Frankie's Standard had shown unmistakable signs of decrepitude at every hill. The time fixed had been one o'clock.

"We don't want to be interrupted when we're staging the thing," Frankie had said. "Hardly anything ever goes down this road, I should imagine, but at lunch time we ought to be perfectly safe."

They proceeded for half a mile on the side road and then Frankie pointed out the place she had selected for the accident to take place.

"It couldn't be better in my opinion," she said. "Straight down this hill, and then, as you see, the road gives a sudden very sharp turn round that bulging bit of wall. The wall is actually the wall of Merroway Court. If we start the car and let it run down the hill it will crash straight into the wall and something pretty drastic ought to happen to it."

"I should say so," Bobby agreed. "But one of us ought to be on the lookout at the corner to be sure nobody is coming round it from the opposite direction."

"Quite right," said Frankie. "We don't want to involve anybody else in a mess up and perhaps maim them for life. George can take his car down there and turn it as though he were coming from the other direction. Then when he waves a handkerchief it will show that all is clear."

"You're looking very pale, Frankie," said Bobby anxiously. "Are you sure you're all right?"

"I'm made up pale," explained Frankie. "Ready for the concussion. You don't want me to be carried into the house blooming with health."

"How wonderful women are!" said Bobby appreciatively. "You look exactly like a sick monkey."

"I think you're very rude," said Frankie. "Now then, I shall go and prospect at the gate into Merroway Court. It's just this side of the bulge. There's no lodge fortunately. When George waves his handkerchief and I wave mine, you start her off."

"Right," said Bobby. "I'll stay on the running board to guide her until the pace gets too hot and then I'll jump off."

"Don't hurt yourself," said Frankie anxiously.

"I shall be extremely careful not to. It would complicate matters to have a real accident on the spot of the faked one."

"Well, start off, George," said Frankie.

George nodded, jumped into the second car and ran slowly down the hill. Bobby and Frankie stood looking after him.

"You'll—look after yourself, won't you, Frankie?" said Bobby with sudden gruffness. "I mean—don't go doing anything foolish."

"I shall be all right. Most circumspect. By the way, I don't think I'd better write to you direct. I'll write to George or my maid or someone or other to pass on to you."

"I wonder if George is going to be a success in his profession?"

"Why shouldn't he?"

"Well, he doesn't seem to have acquired a chatty bedside manner yet."

"I expect that will come," said Frankie. "I'd better be going now. I'll let you know when I want you to come down with the Bentley."

"I'll get busy with the moustache. So long, Frankie."

They looked at each other for a moment and then Frankie nodded and began to walk down the hill.

George had turned the car and then backed it round the bulge.

Frankie disappeared for a moment, then reappeared in the road waving a handkerchief. A second handkerchief waved from the bottom of the road at the turn.

Bobby put the car into third gear, then standing on the footboard he released the brake. The car moved grudgingly forward—impeded by being in gear. The slope, however, was sufficiently steep. The engine started. The car gathered way. Bobby steadied the steering wheel. At the last possible moment he jumped off.

The car went on down the hill and crashed into the wall with considerable force. All was well—the accident had taken place successfully.

Bobby saw Frankie run quickly to the scene of the crime and plop down amid the wreckage. George in his car came round the corner and pulled up.

With a sigh Bobby mounted his motorcycle and rode away in the direction of London.

At the scene of the accident things were busy.

"Shall I roll about in the road a bit?" asked Frankie. "To get myself dusty."

"You might as well," said George. "Here, give me your hat."

He took it and inflicted a terrific dent on it. Frankie gave a faint anguished cry.

"That's the concussion," explained George. "Now then, lie doggo just where you are. I think I heard a bicycle bell."

Sure enough, at that moment, a boy of about seventeen came whistling round the corner. He stopped at once, delighted with the pleasurable spectacle that met his eyes.

"Ooer!" he ejaculated, " 'as there been an accident?"

"No," said George sarcastically. "The young lady ran her car into the wall on purpose."

Accepting, as he was meant to do, this remark as irony rather than the simple truth which it was, the boy said with relish, "Looks bad, don't she? Is she dead?"

"Not yet," said George. "She must be taken somewhere at once. I'm a doctor. What's this place in here?"

"Merroway Court. Belongs to Mr. Bassington-ffrench. He's a J.P., he is."

"She must be carried there at once," said George authoritatively. "Here, leave your bicycle, and lend me a hand."

Only too willing, the boy propped his bicycle against the wall and came to assist. Between them George and the boy carried Frankie up the drive to a pleasant, old-fashioned-looking manor house.

Their approach had been observed, for an elderly butler came out to meet them.

"There's been an accident," said George curtly. "Is there a room I can carry this lady into? She must be attended to at once."

The butler went back into the hall in a flustered way. George and the boy followed him up closely, still carrying the limp body of Frankie. The butler had gone into a room on the left and from there a woman emerged.

She was tall, with red hair, and about thirty years of age.
Her eyes were a light, clear blue.

She dealt with the situation quickly.

"There is a spare bedroom on the ground floor," she
said. "Will you bring her in there? Ought I to telephone
for a doctor?"

"I am a doctor," explained George. "I was passing in
my car and saw the accident occur."

"Oh! How very fortunate. Come this way, will you?"

She showed them the way into a pleasant bedroom
with windows giving on the garden.

"Is she badly hurt?" she inquired.

"I can't tell yet."

Mrs. Bassington-ffrench took the hint and retired. The
boy accompanied her and launched out into a description
of the accident as though he had been an actual witness
of it.

"Run smack into the wall, she did. Car's all smashed
up. There she was lying on the ground with her hat all
dinted in. The gentleman he was passing in his car—"
He proceeded *ad lib*. till got rid of with a half-crown.

Meanwhile Frankie and George were conversing in
careful whispers.

"George, darling, this won't blight your career, will
it? They won't strike you off the register, or whatever it
is, will they?"

"Probably," said George gloomily. "That is, if it ever
comes out."

"It won't," said Frankie. "Don't worry, George. I
shan't let you down." She added thoughtfully, "You did
it very well. I've never heard you talk so much before."

George sighed. He looked at his watch. "I shall give
my examination another three minutes," he said.

"What about the car?"

"I'll arrange with a garage to have that cleared up."

"Good."

George continued to study his watch. Finally he said with an air of relief, "Time!"

"George," said Frankie, "you've been an angel. I don't know why you did it."

"No more do I," said George. "Damn fool thing to do."

He nodded to her.

"Bye-bye. Enjoy yourself."

"I wonder if I shall," said Frankie. She was thinking of that cool impersonal voice with the slight American accent.

George went in search of the owner of it, whom he found waiting for him in the drawing-room.

"Well," he said abruptly. "I'm glad to say it's not so bad as I feared. Concussion very slight and already passing off. She ought to stay quietly where she is for a day or so, though." He paused. "She seems to be a Lady Frances Derwent."

"Oh, fancy!" said Mrs. Bassington-ffrench. "Then I know some cousins of hers, the Draycotts, quite well."

"I don't know if it's inconvenient for you to have her here," said George. "But if she *could* stay where she was for a day or two—" Here George paused.

"Oh, of course. That will be quite all right, Dr.—?"

"Arbuthnot. By the way, I'll see to the car business. I shall be passing a garage."

"Thank you very much, Dr. Arbuthnot. How very lucky you happened to be passing! I suppose a doctor ought to see her to-morrow just to see she's getting on all right."

"Don't think it's necessary," said George. "All she needs is quiet."

"But I should feel happier. And her people ought to know."

"I'll attend to that," said George. "And as to the doctoring business—well, it seems she's a Christian Scientist and won't have doctors at any price. She wasn't too pleased at finding me in attendance."

"Oh, dear!" said Mrs. Bassington-ffrench.

"But she'll be quite all right," said George reassuringly. "You can take my word for it."

"If you really think so, Dr. Arbuthnot," said Mrs. Bassington-ffrench rather doubtfully.

"I do," said George. "Good-bye. Dear me, I left one of my instruments in the bedroom."

He came rapidly into the room and up to the bedside.

"Frankie," he said in a quick whisper, "you're a Christian Scientist. Don't forget."

"But why?"

"I had to do it. Only way."

"All right," said Frankie. "I won't forget."

12

In the Enemy's Camp

"Well, here I am," thought Frankie. "Safely in the enemy's camp. Now it's up to me."

There was a tap on the door and Mrs. Bassington-ffrench entered.

Frankie raised herself a little on her pillows.

"I'm so frightfully sorry," she said in a faint voice. "Causing you all this bother."

"Nonsense," said Mrs. Bassington-ffrench. Frankie heard anew that cool, attractive, drawling voice with a slight American accent, and remembered that Lord Marchington had said that one of the Hampshire Bassington-ffrenches had married an American heiress. "Dr. Arbuthnot says you will be quite all right in a day or two if you just keep quiet."

Frankie felt that she ought at this point to say something about "error" or "mortal mind" but was frightened of saying the wrong thing.

"He seems nice," she said. "He was very kind."

"He seemed a most capable young man," said Mrs. Bassington-ffrench. "It was very fortunate that he just happened to be passing."

"Yes, wasn't it? Not, of couse, that I really needed him."

"But you mustn't talk," continued her hostess. "I'll

send my maid along with some things for you and then she can get you properly into bed."

"It's frightfully kind of you."

"Not at all."

Frankie felt a momentary qualm as the other woman withdrew.

"A nice kind creature," she said to herself. "And beautifully unsuspecting."

For the first time she felt that she was playing a mean trick on her hostess. Her mind had been so taken up with the vision of a murderous Bassington-ffrench pushing an unsuspecting victim over a precipice that lesser characters in the drama had not entered her imagination.

"Oh, well," thought Frankie, "I've got to go through with it now. But I wish she hadn't been so nice about it."

She spent a dull afternoon and evening lying in her darkened room. Mrs. Bassington-ffrench looked in once or twice to see how she was, but she did not stay.

The next day, however, Frankie admitted the daylight and expressed a desire for company and her hostess came and sat with her for some time. They discovered many common acquaintances and friends, and by the end of that day Frankie felt, with a guilty qualm, that they had become friends.

Mrs. Bassington-ffrench referred several times to her husband and to her small boy, Tommy. She seemed a simple woman, deeply attached to her home; yet for some reason or other Frankie fancied that she was not quite happy. There was an anxious expression in her eyes sometimes that did not argue a mind at peace with itself.

On the third day Frankie got up and was introduced to the master of the house.

He was a big man, heavy-jowled, with a kindly but

rather abstracted air. He seemed to spend a good deal of his time shut up in his study. Yet Frankie judged him to be very fond of his wife, though interesting himself very little in her concerns.

Tommy, the small boy, was seven, and a healthy, mischievous child. Sylvia Bassington-ffrench obviously adored him.

"It's so nice down here," said Frankie with a sigh. She was lying out on a long chair in the garden. "I don't know whether it's the bang on the head, or what it is, but I just don't feel I want to move. I'd like to lie here for days and days."

"Well, do," said Sylvia Bassington-ffrench in her calm, incurious tones. "No, really, I mean it. Don't hurry back to town. You see," she went on, "it's a great pleasure to me to have you here. You're so bright and amusing. It quite cheers me up."

"So she needs cheering up," flashed across Frankie's mind. At the same time she felt ashamed of herself.

"I feel we really have become friends," continued the other woman.

Frankie felt still more ashamed. It was a mean thing she was doing—mean—mean—mean. She would give it up! Go back to town—

Her hostess went on. "It won't be too dull here. Tomorrow my brother-in-law is coming back. You'll like him, I'm sure. Everyone likes Roger."

"He lives with you?"

"Off and on. He's a restless creature. He calls himself the ne'er-do-well of the family, and perhaps it's true in a way. He never sticks to a job for long—in fact I don't believe he's ever done any real work in his life. But some people just are like that—especially in old families. And they're usually people with a great charm of manner. Roger is wonderfully sympathetic. I don't know what I should have done without him this Spring when Tommy was ill."

"What was the matter with Tommy?"

"He had a bad fall from the swing. It must have been tied on to a rotten branch, and the branch gave way. Roger was very much upset because he was swinging the child at the time—you know, giving him high ones such as children love. We thought at first Tommy's spine was hurt, but it turned out to be a very slight injury and he's quite all right now."

"He certainly looks it," said Frankie, smiling, as she heard faint yells and whoops in the distance.

"I know. He seems in perfect condition. It's such a relief. He's had bad luck in accidents. He was nearly drowned last winter."

"Was he really?" said Frankie thoughtfully.

She no longer meditated returning to town. The feeling of guilt had abated. Accidents! Did Roger Bassington-ffrench specialize in accidents, she wondered.

She said: "If you're sure you mean it, I'd love to stay a little longer. But won't your husband mind my butting in like this?"

"Henry?" Mrs. Bassington-ffrench's lips curled in a strange expression. "No, Henry won't mind. Henry never minds anything—nowadays."

Frankie looked at her curiously.

"If she knew me better she'd tell me something," she thought to herself. "I believe there are lots of odd things going on in this household."

Henry Bassington-ffrench joined them for tea, and Frankie studied him closely. There was certainly something odd about the man. His type was an obvious one—a jovial, sport-loving, simple country gentleman. But such a man ought not to sit twitching nervously, his nerves obviously on edge, now sunk in an abstraction from which it was impossible to rouse him, now giving out bitter and sarcastic replies to anything said to him. Not that he was always like that. Later that evening, at dinner, he showed out in quite a new light. He joked, laughed, told stories, and was, for a man of his abilities, quite brilliant. Too brilliant, Frankie felt. The brilliance was just as unnatural and out of character.

"He has such queer eyes," she thought. "They frighten me a little."

And yet surely she did not suspect *Henry* Bassington-ffrench of anything? It was his brother, not he, who had been in Marchbolt on that fatal day.

As for the brother, Frankie looked forward to seeing him with eager interest. According to her and to Bobby, the man was a murderer. She was going to meet a murderer face to face.

She felt momentarily nervous. Yet, after all, how could he guess? How could he, in any way, connect her with a successfully accomplished crime?

"You're making a bogy for yourself out of nothing," she reflected.

Roger Bassington-ffrench arrived just before tea on the following afternoon. Frankie did not meet him till tea-time. She was still supposed to "rest" in the afternoon.

When she came out onto the lawn where tea was laid, Sylvia said, smiling: "Here is our invalid. This is my brother-in-law—Lady Frances Derwent."

Frankie saw a tall, slender young man of something over thirty with very pleasant eyes. Although she could see what Bobby meant by saying he ought to have a monocle and a toothbrush moustache, she herself was more inclined to notice the intense blue of his eyes. They shook hands.

He said, "I've been hearing all about the way you tried to break down the park wall."

"I'll admit," said Frankie, "that I'm the world's worst driver. But I was driving an awful old rattle-trap. My own car was laid up, and I bought a cheap one second-hand."

"She was rescued from the ruins by a very good-looking young doctor," said Sylvia.

"He was rather sweet," agreed Frankie.

Tommy arrived at this moment and flung himself upon his uncle with squeaks of joy.

"Have you brought me a Hornby train? You said you would. You said you would!"

"Oh, Tommy, you mustn't ask for things!" said Sylvia.

"That's all right, Sylvia. It was a promise. I've got your train all right, old man." He looked casually at his sister-in-law. "Isn't Henry coming to tea?"

"I don't think so." A constrained note was in her voice. "He isn't feeling awfully well to-day, I imagine." Then she said impulsively, "Oh, Roger, I'm glad you're back!"

He put his hand on her arm for a minute. "That's all right, Sylvia, old girl."

After tea, Roger played trains with his nephew. Frankie watched them, her mind in a turmoil. Surely this wasn't the sort of man to push people over cliffs! This charming young man couldn't be a cold-blooded murderer!

But then—she and Bobby must have been wrong all along. Wrong, that is, about this part of it.

She felt sure now that it wasn't Bassington-ffrench who had pushed Pritchard over the cliff.

Then who was it? She was still convinced he had been

pushed over. Who had done it? And who had put the morphia in Bobby's beer?

With the thought of morphia suddenly the explanation of Henry Bassington-ffrench's peculiar eyes came to her, with their pin-point pupils. Was Henry Bassington-ffrench a drug fiend?

Alan Carstairs

Strangely enough, she received confirmation of this theory no later than the following day, and it came from Roger.

They had been playing a single at tennis against each other and, sitting afterwards sipping iced drinks, had been talking about various indifferent subjects. Frankie had become more and more sensible of the charm of someone who had, like Roger Bassington-ffrench, travelled about all over the world. The family ne'er-do-well, she could not help thinking, contrasted very favorably with his heavy, serious-minded brother.

A pause had fallen while these thoughts were passing through Frankie's mind. It was broken by Roger— speaking this time in an entirely different tone of voice.

"Lady Frances, I'm going to do a rather peculiar thing. I've known you less than twenty-four hours, but I feel instinctively that you're the one person I can ask advice from."

"Advice?" said Frankie, surprised.

"Yes. I can't make up my mind between two different courses of action." He paused. He was leaning forward, swinging a racquet between his knees, a light frown on his forehead. He looked worried and upset. "It's about my brother, Lady Frances."

"Yes?"

"He is taking drugs. I am sure of it."

"What makes you think so?" asked Frankie.

"Everything. His appearance. His extraordinary changes of mood. And have you noticed his eyes? The pupils are like pin-points."

"I had noticed that," admitted Frankie. "What do you think it is?"

"Morphia or some form of opium."

"Has it been going on for long?"

"I date the beginning of it from about six months ago. I remember that he complained of sleeplessness a good deal. How he first came to take the stuff I don't know, but I think it must have begun soon after then."

"How does he get hold of it?" inquired Frankie practically.

"I think it comes to him by post. Have you noticed that he is particularly nervous and irritable some days at tea-time?"

"Yes, I have."

"I suspect that that is when he has finished up his supply and is waiting for more. Then, after the six o'clock post has come, he goes into his study and emerges for dinner in quite a different mood."

Frankie nodded. She remembered that unnatural brilliance of conversation sometimes at dinner.

"But where does the supply come from?" she asked.

"Ah, that I don't know. No reputable doctor would give it to him. There are, I suppose, various sources where one could get it in London by paying a big price."

Frankie nodded thoughtfully. She was remembering having said to Bobby something about a gang of drug-smugglers and his replying that one could not mix up too many crimes. It was queer that so soon in their investigations they should have come upon the traces of such a thing. And it was queerer that it should be the chief suspect who had drawn her attention to the fact. It made her more inclined than ever to acquit Roger Bassington-ffrench of the charge of murder.

And yet there was the inexplicable matter of the changed photograph. The evidence against him, she reminded herself, was still exactly what it had been. On the other side was only the personality of the man himself. And everyone always said that murderers were charming people!

She shook off these reflections and turned to her companion.

"Why exactly are you telling me this?" she asked frankly.

"Because I don't know what to do about Sylvia," he said simply.

"You think she doesn't know?"

"Of course she doesn't know. Ought I to tell her?"

"It's very difficult—"

"It *is* difficult. That's why I thought you might be able to help me. Sylvia has taken a great fancy to you. She doesn't care much for any of the people round about, but she liked you at once, she tells me. What ought I to do, Lady Frances? By telling her I shall add a great burden to her life."

"If she knew, she might have some influence," suggested Frankie.

"I doubt it. When it's a case of drug-taking, nobody, even the nearest and dearest, has any influence."

"That's rather a hopeless attitude, isn't it?"

"It's a fact. There are ways, of course. If Henry would only consent to go in for a cure—there's a place actually near here. Run by a Dr. Nicholson."

"But he'd never consent, would he?"

"He might. You can catch a morphia-taker in a mood of extravagant remorse sometimes when he'd do anything to cure himself. I'm inclined to think that Henry might be got to that frame of mind more easily if he thought Sylvia didn't know—if her knowing were held over him as a kind of threat. If the cure were successful—they'd call it 'nerves,' of course—she would never need to know."

"Would he have to go away for the cure?"

"The place I mean is about three miles from here, the other side of the village. It's run by a Canadian, Dr. Nicholson. A very clever man, I believe. And fortunately Henry likes him. Hush—here comes Sylvia."

Mrs. Bassington-ffrench joined them, observing, "Have you been very energetic?"

"Three sets," said Frankie. "And I was beaten every time."

"You play a very good game," said Roger.

"I'm terribly lazy about tennis," said Sylvia. "We must ask the Nicholsons over one day. She's very fond of a game. Why—what is it?" She had caught the glance the other two had exchanged.

"Nothing—only I just happened to be talking about the Nicholsons to Lady Frances."

"You'd better call her Frankie as I do," said Sylvia. "Isn't it odd how whenever one talks of any person or thing, somebody else does the same immediately afterwards?"

"They are Canadians, aren't they?" inquired Frankie.

"He is, certainly. I rather fancy she is English, but I'm not sure. She's a very pretty little thing—quite charming, with the loveliest big wistful eyes. Somehow or other I fancy she isn't terribly happy. It must be a depressing life."

"He runs a kind of sanitarium, doesn't he?"

"Yes, nerve cases and people who take drugs. He's

very successful, I believe. He's rather an impressive man."

"You like him?"

"No," said Sylvia abruptly. "I don't." And rather vehemently, after a moment or two, she added, "Not at all."

Later on, she pointed out to Frankie a photograph of a charming, large-eyed woman which stood on the piano.

"That's Moira Nicholson. An appealing face, isn't it? A man who came down here with some friends of ours some time ago was quite struck with it. He wanted an introduction to her, I think." She laughed. "I'll ask them to dinner tomorrow night. I'd like to know what you think of him."

"Him?"

"Yes. As I told you, I dislike him, and yet he's quite an attractive-looking man."

Something in her tone made Frankie look at her quickly, but Sylvia Bassington-ffrench had turned away and was taking some dead flowers out of a vase.

"I must collect my ideas," thought Frankie as she drew a comb through her thick dark hair when dressing for dinner that night. "And," she added resolutely, "it's time I made a few experiments."

Was, or was not, Roger Bassington-ffrench the villain she and Bobby assumed him to be?

She and Bobby had agree that whoever had tried to put him out of the way must have easy access to morphia. Now in a way this held good for Roger Bassington-ffrench. If his brother received supplies of morphia by post, it would be easy enough for Roger to abstract a packet and use it for his own purposes.

"Mem.," wrote Frankie on a sheet of paper. "One—

find out where Roger was on 16th—day when Bobby was poisoned."

She thought she saw her way to doing that fairly clearly.

"Two," she wrote. "Produce picture of dead man and observe reactions, if any. Also note whether R. B. F. admits being in Marchbolt then."

She felt slightly nervous over the second resolution. It meant coming out into the open. On the other hand the tragedy had happened in her own part of the world, and to mention it casually would be the most natural thing in the world. She crumpled up the sheet of paper and burnt it.

She managed to introduce the first point fairly naturally at dinner.

"You know," she said frankly to Roger, "I can't help feeling that we've met before. And it wasn't very long ago either. It wasn't, by any chance, at that party of Lady Shane's at Claridge's? On the 16th it was."

"It couldn't have been on the 16th," said Sylvia quickly. "Roger was here then. I remember, because we had a children's party that day, and what I should have done without Roger, I simply don't know."

She gave a grateful glance at her brother-in-law and he smiled back at her.

"I don't feel I've ever met you before," he said thoughtfully to Frankie and added, "I'm sure, if I had, I'd remember it." He said it rather nicely.

"One point settled," thought Frankie. "Roger Bassington-ffrench was not in Wales on the day that Bobby was poisoned."

The second point came up fairly easily later. Frankie led the talk to country places, their dullness, and the interest aroused by any local excitement.

"We had a man fall over the cliff last month," she

remarked. "We were all thrilled to the core. I went to the inquest full of excitement, but it was all rather dull really."

"Was that at a place called Marchbolt?" asked Sylvia suddenly.

Frankie nodded. "Derwent Castle is only about seven miles from Marchbolt," she explained.

"Roger, that must have been your man!" cried Sylvia.

Frankie looked inquiringly at him.

"I was actually in at the death," said Roger. "I stayed with the body till the police came."

"I thought one of the Vicar's sons did that," said Frankie.

"He had to go off to play the organ or something— so I took over."

"How perfectly extraordinary!" said Frankie. "I did hear somebody else had been there too, but I never heard the name. So it was *you.*"

There was a general atmosphere of "How curious! Isn't the world small?" Frankie felt she was doing this rather well.

"Perhaps that's where you saw me before—in Marchbolt?" suggested Roger.

"I wasn't there actually at the time of the accident," said Frankie. "I came back from London a couple of days afterward. Were you at the inquest?"

"No. I went back to London the morning after the tragedy."

"He had some absurd idea of buying a house down there," said Sylvia.

"Utter nonsense," said Henry Bassington-ffrench.

"Not at all," said Roger good-humoredly.

"You know perfectly well, Roger, that as soon as you'd bought it, you'd get a fit of wanderlust and go off abroad again."

"Oh! I shall settle down some day, Sylvia."

"When you do, you'd better settle down near us," said Sylvia. "Not go off to Wales."

Roger laughed. Then he turned to Frankie. "Any points of interest about the accident? It didn't turn out to be suicide or anything?"

"Oh, no, it was all painfully above-board, and some appalling relations came and identified the man. He was on a walking tour, it seems. Very sad really, because he was awfully good-looking. Did you see his picture in the papers?"

"I think I did," said Sylvia vaguely, "but I don't remember."

"I've got a cutting upstairs from our local paper."

Frankie was all eagerness. She ran upstairs and came down with the cutting in her hand. She gave it to Sylvia. Roger came and looked over Sylvia's shoulder.

"Don't you think he's good-looking?" Frankie demanded.

"He is, rather," said Sylvia. "He looks very like that man Alan Carstairs. Don't you think so, Roger? I believe I remember saying so at the time."

"He's got quite a look of him here," agreed Roger. "But there wasn't much real resemblance, you know."

"You can't tell from newspaper pictures, can you?" said Sylvia as she handed the cutting back.

Frankie agreed that you couldn't, and the conversation passed to other matters.

She went to bed undecided. Everyone seemed to have reacted with perfect naturalness. Roger's house-hunting stunt had been no secret.

The only thing she had succeeded in getting was a name—the name of Alan Carstairs.

Dr. Nicholson

Frankie attacked Sylvia the following morning. She started by asking carelessly:

"What was that man's name you mentioned last night? Alan Carstairs, was it? I feel sure I've heard that name before."

"I dare say you have. He's rather a celebrity in his way, I believe. He's a Canadian—a naturalist and big-game hunter and explorer. I don't really know him. Some friends of ours, the Rivingtons, brought him down here one day for lunch. A very attractive man—big and bronzed and nice blue eyes."

"I was sure I'd heard of him."

"He'd never been over to this country before, I believe. Last year he went a tour through Africa with that millionaire man, John Savage—the one who thought he had cancer and killed himself in that tragic way. Carstairs has been all over the world. East Africa, South America—simply everywhere, I believe."

"Sounds a nice adventurous person," said Frankie.

"Oh, he was. Distinctly attractive."

"Funny—his being so like the man who fell over the cliff at Marchbolt," said Frankie.

"I wonder if everyone has a double."

They compared instances, citing Adolf Beck and referring lightly to the Lyons Mail. Frankie was careful to make no further references to Alan Carstairs. To show too much interest in him would be fatal. In her own mind, however, she felt she was getting on now. She was quite convinced that the victim of the cliff tragedy at Marchbolt had been Alan Carstairs. He fulfilled all the conditions. He had no intimate friends or relations in this country, and his disappearance was unlikely to be noticed for some time. A man who frequently ran off to East Africa and South America was not likely to be missed at once. Moreover, Frankie noted, although Sylvia Bassington-ffrench had commented on the resemblance in the newspaper reproduction, it had not occurred to her for a moment that it actually *was* the man. That, Frankie thought, was rather an interesting bit of psychology. We seldom suspect people who are "news" of being people we have actually seen or met.

Very good then. The dead man was Alan Carstairs. The next step was to learn more about Alan Carstairs. His connection with the Bassington-ffrenches seemed to have been of the slightest. He had been brought down there quite by chance by friends. What was the name?— Rivington. Frankie stored it in her memory for future use.

That certainly was a possible avenue of inquiry. But it would be well to go slowly. Inquiries about Alan Carstairs must be very discreetly made.

"I don't want to be poisoned or knocked on the head," thought Frankie with a grimace. "They were ready enough to bump off Bobby for practically nothing at all—"

Her thoughts flew off at a tangent to that tantalizing phrase that had started the whole business. Evans! Who was Evans? Where did Evans fit in?

"A dope gang," decided Frankie. Perhaps some relative of Carstairs was being victimized, and he had de-

termined to bust it up. Perhaps he had come to England
for that purpose. Evans may have been one of the gang
who had retired and gone to Wales to live. Carstairs had
bribed Evans to give the others away, and Evans had
consented and Carstairs went there to see him, and someone followed him and killed him.

Was that somebody Roger Bassington-ffrench? It
seemed very unlikely. The Caymans, now, were far more
what Frankie imagined a gang of dope-smugglers would
be likely to be.

And yet—that photograph. If only there were some
explanation of that photograph!

That evening Dr. Nicholson and his wife were expected to dinner. Frankie was finishing dressing when
she heard their car drive up to the front door. Her window faced that way, and she looked out.

A tall man was just alighting from the driver's seat
of a dark-blue Talbot.

Frankie withdrew her head thoughtfully.

Carstairs had been a Canadian. Dr. Nicholson was a
Canadian. And Dr. Nicholson had a dark-blue Talbot.

Absurd to build anything upon that, of course, but
wasn't it just faintly suggestive?

Dr. Nicholson was a big man with a manner that suggested great reserves of power. His speech was slow,
and on the whole he said very little, but he contrived
somehow to make every word sound significant. He
wore strong glasses, and behind them his very pale blue
eyes glittered reflectively.

His wife was a slender creature of perhaps twenty-
seven, pretty, indeed beautiful. She seemed, Frankie
thought, slightly nervous and chattered rather feverishly
as though to conceal the fact.

"You had an accident, I hear, Lady Frances," said Dr.

Nicholson as he took his seat beside her at the dinner table.

Frankie explained the catastrophe. She wondered why she should feel so nervous in doing so. The Doctor's manner was simple and interested. Why should she feel as though she were rehearsing a defence to a charge that had never been made? Was there any earthly reason why the Doctor should disbelieve in her accident?

"That was too bad," he said, as she finished, having perhaps made a more detailed story of it than seemed strictly necessary. "But you seem to have made a very good recovery."

"We won't admit she's cured yet. We're keeping her with us," said Sylvia.

The Doctor's gaze went to Sylvia. Something like a very faint smile came to his lips, but passed almost immediately.

"I should keep her with you as long as possible," he said gravely.

Frankie was sitting between her host and Dr. Nicholson. Henry Bassington-ffrench was decidedly moody to-night. His hands twitched, he ate next to nothing, and he took no part in the conversation.

Mrs. Nicholson, opposite, had a difficult time with him, and turned to Roger with obvious relief. She talked to him in a desultory fashion, but Frankie noticed that her eyes were never long absent from her husband's face.

Dr. Nicholson was talking about life in the country. "Do you know what a culture is, Lady Frances?"

"Do you mean book-learning?" asked Frankie, rather puzzled.

"No, no. I was referring to germs. They develop, you know, in specially prepared serum. The country, Lady Frances, is a little like that. There is time, and space, and infinite leisure—suitable conditions, you see, for development."

"Do you mean bad things?" asked Frankie.

"That depends, Lady Frances, on the kind of germ cultivated."

Idiotic conversation, thought Frankie. Why should it make her feel creepy? Yet it did! She said flippantly, "I expect I'm developing all sorts of dark qualities."

He looked at her and said calmly: "Oh, no, I don't think so, Lady Frances. I think you would always be on the side of law and order."

Was there a faint emphasis on the word *law?*

Suddenly, across the table Mrs. Nicholson said, "My husband prides himself on summing up character."

Dr. Nicholson nodded his head gently. "Quite right, Moire. Little things interest me." He turned to Frankie again. "I had heard of your accident, you know. One thing about it intrigued me very much."

"Yes?" said Frankie, her heart beating suddenly.

"The doctor who was passing. The one who brought you in here."

"Yes?"

"He must have had a curious character—to turn his car before going to the rescue."

"I don't understand."

"Of course not. You were unconscious. But young Reeves, the message boy, came from Staverley on his bicycle, and no car passed him. Yet he comes round the corner, finds the smash, and the doctor's car pointing the same way he was going—towards London. You see the point? The Doctor did not come from the direction of Staverley, so he must have come the other way, down the hill. But in that case, his car should have been pointing towards Staverley. But it wasn't. Therefore he must have turned it."

"Unless he had come from Staverley some time before," said Frankie.

"Then his car would have been standing there as you came down the hill. Was it?"

The pale-blue eyes were looking at her very intently through the thick glasses.

"I don't remember," said Frankie. "I don't think so."

"You sound like a detective, Jasper," said Mrs. Nicholson. "And all about nothing at all."

"Little things interest me," said Nicholson. He turned to his hostess and Frankie drew a breath of relief.

Why had he catechized her like that? How had he found out all about the accident? "Little things interest me," he had said. Was that all there was to it? Frankie remembered the dark-blue Talbot saloon, and the fact that Carstairs had been a Canadian. It seemed to her that Dr. Nicholson was a sinister man.

She kept out of his way after dinner, attaching herself to the gentle, fragile Mrs. Nicholson. She noticed that all the time Mrs. Nicholson's eyes still watched her husband. Was it love, Frankie wondered, or fear?

Nicholson devoted himself to Sylvia, and at half-past ten he caught his wife's eye and they rose to go.

"Well," said Roger after they had gone, "what do you think of our Dr. Nicholson? A very forceful personality, hasn't he?"

"I'm like Sylvia," said Frankie. "I don't think I like him very much. I like her better."

"Good-looking but rather a little idiot," said Roger. "She either worships him or is scared to death of him, I don't know which."

"That's just what I wondered," agreed Frankie.

"I don't like him," said Sylvia, "but I must admit that he's got a lot of—of *force*. I believe he's cured drug-takers in the most marvellous way. People whose relatives despaired utterly. They've gone there as a last hope and come out absolutely cured."

"Yes," cried Henry Bassington-ffrench suddenly. "And do you know what goes on there? Do you know the awful suffering and mental torment? A man's used to a drug and they cut him off it—cut him off it—till he goes raving mad for the lack of it and beats his head against the wall. That's what he does, your 'forceful' doctor, tortures people—tortures them—sends them to Hell—drives them mad. . . ."

He was shaking violently. Suddenly he turned and left the room.

Sylvia Bassington-ffrench looked startled. "What is the matter with Henry?" she said wonderingly. "He seems very much upset."

Frankie and Roger dared not look at each other.

"He's not looked well all the evening," ventured Frankie.

"No. I noticed that. He's very moody lately. I wish he hadn't given up riding. Oh, by the way, Dr. Nicholson invited Tommy over to-morrow, but I don't like his going there very much—not with all those queer nerve cases and dope-takers."

"I don't suppose the Doctor would allow him to come into contact with them," said Roger. "He seems very fond of children."

"Yes, I think it's a disappointment he hasn't got any of his own. Probably to her too. She looks very sad—and terribly delicate."

"She's like a sad Madonna," said Frankie.

"Yes, that describes her very well."

"If Dr. Nicholson is so fond of children, I suppose he came to your children's party?" said Frankie carelessly.

"Unfortunately he was away for a day or two just

then. I think he had to go to London for some conference."

"I see."

They went up to bed. Before she went to sleep Frankie wrote to Bobby.

15

A Discovery

Bobby had had an irksome time. His enforced inaction was exceedingly trying. He hated staying quietly in London and doing nothing.

He had been rung up on the telephone by George Arbuthnot, who in a few laconic words told him that all had gone well. A couple of days later he had a letter from Frankie delivered to him by her maid, the letter having gone under cover to her at Lord Marchington's town house. Since then he had heard nothing.

"Letter for you!" called out Badger.

Bobby came forward excitedly, but the letter was one addressed in his father's handwriting and postmarked Marchbolt. At that moment, however, he caught sight of the neat, black-gowned figure of Frankie's maid approaching down the mews. Five minutes later he was tearing open Frankie's second letter.

DEAR BOBBY,
I think it's about time you came down. I've given them instructions at home that you're to have the Bentley whenever you ask for it. Get a chauffeur's livery—dark green ours always are. Put it down to Father at Harrod's. It's best to be correct in details. Concentrate on making a good job of the moustache. It makes a frightful difference to anyone's face.

Come down here and ask for me. You might bring me an ostensible note from Father. Report that the car is now in working order again. The garage here only holds two cars and as it's got the family Daimler and Roger Bassington-ffrench's two-seater in it, it is fortunately full up, so you will go to Staverley and put up there.

Get what local information you can when there— particularly about a Dr. Nicholson who runs a place for dope patients. Several suspicious circumstances about him: he has a dark-blue Tablot saloon, he was away from home on the 16th when your beer was doctored, and he takes altogether too detailed an interest in the circumstances of my accident.

I think I've identified the corpse!!!

Au revoir, my fellow sleuth.

> Love from your successfully concussed
> FRANKIE.

P.S. I shall post this myself.

Bobby's spirits rose with a bound.

Discarding his overalls and breaking the news of his immediate departure to Badger, he was about to hurry off when he remembered that he had not yet opened his father's letter. He did so with a rather qualified enthusiasm since the Vicar's letters were actuated by a spirit of duty rather than pleasure and breathed an atmosphere of Christian forbearance which was highly depressing.

The Vicar gave conscientious news of doings in Marchbolt, described his own troubles with the organist and commented on the un-Christian spirit of one of his churchwardens. The rebinding of the hymn-books was also touched upon. And the Vicar hoped that Bobby was sticking manfully to his job and trying to make good, and remained his ever affectionate Father.

There was a postscript.

By the way, someone called who asked for your address in London. I was out at the time, and he did not leave his name. Mrs. Roberts described him as a tall, stooping gentleman with pince-nez. He seemed very sorry to miss you and very anxious to see you again.

A tall stooping man with pince-nez—Bobby tried to think of anyone he knew who was likely to fit that description, but could not. Suddenly a quick suspicion darted into his mind. Was this the forerunner of a new attempt upon his life? Was this mysterious enemy—one or more—trying to track him down?

He sat still and did some serious thinking. They, whoever they were, had only just discovered that he had left the neighborhood. All unsuspecting, Mrs. Roberts had given his new address. So that already they—whoever they were—might be keeping a watch upon the place. If he went out he would be followed—and just as things were at the moment that would never do.

"Badger," said Bobby.

"Yes, old lad."

"Come here."

The next five minutes were spent in genuine hard work. At the end of ten minutes Badger could repeat his instructions by heart.

When he was word-perfect, Bobby got into a two-seater Fiat dating from 1902 and drove dashingly down the mews. He parked the Fiat in St. James's Square and walked straight from there to his club. There he did some telephoning, and a couple of hours later certain parcels were delivered to him. Finally, about half-past three a chauffeur in dark-green livery walked to St. James's Square and went rapidly up to a large Bentley which had been parked there about half an hour previously. The parking attendant nodded to him—the gentleman who had left the car had remarked, stammering slightly as he did so, that his chauffeur would be fetching it shortly.

Bobby let in the clutch and drew neatly out. The abandoned Fiat still stood demurely awaiting its owner. Bobby, despite the intense discomfort of his upper lip, began to enjoy himself. He headed north, not south, and before long, the powerful engine was forging ahead on the Great North Road.

It was only an extra precaution that he was taking. He was pretty sure that he was not being followed. Presently he turned off to the left, and made his way by circuitous roads to Hampshire.

It was just after tea that the Bentley purred up the drive of Merroway Court, a stiff and correct chauffeur at the wheel.

"Hullo," said Frankie lightly. "There's the car."

She went out to the front door. Sylvia and Roger came with her.

"Is everything all right, Hawkins?"

The chauffeur touched his cap. "Yes, m'lady. She's been thoroughly overhauled."

"That's all right, then."

The chauffeur produced a note. "From his lordship, m'lady."

Frankie took it. "You'll put up at the—what is it— Anglers' Arms in Staverley, Hawkins. I'll telephone in the morning if I want the car."

"Very good, your ladyship." Bobby backed, turned and sped down the drive.

"I'm so sorry we haven't room here," said Sylvia. "It's a lovely car."

"You get some pace out of that," said Roger.

"I do," admitted Frankie.

She was satisfied that no faintest quiver of recognition had shown on Roger's face. She would have been surprised if it had. She would not have recognized Bobby herself had she met him casually. The small moustache had a perfectly natural appearance, and that, with the stiff demeanor so uncharacteristic of the natural Bobby, completed the disguise enhanced by the chauffeur's livery.

The voice, too, had been excellent, and quite unlike Bobby's own. Frankie began to think that Bobby was far more talented than she had given him credit for being.

Meanwhile Bobby had successfully taken up his quarters at the Anglers' Arms. It was up to him to create the part of Edward Hawkins, chauffeur to Lady Frances Derwent.

As to the behavior of chauffeurs in private life Bobby was singularly ill-informed, but he imagined that a certain haughtiness would not come amiss. He tried to feel himself a superior being and to act accordingly. The admiring attitude of various young women employed in the Anglers' Arms had a distinctly encouraging effect, and he soon found that Frankie and her accident had provided the principal topic of conversation in Staverley ever since it had happened. Bobby unbent towards the landlord, a stout genial person of the name of Thomas Askew, who permitted information to leak from him.

"Young Reeves, he was there and saw it happen," declared Mr. Askew.

Bobby blessed the natural mendacity of the young. The famous accident was now vouched for by an eye-witness.

"Thought his last moment had come, he did," went on Mr. Askew. "Straight for him down the hill it come—

and then took the wall instead. A wonder the young lady wasn't killed."

"Her ladyship takes some killing," said Bobby.

"Had many accidents, has she?"

"She's been lucky," said Bobby. "But I assure you, Mr. Askew, that when her ladyship's taken over the wheel from me as she sometimes does—well, I've made sure my last hour has come."

Several persons present shook their heads wisely and said they didn't wonder and it's just what they would have thought.

"Very nice little place you have here, Mr. Askew," said Bobby kindly and condescendingly. "Very nice and snug."

Mr. Askew expressed gratification.

"Merroway Court the only big place in the neighborhood?"

"Well, there's the Grange, Mr. Hawkins. Not that you'd call that a place exactly. There's no family living there. No, it had been empty for years until this American doctor took it."

"An American doctor?"

"That's it—Nicholson his name is. And if you ask me, Mr. Hawkins, there are some very queer goings on there."

The barmaid at this point remarked that Dr. Nicholson gave her the shivers, he did.

"Goings on, Mr. Askew?" said Bobby. "Now what do you mean by goings on?"

Mr. Askew shook his head darkly. "There's those there that don't want to be there. Put away by their relations. I assure you, Mr. Hawkins, the moanings and the shrieks and the groans that go on there you wouldn't believe."

"Why don't the police interfere?"

"Oh, well, you see, it's supposed to be all right. Nerve cases, and such-like. Loonies that aren't so very bad. The gentleman's a doctor and it's all all right, so to speak—" Here the landlord buried his face in a pint pot and emerged again to shake his head in a very doubtful fashion.

"Ah!" said Bobby in a dark and meaning way. "If we knew everything that went on in these places. . . ." And he too applied himself to a pewter pot.

The barmaid chimed in eagerly: "That's what I say, Mr. Hawkins. What goes on there? Why, one night a poor young creature escaped—in her nightgown she was—and the Doctor and a couple of nurses out looking for her. 'Oh! don't let them take me back!'—that's what she was crying out. Pitiful it was. And about her being rich really and her relations having her put away. But they took her back they did, and the Doctor he explained that she'd got a persecution mania—that's what he called it. Kind of thinking everyone was against her. But I've often wondered—yes, I have. I've often wondered. . . ."

"Ah!" said Mr. Askew. "It's easy enough to say—"

Somebody present said that there was no knowing what went on in places. And someone else said that was right.

Finally the meeting broke up and Bobby announced his intention of going for a stroll before turning in.

The Grange was, he knew, on the other side of the village from Merroway Court, so he turned his footsteps in that direction. What he had heard that evening seemed to him worthy of attention. A lot of it could, of course, be discounted. Villages are usually prejudiced against newcomers, and still more so if the newcomer is of a different nationality. If Nicholson ran a place for curing drug-takers, there would naturally be strange sounds is-

suing from it—groans and even shrieks might be heard
without any sinister reason for them. But all the same
the story of the escaping girl struck Bobby unpleasantly.
Supposing the Grange were really a place where people
were kept against their will? A certain number of genuine cases might be taken as camouflage.

At this point in his meditations Bobby arrived at a
high wall with an entrace of wrought-iron gates. He
stepped up to the gates and tried one gently. It was
locked. Well, after all, why not?

And yet somehow the touch of that locked gate gave
him a faintly sinister feeling. The place was like a prison.

He moved a little farther along the road, measuring
the wall with his eye. Would it be possible to climb
over? The wall was smooth and high and presented no
accommodating crannies. He shook his head. Suddenly
he came upon a little door. Without much real hope he
tried it. To his surprise it yielded. It was not locked.

"Bit of an oversight here," thought Bobby with a grin.
He slipped through, closing the door softly behind him.

He found himself on a path leading through a shrubbery. He followed the path, which twisted a good deal—
in fact it reminded Bobby of the one in *Alice Through
the Looking-Glass*. Suddenly without any warning it
gave a sharp turn and emerged into an open space close
to the house. It was a moonlit night and the space was
clearly lit. Bobby had stepped full into the moonlight
before he could stop himself.

At the same moment a woman's figure came round
the corner of the house. She was treading very softly,
glancing from side to side with—or so it seemed to the
watching Bobby—the nervous alertness of a hunted animal. Suddenly she stopped dead and stood swaying as
though she would fall.

Bobby rushed forward and caught her. Her lips were

white and it seemed to him that never had he seen such awful fear on any human countenance.

"It's all right," he said reassuringly in a very low voice. "It's quite all right."

The girl, for she was little more, moaned faintly, her eyelids half closed. "I'm so frightened," she murmured. "I'm so terribly frightened."

"What's the matter?" asked Bobby.

The girl only shook her head and repeated faintly, "I'm so frightened. I'm so horribly frightened."

Suddenly some sound seemed to come to her ears. She sprang upright, away from Bobby. Then she turned to him.

"Go away," she said. "Go away at once!"

"I want to help you," said Bobby.

"Do you?" She looked at him for a minute or two, a strange searching and moving glance. It was as though she explored his soul. Then she shook her head.

"No one can help me."

"I can," said Bobby. "I'd do anything. Tell me what it is that frightens you so."

She shook her head. "Not now. Oh, quick! They're coming. You can't help me unless you go now. At once—at once."

Bobby yielded to her urgency. With a whispered "I'm at the Anglers' Arms," he plunged back along the path. The last he saw of her was an urgent gesture bidding him hurry.

Suddenly he heard footsteps on the path in front of him. Someone was coming along the path from the little door. Bobby plunged abruptly into the bushes at the side of the path.

He had not been mistaken. A man was coming along the path. He passed close to Bobby, but it was too dark for the young man to see his face.

When he had passed Bobby resumed his retreat. He felt that he could do nothing more that night. Anyway, his head was in a whirl.

For he had recognized the girl—recognized her beyond any possible doubt.

She was the original of the photograph which had so mysteriously disappeared.

16

Bobby Becomes a Solicitor

"Mr. Hawkins?"

"Yes," said Bobby—his voice slightly muffled owing to a large mouthful of bacon and eggs.

"You're wanted on the telephone."

Bobby took a hasty gulp of coffee, wiped his mouth and rose. The telephone was in a small dark passage. He took up the receiver.

"Hullo," said Frankie's voice.

"Hullo, Frankie," said Bobby incautiously.

"This is Lady Frances Derwent speaking," said the voice coldly. "Is that Hawkins?"

"Yes, m'lady."

"I shall want the car at ten o'clock to take me up to London."

"Very good, your ladyship." Bobby replaced the receiver.

"When does one say 'my lady' and when does one say 'your ladyship'?" he cogitated. "I ought to know, but I don't. It's the sort of thing that will lead a real chauffeur or butler to catch me out."

At the other end, Frankie hung up the receiver and turned to Roger Bassington-ffrench.

"It's a nuisance," she observed lightly, "to have to go up to London to-day. All owing to Father's fuss."

"Still," said Roger, "you'll be back this evening?"

"Oh, yes."

"I'd half thought of asking you if you'd give me a lift to town," said Roger carelessly.

Frankie paused for an infinitesimal second before her answer—given with an apparent readiness.

"Why, of course," she said.

"But on second thoughts I don't think I will go up today," went on Roger. "Henry's looking even odder than usual. Somehow I don't very much like leaving Sylvia alone with him."

"I know," said Frankie.

"Are you driving yourself?" asked Roger casually as they moved away from the telephone.

"Yes, but I shall take Hawkins. I've got some shopping to do as well and it's a nuisance if you're driving yourself—you can't leave the car anywhere."

"Yes, of course."

He said no more, but when the car came around, Bobby at the wheel very stiff and correct of demeanor, he came out on the doorstep to see her off.

"Good-bye," said Frankie.

Under the circumstances she did not think of holding out a hand, but Roger took hers and held it a minute.

"You *are* coming back?" he said with curious insistence.

Frankie laughed. "Of course. I only meant good-bye till this evening."

"Don't have any more accidents."

"I'll let Hawkins drive if you like."

She sprang in beside Bobby, who touched his cap. The car moved off down the drive, Roger still standing on the steps looking after it.

"Bobby," said Frankie, "do you think it possible that Roger might fall for me?"

"Has he?" inquired Bobby.

"Well, I just wondered."

"I expect you know the symptoms pretty well," said Bobby. But he spoke absently.

Frankie shot him a quick glance. "Has anything—happened?" she asked.

"Yes, it has. Frankie, I've found the original of the photograph!"

"You mean—*the* one—the one you talked so much about—the one that was in the dead man's pocket?"

"Yes."

"*Bobby!* I've got a few things to tell you, but nothing to this. Where did you find her?"

Bobby jerked his head back over his shoulder. "In Dr. Nicholson's nursing home."

"Tell me."

Carefully and meticulously Bobby described the events of the previous night. Frankie listened breathlessly.

"Then we *are* on the right track," she said. "And Dr. Nicholson *is* mixed up in all this! Bobby, I'm afraid of that man."

"What is he like?"

"Oh! big and forceful—and he watches you. Very intently behind glasses. And you feel he knows all about you."

"When did you meet him?"

"He came to dinner."

She described the dinner party and Dr. Nicholson's insistent dwelling on the details of her "accident."

"I felt he was suspicious," she ended up.

"It's certainly queer his going into details like that," said Bobby. "What do you think is at the bottom of all this business, Frankie?"

"Well, I'm beginning to think that your suggestion of

a dope gang—which I was so haughty about at the time—isn't such a bad guess after all."

"With Dr. Nicholson as the head of the gang?"

"Yes. This nursing home business would be a very good cloak for that sort of thing. He'd have a certain supply of drugs on the premises quite legitimately. While pretending to cure drug cases he might really be supplying them with the stuff."

"That seems plausible enough," agreed Bobby.

"I haven't told you yet about Henry Bassington-ffrench."

Bobby listened attentively to her description of her host's idiosyncrasies. "His wife doesn't suspect?"

"I'm sure she doesn't."

"What is she like? Intelligent?"

"I never thought exactly. No, I suppose she isn't very. And yet in some ways she seems quite shrewd. A frank, pleasant woman."

"And our Bassington-ffrench?"

"There I'm puzzled," said Frankie slowly. "Do you think, Bobby, that just possibly we might be all wrong about him?"

"Nonsense!" said Bobby. "We worked it all out and decided that he must be the villain of the piece."

"Because of the photograph?"

"Because of the photograph. No one else *could* have changed that photograph for the other."

"I know," said Frankie. "But that one incident is all that we have against him."

"It's quite enough."

"I suppose so. And yet—"

"Well?"

"I don't know. But I have a queer sort of feeling that he's innocent—that he's not concerned in the matter at all."

Bobby looked at her coldly. "Did you say that he had fallen for you, or that you had fallen for him?" he inquired politely.

Frankie flushed. "Don't be so absurd, Bobby. I just wondered if there couldn't be some innocent explanation—that's all."

"I don't see that there can be. Especially now that we've actually found the girl in the neighborhood. That seems to clinch matters. If we only had some inkling as to who the dead man was—"

"Oh, but I have. I told you so in my letter. I'm nearly sure that the murdered man was somebody called Alan Carstairs."

Once more she plunged into narrative.

"You know," said Bobby, "we really are getting on. Now we must try, more or less, to reconstruct the crime. Let's spread out our facts and see what sort of job we can make of it."

He paused for a moment and the car slackened speed as though in sympathy. Then he pressed his foot down once more on the accelerator and at the same time spoke.

"First, we'll assume that you are right about Alan Carstairs. He certainly fulfils the conditions. He's the right sort of man, he led a wandering life, he had very few friends and acquaintances in England, and if he disappeared he wasn't likely to be missed or sought after. So far, so good. Alan Carstairs comes down to Staverley with these people—what did you say their name was—?"

"Rivington. There's a possible channel of inquiry there. In fact I think we ought to follow it up."

"We will. Very well, Carstairs comes down to Staverley with the Rivingtons. Now, is there anything in that?"

"You mean did he get them to bring him down here deliberately?"

"That's what I mean. Or was it just a casual chance? Was he brought down here by them, and did he then come across the girl by accident just as I did? I presume he knew her before or he wouldn't have had her photograph on him."

"The alternative being," said Frankie thoughtfully, "that he was already on the track of Nicholson and his gang."

"And used the Rivingtons as a means of getting to this part of the world naturally?"

"That's quite a possible theory," said Frankie. "He may have been on the track of this gang."

"Or simply on the track of the girl."

"The girl?"

"Yes. She may have been abducted. He may have come over to England to find her."

"Well, but if he had tracked her down to Staverley why should he go off to Wales?"

"Obviously, there's a lot we don't know yet," said Bobby.

"Evans," said Frankie thoughtfully. "We don't get any clues as to Evans. The Evans part of it must have to do with Wales."

They were both silent for a moment or two. Then Frankie woke up to her surroundings.

"My dear, we're actually at Putney Hill. It seems like five minutes. Where are we going and what are we doing?"

"That's for you to say. I don't even know why we've come up to town."

"The journey to town was only an excuse for getting a talk with you. I couldn't very well risk being seen walking the lanes at Staverley deep in conversation with my chauffeur. I used the pseudo-letter from Father as an excuse for driving up to town and talking to you on the way, and even that was nearly wrecked by Bassington-ffrench's suggestion that he should come too."

"That would have torn it severely."

"Not really. We'd have dropped him wherever he liked and then we'd have gone on to Brook Street and talked there. I think we'd better do that anyway. Your garage place may be watched."

Bobby agreed and related the episode of the inquiries made about him at Marchbolt.

"Better go to our town house," suggested Frankie. "There's no one there but my maid and a couple of care-takers."

They drove to Brook Street. Frankie rang the bell and was admitted, Bobby remaining outside. Presently Frankie opened the door again and beckoned him in. They went upstairs to the big drawing-room and pulled up some of the blinds and removed the swathing from one of the sofas.

"There's one other thing I forgot to tell you," said Frankie. "On the 16th, the day you were poisoned, Bassington-ffrench was at Staverley, but Nicholson was away—supposedly at a conference in London. And his car is a dark-blue Talbot."

"And he has access to morphia," said Bobby.

They exchanged significant glances.

"It's not exactly evidence, I suppose," said Bobby, "but it fits in nicely."

Frankie went to a side table and returned with a telephone directory.

"What are you going to do?"

"I'm looking up the name Rivington."

She turned pages rapidly.

"A. Rivington & Sons, builders. B.A.C. Rivington,

dental surgeon. D. Rivington, Shooter's hill—I think not. Miss Florence Rivington. Col. H. Rivington, D.S.O.—that's more like it—Tite Street, Chelsea."

She continued her search.

"There's M. R. Rivington, Onslow Square. He's possible. And there's a William Rivington at Hampstead. I think Onslow Square and Tite Street are the most likely ones. The Rivingtons, Bobby, have got to be seen without delay."

"I think you're right. But what are we going to say? Think up a few good lies, Frankie. I'm not much good at that sort of thing."

Frankie reflected for a minute or two. "I think," she said, "that you'll have to go. Do you feel you could be the junior partner of a solicitor's firm?"

"That seems a most gentlemanly rôle," said Bobby. "I was afraid you might think of something much worse than that. All the same, it's not quite in character, is it?"

"How do you mean?"

"Well, solicitors never do make personal visits, do they? Surely they always write letters at six-and-eightpence a time, or else write and ask someone to keep an appointment at their office."

"This particular firm of solicitors is unconventional," said Frankie. "Wait a minute."

She left the room and returned with a card.

"Mr. Frederick Spragge," she said, handing it to Bobby. "You are a young member of the firm of Spragge, Spragge, Jenkinson and Spragge of Bloomsbury Square."

"Did you invent that firm, Frankie?"

"Certainly not. They're Father's solicitors."

"And suppose they have me up for impersonation?"

"That's all right. There isn't any young Spragge. The only Spragge is about a hundred, and anyway he eats out of my hand. I'll fix him if things go wrong. He's a great snob—he loves lords and dukes however little money he makes out of them."

"What about clothes? Shall I ring up Badger to bring some along?"

Frankie looked doubtful. "I don't want to insult your clothes, Bobby," she said, "or throw your poverty in your teeth, or anything like that. But will they carry conviction? I think, myself, that we'd better raid Father's wardrobe. His clothes won't fit you too badly."

A quarter of an hour later, Bobby, attired in a morning coat and striped trousers of exquisitely correct cut and passable fit, stood surveying himself in Lord Marchington's pier glass.

"Your father does himself well in clothes," he remarked graciously. "With the might of Savile Row behind me, I feel a great increase of confidence."

"I suppose you'll have to stick to your moustache," said Frankie.

"It's sticking to me," said Bobby. "It's a work of art that couldn't be repeated in a hurry."

"You'd better keep it then. Though it's more legal-looking to be clean-shaven."

"It's better than a beard," said Bobby. "Now then, Frankie, do you think your father could lend me a hat?"

17

Mrs. Rivington Talks

"Supposing," said Bobby, pausing on the doorstep, "that Mr. M. R. Rivington of Onslow Square is himself a solicitor? That would be a blow."

"You'd better try the Tite Street colonel first," said Frankie. "He won't know anything about solicitors."

Accordingly Bobby took a taxi to Tite Street. Colonel Rivington was out. Mrs. Rivington, however, was at home. Bobby delivered over to the smart parlormaid his card on which he had written *"From Messrs. Spragge, Spragge, Jenkinson & Spragge. Very urgent."*

The card and Lord Marchington's clothes produced their effect upon the parlormaid. She did not for an instant suspect that Bobby had come to sell miniatures or tout for insurance. He was shown into a beautifully and expensively furnished drawing-room, and presently Mrs. Rivington beautifully and expensively dressed and made up, came into the room.

"I must apologize for troubling you, Mrs. Rivington," said Bobby. "But the matter was rather urgent and we wished to avoid the delay of letters."

That any solicitor could ever wish to avoid delay seemed so transparently impossible that Bobby for a moment wondered anxiously whether Mrs. Rivington would see through the pretence.

Mrs. Rivington, however, was clearly a woman of

more looks than brains, who accepted things as they were presented to her.

"Oh, do sit down," she said. "I got the telephone message just now from your office saying that you were on your way here."

Bobby mentally applauded Frankie for this last-minute flash of brilliance. He sat down and endeavored to look legal.

"It is about our client, Mr. Alan Carstairs," he said.

"Oh, yes?"

"He may have mentioned that we were acting for him."

"Did he now? I believe he did," said Mrs. Rivington, opening very large blue eyes. She was clearly of a suggestible type. "But of course I know about you. You acted for Dolly Maltravers, didn't you, when she shot that dreadful dressmaker man? I suppose you know all the details?"

She looked at him with frank curiosity. It seemed to Bobby that Mrs. Rivington was going to be easy meat.

"We know a lot that never comes into court," he said, smiling.

"Oh, I suppose you must." Mrs. Rivington looked at him enviously. "Tell me, did she really—I mean—was she dressed as that woman said?"

"The story was contradicted in court," said Bobby solemnly. He slightly dropped the corner of his eyelid.

"Oh, I see," breathed Mrs. Rivington, enraptured.

"About Mr. Carstairs," said Bobby, feeling that he had now established friendly relations and could get on with his job. "He left England very suddenly, as perhaps you know?"

Mrs. Rivington shook her head. "Has he left England? I didn't know. We haven't seen him for some time."

"Did he tell you how long he expected to be over here?"

"He said he might be here for a week or two, or it might be six months or a year."

"Where was he staying?"

"At the Savoy."

"And you saw him last—when?"

"Oh, about three weeks or a month ago. I can't remember."

"You took him down to Staverley one day?"

"Of course! I believe that's the last time we saw him. He rang up to know when he could see us. He'd just arrived in London, and Hubert was very put out because we were going up to Scotland the next day, and we were going down to Staverley to lunch and dining out with some dreadful people that we couldn't get out of, and he wanted to see Carstairs because he liked him so much, and so I said, 'My dear, let's take him down to the Bassington-ffrenches with us. They won't mind.' And we did. And, of course, they didn't." She came breathlessly to a pause.

"Did he tell you his reasons for being in England?" asked Bobby.

"No. Did he have any? Oh, yes, I know. We thought it was something to do with that millionaire man, that friend of his, who had such a tragic death. Some doctor told him he had cancer, and he killed himself. A very wicked thing for a doctor to do, don't you think so? And they're often quite wrong. Our doctor said the other day that my little girl has measles, and it turned out to be a sort of heat rash. I told Hubert I should change him."

Ignoring Mrs. Rivington's treatment of doctors as though they were library books, Bobby returned to the point.

"Did Mr. Carstairs know the Bassington-ffrenches?"

"Oh, no. But I think he liked them. Though he was very queer and moody on the way back. I suppose something that had been said must have upset him. He's a Canadian, you know, and I often think Canadians are so touchy."

"You don't know what it was that upset him?"

"I haven't the least idea. The silliest things do it sometimes, don't they?"

"Did he take any walks in the neighborhood?" asked Bobby.

"Oh, no. What a very odd idea!" She stared at him.

Bobby tried again. "Was there a party? Did he meet any of the neighbors?"

"No, it was just ourselves and them. But it's odd your saying that—"

"Yes," said Bobby eagerly, as she paused.

"Because he asked a most frightful lot of questions about some people who lived near there."

"Do you remember the name?"

"No, I don't. It wasn't anyone very interesting—some doctor or other."

"Dr. Nicholson?"

"I believe that was the name. He wanted to know all about him and his wife and when they came there—all sorts of things. It seemed so odd when he didn't know them, and he wasn't a bit a curious man as a rule. But, of course, perhaps he was only making conversation and couldn't think of anything to say. One does do things like that sometimes."

Bobby agreed that one did and asked how the subject of the Nicholsons had come up, but this Mrs. Rivington was unable to tell him. She had been out with Henry Bassington-ffrench in the garden and had come in to find the others discussing the Nicholsons.

So far the conversation had proceeded easily, Bobby

pumping the lady without any camouflage, but she now displayed a sudden curiosity.

"But what is it you want to know about Mr. Carstairs?" she asked.

"I really wanted his address," explained Bobby. "As you know, we act for him and we've just had a rather important cable from New York—you know there's rather a serious fluctuation in the dollar just now—"

Mrs. Rivington nodded with desperate intelligence.

"And so," continued Bobby rapidly, "we wanted to get into touch with him—to get his instructions. And he hasn't left an address—and having heard him mention he was a friend of yours, I thought you might possibly have news of him."

"Oh, I see," said Mrs. Rivington, completely satisfied. "What a pity! But he's always rather a vague man, I should think."

"Oh, distinctly so," said Bobby. "Well—" He rose. "I apologize for taking up so much of your time."

"Oh, not at all," said Mrs. Rivington. "And it's so interesting to know that Dolly Maltravers really did—as you say she did."

"I said nothing at all," said Bobby.

"Yes, but then lawyers are so discreet, aren't they?" said Mrs. Rivington with a little gurgle of laughter.

"So that's all right," thought Bobby, as he walked away down Tite Street. "I seem to have taken Dolly What's-her-name's character away for good, but I daresay she deserves it. And that charming idiot of a woman will never wonder why, if I wanted Carstairs' address, I didn't simply ring up and ask for it!"

Back in Brook Street he and Frankie discussed the matter from every angle.

"It looks as though it were really pure chance that

took him to the Bassington-ffrenches," said Frankie thoughtfully.

"I know. But evidently when he was down there some chance remark directed his attention to the Nicholsons."

"So that, really, it is Nicholson who is at the heart of the mystery, not the Bassington-ffrenches?"

Bobby looked at her. "Still intent on whitewashing your hero?" he inquired coldly.

"My dear, I'm only pointing out what it looks like. It's the mention of Nicholson and his nursing home that excited Carstairs. Being taken down to the Bassington-ffrenches was a pure matter of chance. You must admit that."

"It seems like it."

"Why only 'seems'?"

"Well, there is just one other possibility. In some way, Carstairs may have found out that the Rivingtons were going down to lunch with the Bassington-ffrenches. He may have overheard some chance remark in a restaurant—at the Savoy perhaps. So he rings them up, very urgent to see them, and what he hopes may happen does happen. They're very booked up and they suggest his coming down with them—their friends won't mind and they do so want to see him. That is possible, Frankie."

"It is *possible*, I suppose. But it seems a very round-about method of doing things."

"No more roundabout than your accident," said Bobby.

"My accident was vigorous direct action," said Frankie coldly.

Bobby removed Lord Marchington's clothes and replaced them where he had found them. Then he donned his chauffeur's uniform once more, and they were soon speeding back to Staverley.

"If Roger has fallen for me," said Frankie demurely,

"he'll be pleased I've come back so soon. He'll think I can't bear to be away from him for long."

"I'm not sure that you can bear it, either," said Bobby. "I've always heard that really dangerous criminals are singularly attractive."

"Somehow I can't believe he is a criminal."

"So you remarked before."

"Well, I feel like that."

"You can't get over the photograph."

"Damn the photograph!" said Frankie.

Bobby drove up the drive in silence. Frankie sprang out and went into the house without a backward glance. Bobby drove away.

The house seemed very silent. Frankie glanced at the clock. It was half-past two.

"They don't expect me back for hours yet," she thought. "I wonder where they are."

She opened the door of the library and went in, stopping suddenly on the threshold.

Dr. Nicholson was sitting on the sofa holding both Sylvia Bassington-ffrench's hands in his.

Sylvia jumped to her feet and came across the room towards Frankie.

"He's been telling me," she said. Her voice was stifled. She put both hands to her face as though to hide it from view.

"It's too terrible!" she sobbed, and brushing past Frankie, she ran out of the room.

Dr. Nicholson had risen. Frankie advanced a step or two towards him. His eyes, watchful as ever, met hers.

"Poor lady!" he said suavely. "It has been a great shock to her."

The muscles at the corner of his mouth twitched. For a moment or two Frankie fancied that he was amused.

And then, quite suddenly, she realized that it was quite a different emotion.

The man was angry. He was holding himself in, hiding his anger behind a suave, bland mask, but the emotion was there. It was all he could do to hold that emotion in.

There was a moment's pause.

"It was best that Mrs. Bassington-ffrench should know the truth," said the Doctor. "I want her to induce her husband to place himself in my hands."

"I'm afraid," said Frankie gently, "that I interrupted you." She paused. "I came back sooner than I meant."

18

The Girl of the Photograph

On Bobby's return to the inn he was greeted with the information that someone was waiting to see him.

"It's a lady. You'll find her in Mr. Askew's little sitting-room."

Bobby made his way there slightly puzzled. Unless she had flown there on wings he could not see how Frankie could possibly have got to the Anglers' Arms ahead of him, and that his visitor could be anyone but Frankie never occurred to him.

He opened the door of the small room which Mr. Askew kept as his private sitting-room. Sitting bolt upright in a chair was a slender figure dressed in black—the girl of the photograph.

Bobby was so astonished that for a moment or two he could not speak. Then he noticed that the girl was terribly nervous. Her small hands were trembling and closed and unclosed themselves on the arm of the chair. She seemed too nervous even to speak, but her large eyes held a kind of terrified appeal.

"So it's you," said Bobby at last. He shut the door behind him and came forward to the table.

Still the girl did not speak—still those large, terrified eyes looked into his. At last words came—a mere hoarse whisper.

"You said—you said—you'd help me. Perhaps I shouldn't have come—"

Here Bobby broke in, finding words and assurance at the same time. "Shouldn't have come? Nonsense! You did quite right to come. Of course you should have come. And I'll do anything—anything in the world to help you. Don't be frightened. You're quite safe now."

The color rose a little in the girl's face. She said abruptly: "Who are you? You're—you're—not a chauffeur. I mean you may be a chauffeur, but you're not one really."

Bobby understood her meaning in spite of her confused words.

"One does all sorts of jobs nowadays," he said. "I used to be in the Navy. As a matter of fact I'm not exactly a chauffeur—but that doesn't matter now. Anyway, I assure you you can trust me and—and tell me all about it."

Her flush had deepened. "You must think me mad," she murmured. "You must think me quite mad."

"No, no."

"Yes—coming here like this. But I was so frightened—so terribly frightened—" Her voice died away. Her eyes widened as though they saw some vision of terror.

Bobby seized her hand firmly.

"Look here," he said. "It's quite all right. Everything's going to be all right. You're safe now—with—with a friend. Nothing shall happen to you."

He felt the answering pressure of her fingers.

"When you stepped out into the moonlight the other night," she said in a low hurried voice, "it was—it was like a dream—a dream of deliverance. I didn't know who you were or where you came from. But it gave me hope and I determined to come and find you—and—and tell you."

"That's right," said Bobby encouragingly. "Tell me. Tell me everything."

She drew her hand away suddenly. "If I do, you'll think I'm mad—that I've gone wrong in my head from being in that place with those others."

"No, I shan't. I shan't really."

"You will. It *sounds* mad."

"I shall know it isn't. Tell me. Please tell me."

She drew a little farther away from him, sitting very upright, her eyes staring straight in front of her. "It's just this," she said. "I'm afraid I'm going to be murdered."

Her voice was dry and hoarse. She was speaking with obvious self-restraint, but her hands were trembling.

"Murdered?"

"Yes, that sounds mad, doesn't it? Like—what do they call it?—persecution mania."

"No," said Bobby. "You don't sound mad at all—just frightened. Tell me who wants to murder you and why?"

She was silent a minute or two, twisting and untwisting her hands. Then she said in a low voice, "My husband."

"Your husband?" Thoughts whirled round in Bobby's head. "Who are you?" he said abruptly.

It was her turn to look surprised. "Don't you know?"

"I haven't the least idea."

She said: "I'm Moira Nicholson. My husband is Dr. Nicholson."

"Then you're not a patient there?"

"A patient? Oh, no." Her face darkened suddenly. "I suppose you think I speak like one."

"No, no, I didn't mean that at all." He was at pains to reassure her. "Honestly, I didn't mean it that way. I was only surprised at finding you married—and—all that. Now go on with what you're telling me. About your husband wanting to murder you."

"It sounds mad, I know. But it isn't—it isn't! I see it in his eyes when he looks at me. And queer things have happened—accidents."

"Accidents?" said Bobby sharply.

"Yes. Oh, I know it sounds hysterical and as though I were making it all up—"

"Not a bit," said Bobby. "It sounds perfectly reasonable. Go on. About these accidents."

"They were just accidents. He backed the car, not seeing I was there—I just jumped aside in time. And some stuff that was in the wrong bottle—oh, stupid things—and things that people would think quite all right, but they weren't—they were *meant*. I know it. And it's wearing me out—watching for them—being on my guard—trying to save my life." She swallowed convulsively.

"Why does your husband want to do away with you?" asked Bobby.

Perhaps he hardly expected a definite answer—but the answer came promptly.

"Because he wants to marry Sylvia Bassington-ffrench."

"What? But she's married already."

"I know. But he's arranging for that."

"How do you mean?"

"I don't know exactly. But I know that he's trying to get Mr. Bassington-ffrench brought to the Grange as a patient."

"And then?"

"I don't know, but I think something would happen." She shuddered. "He's got some hold over Mr. Bassington-ffrench. I don't know what it is."

"Bassington-ffrench takes morphia," said Bobby.

"Is that it? Jasper gives it to him, I suppose."

"It comes by post."

"Perhaps Jasper doesn't do it directly—he's very cunning. Mr. Bassington-ffrench mayn't know it comes from Jasper—but I'm sure it does. And then Jasper would have him at the Grange and pretend to cure him—and once he was there—" She paused and shivered. "All sorts of things happen at the Grange," she went on. "Queer things. People come there to get better, and they don't get better—they get worse."

As she spoke Bobby was aware of a glimpse into a strange evil atmosphere. He felt something of the terror that had enveloped Moira Nicholson's life so long.

He said abruptly, "You say your husband wants to marry Mrs. Bassington-ffrench?"

Moira nodded. "He's crazy about her."

"And she?"

"I don't know," said Moira slowly. "I can't make up my mind. On the surface she seems fond of her husband and little boy, and content and peaceful. She seems a very simple woman. But sometimes I fancy that she isn't so simple as she seems. I've even wondered sometimes whether she is an entirely different woman from what we all think she is . . . whether perhaps she isn't playing a part and playing it very well. But really, I think, that's nonsense—foolish imagination on my part. When you've lived at a place like the Grange your mind gets distorted and you do begin imagining things."

"What about the brother Roger?" asked Bobby.

"I don't know much about him. He's nice, I think, but he's the sort of person who would be very easily deceived. He's quite taken in by Jasper, I know. Jasper is working on him to persuade Mr. Bassington-ffrench to come to the Grange. I believe he thinks it's all his own idea." She leaned forward suddenly and caught

Bobby's sleeve. "Don't let him come to the Grange," she implored. "If he does, something awful will happen. I know it will."

Bobby was silent a minute or two, turning over the amazing story in his mind.

"How long have you been married to Nicholson?" he said at last.

"Just over a year—" She shivered.

"Haven't you ever thought of leaving him?"

"How could I? I've nowhere to go. I've no money. If anyone took me in, what sort of story could I tell? A fantastic tale that my husband wanted to murder me? Who would believe me?"

"Well, I believe you," said Bobby.

He paused a moment, as though making up his mind to a certain course of action. Then he went on.

"Look here," he said bluntly. "I'm going to ask you a question straight out. Did you know a man called Alan Carstairs?"

He saw the color come up in her cheeks. "Why do you ask me that?"

"Because it's rather important that I should know. My idea is that you did know Alan Carstairs, that perhaps at some time or other you gave him your photograph."

She was silent a moment, her eyes downcast. Then she lifted her head and looked him in the face. "That's quite true," she said.

"You knew him before you were married?"

"Yes."

"Has he been down here to see you since you were married?"

She hesitated, then said, "Yes, once."

"About a month ago, would that be?"

"Yes. I suppose it would be about a month."

"He knew you were living down here?"

"I don't know how he knew—I hadn't told him. I had never even written to him since my marriage."

"But he found out and came here to see you. Did your husband know that?"

"No."

"You think not. But he might have known all the same?"

"I suppose he might, but he never said anything."

"Did you discuss your husband at all with Carstairs? Did you tell him of your fears as to your safety?"

She shook her head. "I hadn't begun to suspect them."

"But you were unhappy?"

"Yes."

"And you told him so?"

"No, I tried not to show in any way that my marriage hadn't been a success."

"But he might have guessed it all the same," said Bobby gently.

"I suppose he might," she admitted in a low voice.

"Do you think—I don't know how to put it—but do you think that he knew anything about your husband— that he suspected, for instance, that this nursing home place mightn't be quite what it seemed to be?"

Her brows furrowed as she tried to think.

"It's possible," she said at last. "He asked one or two rather peculiar questions—but—no—I don't think he can really have known anything about it."

Bobby was silent again for a few minutes. Then he asked, "Would you call your husband a jealous man?"

Rather to his surprise she answered, "Yes. Very jealous."

"Jealous, for instance, of you?"

"You mean even though he doesn't care? But yes, he would be jealous, just the same. I'm his property, you see. He's a queer man—a very queer man."

She shivered. Then she asked suddenly, "You're not connected with the police in any way, are you?"

"I? Oh, no."

"I wondered. I mean—"

Bobby looked down at his chauffeur's livery.

"It's rather a long story," he said.

"You are Lady Frances Derwent's chauffeur, aren't you? So the landlord here said. I met her at dinner the other night."

"I know." He paused. "We've got to get hold of her," he said. "And it's a bit difficult for me to do. Do you think you could ring up and ask to speak to her and then get her to come and meet you somewhere outdoors?"

"I suppose I could," said Moira slowly.

"I know it must seem frightfully odd to you. But it won't when I've explained. We must get hold of her as soon as possible. It's essential."

Moira rose. "Very well," she said.

With her hand on the door-handle she hesitated. "Alan," she said. "Alan Carstairs. Did you say you'd seen him?"

"I have seen him," said Bobby slowly. "But not lately." And he thought, with a shock, "Of course—she doesn't know he's dead. . . ."

He said, "Ring up Lady Frances. Then I'll tell you everything."

19

A Council of Three

Moira returned a few minutes later.

"I got her," she said. "I've asked her to come and meet me at a little summer house down near the river. She must have thought it very odd, but she said she'd come."

"Good," said Bobby. "Now just where is this place exactly?"

Moira described it carefully, and the way to get to it.

"That's all right," said Bobby. "You go first. I'll follow on."

They adhered to this program, Bobby lingering to have a word with Mr. Askew.

"Odd thing," he said casually. "That lady—Mrs. Nicholson—I used to work for an uncle of hers. Canadian gentleman."

Moira's visit to him might, he felt, give rise to gossip, and the last thing he wanted was to let gossip of that kind get about and possibly find its way to Dr. Nicholson's ears.

"So that's it, is it?" said Mr. Askew. "I rather wondered."

"Yes," said Bobby. "She recognized me and came along to hear what I was doing now. A nice, pleasant-spoken lady."

"Very pleasant indeed. She can't have much of a life living at the Grange."

"It wouldn't be *my* fancy," agreed Bobby.

Feeling that he had achieved his object, he strolled out into the village and with an aimless air betook himself in the direction indicated by Moira.

He reached the rendezvous successfully and found her there waiting for him. Frankie had not yet put in an appearance.

Moira's glance was frankly inquiring and Bobby felt he must attempt the somewhat difficult task of explanation.

"There's an awful lot I've got to tell you," he said, and stopped awkwardly.

"Yes."

"To begin with," said Bobby, plunging, "I'm not really a chauffeur although I do work in a garage in London. And my name isn't Hawkins—it's Jones—Bobby Jones. I come from Marchbolt in Wales."

Moira was listening attentively, but clearly the name Marchbolt meant nothing to her. Bobby set his teeth and went bravely to the heart of the matter.

"Look here, I'm afraid I'm going to give you rather a shock. This friend of yours, Alan Carstairs—he's—well, you've got to know—he's dead."

He felt the start she gave and tactfully he averted his eyes from her face. Did she mind very much? Had she been—dash it all—keen on the fellow?

She was silent a moment or two, then she said in a low thoughtful voice, "So that's why he never came back. I wondered."

Bobby ventured to steal a look at her. His spirits rose. She looked sad and thoughtful—but that was all.

"Tell me about it," she said.

Bobby complied.

"He fell over the cliff at Marchbolt—the place where I live. I and the doctor there happened to be the ones to find him." He paused and then added: "He had your photograph in his pocket."

"Did he?" She gave a sweet, rather sad smile. "Dear Alan, he was—very faithful."

There was silence for a moment or two and then she asked, "When did all this happen?"

"About a month ago. October 3rd, to be exact."

"That must have been just after he came down here."

"Yes. Did he mention that he was going to Wales?"

She shook her head.

"You don't know anyone called Evans, do you?" said Bobby.

"Evans?" Moira frowned, trying to think. "No, I don't think so. It's a very common name, of course, but I can't remember anybody. What is he?"

"That's just what we don't know—Oh, hullo! Here's Frankie."

Frankie came hurrying along the path. Her face, at the sight of Bobby and Mrs. Nicholson sitting chatting together, was a study in conflicting expressions.

"Hullo, Frankie," said Bobby. "I'm glad you've come. We've got to have a great powwow. To begin with, it's Mrs. Nicholson who is the original of *the* photograph."

"Oh!" said Frankie blankly. She looked at Moira and suddenly laughed.

"My dear," she said to Bobby, "now I see why the sight of Mrs. Cayman at the inquest was such a shock to you!"

"Exactly," said Bobby.

What a fool he had been! However could he have imagined for one moment that any space of time could turn a Moira Nicholson into an Amelia Cayman?

"Lord, what a fool I've been!" he exclaimed.

Moira was looking bewildered.

"There's such an awful lot to tell," said Bobby. "And I don't quite know how to put it all."

He described the Caymans and their identification of the body.

"But I don't understand," said Moira, bewildered. "Whose body was it really, her brother's, or Alan Carstairs'?"

"That's where the dirty work comes in," explained Bobby.

"And then," continued Frankie, "Bobby was poisoned."

"Eight grains of morphia," said Bobby reminiscently.

"Don't start on that," said Frankie. "You're capable of going on for hours on the subject, and it's really very boring to other people. Let me explain."

She took a long breath.

"You see," she said, "these Cayman people came to see Bobby after the inquest, to ask him if the brother (supposed) had said anything before he died, and Bobby said 'No.' But afterwards he remembered that the man had said something about somebody called Evans—so Bobby wrote and told them so. And a few days afterwards he got a letter offering him a job in Peru or somewhere, and when he wouldn't take it, the next thing was that someone put a lot of morphia—"

"Eight grains," said Bobby.

"—in his beer. Only, as Bobby has a most extraordinary inside or something, it didn't kill him. And so then we saw at once that Pritchard—or Carstairs, you know—must have been pushed over the cliff."

"But why?" asked Moira.

"Don't you see? Why, it seems perfectly clear to us. I expect I haven't told it very well. Anyway, we decided that he had been, and that Roger Bassington-ffrench had probably done it."

"Roger Bassington-ffrench?" Moira spoke in tones of the liveliest amazement.

"We worked it out that way. You see he was there at the time, and your photograph disappeared, and he seemed to be the only one who could have taken it."

"I see," said Moira thoughtfully.

"And then," continued Frankie, "I happened to have an accident just here. An amazing coincidence, wasn't it?" She looked hard at Bobby with an admonishing eye. "So I telephoned to Bobby and suggested that he should come down here pretending to be my chauffeur and we'd look into the matter."

"So now you see how it was," said Bobby, accepting Frankie's one discreet departure from the truth. "And the climax was when last night I strolled into the grounds of the Grange and ran right into you—the original of the mysterious photograph!"

"You recognized me very quickly," said Moira with a faint smile.

"Yes," said Bobby. "I would have recognized the original of that photograph anywhere."

For no particular reason Moira blushed. Then an idea seemed to strike her and she looked sharply from one to the other.

"Are you telling me the truth?" she asked. "Is it really true that you came down here—by accident? Or did you come because—because—" her voice quavered in spite of herself—"You suspected my husband?"

Bobby and Frankie looked at each other. Then Bobby said:

"I give you my word of honor that we'd never even heard of your husband till we came down here."

"Oh, I see." She turned to Frankie. "I'm sorry, Lady

Frances, but you see I remembered that, on the evening when we came to dinner, Jasper—my husband—went on and on at you, asking you things about your accident. I couldn't think why. But I think now that perhaps he suspected it wasn't genuine."

"Well, if you really want to know, it wasn't," said Frankie. "Whoof—now I feel better! It was all camouflaged very carefully. But it had nothing to do with your husband. The whole thing was staged because we wanted to—to—what does one call it?—get a line on Roger Bassington-ffrench."

"Roger?" Moira frowned and smiled perplexedly. "It seems absurd," she said frankly.

"All the same, facts are facts," said Bobby.

"Roger? Oh, no." She shook her head. "He might be weak—or wild. He might get into debt or get mixed up in a scandal. But pushing someone over a cliff?—no, I simply can't imagine it."

"Do you know," said Frankie, "I can't very well imagine it either."

"But he must have taken that photograph," said Bobby stubbornly. "Listen, Mrs. Nicholson, while I go over the facts."

He did so slowly and carefully. When he had finished, she nodded her head comprehendingly.

"I see what you mean. It seems very queer." She paused a minute and then asked unexpectedly, "Why don't you ask him?"

20

Council of Two

For a moment the bold simplicity of the question quite took their breaths away. Both Frankie and Bobby started to speak at once.

"That's impossible—" began Bobby, just as Frankie said, "That would never do."

Then they both stopped dead as the possibilities of the idea sank in.

"You see," said Moira eagerly, "I do understand what you mean. It does seem as though Roger *must* have taken that photograph. But I don't believe for one moment that he pushed Alan over. Why should he? He didn't even know him. They'd only met once—at lunch down here. They'd never come across each other in any way. There's no motive."

"Then who *did* push him over?" asked Frankie bluntly.

A shadow crossed Moira's face. "I don't know," she said constrainedly.

"Look here," said Bobby. "Do you mind if I tell Frankie what you told me? About what you're afraid of?"

Moira turned her head away. "If you like. But it sounds so melodramatic and hysterical. I can't believe it myself this minute."

And indeed the bald statement, made unemotionally

in the open air of the quiet English countryside, did seem curiously lacking in reality.

Moira got up abruptly. "I really feel I've been terribly silly," she said, her lip trembling. "Please don't pay any attention to what I said, Mr. Jones. It was just—nerves. Anyway, I must be going now. Good-bye."

She moved rapidly away. Bobby sprang up to follow her, but Frankie pushed him firmly back.

"Stay there, idiot, leave this to me."

She went rapidly off after Moira. She returned a few minutes later.

"Well," queried Bobby anxiously.

"That's all right. I calmed her down. It was a bit hard on her, having her private fears blurted out in front of her to a third person. I made her promise we'd have a meeting—all three of us—again soon. Now that you're not hampered by her being here, tell us all about it."

Bobby did so. Frankie listened attentively. Then she said:

"It fits in with two things. First of all, I came back just now to find Nicholson holding both Sylvia Bassington-ffrench's hands—and didn't he look daggers at me! If looks could kill, I feel sure he'd have made me a corpse then and there."

"What's the second thing?" asked Bobby.

"Oh, just an incident. Sylvia described how Moira's photograph had made a great impression on some stranger who had come to the house. Depend upon it, that was Carstairs. He recognizes the photograph, Mrs. Bassington-ffrench tells him that it is a portrait of a Mrs. Nicholson, and that explains how he came to find out where she was. But you know, Bobby, I don't see yet where Nicholson comes in. Why should he want to do away with Alan Carstairs?"

"You think it was he and not Bassington-ffrench?

Rather a coincidence if he and Bassington-ffrench should both be in Marchbolt on the same day."

"Well, coincidences do happen. But if it was Nicholson, I don't yet see the motive. Was Carstairs on the track of Nicholson as the head of a dope gang? Or is your new lady friend the motive for the murder?"

"It might be both," suggested Bobby. "He may know that Carstairs and his wife had an interview, and he may have believed that his wife gave him away somehow."

"Now that is a possibility," said Frankie. "But the first thing is to make sure about Roger Bassington-ffrench. The only thing we've got against him is the photograph business. If he can clear that up satisfactorily—"

"You're going to tackle him on the subject? Frankie, is that wise? If he is the villain of the piece, as we decided he must be, it means that we're going to show him our hand."

"Not quite—not the way I shall do it. After all, in every other way he's been perfectly straightforward and above-board. We've taken that to be super-cunning—but suppose it just happens to be innocence? *If* he can explain the photograph—and I shall be watching him when he does explain—and if there's the least sign of hesitation or guilt, I shall see it—as I say, *if* he can explain the photograph, then he may be a very valuable ally."

"How do you mean, Frankie?"

"My dear, your little friend may be an emotional scare-monger who likes to exaggerate, but supposing she isn't—that all she says is gospel truth—that her husband wants to get rid of her and marry Sylvia. Don't you realize that in that case, Henry Bassington-ffrench is in mortal danger too? At all costs, we've got to prevent his being sent to the Grange. And at present, Roger Bassington-ffrench is on Nicholson's side."

"Good for you, Frankie," said Bobby quietly. "Go ahead with your plan."

Frankie got up to go, but before departing she paused for a moment.

"Isn't it odd?" she said. "We seem somehow to have got in between the covers of a book. We're in the middle of someone else's story. It's a frightfully queer feeling."

"I know what you mean," said Bobby. "There is something rather uncanny about it. I should call it a play rather than a book. It's as though we'd walked onto the stage in the middle of the second act, and we haven't really got parts in the play at all, but we have to pretend, and what makes it so frightfully hard is that we haven't the faintest idea what the first act was about."

Frankie nodded eagerly. "I'm not even sure it's the second act—I think it's more like the third. Bobby, I'm sure we've got to go back a long way. . . . And we've got to be quick because I fancy the play is frightfully near the final curtain."

"With corpses strewn everywhere," said Bobby. "And what brought us into the show was a regular cue—five words, quite meaningless as far as we are concerned."

" '*Why didn't they ask Evans?*' Isn't it odd, Bobby, that though we've found out a good deal, and more and more characters come into the thing, we never get any nearer to the mysterious Evans?"

"I've got an idea about Evans. I've a feeling that Evans doesn't really matter at all—that although he's been the starting point as it were, in himself he's probably quite unessential. It will be like that story of Wells' where a prince built a marvellous palace or temple round the tomb of his beloved. And when it was finished there was just one little thing that jarred. So he said, 'Take it away'—and the thing was actually the tomb itself."

"Sometimes," said Frankie, "I don't believe there is an Evans."

Saying which she nodded to Bobby and retraced her steps towards the house.

21

Roger Answers a Question

Fortune favored her, for she fell in with Roger not far from the house.

"Hullo," he said. "You're back early from London."

"I wasn't in the mood for London," said Frankie.

"Have you been to the house yet?" he asked. His face grew grave. "Nicholson, I find, has been telling Sylvia the truth about poor old Henry. Poor girl, she's taken it hard. It seems she had absolutely no suspicion."

"I know," said Frankie. "They were both together in the library when I came in. She was—very much upset."

"Look here, Frankie," said Roger. "Henry has absolutely got to be cured. It isn't as though this drug habit had a real hold on him. He hasn't been taking it so very long. And he's got every incentive in the world to make him keen on being cured—Sylvia, Tommy, his home. He's got to be made to see the position clearly. Nicholson is just the man to put the thing through. He was talking to me the other day. He's had some amazing successes—even with people who have been slaves for years to the beastly stuff. If Henry will only consent to go to the Grange—"

Frankie interrupted.

"Look here," she said. "There's something I want to ask you. Just a question. I hope you won't think I'm simply frightfully impertinent."

"What is it?" asked Roger, his attention arrested.

"Do you mind telling me whether you took a photograph out of that man's pocket—the one who fell over the cliff at Marchbolt?"

She was studying him closely, watching every detail of his expression. She was satisfied with what she saw.

Slight annoyance, a trace of embarrassment—no flash of guilt or dismay.

"Now how on earth did you come to guess that?" he said. "Or did Moira tell you?—But then, she doesn't know—"

"You did then?"

"I suppose I'll have to admit it."

"Why?"

Roger seemed embarrassed again. "Well, look at it as I did. Here I am mounting guard over a strange dead body. Something is sticking out of his pocket. I look at it. By an amazing coincidence it's the photograph of a woman I know—a married woman—and a woman who I guess is not too happily married. What's going to happen? An inquest. Publicity. Possibly the wretched girl's name in all the papers. I acted on impulse. Took the photograph and tore it up. I dare say I acted wrongly, but Moira Nicholson is a nice little soul and I didn't want her to get landed in a mess."

Frankie drew a deep breath. "So that was it," she said. "If you only knew—"

"Knew what?" said Roger, puzzled.

"I don't know that I can tell you just now," said Frankie. "I may later. It's all rather complicated. I can quite see why you took the photograph, but was there any objection to your saying you recognized the man? Oughtn't you to have told the police who he was?"

"Recognized him?" said Roger. He looked bewildered. "How could I recognize him? I didn't know him."

"But you'd met him down here—only about a week before."

"My dear girl, are you quite mad?"

"Alan Carstairs—you did meet Alan Carstairs?"

"Oh, yes. Man who came down with the Rivingtons. But the dead man wasn't Alan Carstairs."

"But he *was!*"

They stared at each other. Then Frankie said, with a renewal of suspicion, "Surely you must have recognized him?"

"I never saw his face," said Roger.

"What?"

"No. There was a handkerchief spread over it."

Frankie stared at him. Suddenly she remembered that in Bobby's first account of the tragedy he had mentioned putting a handkerchief over the face of the dead man.

"You never thought of looking?" went on Frankie.

"No. Why should I?"

"Of course," thought Frankie, "If *I'd* found a photograph of somebody I knew in a dead person's pocket, I should simply have had to look at the person's face. How beautifully incurious men are!" She paused for a moment. "Poor little thing," she went on. "I'm so terribly sorry for her."

"Whom do you mean? Moira Nicholson? Why are you so sorry for her?"

"Because she's frightened," said Frankie slowly.

"She always looks half scared to death. But what is she frightened of?"

"Her husband."

"I don't know that I'd care to be up against Jasper Nicholson myself," admitted Roger.

"She's sure he's trying to murder her," said Frankie abruptly.

"Oh, my dear!" he protested.

"Sit down," said Frankie. "I'm going to tell you a lot of things. I've got to prove to you that Dr. Nicholson is a dangerous criminal."

"A criminal?" Roger's tone was frankly incredulous.

"Wait till you've heard the whole story."

She gave him a clear and careful narrative of all that had occurred since the day Bobby and Dr. Thomas had found the body. She kept back only the fact that her accident had not been genuine, but she let it appear that she had lingered at Merroway Court through her intense desire to get to the bottom of the mystery.

She could complain of no lack of interest on the part of her listener. Roger seemed quite fascinated by the story.

"Is this really true?" he demanded. "All this about the fellow Jones being poisoned and all that?"

"Absolute gospel truth."

"Sorry for my incredulity—but the facts do take a bit of swallowing, don't they?"

He was silent for a minute, frowning.

"Look here," he said at last. "Fantastic though the whole thing sounds, I think you must be right in your first deduction. This man, Alex Pritchard, or Alan Carstairs, must have been murdered. If he wasn't, there seems no point in the attack upon Jones. Whether or not the key to the situation is the phrase *'Why didn't they ask Evans?'* doesn't seem to me to matter much, since you've no clue to who Evans is or what he was to have been asked. Let's put it that the murderer or murderers assumed that Jones was in possession of some knowledge, whether he knew it himself or not, which was dangerous to them. So they accordingly tried to eliminate him, and probably would try again if they got on his track. So far that seems sense—but I don't see by what process of reasoning you fix on Nicholson as the criminal."

"He's such a sinister man, and he's got a dark-blue Talbot, and he was away from here on the day that Bobby was poisoned."

"That's all pretty thin as evidence."

"There are all the things Mrs. Nicholson told Bobby." She recited them—and once again they sounded melodramatic and unsubstantial repeated aloud against the background of the peaceful English landscape.

Roger shrugged his shoulders.

"She thinks he supplies Henry with the drug—but that's pure conjecture. She's not a particle of evidence that he does so. She thinks he wants to get Henry to the Grange as a patient—well, that's a very natural wish for a doctor to have. A doctor wants as many patients as he can get. She thinks he's in love with Sylvia. Well, as to that, of course, I can't say."

"If she thinks so, she's probably right," interrupted Frankie. "A woman would know all right about her own husband."

"Well, granting that that's the case, it doesn't necessarily mean that the man's a dangerous criminal. Lots of respectable citizens fall in love with other people's wives."

"There's her belief that he wants to murder her," urged Frankie.

Roger looked at her quizzically. "You take that seriously?"

"She believes it, anyhow."

Roger nodded and lit a cigarette. "The question is, how much attention to pay that belief of hers," he said. "It's a creepy sort of place, the Grange, full of queer customers. Living there would tend to upset a woman's balance, especially if she were of the timid, nervous type."

"Then you don't think it's true?"

"I don't say that. She probably believes quite honestly that he is trying to kill her. But is there any foundation in fact for that belief? There doesn't seem to be."

Frankie remembered with curious clearness Moira's saying, "It's just nerves." And somehow the mere fact that she had said that seemed to Frankie to point to the fact that it was *not* nerves; but she did not know how to explain her point of view to Roger.

Meanwhile the young man was going on:

"Mind you, if you could show that Nicholson had been in Marchbolt on the day of the cliff tragedy, that would be very different—or if we could find any definite motive linking him with Carstairs. But it seems to me you're ignoring the real suspects."

"What real suspects?"

"The—what did you call them—Haymans?"

"Caymans."

"That's it. Now, they are undoubtedly in it up to the hilt. First, there's the false identification of the body. Then there's their insistence on the point of whether the poor fellow said anything before he died. And I think it's logical to assume, as you did, that the Buenos Aires offer came from them or was arranged for by them."

"It's a bit annoying," said Frankie, "to have the most strenuous efforts made to get you out of the way because you know something—and not to know yourself what the something you know is. Bother—what a mess one gets into with words!"

"Yes," said Roger grimly, "that was a mistake on their part. A mistake that it's going to take them all their time to remedy."

"Oh!" cried Frankie, "I've just thought of something.

Up to now, you see, I've been assuming that the photograph of Mrs. Cayman was substituted for the one of Moira Nicholson."

"I can assure you," said Roger gravely, "that I have never treasured the likeness of a Mrs. Cayman against my heart. She sounds a most repulsive creature."

"Well, she was handsome in a way," admitted Frankie. "A sort of bold, coarse, vampish way. But the point is this: Carstairs must have had *her* photograph on him as well as Mrs. Nicholson's."

Roger nodded. "And you think—" he suggested.

"I think one was love and the other was business! Carstairs was carrying about the Cayman's photograph for a reason. He wanted it identified by somebody, perhaps. Now listen—what happens? Someone, the male Cayman perhaps, is following him and seeing a good opportunity, steals up behind him in the mist and gives him a shove. Carstairs goes over the cliff with a startled cry. Male Cayman makes off as fast as he can—he doesn't know who may be about. We'll say that he doesn't know that Alan Carstairs is carrying about that photograph. What happens next? The photograph is published—"

"Consternation in the Cayman ménage," said Roger helpfully.

"Exactly. What is to be done? The bold thing—grasp the nettle. Who knows Carstairs as Carstairs? Hardly anyone in this country. Down goes Mrs. Cayman, weeping crocodile tears and recognizing the body as that of a convenient brother. The two also do a little hocus-pocus of posting parcels to bolster up the walking-tour story."

"You know, Frankie, I think that's positively brilliant," said Roger with admiration.

"I think it's pretty good myself," said Frankie. "And

you're quite right. We ought to get busy on the track of the Caymans. I can't think why we haven't done so before."

This was not quite true, since Frankie knew the reason quite well—namely, that they had been on the track of Roger himself. However, she felt it would be tactless, just at this stage, to reveal the fact.

"What are we going to do about Mrs. Nicholson?" she asked abruptly.

"What do you mean—do about her?"

"Well, the poor thing is terrified to death. I do think you're callous about her, Roger."

"I'm not really, but people who can't help themselves always irritate me."

"Oh, but do be fair! What can she do? She's no money and nowhere to go."

Roger said unexpectedly, "If you were in her place, Frankie, you'd find something to do."

"Oh!" Frankie was rather taken aback.

"Yes, you would. If you really thought somebody was trying to murder you, you wouldn't just stay there tamely waiting to be murdered. You'd run away and make a living somehow, or you'd murder the other person first! You'd do *something*."

Frankie tried to think what she would do.

"I'd certainly do something," she said thoughtfully.

"The truth of the matter is that you've got guts and she hasn't," said Roger with decision.

Frankie felt complimented. Moira Nicholson was not really the type of woman she admired, and she had also felt just slightly ruffled by Bobby's absorption in her. "Bobby," she thought to herself, "likes them helpless." And she remembered the curious fascination that the photograph had had for him from the start of the affair.

"Oh, well," thought Frankie, "at any rate Roger's different."

Roger, it was clear, did not like them helpless. Moira, on the other hand, clearly did not think very much of Roger. She had called him weak and had scouted the possibility of his having the guts to murder anyone. He was weak, perhaps—but undeniably he had charm. She had felt it from the first moment of arriving at Merroway Court.

Roger said quietly, "If you liked, Frankie, you could make anything you chose of a man. . . ."

Frankie felt a sudden little thrill—and at the same time an acute embarrassment. She changed the subject hastily.

"About your brother," she said. "Do you still think he should go to the Grange?"

22

Another Victim

"No," said Roger. "I don't. After all, there are heaps of other places where he can be treated. The really important thing is to get Henry to agree."

"Do you think that will be difficult?" asked Frankie.

"I'm afraid it may be. You heard him the other night. On the other hand, if we just catch him in the repentant mood, that's very different. Hullo—here comes Sylvia."

Mrs. Bassington-ffrench emerged from the house and looked about her. Then seeing Roger and Frankie she walked across the grass towards them. They could see that she was looking terribly worried and strained.

"Roger," she began, "I've been looking for you everywhere." Then, as Frankie made a movement to leave them—"No, my dear, don't go. Of what use are concealments? In any case, I think you know all there is to know. You've suspected this business for some time, haven't you?"

Frankie nodded.

"While I've been blind—blind," said Sylvia bitterly. "Both of you saw what I never even suspected. I only wondered why Henry had changed so to all of us. It made me very unhappy, but I never suspected the reason."

She paused, then went on again with a slight change of tone.

"As soon as Dr. Nicholson told me the truth, I went straight to Henry. I've only just left him now." She paused, swallowing a sob. "Roger—it's going to be all right. He's agreed. He will go to the Grange and put himself in Dr. Nicholson's hands to-morrow."

"Oh, no!" The exclamation came from Roger and Frankie simultaneously. Sylvia looked at them, astonished.

Roger spoke awkwardly. "Do you know, Sylvia, I've been thinking it over, and I don't believe the Grange would be a good plan, after all."

"You think he can fight it by himself?" asked Sylvia doubtfully.

"No, I don't. But there are other places—places not—so—well, not so near at hand. I'm convinced that staying in this district would be a mistake."

"I'm sure of it," said Frankie, coming to his rescue.

"Oh, I don't agree," said Sylvia. "I couldn't bear to have him go away somewhere. And Dr. Nicholson has been so kind and understanding. I shall feel happy about Henry's being under his charge."

"I thought you didn't like Nicholson, Sylvia," said Roger.

"I've changed my mind." She spoke simply. "Nobody could have been nicer or kinder than he was this afternoon. My silly prejudice against him has quite vanished."

There was a moment's silence. The position was awkward. Neither Roger nor Sylvia knew quite what to say next.

"Poor Henry," said Sylvia. "He broke down. He was terribly upset at my knowing. He agreed that he must fight this awful craving for my sake and Tommy's, but he said I hadn't a conception of what it meant. I suppose I haven't, though Dr. Nicholson explained very fully. It becomes a kind of obsession—people aren't responsible for their actions, so he said. Oh, Roger, it seems so awful! But Dr. Nicholson was really kind. I trust him."

"All the same, I think it would be better—" began Roger.

Sylvia turned on him. "I don't understand you, Roger. Why have you changed your mind? Half an hour ago you were all for Henry's going to the Grange."

"Well—I've—I've had time to think the matter over since—"

Again Sylvia interrupted. "Anyway, I've made up my mind. Henry shall go to the Grange and nowhere else."

They confronted her in silence. Then Roger said: "Do you know, I think I will ring up Nicholson. He will be home now. I'd like—just to have a talk with him about matters."

Without waiting for her reply he turned away and went rapidly into the house. The two women stood looking after him.

"I cannot understand Roger," said Sylvia impatiently. "About a quarter of an hour ago he was positively urging me to arrange for Henry to go to the Grange." Her tone held a distinct note of anger.

"All the same," said Frankie, "I agree with him. I'm sure I've read somewhere that people ought always to go for a cure somewhere far away from their homes."

"I think that's just nonsense," said Sylvia.

Frankie felt in a dilemma. Sylvia's unexpected obstinacy was making things difficult, and also she seemed suddenly to have become as violently pro-Nicholson as she formerly had been against him. It was very hard to know what arguments to use. Frankie considered telling the whole story to Sylvia—but would Sylvia believe it? Even Roger had not been very impressed by the theory of Dr. Nicholson's guilt. Sylvia, with her new-found partisanship where the Doctor was concerned, would probably be even less so. She might even go and repeat the whole thing to him. It was certainly difficult.

An airplane passed low overhead in the gathering dusk, filling the air with its loud beat of engines. Both Sylvia and Frankie stared up at it, glad of the respite it afforded, since neither of them quite knew what to say next. It gave Frankie time to collect her thoughts, and Sylvia time to recover from her fit of sudden anger.

As the airplane disappeared over the trees and its roar receded into the distance, Sylvia turned abruptly to Frankie.

"It's been so awful—" she said brokenly. "And you all seem to want to send Henry far away from me."

"No, no," said Frankie. "It wasn't that at all."

She cast about for a minute.

"It was only that I thought he ought to have the best treatment. And I do think that Dr. Nicholson is rather— well, rather a quack."

"I don't believe it," said Sylvia. "I think he's a very clever man and just the kind of man Henry needs."

She looked defiantly at Frankie. Frankie marvelled at the hold Dr. Nicholson had acquired over her in such a short time. All her former distrust of the man seemed to have vanished completely.

At a loss what to say or do next, Frankie relapsed into silence. Presently Roger came out again from the house. He seemed slightly breathless.

"Nicholson isn't in yet," he said. "I left a message."

"I don't see why you want to see Dr. Nicholson so urgently," said Sylvia. "You suggested this plan, and it's all arranged, and Henry has consented."

"I think I've got some say in the matter, Sylvia," said Roger gently. "After all, I'm Henry's brother."

"You suggested the plan yourself," said Sylvia obstinately.

"Yes, but I've heard a few things about Nicholson since."

"What things? Oh, I don't believe you!"

She bit her lip, turned away, and went into the house.

Roger looked at Frankie. "This is a bit awkward," he said.

"Very awkward indeed."

"Once Sylvia has made her mind up she can be obstinate as the devil."

"What are we going to do?"

They sat down again on the garden seat and went into the matter carefully. Roger agreed with Frankie that to tell the whole story to Sylvia would be a mistake. The best plan, in his opinion, would be to tackle the Doctor.

"But what are you going to say exactly?"

"I don't know that I shall say much—but I shall hint a good deal. At any rate, I agree with you about one thing—Henry mustn't go to the Grange. Even if we come right out into the open, we've got to stop that."

"We give the whole show away if we do," Frankie reminded him.

"I know. That's why we've got to try everything else first. Curse Sylvia, why must she turn obstinate just at this minute?"

"It shows the power of the man," Frankie said.

"Yes. You know, it inclines me to believe that, evidence or no evidence, you may be right about him after all—What's that?"

They both sprang up.

"It sounded like a shot," said Frankie. "From the house."

They looked at each other, then raced towards the building. They went in by the French window of the drawing-room and passed through into the hall. Sylvia Bassington-ffrench was standing there, her face white as paper.

"Did you hear?" she said. "It was a shot—from Henry's study."

She swayed, and Roger put an arm round her to steady her. Frankie went to the study and turned the handle.

"It's locked," she said.

"The window," said Roger.

He deposited Sylvia, who was in a half-fainting condition, on a convenient settee and raced out again through the drawing-room, Frankie on his heels. They went round the house till they came to the study window. It was closed but they put their faces close to the glass and peered in. The sun was setting and there was not much light—but they could see plainly enough.

Henry Bassington-ffrench was lying sprawled out across his desk. There was a bullet wound plainly visible in his temple, and a revolver lay on the floor where it had dropped from his hand.

"He's shot himself," said Frankie. "How ghastly. . . ."

"Stand back a little," said Roger. "I'm going to break the window."

He wrapped his hand in his coat and struck the pane of glass a heavy blow that shattered it. Roger picked out the pieces carefully, then he and Frankie stepped into the room. As they did so, Mrs. Bassington-ffrench and Dr. Nicholson came hurrying along the terrace.

"Here's the Doctor," said Sylvia. "He's just come. Has—has anything happened to Henry?"

Then she saw the sprawling figure and uttered a cry.

Roger stepped quickly out again through the window, and Dr. Nicholson thrust Sylvia into his arms.

"Take her away," he said briefly. "Look after her.

Give her some brandy if she'll take it. Don't let her see more than you can help." He himself stepped through the window and joined Frankie.

He shook his head slowly. "This is a tragic business," he said. "Poor fellow. So he felt he couldn't face the music. Too bad. Too bad."

He bent over the body, then straightened himself up again.

"Nothing to be done. Death must have been instantaneous. I wonder if he wrote something first. They usually do."

Frankie advanced till she stood beside them. A piece of paper with a few scrawled words on it, evidently freshly written, lay at Bassington-ffrench's elbow. Their purport was clear enough.

I feel this is the best way out [Henry Bassington-ffrench had written]. This fatal habit has taken too great a hold on me for me to fight it now. Want to do the best I can for Sylvia—Sylvia and Tommy. God bless you both, my dears. Forgive me.

Frankie felt a lump rise in her throat.

"We mustn't touch anything," said Dr. Nicholson. "There will have to be an inquest, of course. We must ring up the police."

In obedience to his gesture, Frankie went towards the door. Then she stopped.

"The key's not in the lock," she said.

"No? Perhaps it's in his pocket."

He knelt down, investigating delicately. From the dead man's coat pocket he drew out a key. He tried it in the lock and it fitted. Together they passed out into the hall. Dr. Nicholson went straight to the telephone.

Frankie, her knees shaking under her, felt suddenly sick.

23

Moira Disappears

Frankie rang up Bobby about an hour later.

"Is that Hawkins? Hullo, Bobby—have you heard what has happened? You have? Quick, we must meet somewhere. Early to-morrow morning would be best, I think. I'll stroll out before breakfast. Say eight o'clock—the same place we met to-day."

She rang off as Bobby uttered his third respectful "Yes, your ladyship," for the benefit of any curious ears.

Bobby arrived at the rendezvous first, but Frankie did not keep him waiting long. She looked pale and upset.

"Hullo, Bobby, isn't it awful? I wasn't able to sleep last night."

"I haven't heard any details," said Bobby. "Just that Mr. Bassington-ffrench had shot himself. That's right, I suppose?"

"Yes. Sylvia had been talking to him—persuading him to agree to a course of treatment, and he had said he would. Afterwards, I suppose, his courage must have failed him. He went into his study, locked the door, wrote a few words on a sheet of paper—and—and shot himself. Bobby, it's too ghastly. It's—it's grim."

"I know," said Bobby quietly.

They were both silent for a little.

"I shall have to leave to-day, of course," said Frankie presently.

"Yes, I suppose you will. How is she—Mrs. Bassington-ffrench, I mean?"

"She's collapsed, poor soul. I haven't seen her since we—we found the body. The shock to her must have been awful."

Bobby nodded.

"You'd better bring the car round about eleven," continued Frankie.

Bobby did not answer. Frankie looked at him impatiently.

"What's the matter with you, Bobby? You look as though you were miles away."

"Sorry. As a matter of fact—"

"Yes?"

"Well, I was just wondering. I suppose—well, I suppose it's all right?"

"What do you mean—all right?"

"I mean it's quite certain that he *did* commit suicide?"

"Oh!" said Frankie. "I see." She thought a minute. "Yes," she said, "it was suicide all right."

"You're quite sure? You see, Frankie, we have Moira's word for it that Nicholson wanted two people out of the way. Well, *here's one of them gone*."

Frankie thought again, but once more she shook her head.

"It must be suicide," she said. "I was in the garden with Roger when we heard the shot. We both ran straight in through the drawing-room to the hall. The study door was locked on the inside. We went round to the window. That was fastened also and Roger had to smash it. It wasn't till then that Nicholson appeared upon the scene."

Bobby reflected upon this information.

"It looks all right," he agreed. "But Nicholson seems to have appeared on the scene very suddenly."

"He'd left a stick behind earlier in the afternoon and had come back for it."

Bobby was frowning with the process of thought.

"Listen, Frankie. Suppose that actually Nicholson shot Bassington-ffrench—"

"Having induced him first to write a suicide's letter of farewell?"

"I should think that would be the easiest thing in the world to fake. Any alteration in handwriting would be put down to agitation."

"Yes, that's true. Go on with your theory."

"Nicholson shoots Bassington-ffrench, leaves the farewell letter, and nips out, locking the door—to appear again a few minutes later as though he had just arrived."

Frankie shook her head regretfully.

"It's a good idea—but it won't work. To begin with, the key was in Henry Bassington-ffrench's pocket—"

"Who found it there?"

"Well, as a matter of act, Nicholson did."

"There you are! What's easier for him than to pretend to find it there?"

"I was watching him—remember. I'm sure the key was in the pocket."

"That's what one says when one watches a conjurer. You *see* the rabbit being put into the hat! If Nicholson is a high-class criminal a simple little bit of sleight-of-hand like that would be child's play to him."

"Well, you may be right about that, but honestly, Bobby, the whole thing's impossible. Sylvia Bassington-ffrench was actually in the house when the shot was fired. The moment she heard it she ran out into the hall. If Nicholson had fired the shot and come out through the study door she would have been bound to see him. Besides, she told us that he actually came up the drive to the front door. She saw him coming as we ran round the house, and went to meet him and brought him round to the study window. No, Bobby, I hate to say it, but the man has an alibi."

"On principle I distrust people who have alibis," said Bobby.

"So do I. But I don't see how you can get round this one."

"No. Sylvia Bassington-ffrench's word ought to be good enough."

"Yes, indeed."

"Well," said Bobby with a sigh, "I suppose we'll have to leave it at suicide. Poor devil. What's the next angle of attack, Frankie?"

"The Caymans," said Frankie. "I can't think how we've been so remiss as not to have looked them up before. You've kept the address Cayman wrote from, haven't you?"

"Yes. It's the same they gave at the inquest. Number 17 St. Leonard's Gardens, Paddington."

"Don't you agree that we've rather neglected that channel of inquiry?"

"Absolutely. All the same, you know, Frankie, I've got a very shrewd idea that you'll find the birds flown. I should imagine that the Caymans weren't exactly born yesterday."

"Even if they have gone off, I may find out something about them."

"Why *I*?"

"Because, once again, I don't think you'd better appear in the matter. It's like coming down here when we thought Roger was the bad man of the show. You are known to them and I am not."

"And how do you propose to make their acquaintance?" asked Bobby.

"I shall be something political," said Frankie. "Canvassing for the Conservative party. I shall arrive with leaflets."

"Good enough," said Bobby. "But, as I said before, I think you'll find the birds flown. Now there's another thing that requires to be thought of—Moira."

"Goodness!" said Frankie. "I'd forgotten all about her."

"So I noticed," said Bobby with a trace of coldness in his manner.

"You're right," said Frankie thoughtfully. "Something must be done about her."

Bobby nodded. The strange haunting face came up before his eyes. There was something tragic about it. He had always felt this from the first moment when he had taken the photograph from Alan Carstairs' pocket.

"If you'd seen her that night when I first went to the Grange!" he said. "She was crazy with fear—and I tell you, Frankie, *she's right*. It's not nerves nor imagination nor anything like that. If Nicholson wants to marry Sylvia Bassington-ffrench, two obstacles have got to go. One's gone. I've a feeling that Moira's life is hanging by a hair and that any delay may be fatal."

Frankie was sobered by the earnestness of his words.

"My dear, you're right," she said. "We must act quickly. What shall we do?"

"We must persuade her to leave the Grange—at once."

Frankie nodded. "I tell you what," she said. "She'd better go down to Wales—to the Castle. Heaven knows she ought to be safe enough there."

"If you can fix that, Frankie, nothing could be better."

"Well, it's simple enough. Father never notices who goes or comes. He'll like Moira—nearly any man would, she's so feminine. It's extraordinary how men like helpless women."

"I don't think Moira is particularly helpless," said Bobby.

"Nonsense. She's like a little bird that sits and waits to be eaten by a snake without doing anything about it."

"What could she do?"

"Heaps of things," said Frankie vigorously.

"Well, I don't see it. She's got no money, no friends—"

"My dear, don't drone on as though you were recommending a case to the Girls' Friendly Society."

"Sorry," said Bobby.

There was an offended pause.

"Well," said Frankie, recovering her temper. "As you were. I think we'd better get on to this business as soon as possible."

"So do I," said Bobby. "Really, Frankie, it's awfully decent of you to—"

"That's all right," said Frankie, interrupting him. "I don't mind befriending the girl so long as you don't drivel on about her as though she had no hands or feet or tongue or brains."

"I simply don't know what you mean," said Bobby.

"Well, we needn't talk about it," said Frankie. "Now my idea is that whatever we're going to do we'd better do it quickly. Is that a quotation?"

"It's a paraphrase of one. Go on, Lady Macbeth."

"You know I've always thought," said Frankie, suddenly digressing wildly from the matter in hand, "that Lady Macbeth incited Macbeth to do all those murders simply and solely because she was so frightfully bored with life—and incidentally with Macbeth. I'm sure he was one of those meek, inoffensive men who drive their wives distracted with boredom. But having once committed a murder for the first time in his life he felt the hell of a fine fellow and began to develop egomania as a compensation for his former inferiority complex."

"You ought to write a book on the subject, Frankie."

"I can't spell. Now, where were we? Oh, yes, rescue of Moira. You'd better bring the car round at half-past ten. I'll drive over to the Grange, ask for Moira, and, if Nicholson's there when I see her, I'll remind her of her promise to come and stay with me and carry her off then and there."

"Excellent, Frankie. I'm glad we're not going to waste any time. I've a horror of another accident happening."

"Half-past ten, then," said Frankie.

By the time she got back to Merroway Court it was half-past nine. Breakfast had just been brought in, and Roger was pouring himself out some coffee. He looked ill and worn.

"Good-morning," said Frankie. "I slept awfully badly. In the end I got up about seven and went for a walk."

"I'm frightfully sorry you should have been let in for all this worry," said Roger.

"How's Sylvia?"

"They gave her an opiate last night. She's still asleep, I believe. Poor girl, I'm most terribly sorry for her. She was simply devoted to Henry."

"I know."

Frankie paused, and then explained her plans for departure.

"I suppose you'll have to go," said Roger resentfully. "The inquest's on Friday. I'll let you know if you're wanted for it. It all depends on the Coroner."

He swallowed a cup of coffee and a piece of toast and then went off to see to the many things requiring his attention. Frankie felt very sorry for him. The amount of gossip and curiosity created by a suicide in a family she could imagine only too well. Tommy appeared and she devoted herself to amusing the child.

Bobby brought the car round at half-past ten. Frankie's luggage was brought down. She said good-bye to Tommy and left a note for Sylvia. The Bentley drove away.

They covered the distance to the Grange in a very short time. Frankie had never been there before, and the big iron gates and the overgrown shrubbery depressed her spirits.

"It's a creepy place," she observed. "I don't wonder Moira gets the horrors here."

They drove up to the front door and Bobby got down and rang the bell. It was not answered for some minutes. Finally a woman in nurse's kit opened it.

"Mrs. Nicholson?" said Bobby.

The woman hesitated, then withdrew into the hall and opened the door wider. Frankie jumped out of the car and passed into the house. The door closed behind her. It had a nasty echoing clang as it shut. Frankie noticed that it had heavy bolts and bars across it. Quite irrationally she felt afraid—as though she were here, in this sinister house, a prisoner.

"Nonsense!" she told herself. "Bobby's outside in the car. I've come here openly. Nothing can happen to me." And, shaking off the ridiculous feeling, she followed the nurse upstairs and along a passage. The nurse threw open a door and Frankie passed into a small sitting-room daintily furnished with cheerful chintzes and flowers in vases. Her spirits rose. Murmuring something, the nurse withdrew.

About five minutes passed and then the door opened and Dr. Nicholson came in.

Frankie was quite unable to control a slight nervous

start, but she masked it by a welcoming smile and shook hands.

"Good-morning," she said.

"Good-morning, Lady Frances. You have not come to bring me bad news of Mrs. Bassington-ffrench, I hope?"

"She was still asleep when I left," said Frankie.

"Poor lady. Her own doctor is, of course, looking after her?"

"Oh, yes." She paused, then said, "I'm sure you're busy. I mustn't take up your time, Dr. Nicholson. I really called to see your wife."

"To see Moira? That was very kind of you."

Was it only a fancy, or did the pale-blue eyes behind the strong glasses harden ever so slightly?

"Yes," he repeated. "That was very kind."

"If she isn't up yet," said Frankie, smiling pleasantly, "I'll sit down and wait."

"Oh, she's up," said Dr. Nicholson.

"Good," said Frankie. "I want to persuade her to come to me for a visit. She's practically promised to." She smiled again.

"Why, now, that's really very kind of you, Lady Frances—very kind indeed. I'm sure Moira would have enjoyed that very much."

" 'Would have'?" asked Frankie sharply.

Dr. Nicholson smiled, showing his fine set of even white teeth.

"Unfortunately my wife went away this morning."

"Went away?" said Frankie blankly. "Where?"

"Oh, just for a little change. You know what women are, Lady Frances. This is rather a gloomy place for a young woman. Occasionally Moira feels she must have a little excitement and then off she goes."

"You don't know where she has gone?" said Frankie.

"London, I imagine. Shops and theatres. You know the sort of thing."

Frankie felt that his smile was the most disagreeable thing she had ever come across.

"I am going up to London to-day," she said lightly. "Will you give me her address?"

"She usually stays at the Savoy," said Dr. Nicholson. "But in any case I shall probably hear from her in a day or so. She's not a very good correspondent, I'm afraid, and I believe in perfect liberty between husband and wife. But I think the Savoy is the most likely place for you to find her."

He held the door open and Frankie found herself shaking hands with him and being ushered to the front door. The nurse was standing there to let her out. The last thing Frankie heard was Dr. Nicholson's voice— suave and perhaps just a trifle ironical.

"So very kind of you to think of asking my wife to stay, Lady Frances."

24

On the Track of the Caymans

Bobby had some ado to preserve his impassive chauffeur's demeanor as Frankie came out alone.

She said: "Back to Staverley, Hawkins," for the benefit of the nurse.

The car swept down the drive and out through the gates. Then, when they came to an empty bit of road, Bobby pulled up and looked inquiringly at his companion.

"What about it?" he asked.

Rather pale, Frankie replied, "Bobby, I don't like it. Apparently, she's gone away."

"Gone *away?* This morning?"

"Or last night."

"Without a word to us?"

"Bobby, I just don't believe it. The man was lying, I'm sure of it."

Bobby looked distressed. He murmured: "Too late! Idiots that we've been! We should never have let her go back there yesterday."

"You don't think she's—dead, do you?" whispered Frankie in a shaky voice.

"No," said Bobby in a violent voice, as though to reassure himself.

They were both silent for a minute or two, then Bobby stated his deductions in a calmer tone.

"She must be still alive because of disposing of the body and all that. Her death would have to seem natural and accidental. No, she's either been spirited away somewhere against her will, or else—and this is what I believe—she's still there."

"At the Grange?"

"At the Grange."

"Well," said Frankie, "what are we going to do?"

Bobby thought for a minute. "I don't think you can do anything," he said at last. "You'd better go back to London. You suggested trying to trace the Caymans. Go on with that."

"Oh, Bobby!"

"My dear, you can't be of any use down here. You're known—very well known by now. You've announced that you're going—what can you do? You can't stay on at Merroway. You can't come and stay at the Anglers' Arms. You'd set every tongue in the neighborhood wagging. No, you must go. Nicholson may suspect, but he can't be *sure* that you know anything. You go back to town and I'll stay."

"At the Anglers' Arms?"

"No, I think your chauffeur will now disappear. I shall take up my headquarters at Ambledever—that's ten miles away—and if Moira's still in that beastly house I shall find her."

Frankie demurred a little. "Bobby, you will be careful?"

"I shall be cunning as the serpent."

With rather a heavy heart Frankie gave in. What Bobby said was certainly sensible enough. She herself could do no further good down here. Bobby drove her up to town and Frankie, letting herself into the Brook Street house, felt suddenly forlorn.

She was not one, however, to let the grass grow under

her feet. At three o'clock that afternoon, a fashionably but soberly dressed young woman with pince-nez and an earnest frown might have been seen approaching St. Leonard's Gardens, a sheaf of pamphlets and papers in her hand.

St. Leonard's Gardens, Paddington, was a distinctly gloomy collection of houses, most of them in a somewhat dilapidated condition. The place had a general air of having seen "better days" a long time ago.

Frankie walked along looking up at the numbers. Suddenly she came to a halt with a grimace of vexation.

No. 17 had a board up announcing that it was to be sold or let unfurnished.

Frankie immediately removed the pince-nez and the earnest air.

It seemed that the political canvasser would not be required.

The names of several house agents were given. Frankie selected two and wrote them down. Then, having determined on her plan of campaign, she proceeded to put it into action.

The first agents were Messrs. Gordon & Porter of Praed Street.

"Good-morning," said Frankie. "I wonder if you can give me the address of a Mr. Cayman? He was until recently at 17 St. Leonard's Gardens."

"That's right," said the young man to whom Frankie had addressed herself. "Only there a short time, though, wasn't he? We act for the owners, you see. Mr. Cayman took it on a quarterly tenancy as he might have to take up a post abroad any moment. I believe he's actually done so."

"Then you haven't got his address?"

"I'm afraid not. He settled up with us and that was all."

"But he must have had some address originally when he took the house."

"A hotel—I think it was the G.W.R. Paddington Station, you know."

"References?" suggested Frankie.

"He paid the quarter's rent in advance and a deposit to cover the electric light and gas."

"Oh!" said Frankie, feeling despairing.

She saw the young man looking rather curiously at her. House agents are adept at summing up the "class" of clients. He obviously found Frankie's interest in the Caymans rather unexpected.

"He owes me a good deal of money," said Frankie mendaciously.

The young man's face immediately assumed a shocked expression. Thoroughly sympathetic with beauty in distress, he hunted up files of correspondence and did all he could, but no trace of Mr. Cayman's present or late abode could be found.

Frankie thanked him and departed. She took a taxi to the next firm of house agents. She wasted no time in repeating the process. The first agents were the ones who had let Cayman the house. These people would be merely concerned to let it again on behalf of the owner. Frankie asked for an order to view.

This time, to counteract the expression of surprise that she saw appear on the clerk's face, she explained that she wanted a cheap property to open as a hostel for girls. The surprised expression disappeared, and Frankie emerged with the key of 17 St. Leonard's Gardens, the keys of two more "properties" which she had no wish to see, and an order to view yet a fourth.

It was a bit of luck, Frankie thought, that the clerk had not wished to accompany her, but perhaps they only did that when it was a question of a furnished tenancy.

The musty smell of a closed-up house assailed Frankie's nostrils as she unlocked and pushed open the front door of No. 17.

It was an unappetizing house, cheaply decorated, and with blistered, dirty paint. Frankie went over it methodically from garret to basement. The house had not been cleaned up on departure. There were bits of string, old newspapers and some odd nails and tools. But as for anything of a personal nature, Frankie could not find so much as the scrap of a torn-up letter.

The only thing that struck her as having a possible significance was an A.B.C. railway guide which lay open on one of the window seats. There was nothing to indicate that any of the names on the open page was of special significance, but Frankie copied the lot down in a little notebook as a poor substitute for all she had hoped to find.

As far as tracing the Caymans was concerned she had drawn a blank.

She consoled herself with the reflection that this was only to be expected. If Mr. and Mrs. Cayman were associated with the wrong side of the law they would take particularly good care that no one should be able to trace them. It was at least a kind of negative confirmatory evidence.

Still, Frankie felt definitely disappointed as she handed back the keys to the house agents and uttered mendacious statements as to communicating with them in a few days.

She walked down towards the Park feeling rather depressed and wondering what on earth she was going to do next. These fruitless meditations were interrupted by a sharp and violent squall of rain. No taxi was in sight and Frankie hurriedly preserved a favorite hat by hurrying into the Tube which was close at hand. She took a ticket to Piccadilly Circus and bought a couple of papers at the bookstall.

When she had entered the train—almost empty at this time of day—she resolutely banished thoughts of the vexing problem and opening her paper strove to concentrate her attention on its contents.

She read desultory snippets here and there.

Number of Road Deaths. Mysterious Disappearance of a Schoolgirl. Lady Peterhampton's Party at Claridge's. Sir John Milkington's convalescence after his yachting accident on the *Astradora*, the famous yacht which had belonged to the late Mr. John Savage, the millionaire. Was she an unlucky boat? The man who had designed her had met with a tragic death—Mr. Savage had committed suicide—Sir John Milkington had just escaped death by a miracle.

Frankie lowered the paper, frowning in an effort of remembrance.

Twice before, the name of John Savage had been mentioned—once by Sylvia Bassington-ffrench when she was speaking of Alan Carstairs, and once by Bobby when he was repeating the conversation he had had with Mrs. Rivington.

Alan Carstairs had been a friend of John Savage's. Mrs. Rivington had had a vague idea that Carstairs' presence in England had something to do with the death of Savage. Savage had—what was it?—he had committed suicide because he thought he had cancer.

Supposing—supposing Alan Carstairs had not been satisfied with the account of his friend's death? Supposing he had come over to inquire into the whole thing? Supposing that here, in the circumstances surrounding Savage's death, was the first act of the drama that she and Bobby were acting in?

"It's possible," thought Frankie. "Yes, it's possible."

She thought deeply, wondering how best to attack this new phase of the matter. She had no idea who John Savage's friends or intimates had been.

Then an idea struck her—his will. If there had been something suspicious about the way he met his death, his will would give a possible clue. Somewhere in London, Frankie knew, was a place where you went and read wills if you paid a shilling. But she couldn't remember where it was.

The train drew up at a station and Frankie saw that it was the British Museum. She had overshot Oxford Circus, where she had meant to change, by two stations.

She jumped up and left the train. As she emerged into the street an idea came to her. Five minutes' walk brought her to the office of Messrs. Spragge, Spragge, Jenkinson & Spragge.

Frankie was received with deference and was at once ushered into the private fastness of Mr. Spragge, the senior member of the firm.

Mr. Spragge was exceedingly genial. He had a rich, mellow, persuasive voice which his aristocratic clients had found extremely soothing when they had come to him to be extricated from some mess. It was rumored that Mr. Spragge knew more discreditable secrets about noble families than any other man in London.

"This is a pleasure indeed, Lady Frances," he said. "Do sit down. Now are you sure that chair is quite comfortable? Yes, yes. The weather is very delightful just now, is it not?—a St. Martin's summer. And how is Lord Marchington? Well, I trust?"

Frankie answered these and other inquiries in a suitable manner.

Then Mr. Spragge removed his pince-nez from his nose and became more definitely the legal guide and adviser.

"And now, Lady Frances," he said, "what is it gives me the pleasure of seeing you in my—hm—dingy office this afternoon?"

("Blackmail?" asked his eyebrows. "Indiscreet letters? An entanglement with an undesirable young man? Sued by your dressmaker?" But the eyebrows asked these questions in a very discreet manner as befitted a solicitor of Mr. Spragge's experience and income.)

"I want to look at a will," said Frankie. "And I don't know where you go and what you do. But there is some place where you can pay a shilling, isn't there?"

"Somerset House," said Mr. Spragge. "But what will is it? I think I can probably tell you anything you want to know about—er—wills in your family. I may say that I believe our firm has had the honor of drawing them up for many years past."

"It isn't a family will," said Frankie.

"No?" said Mr. Spragge.

And so strong was his almost hypnotic power of drawing confidences out of his clients that Frankie, who had not meant to do so, succumbed to the manner and told him.

"I wanted to see the will of Mr. Savage—John Savage."

"In-deed." A very real astonishment showed in Mr. Spragge's voice. He had not expected this. "Now that is very extraordinary—very extraordinary indeed."

There was something so unusual in his voice that Frankie looked at him in surprise.

"Really," said Mr. Spragge, "really I do not know what to do. Perhaps, Lady Frances, you can give me your reasons for wanting to see that will?"

"No," said Frankie slowly. "I'm afraid I can't."

It struck her that Mr. Spragge was, for some reason,

behaving quite unlike his usual benign omniscient self. He looked actually worried.

"I really believe," said Mr. Spragge, "that I ought to warn you."

"Warn me?" said Frankie.

"Yes. The indications are vague, very vague—but clearly there is something afoot. I would not for the world have you involved in any questionable business."

As far as that went Frankie could have told him that she was already involved up to the neck in a business of which he would have decidedly disapproved. But she merely stared at him inquiringly.

"The whole thing is rather an extraordinary coincidence," Mr. Spragge was going on. "Something is clearly afoot—clearly. But what it is I am not at present at liberty to say."

Frankie continued to look inquiring.

"A piece of information has just come to my knowledge," continued Mr. Spragge. His chest swelled with indignation. "I have been impersonated, Lady Frances. Deliberately impersonated. What do you say to that?"

But for just one panic-stricken minute Frankie could say nothing at all.

25

Mr. Spragge Talks

At last she stammered, "How did you find out?"

It was not at all what she meant to say. She could, in fact, have bitten out her tongue for stupidity a moment later, but the words had been said, and Mr. Spragge would have been no lawyer had he failed to perceive that they contained an admission.

"So you know something of this business, Lady Frances?"

"Yes," said Frankie.

She paused, drew a deep breath and said, "The whole thing is really my doing, Mr. Spragge."

"I am amazed," said Mr. Spragge.

There was a struggle in his voice—the outraged lawyer was at war with the fatherly family solicitor.

"How did this come about?" he asked.

"It was just a joke," said Frankie weakly. "We—we wanted something to do."

"And who," demanded Mr. Spragge, "had the idea of passing himself off as Me?"

Frankie looked at him and, her wits working once more, made a rapid decision.

"It was the young Duke of—no—" she broke off. "I—really mustn't mention names. It isn't fair."

But she knew that the tide had turned in her favor. It was doubtful whether Mr. Spragge could have forgiven a mere vicar's son such audacity, but his weakness for noble names led him to look softly on the impertinences of a duke. His benign manner returned.

"Oh! you Bright Young People—you Bright Young People," he murmured, wagging a forefinger. "What trouble you land yourselves in! You would be surprised, Lady Frances, at the amount of legal complications that may ensue from an apparently harmless practical joke determined upon the spur of the moment. Just high spirits—but sometimes extremely difficult to settle out of court."

"I think you're too marvellous, Mr. Spragge," said Frankie earnestly. "I do really. Not one person in a thousand would have taken it as you have done. I feel really terribly ashamed."

"No, no, Lady Frances," said Mr. Spragge paternally.

"Oh, but I do. I suppose it was the Rivington woman—what exactly did she tell you?"

"I think I have the letter here. I opened it only half an hour ago."

Frankie held out a hand, and Mr. Spragge put the letter into it with the air of one saying: "There, see for yourself what your foolishness has led you into."

DEAR MR. SPRAGGE, [Mrs. Rivington had written] It's really too stupid of me, but I've just remembered something that might have helped you the day you called on me. Alan Carstairs mentioned that he was going down to a place called Chipping Somerton. I don't know whether this will be any help to you?

I was *so* interested in what you told me about the Maltravers case.

> With kind regards,
> Yours sincerely,
> EDITH RIVINGTON

"You can see that the matter might have been very grave," said Mr. Spragge severely—but with a severity tempered by benevolence. "I took it that some extremely questionable business was afoot. Whether connected with the Maltravers case or with my client, Mr. Carstairs—"

Frankie interrupted him.

"Was Alan Carstairs a client of yours?" she inquired excitedly.

"He was. He consulted me when he was last in England a month ago. You know Mr. Carstairs, Lady Frances?"

"I think I may say I do," replied Frankie.

"A most attractive personality," said Mr. Spragge. "He brought quite a breath of the—er—wide open spaces into my office."

"He came to consult you about Mr. Savage's will, didn't he?" said Frankie.

"Ah!" said Mr. Spragge. "So it was you who advised him to come to me? He couldn't remember just who it was. I'm sorry I couldn't do more for him."

"Just what did you advise him to do?" asked Frankie. "Or would it be unprofessional to tell me?"

"Not in this case," said Mr. Spragge, smiling. "My opinion was that there was nothing to be done—nothing, that is, unless Mr. Savage's relatives were prepared to spend a lot of money on fighting the case—which I gather they were not prepared, or indeed in a position, to do. I never advise bringing a case into court unless there is every hope of success. The law, Lady Frances, is an uncertain animal. It has twists and turns that surprise the non-legal mind. Settle out of court has always been my motto."

"The whole thing was very curious," said Frankie thoughtfully.

She had a little the sensation of walking barefoot over a floor covered with tin tacks. At any minute she might step on one—and the game would be up.

"Such cases are less uncommon than you might think," said Mr. Spragge.

"Cases of suicide?" inquired Frankie.

"No, no, I meant cases of undue influence. Mr. Savage was a hard-headed business man, and yet he was clearly as wax in this woman's hands. I've no doubt she knew her business thoroughly."

"I wish you'd tell me the whole story properly," said Frankie boldly. "Mr. Carstairs was—well, was so heated, that I never seemed to get the thing clearly."

"The case was extremely simple," said Mr. Spragge. "I can run over the facts to you—they are accessible to everyone—so there is no objection to my doing so."

"Then tell me all about it," said Frankie.

"Mr. Savage happened to be travelling back from the United States to England in November of last year. He was, as you know, an extremely wealthy man with no near relatives. On this voyage he made the acquaintance of a certain lady—a—er—Mrs. Templeton. Nothing much is known about Mrs. Templeton except that she was a very good-looking woman and had a husband somewhere conveniently in the background."

"The Caymans," thought Frankie.

"These ocean trips are dangerous," went on Mr. Spragge, smiling and shaking his head. "Mr. Savage was clearly very much attracted. He accepted the lady's invitation to come down and stay at her little cottage at Chipping Somerton. Exactly how often he went there I have not been able to ascertain, but there is no doubt that he came more and more under this Mrs. Templeton's influence.

"Then came the tragedy. Mr. Savage had for some

time been uneasy about his state of health. He feared
that he might be suffering from a certain disease—"

"Cancer?" said Frankie.

"Well, yes, as a matter of fact, cancer. The idea became quite an obsession with him. He was staying with
the Templetons at the time. They persuaded him to go
up to London and consult a specialist. He did so. Now
here, Lady Frances, I preserve an open mind. That specialist, a very distinguished man who has been at the top
of his profession for many years, swore at the inquest
that Mr. Savage was not suffering from cancer and that
he had told him so, but that Mr. Savage was so obsessed
by his own belief that he could not accept the truth when
he was told it. Now, strictly without prejudice, Lady
Frances, and knowing the medical profession, I think
things may have gone a little differently. If Mr. Savage's
symptoms puzzled the doctor he may have spoken seriously, pulled a long face, talked of certain expensive
treatments, and while reassuring him as to cancer yet
have conveyed the impression that something was seriously wrong. Mr. Savage, having heard that doctors usually conceal from a patient the fact that he is suffering
from that disease, would interpret this according to his
own lights. The doctor's reassuring words were *not*
true—he *had* got the disease he thought he had.

"Anyway, Mr. Savage came back to Chipping Somerton in a state of great mental distress. He saw ahead of
him a painful and lingering death. I understand some
members of his family had died of cancer, and he determined not to go through what he had seen them suffer.
He sent for a solicitor—a very reputable member of an
eminently respectable firm, and the latter drew up a will
there and then which Mr. Savage signed and which he
then delivered over to the solicitor for safe-keeping. On
that same evening Mr. Savage took a large overdose of

chloral, leaving a letter behind in which he explained that he preferred a quick and painless death to a long and painful one.

"By his will Mr. Savage left the sum of seven hundred thousand pounds free of legacy duty to Mrs. Templeton, and the remainder to certain specified charities."

Mr. Spragge leaned back in his chair. He was now enjoying himself.

"The jury brought in the usual sympathetic verdict of 'suicide while of unsound mind,' but I do not think that we can argue from that that he was necessarily of unsound mind when he made the will. I do not think that any jury would take it so. The will was made in the presence of a solicitor in whose opinion the deceased was undoubtedly sane and in possession of his senses. Nor do I think we can prove undue influence. Mr. Savage did not disinherit anyone near and dear to him—his only relatives were distant cousins whom he seldom saw. They actually live in Australia, I believe."

Mr. Spragge paused.

"Mr. Carstairs' contention was that such a will was completely uncharacteristic of Mr. Savage. Mr. Savage had no liking for organized charities and had always held very strong opinions as to money passing by blood relationship. However, Mr. Carstairs had no documentary proof of these assertions and, as I pointed out to him, men change their opinions. In contesting such a will there would be the charitable organizations to deal with as well as Mrs. Templeton. Also the will had been admitted to probate."

"There was no fuss made at the time?" asked Frankie.

"As I say, Mr. Savage's relatives were not living in this country and they knew very little about the matter. It was Mr. Carstairs who took the matter up. He returned from a trip into the interior of Africa, gradually learnt

the details of this business and came over to this country
to see if something could be done about it. I was forced
to tell him that in my view there was nothing to be done.
Possession is nine points of the law, and Mrs. Templeton
was in possession. Moreover, she had left the country
and gone, I believe, to the south of France to live. She
refused to enter into any communication on the matter.
I suggested getting counsel's opinion, but Mr. Carstairs
decided that it was not necessary and took my view that
there was nothing to be done—or, alternatively, that
though something might have been done at the time (and
in my opinion that was exceedingly doubtful) it was now
too late to do it."

"I see," said Frankie. "And nobody knows anything
about this Mrs. Templeton?"

Mr. Spragge shook his head and pursed his lips.

"A man like Mr. Savage, with his knowledge of life,
ought to have been less easily taken in, but—" Mr.
Spragge shook his head sadly as a vision of innumerable
clients, who ought to have known better and who had
come to him to have their cases settled out of court,
passed across his mind.

Frankie rose.

"Men are extraordinary creatures," she said.

She held out a hand.

"Good-bye, Mr. Spragge," she said. "You've been
wonderful—simply wonderful. I feel too ashamed."

"You Bright Young People must be more careful,"
said Mr. Spragge, shaking his head at her.

"You've been an angel," said Frankie.

She squeezed his hand fervently and departed.

Mr. Spragge sat down again before his table.

He was thinking. "The young Duke of—"

There were only two dukes who could be so described. Which was it?

He picked up a *Peerage*.

26

Nocturnal Adventure

The inexplicable absence of Moira worried Bobby more than he cared to admit. He told himself repeatedly that it was absurd to jump to conclusions—that it was fantastic to imagine that Moira had been done away with in a house full of possible witnesses—that there was probably some perfectly simple explanation and that at the worst she could only be a prisoner in the Grange.

That she had left Staverley of her own free will Bobby did not for one minute believe. He was convinced that she would never have gone off like that without sending him a word of explanation. Besides, she had stated emphatically that she had nowhere to go.

No, the sinister Dr. Nicholson was at the bottom of this. Somehow or other he must have become aware of Moira's activities, and this was his counter-move. Somewhere within the sinister walls of the Grange, Moira was a prisoner, unable to communicate with the outside world.

But she might not remain a prisoner long. Bobby believed implicitly every word Moira had uttered. Her fears were neither the result of a vivid imagination nor the result of nerves. They were simple stark truth.

Nicholson meant to get rid of his wife. Several times his plans had miscarried. Now Moira, by communicating her fears to others, had forced his hand. He must act quickly or not at all. Would he have the nerve to act?

Bobby believed he would. He must know that, even if these strangers had listened to his wife's fears, they had no evidence. Also, he would believe that he had only Frankie to deal with. It was possible that he had suspected her from the first—his pertinent questioning as to her "accident" seemed to point to that. But as Lady Frances' chauffeur Bobby did not believe that he himself was suspected of being anything other than he appeared to be.

Yes, Nicholson would act. Moira's body would probably be found in some district far from Staverley. It might, perhaps, be washed up by the sea. Or it might be found at the foot of a cliff. The thing would appear to be, Bobby was almost sure, an "accident." Nicholson specialized in "accidents."

Nevertheless, Bobby believed that the planning and carrying out of such an accident would need time—not much time, but a certain amount. Nicholson's hand was being forced—he had to act more quickly than he had anticipated. It seemed reasonable to suppose that twenty-four hours at least must elapse before he could put any plan into operation.

Before that interval had elapsed Bobby meant to have found Moira if she were in the Grange.

After he had left Frankie in Brook Street, he started to put his plans into operation. He judged it wise to give the mews a wide berth. For all he knew a watch might be being kept on it. As Hawkins, he believed himself to be still unsuspected. Now "Hawkins" in turn was about to disappear.

That evening a young man with a moustache, dressed in a cheap dark-blue suit, arrived at the bustling little town of Ambledever. He put up at a hotel near the station, registering as George Parker. Having deposited his suitcase there, he strolled out and entered into negotiations for hiring a motorcycle.

At ten o'clock that evening a motorcyclist in cap and goggles passed through the village of Staverley and came to a halt at a deserted part of the road not far from the Grange.

Hastily shoving the bicycle behind some convenient bushes, Bobby looked up and down the road. It was quite deserted.

Then he sauntered along the wall till he came to the little door. As before it was unlocked. With another look up and down the road to make sure he was not observed, Bobby slipped quietly inside. He put his hand into the pocket of his coat where a bulge showed the presence of his Service revolver. The feel of it was reassuring.

Inside the grounds of the Grange everything seemed quiet.

Bobby grinned to himself as he recalled blood-curdling stories where the villain of the piece kept a cheetah or some exciting beast of prey about the place to deal with intruders.

Dr. Nicholson seemed content with mere bolts and bars, and even there he seemed to be somewhat remiss. Bobby felt certain that this little door should not have been left open. As the villain of the piece Dr. Nicholson seemed regrettably careless.

"No tame pythons," thought Bobby, "no cheetahs, no electrically charged wires—the man is shamefully behind the times."

He made these reflections more to cheer himself up than for any other reason. Every time he thought of Moira a queer constriction seemed to tighten round his heart.

Her face rose in the air before him—the trembling lips—the wide terrified eyes. It was just about here that he had first seen her in the flesh. A little thrill ran through him as he remembered how he had put his arm round her to steady her. . . .

Moira—where was she now? What had that sinister doctor done with her? If only she were still alive. . . .

"She must be," said Bobby grimly between set lips. "I'm not going to think anything else."

He made a careful reconnaissance round the house. Some of the upstairs windows had lights in them and there was one lighted window on the ground floor. Towards this window Bobby crept. The curtains were drawn across it, but there was a slight chink between them. Bobby put a knee on the window-sill and hoisted himself noiselessly up. He peered through the slit.

He could see a man's arm and shoulder moving along as though writing. Presently the man shifted his position and his profile came into view. It was Dr. Nicholson.

It was a curious situation. Quite unconscious that he was being watched, the Doctor wrote steadily on. A queer sort of fascination stole over Bobby. The man was so near him that, but for the intervening glass, Bobby could have stretched out his arm and touched him.

For the first time, Bobby felt, he was really seeing the man. It was a forceful profile—the big bold nose, the jutting chin, the crisp, well-shaven line of the jaw. The ears, Bobby noted, were small and laid flat to the head, and the lobe of the ear was actually joined to the cheek. He had an idea that ears like these were said to have some special significance.

The Doctor wrote on, calm and unhurried. Now pausing for a moment or two as though to think of the right word—then setting to once more. His pen moved over the paper, precisely and evenly. Once he took off his pince-nez, polished them, and put them on again.

At last with a sigh, Bobby let himself slide noiselessly

to the ground. From the look of it Nicholson would be writing for some time to come. Now was the moment to gain admission to the house.

If Bobby could force an entrance by an upstairs window while the Doctor was writing in his study, he could explore the building at his leisure later in the night.

He made a circuit of the house again and singled out a window on the first floor. The sash was open at the top, but there was no light in the room, so that it was probably unoccupied at the moment. Moreover a very convenient tree seemed to promise an easy means of access.

In another minute Bobby was swarming up the tree. All went well and he was just stretching out his hand to take a grip of the window ledge when an ominous crack came from the branch he was on, and the next minute the bough, a rotten one, had snapped and Bobby was pitchforked head-first into a clump of hydrangea bushes below, which fortunately broke his fall.

The window of Nicholson's study was farther along on the same side of the house. Bobby heard an exclamation in the Doctor's voice, and the window was flung up. Bobby, recovering from the first shock of his fall, sprang up, disentangled himself from the hydrangeas and bolted across a dark patch of shadow into the pathway leading to the little door. He went a short way along it, then dived into the bushes.

He heard the sound of voices and saw lights moving near the trampled and broken hydrangeas. Bobby kept still and held his breath. They might come along the path. If so, finding the door open, they would probably conclude that the intruder had escaped that way and would not prosecute the search further.

However, the minutes passed, and nobody came. Presently Bobby heard Nicholson's voice raised in a question. He did not hear the words but he heard an answer given in a hoarse, rather uneducated voice.

"All present and correct, sir. I've been the rounds."

The sounds gradually died down, the lights disappeared. Everyone seemed to have returned to the house.

Very cautiously Bobby came out of his hiding place. He emerged onto the path listening. All was still. He took a step or two towards the house.

And then out of the darkness, something struck him on the back of the neck. He fell forward . . . into darkness.

27

"My Brother Was Murdered"

On Friday morning the green Bentley drew up outside the Station Hotel at Ambledever.

Frankie had wired Bobby under the name they had agreed upon—George Parker—that she would be required to give evidence at the inquest on Henry Bassington-ffrench and would call in at Ambledever on the way down from London. She had expected a wire in reply appointing some rendezvous, but nothing had come, so she had come to the hotel.

"Mr. Parker, miss?" said the boots. "I don't think there's any gentleman of that name stopping here, but I'll see."

He returned a few minutes later.

"Come here Wednesday evening, miss. Left his bag and said he mightn't be in till late. His bag's still here but he hasn't been back to fetch it."

Frankie felt suddenly rather sick. She clutched at a table for support. The man was looking at her sympathetically.

"Feeling bad, miss?" he inquired.

Frankie shook her head. "It's all right," she managed to say. "He didn't leave any message?"

The man went away again and returned shaking his head.

"There's a telegram come for him," he said. "That's all."

He looked at her curiously. "Anything I can do, miss?" he asked.

Frankie shook her head. At the moment she only wanted to get away. She must have time to think what to do next.

"It's all right," she said, and getting into the Bentley she drove away.

The man nodded his head wisely as he looked after her.

"He's done a bunk, he has," he said to himself. "Disappointed her. Given her the slip. A fine rakish piece of goods she is. Wonder what he was like?"

He asked the young lady in the reception office, but the young lady couldn't remember.

"A couple of nobs," said the boots wisely. "Going to get married on the quiet—and he's hooked it."

Meanwhile Frankie was driving in the direction of Staverley, her mind a maze of conflicting emotions.

Why had Bobby not returned to the Station Hotel? There could be only two reasons. Either he was on the trail—and that trail had taken him away somewhere; or else—or else something had gone wrong. The Bentley swerved dangerously. Frankie recovered control just in time.

She was being an idiot—imagining things. Of course Bobby was all right. He was on the trail—that was all—on the trail.

But why, asked another voice, hadn't he sent her a word of reassurance?

That was more difficult to explain, but there were explanations. Difficult circumstances—no time or opportunity—Bobby would know that she, Frankie, wouldn't get the wind up about him. Everything was all right—bound to be.

The inquest passed like a dream. Roger was there, and Sylvia—looking quite beautiful in her widow's weeds. She made an impressive figure and a moving one. Frankie found herself admiring her as though she were admiring a performance at a theater.

The proceedings were very tactfully conducted. The Bassington-ffrenches were popular locally and everything was done to spare the feelings of the widow and the brother of the dead man.

Frankie and Roger gave their evidence—Dr. Nicholson gave his—the dead man's farewell letter was produced. The thing seemed over in no time, and the verdict was given as "Suicide while of unsound mind." The "sympathetic" verdict, as Mr. Spragge had called it.

The two events connected themselves in Frankie's mind. Two suicides "while of unsound mind." Was there—could there be a connection between them?

That this suicide was genuine enough she knew, for she had been on the scene. Bobby's theory of murder had had to be dismissed as untenable. Dr. Nicholson's alibi was cast-iron—vouched for by the widow herself.

Frankie and Dr. Nicholson remained behind after the other people departed, the Coroner having shaken hands with Sylvia and uttered a few words of sympathy.

"I think there are some letters for you, Frankie dear," said Sylvia. "You won't mind if I leave you now and go and lie down. It's all been so awful."

She shivered and left the room. Nicholson went with her, murmuring something about a sedative.

Frankie turned to Roger. "Roger, Bobby's disappeared."

"Disappeared?"

"Yes!"

"Where and how?"

Frankie explained in a few rapid words.

"And he's not been seen since?" said Roger.

"No. What do you think?"

"I don't like the sound of it," said Roger slowly.

Frankie's heart sank. "You don't think—?"

"Oh! it may be all right, but—Sh, here comes Nicholson."

The Doctor entered the room with his noiseless tread. He was rubbing his hands together and smiling.

"That went off very well," he said. "Very well indeed. Dr. Davidson was most tactful and considerate. We may consider ourselves very lucky to have had him as our local Coroner."

"I suppose so," said Frankie mechanically.

"It makes a lot of difference, Lady Frances. The conduct of an inquest is entirely in the hands of the Coroner. He has wide powers. He can make things easy or difficult as he pleases. In this case everything went off perfectly."

"A good stage performance, in fact," said Frankie in a hard voice.

Nicholson looked at her in surprise.

"I know what Lady Frances is feeling," said Roger. "I feel the same. My brother was murdered, Dr. Nicholson."

He was standing behind the other and did not see, as Frankie did, the startled expression that sprang into the Doctor's eyes.

"I mean what I say," said Roger, interrupting Nicholson as he was about to reply. "The law may not regard it as such, but murder it was. The criminal brutes who induced my brother to become a slave to that drug murdered him just as truly as if they had struck him down."

He had moved a little and his angry eyes now looked straight into the Doctor's.

"I mean to get even with them," he said, and the words sounded like a threat.

Dr. Nicholson's pale-blue eyes fell before his. He shook his head sadly.

"I cannot say I disagree with you," he said. "I know more about drug-taking than you do, Mr. Bassington-ffrench. To induce a man to take drugs is indeed a most terrible crime."

Ideas were whirling through Frankie's head—one idea in particular.

"It can't be," she was saying to herself. "That would be too monstrous. And yet—his whole alibi depends on her word. But in that case—"

She roused herself to find Nicholson speaking to her.

"You came down by car, Lady Frances? No accident this time?"

Frankie felt she simply hated that smile.

"No," she said. "I think it's a pity to go in too much for accidents—don't you?"

She wondered whether she had imagined it, or whether his eyelids really flickered for a moment.

"Perhaps your chauffeur drove you this time?"

"My chauffeur," said Frankie, "has disappeared."

She looked straight at Nicholson.

"Indeed?"

"He was last seen heading for the Grange," went on Frankie.

Nicholson raised his eyebrows.

"Really? Have I—some attraction in the kitchen?" His voice sounded amused. "I can hardly believe it."

"At any rate that is where he was last seen," said Frankie.

"You sound quite dramatic," said Nicholson. "Possibly you are paying too much attention to local gossip. Local gossip is very unreliable. I have heard the wildest stories." He paused. His voice altered slightly in tone. "I have even had a story brought to my ears that my wife and your chauffeur had been seen talking together down by the river." Another pause. "He was, I believe, a very superior young man, Lady Frances."

"Is that it?" thought Frankie. "Is he going to pretend that his wife has run off with my chauffeur? Is that his little game?"

Aloud she said, "Hawkins is quite above the average chauffeur."

"So it seems," said Nicholson. He turned to Roger. "I must be going. Believe me, all my sympathies are with you and Mrs. Bassington-ffrench."

Roger went out into the hall with him. Frankie followed. On the hall table were a couple of letters addressed to her. One was a bill. The other—

Her heart gave a leap.

The other was in Bobby's handwriting.

Nicholson and Roger were on the doorstep.

She tore it open.

DEAR FRANKIE, [wrote Bobby]
I'm on the trail at last. Follow me as soon as possible to Chipping Somerton. You'd better come by train and not by car. The Bentley is too noticeable. The trains aren't too good, but you can get there all right. You're to come to a house called Tudor Cottage. I'll explain to you just exactly how to find it. Don't ask the way. [Here followed some minute directions.] Have you got that clear? Don't *tell anyone*. [This was heavily underlined.] *No one at all.*

Yours ever,
BOBBY

Frankie crushed the letter excitedly in the palm of her hand. So it was all right! Nothing dreadful had overtaken Bobby.

He was on the trail—and by a coincidence on the same trail as herself. She had been to Somerset House to look up the will of John Savage. "Rose Emily Templeton" was given as the wife of Edgar Templeton of Tudor Cottage, Chipping Somerton. And that again had fitted in with the open A.B.C. in the St. Leonard's Gardens house. Chipping Somerton had been one of the stations on the open page. The Caymans had gone to Chipping Somerton.

Everything was falling into place. They were nearing the end of the chase.

Roger Bassington-ffrench turned and came towards her.

"Anything interesting in your letter?" he inquired casually.

For a moment Frankie hesitated. Surely Bobby had not meant Roger when he adjured her to tell nobody?

Then she remembered the heavy underlining—remembered, too, her recent monstrous idea. If *that* were true, Roger might betray them both in all innocence. She dared not hint to him her own suspicions.

So she made up her mind. "No," she said. "Nothing at all."

She was to repent her decision bitterly before twenty-four hours had passed.

More than once in the course of the next few hours did she regret Bobby's dictum that the car was not to be used. Chipping Somerton was no very great distance as the crow flies, but the journey involved changing three times, with a long, dreary wait at a country station each time, and to one of Frankie's impatient temperament this

slow method of procedure was extremely hard to endure
with fortitude.

Still, she felt bound to admit that there was something
in what Bobby had said. The Bentley *was* a noticeable
car. Her excuses for leaving it at Merroway had been of
the flimsiest, but she had been unable to think if anything
brilliant on the spur of the moment.

It was getting dark when Frankie's train, an extremely
deliberate and thoughtful train, drew into the little station
of Chipping Somerton. To Frankie it seemed more like
midnight. The train seemed to her to have been ambling
on for hours and hours. It was just beginning to rain,
too, which was additionally trying.

She buttoned up her coat to her neck, took a last look
at Bobby's letter by the light of the station lamp, got the
directions clearly in her head and set off.

The instructions were quite easy to follow. Frankie
saw the lights of the village ahead and turned off to the
left up a lane which led steeply up hill. At the top of
the lane she took the right-hand fork and presently saw
the little cluster of houses that formed the village lying
below her and a belt of pine trees ahead. Finally, she
came to a neat wooden gate and striking a match saw
"Tudor Cottage" written on it.

There was no one about. Frankie slipped up the latch
and passed inside. She could make out the outlines of
the house behind a belt of pine trees. She took up her
post within the trees where she could get a clear view
of the house. Then, her heart beating a little faster, she
gave the best imitation she could of the hoot of an owl.
A few minutes passed and nothing happened. She repeated the call.

The door of the cottage opened and she saw a figure
in chauffeur's dress peer cautiously out. Bobby! He

made a beckoning gesture, then withdrew inside, leaving the door ajar.

Frankie came out from the trees and up to the door. There was no light in any window. Everything was perfectly dark and silent.

Frankie stepped gingerly over the threshold into a dark hall. She stopped, peering about her.

"Bobby?" she whispered.

It was her nose that gave her warning. Where had she known that smell before—that heavy, sweet odor?

Just as her brain gave the answer "Chloroform," strong arms seized her from behind. She opened her mouth to scream and a wet pad was clapped over it. The sweet, cloying smell filled her nostrils.

She fought desperately, twisting and turning, kicking. But it was of no avail. Despite the fight she put up she felt herself succumbing. There was a drumming in her ears, she felt herself choking. And then she knew no more. . . .

28

At the Eleventh Hour

When Frankie came to herself the immediate reactions were depressing. There is nothing romantic about the after-effects of chloroform. She was lying on an extremely hard wooden floor and her hands and feet were tied. She managed to roll herself over, and her head nearly collided violently with a battered coal-box. Various distressing events then occurred.

A few minutes later Frankie was able, if not to sit up, at least to take notice.

Close at hand she heard a faint groan. She peered about her. As far as she could make out she seemed to be in a kind of attic. The only light came from a skylight in the roof, and at this moment there was very little of that. In a few minutes it would be quite dark. There were a few broken pictures lying against the wall—a dilapidated iron bed, and some broken chairs, and the coal-scuttle before mentioned.

The groan seemed to have come from the corner.

Frankie's bonds were not very tight. They permitted motion of a somewhat crablike type. She wormed her way across the dusty floor.

"Bobby!" she ejaculated.

Bobby it was, also tied hand and foot. In addition he had a piece of cloth bound round his mouth. This he had almost succeeded in working lose. Frankie came to his assistance. In spite of being bound together her hands were still of some use, and a final vigorous pull with the teeth finally did the job.

Rather stiffly Bobby managed to ejaculate, "Frankie!"

"I'm glad we're together," said Frankie. "But it does look as though we'd been had for mugs."

"I suppose," said Bobby gloomily, "it's what they call a 'fair cop.' "

"How did they get you?" demanded Frankie. "Was it after you wrote that letter to me?"

"What letter? I never wrote any letter!"

"Oh, I see!" said Frankie, her eyes opening. "What an idiot I have been! And all that stuff in it about not telling a soul."

"Look here, Frankie, I'll tell you what happened to me and then you carry on the good work and tell me what happened to you."

He described his adventures at the Grange and their sinister sequel.

"I came to in this beastly hole," he said. "There was some food and drink on a tray. I was frightfully hungry and I had some. I think it must have been doped for I fell asleep almost immediately. What day is it?"

"Friday."

"And I was knocked out on Wednesday evening. Dash it all, I've been pretty well unconscious all the time. Now tell me what happened to you."

Frankie recounted her adventures beginning with the story she had heard from Mr. Spragge and carrying on until she thought she recognized Bobby's figure in the doorway.

"And then they chloroformed me," she finished. "And, oh, Bobby, I've just been sick in a coal-bucket!"

"I call that very resourceful of you, Frankie," said Bobby approvingly. "With your hands tied and everything. The thing is—what are we going to do now? We've had it our own way for a long time, but now the tables are turned."

"If only I'd told Roger about your letter," lamented Frankie. "I did think of it and wavered—and then I decided to do exactly what you said and tell nobody at all."

"With the result that no one knows where we are," said Bobby, gravely. "Frankie, my dear, I'm afraid I've landed you in a mess."

"We got a bit too sure of ourselves," said Frankie sombrely.

"The only thing I can't make out is why they didn't knock us both on the head straight away," mused Bobby. "I don't think Nicholson would stick at a little trifle like that."

"He's got a plan," said Frankie with a slight shiver.

"Well, we'd better have one too. We've got to get out of this, Frankie. How are we going to do it?"

"We can shout," said Frankie.

"Ye-es," said Bobby. "Somebody might be passing and hear. But from the fact that Nicholson didn't gag you I should say that the chances in that direction are pretty poor. Your hands are more loosely tied than mine. Let's see if I can get them undone with my teeth."

The next five minutes were spent in a struggle that did credit to Bobby's dentist.

"Extraordinary how easy these things sound in books," he panted. "I don't believe I'm making the slightest impression."

"You are," said Frankie. "It's loosening. Look out, there's somebody coming."

She rolled away from him. A step could be heard mounting a stair, a ponderous tread. A gleam of light appeared under the door. Then there was the sound of a key being turned in the lock. The door swung slowly open.

"And how are my two little birds?" said the voice of Dr. Nicholson.

He carried a candle in one hand, and though he was wearing a hat pulled down over his eyes and a heavy overcoat with the collar turned up, his voice would have betrayed him anywhere. His eyes glittered palely behind the strong glasses.

He shook his head at them playfully.

"Unworthy of you, my dear young lady," he said. "To fall into the trap so easily."

Neither Bobby nor Frankie made any reply. The honors of the situation so obviously lay with Nicholson that it was difficult to know what to say.

Nicholson put the candle down on a chair.

"At any rate," he said, "let me see if you are comfortable."

He examined Bobby's fastenings, nodded his head approvingly and passed on to Frankie. There he shook his head.

"As they truly used to say to me in my youth," he remarked, "fingers were made before forks—and teeth were used before fingers. Your young friend's teeth, I see, have been active."

A heavy, broken-backed oak chair was standing in a corner.

Nicholson picked up Frankie, deposited her on the chair and tied her securely to it.

"Not too uncomfortable, I trust?" he said. "Well, it isn't for long."

Frankie found her tongue. "What are you going to do with us?" she demanded.

Nicholson walked to the door and picked up his candle.

"You taunted me, Lady Frances, with being too fond of accidents. Perhaps I am. At any rate, I am going to risk one more accident."

"What do you mean?" said Bobby.

"Shall I tell you? Yes, I think I will. Lady Frances Derwent, driving her car, her chauffeur beside her, mistakes a turning and takes a disused road leading to a quarry. The car crashes over the edge. Lady Frances and her chauffeur are killed."

There was a slight pause, then Bobby said:

"But we mightn't be. Plans go awry sometimes. One of yours did down in Wales."

"Your tolerance of morphia was certainly very remarkable, and—from our point of view—regrettable," said Nicholson. "But you need have no anxiety on my behalf this time. You and Lady Frances will be quite dead when your bodies are discovered."

Bobby shivered in spite of himself. There had been a queer note in Nicholson's voice—it was the tone of an artist contemplating a masterpiece.

"He enjoys this," thought Bobby. "Really enjoys it."

He was not going to give Nicholson any more cause for enjoyment than he had to, so he said in a casual tone of voice, "You're making a mistake—especially where Lady Frances is concerned."

"Yes," said Frankie. "In that very clever letter you forged you told me to tell nobody. Well, I made just one exception. I told Roger Bassington-ffrench. He knows all about you. If anything happens to us, he will know who is responsible for it. You'd better let us go and clear out of the country as fast as you can."

Nicholson was silent for a moment. Then he said, "A good bluff—but I call it."

He turned to the door.

"What about your wife, you swine?" cried Bobby. "Have you murdered her too?"

"Moira is still alive," said Nicholson. "How much longer she will remain so, I do not really know. It depends on circumstances."

He made them a mocking little bow.

"Au revoir," he said. "It will take me a couple of hours to complete my arrangements. You may enjoy talking the matter over. I shall not gag you unless it becomes necessary. You understand? Any calls for help and I return and deal with the matter."

He went out and closed and locked the door behind him.

"It isn't true," said Bobby. "It can't be true. These things don't happen."

But he could not help feeling that they were going to happen—and to him and Frankie.

"In books there's always an eleventh-hour rescue," said Frankie, trying to speak hopefully.

But she was not feeling very hopeful. In fact, her morale was decidedly low.

"The whole thing's so impossible," said Bobby as though pleading with someone. "So fantastic. Nicholson himself was absolutely unreal. I wish an eleventh-hour rescue were possible, but I can't see who's going to rescue us."

"If only I'd told Roger!" wailed Frankie.

"Perhaps in spite of everything Nicholson believes you have," suggested Bobby.

"No," said Frankie. "The suggestion didn't go down at all. The man's too damned clever."

"He's been too clever for us," said Bobby gloomily. "Frankie, do you know what annoys me most about this business?"

"No. What?"

"That even now, when we're going to be hurled into the next world, we still don't know who Evans is."

"Let's ask him," said Frankie. "You know—a last-minute boon. He can't refuse to tell us. I agree with you that I simply can't die without having my curiosity satisfied."

There was a silence, then Bobby asked: "Do you think we ought to yell for help—a sort of last chance? It's about the only chance we've got."

"Not yet," said Frankie. "In the first place I don't believe anyone would hear—he would never have risked keeping us here if anybody could—and in the second place I feel I just can't bear waiting here to be killed without being able to speak or be spoken to. Let's leave shouting till the last possible moment. It's—it's so comforting having you to talk to." Her voice wavered a little over the last words.

"I've got you into an awful mess, Frankie."

"Oh, that's all right. You couldn't have kept me out. I wanted to come in. Bobby, do you think he'll really pull it off? Us, I mean."

"I'm terribly afraid he will. He's so damnably efficient."

"Bobby, do you believe now that it was he who killed Henry Bassington-ffrench?"

"If it were possible—"

"It is possible, granted one thing—*that Sylvia Bassington-ffrench is in it too.*"

"Frankie!"

"I know. I was just as horrified when the idea occurred to me. But it fits. Why was Sylvia so dense about the morphia? Why did she resist so obstinately when we wanted her to send her husband somewhere else instead of the Grange? And then she was in the house when the shot was fired—"

"She might have done it herself."

"Oh, no—surely!"

"Yes, she might. And then have given the key of the study to Nicholson to put in Henry's pocket."

"It's all crazy," said Frankie in a hopeless voice. "Like looking through a distorting mirror. All the people who seemed most all right are really all wrong—all the nice, everyday people. There ought to be some way of telling criminals—eyebrows or ears or something."

"My God!" cried Bobby.

"What is it?"

"Frankie, that wasn't Nicholson who came here just now!"

"Have you gone quite mad? Who was it then?"

"I don't know—but it wasn't Nicholson. All along I felt there was something wrong—but couldn't spot it, and your saying 'ears' has given me the clue. When I was watching Nicholson the other evening through the window I specially noticed his ears—the lobes are joined to his face. But this man to-night—his ears weren't like that."

"But what does it mean?" Frankie asked hopelessly.

"This is a very clever actor impersonating Nicholson."

"But why—and who could it be?"

"Bassington-ffrench," breathed Bobby. *"Roger Bassington-ffrench.* We spotted the right man at the beginning and then—like idiots, we went astray after red herrings."

"Bassington-ffrench?" whispered Frankie. "Bobby, you're right. It must be. He was the only person there when I taunted Nicholson about accidents."

"Then it really *is* all up," said Bobby. "I've still had a kind of sneaking hope that possibly Roger Bassington-ffrench might nose out our trail by some miracle. But now the last hope's gone. Moira's a prisoner, you and I are tied hand and foot. Nobody else has the least idea where we are. The game's up Frankie."

As he finished speaking there was a sound overhead. The next minute, with a terrific crash, a heavy body fell through the skylight.

It was too dark to see anything.

"What the devil—" began Bobby.

From amidst a pile of broken glass a voice spoke.

"B-B-B-Bobby," it said.

"Well, I'm damned," said Bobby. "It's Badger!"

29

Badger's Story

There was not a minute to be lost. Already sounds could be heard on the floor below.

"Quick, Badger, you fool!" said Bobby. "Pull one of my boots off. Don't argue or ask questions! Haul it off somehow. Chuck it down in the middle there and crawl under that bed. *Quick*—I tell you."

Steps were ascending the stairs. The key turned.

Nicholson—the pseudo-Nicholson—stood in the doorway, candle in hand.

He saw Bobby and Frankie as he had left them, but in the middle of the floor was a pile of broken glass and in the middle of the broken glass was a boot!

Nicholson stared in amazement from the boot to Bobby. Bobby's left foot was bootless.

"Very clever, my young friend," he said drily. "Extremely acrobatic."

He came over to Bobby, examined the ropes that bound him and tied a couple of extra knots. He looked at him curiously.

"I wish I knew how you managed to throw that boot through the skylight. It seems almost incredible. A touch of the Houdini about you, my friend."

He looked at them both, up at the broken skylight, then shrugging his shoulders he left the room.

"Quick, Badger."

Badger crawled out from under the bed. He had a pocket-knife and with its aid he soon cut the other two free.

"That's better," said Bobby, stretching himself "Whew! I'm stiff. Well, Frankie? What about our friend Nicholson?"

"You're right," said Frankie. "It's Roger Bassington-ffrench. Now that I *know* he's Roger playing the part of Nicholson, I can *see* it. But it's a pretty good performance all the same."

"Entirely voice and prince-nez," said Bobby.

"I was at Oxford with a B-B-B-Bassington-ffrench," said Badger. "M-m-m-marvellous actor. B-b-b-bad hat, though. B-b-b-bad business about forging his p-p-p-pater's n-n-n-name to a cheque. Old m-m-man hushed it up."

In the minds of both Bobby and Frankie was the same thought. Badger, whom they had judged it wiser not to take into their confidence, could all along have given them valuable information!

"Forgery," said Frankie thoughtfully. "That letter from you, Bobby, was remarkably well done. I wonder how he knew your handwriting?"

"If he's in with the Caymans he probably saw my letter about the Evans business."

The voice of Badger rose plaintively.

"W-w-w-what are we going to do next?" he inquired.

"We're going to take up a comfortable position behind this door," said Bobby. "And when our friend returns—which I imagine won't be for a little while yet—you and I are going to spring on him from behind and give him the surprise of his life. How about it, Badger? Are you game?"

"Oh, absolutely!"

"As for you, Frankie, when you hear his step you'd

better get back onto your chair. He'll see you as soon as he opens the door and will come in without any suspicion."

"All right," said Frankie. "And once you and Badger have got him down I'll join in and bite his ankles or something."

"That's the true womanly spirit," said Bobby approvingly. "Now, let's all sit close together on the floor here and hear all about things. I want to know what miracle brought Badger through that skylight just in the nick of time."

"Well, you s-s-see," said Badger, "after you w-w-went off, I got into a bit of a m-m-m-mess."

He paused. Gradually the story was extracted—a tale of liabilities, creditors, and bailiffs—a typical Badger catastrophe. Bobby had gone off leaving no address, only saying that he was driving the Bentley down to Staverley. So to Staverley came Badger.

"I thought p-p-p-perhaps you m-m-m-might be able to let me have a f-f-fiver," he explained.

Bobby's heart smote him. To aid Badger in his enterprise he had come to London and had promptly deserted his post to go off sleuthing with Frankie. And even now the faithful Badger uttered no word of reproach.

Badger had no wish to endanger Bobby's mysterious enterprises, but he was of the opinion that a car like the green Bentley would not be difficult to find in a place the size of Staverley. As a matter of fact he came across the car before he got to Staverley, for it was standing outside a pub—empty.

"S-s-so I thought," went on Badger, "that I'd give you a little s-s-s-surprise, don't you know? There were some r-r-rugs and things in the b-b-back and nobody about. I g-g-got in and p-p-p-pulled them over me. I thought I'd give you the s-s-surprise of your life."

What actually happened was that a chauffeur in green livery had emerged from the pub and that Badger, peering from his place of concealment, was thunderstruck to perceive that this chauffeur was not Bobby. He had an idea that the face was in some way familiar to him but couldn't place the man. The stranger got into the car and drove off.

Badger was in a predicament. He did not know what to do next. Explanations and apologies were difficult, and in any case it is not easy to explain to someone who is driving a car at sixty miles an hour. Badger decided to lie low and sneak out of the car when it stopped.

The car finally reached its destination—Tudor Cottage. The chauffeur drove it into the garage and left it there, but on going out he shut the garage doors. Badger was a prisoner. There was a small window at one side of the garage and through this, about half an hour later, Badger had observed Frankie's approach, her whistle and her admission into the house.

The whole business puzzled Badger greatly. He began to suspect that something was wrong. At any rate he determined to have a look round for himself and see what it was all about.

With the help of some tools lying about in the garage he succeeded in picking the lock of the garage door and set out on a tour of inspection. The windows on the ground floor were all shuttered, but he thought that by getting onto the roof he might manage to have a look into some of the upper windows. The roof presented no difficulties. There was a convenient pipe running up the garage, and from the garage roof to the roof of the cottage was an easy climb. In the course of his prowling

Badger had come upon the sky-light. Nature and Badger's weight had done the rest.

Bobby drew a long breath as the narrative came to an end.

"All the same," he said reverently, "you are a miracle—a singularly beautiful miracle! But for you, Badger, my lad, Frankie and I would have been little corpses in about an hour's time."

He gave Badger a condensed account of the activities of himself and Frankie. Towards the end, he broke off.

"Someone's coming. Get to your post, Frankie. Now then, this is where our play-acting Bassington-ffrench gets the surprise of his life."

Frankie arranged herself in a depressed attitude on the broken chair. Badger and Bobby stood ready behind the door.

The steps came up the stairs, a line of candle-light showed underneath the door. The key was put in the lock and turned, the door swung open. The light of the candle disclosed Frankie drooping dejectedly on her chair. Their jailor stepped through the doorway.

Then, joyously, Badger and Bobby sprang.

The proceedings were short and decisive. Taken utterly by surprise, the man was knocked down, the candle flew wide and was retrieved by Frankie, and a few seconds later the three friends stood looking down with malicious pleasure at a figure securely bound with the same ropes that had previously secured two of them.

"Good-evening, Mr. Bassington-ffrench," said Bobby, and if the exultation in his voice was a little crude, who shall blame him?—"It's a nice night for the funeral."

30

Escape

The man on the floor stared up at them. His pince-nez had flown off and so had his hat. There could be no further attempt at disguise. Slight traces of make-up were visible about the eyebrows, but otherwise the face was the pleasant, slightly vacuous face of Roger Bassington-ffrench.

He spoke in his own agreeable tenor voice, its note that of pleasant soliloquy.

"Very interesting," he said. "I really knew quite well that no man tied up as you were *could* have thrown a boot through that skylight. But because the boot was there among the broken glass I took it for cause and effect and assumed that, though it was impossible, the impossible had been achieved. An interesting light on the limitations of the brain."

As nobody spoke, he went on still in the same reflective voice.

"So, after all, you've won the round. Most unexpected and extremely regrettable. I thought I'd got you all fooled nicely."

"So you had," said Frankie. "You forged that letter from Bobby, I suppose?"

"I have a talent that way," said Roger modestly.

"And Bobby?"

Lying on his back, smiling agreeably, Roger seemed

to take a positive pleasure in enlightening them.

"I knew he'd go to the Grange. I only had to wait about in the bushes near the path. I was just behind him there when he retreated after rather clumsily falling off a tree. I let the hubbub die down and then got him neatly on the back of the neck with a sandbag. All I had to do was to carry him out to where my car was waiting, shove him in the dickey and drive him here. I was at home again before morning."

"And Moira?" demanded Bobby. "Did you entice her away somehow?"

Roger chuckled. The question seemed to amuse him. "Forgery is a very useful art, my dear Jones," he said.

"You swine," said Bobby.

Frankie intervened. She was still full of curiosity, and their prisoner seemed in an obliging mood.

"Why did you pretend to be Dr. Nicholson?" she asked.

"Why did I now?" Roger seemed to be asking the question of himself. "Partly, I think, the fun of seeing whether I could spoof you both. You were so very sure that poor old Nicholson was in it up to the neck." He laughed, and Frankie blushed. "Just because he cross-questioned you a bit about the details of your accident—in his pompous way. It was an irritating fad of his—accuracy in details."

"And really," said Frankie slowly, "he was quite innocent?"

"As a child unborn," said Roger. "But he did *me* a good turn. He drew my attention to that accident of yours. That and another incident made me realize that you mightn't be quite the innocent young thing you seemed to be. And then I was standing by you when you telephoned one morning and I heard your chauffeur's voice say 'Frankie.' I've got pretty good hearing. I sug-

gested coming up to town with you and you agreed—
but you were very much relieved when I changed my
mind. After that—" He stopped and as far as he was
able shrugged his bound shoulders. "It was rather fun
seeing you get all worked up about Nicholson. He's a
harmless old ass, but he does look exactly like a scien-
tific super-criminal on the films. I thought I might as
well keep the deception up. After all, you never know.
The best-laid plans go wrong, as my present predicament
shows."

"There's one thing you *must* tell me," said Frankie.
"I've been driven nearly mad with curiosity. Who is
Evans?"

"Oh!" said Bassington-ffrench. "So you don't know
that?"

He laughed—and laughed again.

"That's rather amusing," he said. "It shows what a
fool one can be."

"Meaning us?" asked Frankie.

"No," said Roger. "In this case, meaning me. Do you
know, if you don't know who Evans is, I don't think I
shall tell you. I'll keep that to myself as my own little
secret."

The position was a curious one. They had turned the
tables on Bassington-ffrench, and yet, in some peculiar
way, he had robbed them of their triumph. Lying on the
floor, bound and a prisoner, it was he who dominated
the situation.

"And what are your plans now, may I ask?" he inquired.

Nobody had as yet evolved any plans. Bobby rather
doubtfully murmured something about police.

"Much the best thing to do," said Roger cheerfully.
"Ring them up and hand me over to them. The charge
will be abduction, I suppose. I can't very well deny

that." He looked at Frankie. "I shall plead a guilty passion."

Frankie reddened. "What about murder?" she asked.

"My dear, you haven't any evidence. Positively none. Think it over and you'll see you haven't."

"Badger," said Bobby, "you'd better stay here and keep an eye on him. I'll go down and ring up the police."

"You'd better be careful," said Frankie. "We don't know how many of them there may be in the house."

"No one but me," said Roger. "I was carrying this through single-handed."

"I'm not prepared to take your word for that," said Bobby gruffly.

He bent over and tested the knots.

"He's all right," he said. "Safe as houses. We'd better all go down together. We can lock the door."

"Terribly distrustful, aren't you, my dear chap?" said Roger. "There's a pistol in my pocket if you'd like it. It may make you feel happier, and it's certainly no good to me in my present position."

Ignoring the other's mocking tone, Bobby bent down and extracted the weapon.

"Kind of you to mention it," he said. "If you want to know, it does make me feel happier."

"Good," said Roger. "It's loaded."

Bobby took the candle and they filed out of the attic, leaving Roger lying on the floor. Bobby locked the door and put the key in his pocket. He held the pistol in his hand.

"I'll go first," he said. "We've got to be quite sure and not make a mess of things now."

"He's a qu-qu-queer chap, isn't he?" said Badger with a jerk of his head backwards in the direction of the room they had left.

"He's a damned good loser," said Frankie.

Even now, she was not quite free from the charm of that very remarkable young man, Roger Bassington-ffrench.

A rather rickety flight of steps led down to the main landing. Everything was quiet. Bobby looked over the banisters. The telephone was in the hall below.

"We'd better look into these rooms first," he said. "We don't want to be taken in the rear."

Badger flung open each door in turn. Of the four bedrooms, three were empty. In the fourth a slender figure was lying on the bed.

"It's Moira!" cried Frankie.

The others crowded in. Moira was lying like one dead except that her breast moved up and down ever so slightly.

"Is she asleep?" asked Bobby.

"She's drugged, I think," said Frankie.

She looked round. A hypodermic syringe lay on a little enamel tray on a table near the window. There was also a little spirit-lamp and a type of morphia hypodermic needle.

"She'll be all right, I think," she said. "But we ought to get a doctor."

"Let's go down and telephone," said Bobby.

They adjourned to the hall below. Frankie had a half fear that the telephone wires might be cut, but her fears proved quite unfounded. They got through to the police station quite easily, but found a good deal of difficulty in explaining matters. The local police were highly disposed to regard the summons as a practical joke.

However, they were convinced at last, and Bobby replaced the receiver with a sigh. He had explained that they also wanted a doctor, and the police constable promised to bring one along.

Ten minutes later a car arrived with an inspector, a

constable, and an elderly man who had his profession stamped all over him.

Bobby and Frankie received them and after explaining matters once more in a somewhat perfunctory fashion led the way to the attic. Bobby unlocked the door—then stood dumbfounded in the doorway. In the middle of the floor was a heap of severed ropes. Underneath the broken skylight a chair had been placed on the bed which had been dragged out till it was under the skylight.

Of Roger Bassington-ffrench there was no sign.

"Talk of Houdini," said Bobby. "He must have out-Houdini'd Houdini. How the devil did he cut these cords?"

"He must have had a knife in his pocket," said Frankie.

"Even then, how could he get at it? Both hands were bound together behind his back."

The inspector coughed. All his former doubts had returned. He was more strongly disposed than ever to regard the whole thing as a hoax.

Frankie and Bobby found themselves telling a long story which sounded more impossible every minute.

The doctor was their salvation. On being taken to the room where Moira was lying he declared at once that she had been drugged with morphia or some preparation of opium. He did not consider her condition serious and thought she would awake naturally in four or five hours' time.

He suggested taking her off then and there to a good nursing home in the neighborhood.

To this Bobby and Frankie agreed, not seeing what else could be done. Having given their own names and addresses to the inspector, who appeared to disbelieve utterly in Frankie's, they themselves were allowed to leave Tudor Cottage, and with the assistance of the inspector succeeded in gaining admission to the "Seven Stars" in the village.

Here, still feeling that they were regarded as criminals, they were only too thankful to go to their rooms, a double one for Bobby and Badger, and a very minute single one for Frankie.

A few minutes after they had all retired, a knock came on Bobby's door. It was Frankie.

"I've thought of something," she said. "If that fool of a police inspector persists in thinking that we made all this up, at any rate I've got evidence that I was chloroformed."

"Have you? Where?"

"In the coal-bucket," said Frankie with decision.

31

Frankie Asks a Question

Exhausted by all her adventures, Frankie slept late the next morning. It was half-past ten when she came down to the small coffee-room to find Bobby waiting for her.

"Hullo, Frankie, here you are at last."

"Don't be so horribly vigorous, my dear!" Frankie subsided onto a chair.

"What will you have? They've got haddock and eggs and bacon and cold ham."

"I shall have some toast and weak tea," said Frankie, quelling him. "What is the matter with you?"

"It must be the sandbagging," said Bobby. "It's probably broken up adhesions in the brain. I feel absolutely full of pep and vim and bright ideas and a longing to dash out and do things."

"Well, why not dash?" said Frankie languidly.

"I have dashed. I've been with Inspector Hammond for the last half-hour. We'll have to let it go as a practical joke, Frankie, for the moment."

"Oh, but, Bobby—"

"I said *for the moment*. We've got to get to the bottom of this, Frankie. We're on the right spot and all we've got to do is to get down to it. We don't want Roger Bassington-ffrench for abduction. We want him for *murder*."

"And we'll get him," said Frankie with a revival of spirit.

"That's more like it," said Bobby approvingly. "Drink some more tea."

"How's Moira?"

"Pretty bad. She came round in the most awful state of nerves. Scared stiff apparently. She's gone up to London—to a nursing home place in Queen's Gate. She says she'll feel safe there. She was terrified here."

"She never did have much nerve," said Frankie.

"Well, anyone might be scared stiff with a queer cold-blooded murderer like Roger Bassington-ffrench loose in the neighborhood."

"He doesn't want to murder *her*. We're the ones he's after."

"He's probably too busy taking care of himself to worry about us for the moment," said Bobby. "Now, Frankie, we've got to get down to it. The start of the whole thing must be John Savage's death and will. There's something wrong about it. Either that will was forged or Savage was murdered or something."

"It's quite likely the will was forged if Bassington-ffrench was concerned," said Frankie thoughtfully. "Forgery seems to be his speciality."

"It may have been forgery *and* murder. We've got to find out."

Frankie nodded. "I've got the notes I made after looking at the will. The witnesses were Rose Chudleigh, cook, and Albert Mere, gardener. They ought to be quite easy to find. Then there are the lawyers who drew it up—Elford & Leigh—a very respectable firm, as Mr. Spragge said."

"Right, we'll start from there. I think you'd better take the lawyers. You'll get more out of them than I would. I'll hunt up Rose Chudleigh and Albert Mere."

"What about Badger?"

"Badger never gets up till lunch time—you needn't worry about him."

"We must get his affairs straightened out for him some time," said Frankie. "After all, he did save my life."

"They'll soon get tangled again," said Bobby. "Oh, by the way, what do you think of this?"

He held out a dirty piece of cardboard for her inspection. It was a photograph.

"Mr. Cayman," said Frankie immediately. "Where did you get it?"

"Last night. It had slipped down behind the telephone."

"Then it seems pretty clear who Mr. and Mrs. Templeton were. Wait a minute."

A waitress had just approached bearing toast. Frankie displayed the photograph.

"Do you know who that is?" she asked.

The waitress regarded the photograph, her head a little on one side. "Now, I've seen the gentleman—but I can't quite call to mind. Oh, yes—it's the gentleman who had Tudor Cottage—Mr. Templeton. They've gone away now—somewhere abroad, I believe."

"What sort of man was he?" asked Frankie.

"I really couldn't say. They didn't come down here very often—just week-ends now and then. Nobody saw much of him. Mrs. Templeton was a very nice lady. But they hadn't had Tudor Cottage very long—only about six months—when a very rich gentleman died and left Mrs. Templeton all his money, and they went to live abroad. They never sold Tudor Cottage, though. I think they sometimes lend it to people for week-ends. But I don't suppose with all that money they'll ever come back here and live in it themselves."

"They had a cook called Rose Chudleigh, didn't they?" asked Frankie.

But the girl seemed uninterested in cooks. Being left a fortune by a rich gentleman was what really stirred her imagination. In answer to Frankie's question she replied that she couldn't say, she was sure, and withdrew carrying an empty toast-rack.

"That's all plain sailing," said Frankie. "The Caymans have given up coming here, but they keep the place on for the convenience of the gang."

They agreed to divide the labor as Bobby had suggested. Frankie went off in the Bentley, having smartened herself up by a few local purchases, and Bobby went off in quest of Albert Mere, gardener.

They met at lunch time.

"Well?" demanded Bobby.

Frankie shook her head. "Forgery's out of the question." She spoke in a dispirited voice. "I spent a long time with Mr. Elford—he's rather an old dear. He'd got wind of some of our doings last night and was wild to hear a few details. I don't suppose they get much excitement down here. Anyway, I soon got him eating out of my hand. Then I discussed the Savage case—pretended I'd met some of the Savage relations and that they'd hinted at forgery. At that my old dear bristled up—absolutely out of the question! It wasn't a question of letters or anything like that. He saw Mr. Savage himself, and Mr. Savage insisted on the will's being drawn up then and there. Mr. Elford wanted to go away and do it properly—you know how they do—sheets and sheets all about nothing—"

"I don't know," said Bobby. "I've never made any wills."

"I have—two. The second was this morning. I had to have some excuse for seeing a lawyer."

"Whom did you leave your money to?"

"You."

"That was a bit thoughtless, wasn't it? If Roger-Bassington-ffrench succeeded in bumping you off I should probably be hanged for it!"

"I never thought of that," said Frankie. "Well, as I was saying, Mr. Savage was so nervous and wrought up that Mr. Elford wrote out the will then and there, and the servant and the gardener came and witnessed it, and Mr. Elford took it away with him for safe keeping."

"That does seem to knock out forgery," agreed Bobby.

"I know. You can't have forgery when you've actually seen the man sign his name. As to the other business—murder, it's going to be hard to find out anything about that now. The doctor who was called in has died since. The man we saw last night is a new man. He's been here only about two months."

"We seem to have rather an unfortunate number of deaths," said Bobby.

"Why, who else is dead?"

"Albert Mere."

"Do you think they've *all* been put out of the way?"

"That seems rather wholesale. We might give Albert Mere the benefit of the doubt—he was seventy-two, poor old man."

"All right," said Frankie. "I'll allow you Natural Causes in his case. Any luck with Rose Chudleigh?"

"Yes. After she left the Templetons she went to the north of England to a place, but she's come back and married a man down here whom it seems she's been walking out with for the last seventeen years. Unfortunately she's a bit of a nitwit. She doesn't seem to remember anything about anyone. Perhaps you could do something with her."

"I'll have a go," said Frankie. "I'm rather good with nitwits. Where's Badger, by the way?"

"Good Lord, I've forgotten all about him." said Bobby.

He got up and left the room, returning a few minutes later.

"He was still asleep," he explained. "He's getting up now. A chambermaid seems to have called him four times, but it didn't make any impression."

"Well, we'd better go and see the nitwit," said Frankie, rising. "And then I *must* buy a toothbrush and a nightgown and a sponge and a few other necessities of civilized existence. I was so close to Nature last night that I didn't think about any of them. I just stripped off my outer covering and fell upon the bed."

"I know," said Bobby. "So did I."

"Let's go and talk to Rose Chudleigh," said Frankie.

Rose Chudleigh, now Mrs. Pratt, lived in a small cottage that seemed to be overflowing with china dogs and furniture. Mrs. Pratt herself was a bovine-looking woman of ample proportions, with fish-like eyes and every indication of adanoids.

"You see, I've come back," said Bobby breezily.

Mrs. Pratt breathed hard and looked at them both incuriously.

"We were so interested to hear that you had lived with Mrs. Templeton," explained Frankie.

"Yes, ma'am," said Mrs. Pratt.

"She's living abroad now, I believe," continued Frankie, trying to give an impression of being an intimate of the family.

"I've heard so," agreed Mrs. Pratt.

"You were with her for some time, weren't you?" asked Frankie.

"Were I which, ma'am?"

"With Mrs. Templeton for some time," said Frankie, speaking slowly and clearly.

"I wouldn't say that, ma'am. Only two months."

"Oh! I thought you'd been with her longer than that."

"That was Gladys, ma'am. The house-parlormaid. She was there six months."

"There were two of you?"

"That's right. House-parlormaid she was, and I was cook."

"You were there when Mr. Savage died, weren't you?"

"I beg your pardon, ma'am?"

"You were there when Mr. Savage died?"

"Mr. Templeton didn't die—at least I haven't heard so. He went abroad."

"Not Mr. Templeton—Mr. Savage," said Bobby.

Mrs. Pratt looked at him vacantly.

"The gentleman who left her all the money," said Frankie.

A gleam of something like intelligence passed across Mrs. Pratt's face.

"Oh, yes, ma'am—the gentleman there was the inquest on."

"That's right," said Frankie, delighted with her success. "He used to come and stay quite often, didn't he?"

"I couldn't say as to that, ma'am. I'd only just come, you see. Gladys would know."

"But you had to witness his will, didn't you?"

Mrs. Pratt looked blank.

"You went and saw him sign a paper, and you had to sign it too?"

Again the gleam of intelligence. "Yes, ma'am. Me and Albert. I'd never done such a thing before, and I didn't like it. I said to Gladys, 'I don't like signing a paper, and that's a fact,' and Gladys she said it must be all right because Mr. Elford was there and he was a very nice gentleman as well as being a lawyer."

"What happened exactly?" asked Bobby.

"I beg your pardon, sir?"

"Who called you to sign your name?" asked Frankie.

"The mistress, sir. She came into the kitchen and said would I go outside and call Albert, and would we both come up to the best bedroom (which she'd moved out of for Mr.—the gentleman—the night before), and there was the gentleman sitting up in bed—he'd come back from London and gone straight to bed—and a very ill-looking gentleman he was. I hadn't seen him before, but he looked something ghastly. And Mr. Elford was there too, and he spoke very nice and said there was nothing to be afraid of and I was to sign my name where the gentleman had signed his, and I did and put 'cook' after it, and the address. And Albert did the same, and I went down to Gladys all of a tremble and said I'd never seen a gentleman look so like death, and Gladys said he'd looked all right the night before, and that it must have been something in London that had upset him. He'd gone up to London very early before anyone was up. And then I said about not liking to write my name to anything, and Gladys said it was all right because Mr. Elford was there."

"And Mr. Savage—the gentleman—died—when?"

"Next morning as ever was, ma'am. He shut himself up in his room that night and wouldn't let anyone go near him, and when Gladys called him in the morning he was all stiff and dead, and a letter propped up by his bedside—'To the Coroner,' it said. Oh, it gave Gladys a regular turn! And then there was an inquest and everything. And two months later Mrs. Templeton told me she was going abroad to live. But she got me a very good place up north with big wages, and she gave me a nice present and everything. A very nice lady, Mrs. Templeton."

Mrs. Pratt was by now thoroughly enjoying her own loquacity.

Frankie rose.

"Well," she said, "it's been very nice to hear all this." She slipped a note out of her purse. "You must let me leave you a—er—little present. I've taken up so much of your time."

"Well, thank you kindly, I'm sure, ma'am. Good-day to you and your good gentleman."

Frankie blushed and retreated rather rapidly. Bobby followed her after a few minutes. He looked preoccupied.

"Well," he said, "we seem to have got at all she knows."

"Yes," said Frankie. "And it hangs together. There seems no doubt that Savage *did* make that will, and I suppose his fear of cancer was genuine enough. They couldn't very well bribe a Harley Street doctor. I suppose they just took advantage of his having made that will to do away with him quickly before he changed his mind. But how we or anyone else can prove they *did* make away with him I can't see."

"I know. We may suspect that Mrs. T. gave him 'something to make him sleep,' but we can't prove it. Bassington-ffrench may have forged the letter to the Coroner, but that again we can't prove by now. I expect the letter is destroyed long ago after being put in as evidence at the inquest."

"So we come back to the old problem—what on earth are Bassington-ffrench & Co. so afraid of our discovering?"

"Nothing strikes you as odd particularly?"

"No, I don't think so—or at least only one thing. Why

did Mrs. Templeton send out for the gardener to come and witness the will, when the house-parlormaid was in the house? Why didn't they ask the parlor-maid?"

"It's odd your saying that, Frankie," said Bobby.

His voice sounded so queer that Frankie looked at him in surprise. "Why?"

"Because I stayed behind to ask Mrs. Pratt for Gladys's name and address."

"Well?"

"The parlormaid's name was Evans."

32

Evans

Frankie gasped.

Bobby's voice rose excitedly. "You see, you've asked the same question that Carstairs asked. *Why didn't they ask the parlormaid? Why didn't they ask Evans?*"

"Oh, Bobby, we're getting there at last!"

"The same thing must have struck Carstairs. He was nosing round, just as we were looking for something fishy—and this point struck him, just as it struck us. And moreover I believe he came to Wales for that reason. Gladys Evans is a Welsh name—Evans was probably a Welsh girl. He was following her to Marchbolt. And someone was following him—and so he never got to her."

"Why *didn't* they ask Evans?" said Frankie. "There *must* be a reason. It's such a silly little point—and yet it's important. With a couple of maids in the house, why send out for a gardener?"

"Perhaps because both Chudleigh and Albert Mere were chumps, whereas Evans was rather a sharp girl."

"It can't be only that. Mr. Elford was there and he's quite shrewd. Oh, Bobby, the whole situation is there—I know it is. If we could just get at the reason. Evans. Why Chudleigh and Mere and not Evans?"

Suddenly she stopped and put both hands over her eyes.

"It's coming," she said. "Just a sort of flicker. It'll come in a minute."

She stayed dead still for a minute or two, then removed her hands and looked at her companion with an odd flicker in her eyes.

"Bobby," she said, "if you're staying in a house with two servants which do you tip?"

"The house-parlormaid, of course," said Bobby, surprised. "One never tips a cook. One never sees her, for one thing."

"No, and she never sees you. At most she might catch a glimpse of you if you were there for some time. But a house-parlormaid waits on you at dinner and calls you and hands you coffee."

"What are you getting at, Frankie?"

"They couldn't have Evans witnessing that will—*because Evans would have known that it wasn't Mr. Savage who was making it.*"

"Good Lord, Frankie, what do you mean? Who was it then?"

"Bassington-ffrench, of course! Don't you see, he impersonated Savage? I bet it was Bassington-ffrench who went to that doctor and made all that fuss about having cancer. Then the lawyer is sent for—a stranger who doesn't know Mr. Savage but who will be able to swear that he saw 'Mr. Savage' sign that will, and it's witnessed by two people, one of whom hadn't seen him before and the other an old man who was probably pretty blind and who probably had never seen Savage either. Now do you see?"

"But where was the real Savage all that time?"

"Oh, he arrived all right, and then I suspect they drugged him and put him in the attic, perhaps, and kept him there for twelve hours while Bassington-ffrench did his impersonation stunt. Then he was put back in his bed and given chloral, and Evans finds him dead in the morning."

"My God, I believe you've hit it, Frankie! But can we prove it?"

"Yes—no—I don't know. Supposing Rose Chudleigh—Pratt, I mean—were shown a photograph of the real Savage? Would she be able to say, 'That wasn't the man who signed the will'?"

"I doubt it," said Bobby. "She is such a nitwit."

"Chosen for that purpose, I expect. But there's another thing: an expert ought to be able to detect that the signature is a forgery."

"They didn't before."

"Because nobody ever raised the question. There didn't seem any possible moment when the will *could* have been forged. But now it's different."

"One thing we must do," said Bobby. "Find Evans. She may be able to tell us a lot. She was with the Templetons for six months, remember."

Frankie groaned. "That's going to make it even more difficult."

"How about the post office?" suggested Bobby.

They were just passing it. In appearance it was more of a general store than a post office.

Frankie darted inside and opened the campaign. There was no one in the shop except the postmistress, a young woman with an inquisitive nose.

Frankie bought a two-shilling book of stamps, commented on the weather and then said:

"But I expect you always have better weather here than we do in my part of the world. I live in Wales—Marchbolt. You wouldn't believe the rain we have."

The young woman with the nose said that they had a good deal of rain themselves and last Bank Holiday it had rained something cruel.

Frankie said, "There's someone in Marchbolt who comes from this part of the world. I wonder if you know her. Her name was Evans—Gladys Evans."

The young woman was quite unsuspicious.

"Why, of course," she said. "She was in service here. At Tudor Cottage. But she didn't come from these parts. She came from Wales, and she went back there and married—Roberts her name is now."

"That's right," said Frankie. "You can't give me her address, I suppose? I borrowed a raincoat from her and forgot to give it back. If I had her address I'd post it to her."

"Well, now," the other replied, "I believe I can. I get a p.c. from her now and again. She and her husband have gone into service together. Wait a minute now."

She went away and rummaged in a corner. Presently she returned with a piece of paper in her hand.

"Here you are," she said, pushing it across the counter.

Bobby and Frankie read it together. It was the last thing in the world they expected.

Mrs. Roberts,
The Vicarage,
Marchbolt,
Wales.

33

Sensation in the Orient Café

How Bobby and Frankie got out of the post office without disgracing themselves neither of them ever knew.

Outside, with one accord, they looked at each other and shook with laughter.

"At the Vicarage—all the time!" gasped Bobby.

"And I looked through four hundred and eighty Evanses!" lamented Frankie.

"*Now* I see why Bassington-ffrench was so amused when he realized we didn't know in the least who Evans was!"

"And of course it was dangerous from their point of view. You and Evans were actually under the same roof."

"Come on," said Bobby. "Marchbolt's the next place."

"Like where the rainbow ends," said Frankie. "Back to the dear old home."

"Dash it all," said Bobby, "we must do something about Badger. Have you any money, Frankie?"

Frankie opened her bag and took out a handful of notes.

"Give these to him and tell him to make some arrangement with his creditors, and say that Father will buy the garage and put him in as manager."

"All right," said Bobby. "The great thing is to get off quickly."

"Why this frightful haste?"

"I don't know—but I've a feeling something might happen."

"How awful! Let's go ever so quickly."

"I'll settle Badger. You go and start the car."

"I shall never buy that toothbrush," said Frankie.

Five minutes saw them speeding out of Chipping Somerton. Bobby had no occasion to complain of lack of speed.

Nevertheless, Frankie suddenly said, "Look here, Bobby, this isn't quick enough."

Bobby glanced at the speedometer needle, which was, at the moment, registering eighty, and remarked drily, "I don't see what more we can do."

"We can take an air taxi," said Frankie. "We're only about seven miles from Medeshot Aerodrome."

"My dear girl!" said Bobby.

"If we do that we'll be home in a couple of hours."

"Good," said Bobby. "Let's take an air taxi."

The whole proceeding was beginning to take on the fantastic character of a dream. Why this wild hurry to get to Marchbolt? Bobby didn't know. He suspected that Frankie didn't know either. It was just a feeling.

At Medeshot Frankie asked for Mr. Donald King, and an untidy-looking young man was produced who appeared languidly surprised at the sight of her.

"Hullo, Frankie," he said. "I haven't seen you for an age. What do you want?"

"I want an air taxi," said Frankie. "You do that sort of thing, don't you?"

"Oh, yes. Where do you want to go?"

"I want to get home quickly," said Frankie.

Mr. Donald King raised his eyebrows. "Is that all?" he asked.

"Not quite," said, Frankie. "But it's the main idea."

"Oh, well, we can soon fix you up."

"I'll give you a cheque," said Frankie.

Five minutes later they were off.

"Frankie," said Bobby, "why are we doing this?"

"I haven't the faintest idea," said Frankie. "But I feel we must. Don't you?"

"Curiously enough, I do. But I don't know why. After all, our Mrs. Roberts won't fly away on a broomstick."

"She might. Remember, we don't know what Bassington-ffrench is up to."

"That's true," said Bobby thoughtfully.

It was growing late when they reached their destination. The plane landed them in the Park, and five minutes later Bobby and Frankie were driving into Marchbolt in Lord Marchington's Chrysler.

They pulled up outside the Vicarage gate, the Vicarage drive not lending itself to the turning of expensive cars.

Then jumping out they ran up the drive.

"I shall wake up soon," thought Bobby. "What are we doing and why?"

A slender figure was standing on the doorstep. Frankie and Bobby recognized her at the same minute.

"Moira!" cried Frankie.

Moira turned. She was swaying slightly. "Oh, I'm so glad to see you. I don't know what to do."

"But what on earth brings you here?"

"The same thing that has brought you, I expect."

"You have found out who Evans is?" asked Bobby.

Moira nodded. "Yes, it's a long story—"

"Come inside," said Bobby.

But Moira shrank back. "No, no," she said hurriedly.

"Let's go somewhere and talk. There's something I must tell you—before we go into the house. Isn't there a café or some place like that in the town? Somewhere where we could go?"

"All right," said Bobby, moving unwillingly away from the door. "But why—"

Moira stamped her foot. "You'll see when I tell you. Oh, do come! There's not a minute to lose."

They yielded to her urgency. About halfway down the main street was the Orient Café, whose somewhat grand name was not borne out by the interior decoration. The three of them filed in. It was a slack moment—half-past six.

They sat down at a small table in the corner, and Bobby ordered three coffees.

"Now then?" he said.

"Wait till she's brought the coffee," said Moira.

The waitress returned and listlessly deposited three cups of tepid coffee in front of them.

"Now then," said Bobby again.

"I hardly know where to begin," said Moira. "It was in the train going to London. Really the most amazing coincidence. I went along the corridor and—"

She broke off. Her seat faced the door and she leant forward staring.

"He must have followed me," she said.

"Who?" cried Frankie and Bobby together.

"Bassington-ffrench," whispered Moira.

"You've seen him?"

"He's outside. I saw him. With a woman with red hair."

"Mrs. Cayman," cried Frankie.

She and Bobby jumped and ran to the door. A protest came from Moira, but neither of them heeded it. They looked up and down the street but Bassington-ffrench was nowhere in sight.

Moira joined them.

"Has he gone?" she asked, her voice trembling. "Oh! do be careful. He's dangerous—horribly dangerous."

"He can't do anything so long as we're all together," said Bobby.

"Brace up, Moira," said Frankie. "Don't be such a rabbit."

"Well, we can't do anything for the moment," said Bobby, leading the way back to the table. "Go on with what you were telling us, Moira."

He picked up his cup of coffee. Frankie lost her balance and fell against him, and the coffee poured over the table.

"Sorry," said Frankie.

She stretched over to the adjoining table, which was laid for possible diners. There was a cruet on it with two glass-stoppered bottles containing oil and vinegar.

The oddity of Frankie's proceedings riveted Bobby's attention. She took the vinegar bottle, emptied out the vinegar into the slop-bowl and began to pour coffee into it from her cup.

"Have you gone batty, Frankie?" asked Bobby. "What the devil are you doing?"

"Taking a sample of this coffee for George Arbuthnot to analyze," said Frankie.

She turned to Moira.

"*The game's up, Moira!* The whole thing came to me in a flash as we stood at the door just now! When I jogged Bobby's elbow and made him spill his coffee I saw your face. You put something in our cups when you sent us running to the door to look for Bassington-ffrench. The game's up, *Mrs. Nicholson or Templeton or whatever you like to call yourself!*"

"Templeton?" cried Bobby.

"Look at her face," cried Frankie. "If she denies it, ask her to come to the Vicarage and see if Mrs. Roberts doesn't identify her."

Bobby did look at her. He saw that face—that haunting, wistful face—transformed by a demoniac rage. The beautiful mouth opened and a stream of foul and hideous curses poured out. She fumbled in her handbag.

Bobby was still dazed, but he acted in the nick of time. It was his hand that struck the pistol up.

The bullet passed over Frankie's head and buried itself in the wall of the Orient Café.

For the first time in its history one of the waitresses hurried. With a wild scream she shot out into the street calling: "Help! *Murder!* POLICE!"

Letter from South America

It was some weeks later.

Frankie had just received a letter. It bore the stamp of one of the less-known South American republics.

After reading it through, she passed it to Bobby.

It ran as follows:

DEAR FRANKIE:

Really, I congratulate you! You and your young Naval friend have shattered the plans of a lifetime. I had everything so nicely arranged.

Would you really like to hear all about it? My lady friend has given me away so thoroughly (spite, I'm afraid—women are invariably spiteful!) that my most damaging admissions won't do me any further harm. Besides, I am starting life again. Roger Bassington-ffrench is dead.

I fancy I've always been what they call a "wrong 'un." Even at Oxford I had a little lapse. Stupid, because it was bound to be found out. The Pater didn't let me down. But he sent me to the Colonies.

I fell in with Moira and her lot fairly soon. She was the real thing. She was an accomplished criminal by the time she was fifteen. When I met her things were getting a bit too hot for her. The American police were on her trail.

She and I liked each other. We decided to make a match of it, but we'd a few plans to carry through first.

To begin with, she married Nicholson. By doing so she removed herself to another world, and the police lost sight of her. Nicholson was just coming over to England to start a place for nerve patients. He was looking for a suitable house to buy cheap. Moira got him on to the Grange.

She was still working in with her gang in the dope business. Without knowing it, Nicholson was very useful to her.

I had always had two ambitions. I wanted to be the owner of Merroway, and I wanted to command an immense amount of money. A Bassington-ffrench played a great part in the reign of Charles II. Since then the family has dwindled down to mediocrity. I felt capable of playing a great part again. But I had to have money.

Moira made several trips across to Canada to "see her people." Nicholson adored her and believed anything she told him. Most men did. Owing to the complications of the drug business she travelled under various names. She was travelling as Mrs. Templeton when she met Savage. She knew all about Savage and his enormous wealth, and she went all out for him. He was attracted, but he wasn't attracted enough to lose his common sense.

However, we concocted a plan. You know pretty well the story of that. The man you know as Cayman acted the part of the unfeeling husband. Savage was induced to come down and stay at Tudor Cottage more than once. The third time he came our plans were laid. I needn't go into all that—you know it. The whole thing went with a bang. Moira cleared the money and went off—ostensibly abroad—in reality back to Staverley and the Grange.

In the meantime I was perfecting my own plans. Henry and young Tommy had to be got out of the way. I had bad luck over Tommy. A couple of perfectly good accidents went wrong. I wasn't going to fool about with accidents in Henry's case. He had a good deal of rheumatic pain after an accident in the hunting field. I introduced him to morphia. He took it in all good faith. Henry was a simple soul. He soon became an addict. Our plan was that he should go to the Grange for treatment and should there either "commit suicide" or get hold of an overdose of morphia. Moira would do the business. I shouldn't be connected with it in any way.

And then that fool Carstairs began to be active. It seems that Savage had written him a line on board ship mentioning Mrs. Templeton and even enclosing a snapshot of her. Carstairs went on a shooting trip soon afterwards. When he came back from the wilds and heard the news of Savage's death and will, he was frankly incredulous. The story didn't ring true to him. He was certain that Savage wasn't worried about his health and didn't believe he had any special fear of cancer. Also the wording of the will sounded to him highly uncharacteristic. Savage was a hard-headed business man, and while he might be quite ready to have an affair with a pretty woman, Carstairs didn't believe he would leave a vast sum of money to her and the rest to charity. The charity touch was my idea. It sounded so respectable and unfishy.

Carstairs came over here determined to look into the business. He began to poke about.

And straightaway we had a piece of bad luck. Some friends brought him down to lunch, and he saw a picture of Moira on the piano—and recognized it as the woman of the snapshot that Savage had sent him. He went down to Chipping Somerton and started to poke about there.

Moira and I began to get the wind up—I sometimes think unnecessarily. But Carstairs was a shrewd chap.

I went down to Chipping Somerton after him. He failed to trace the cook—Rose Chudleigh. She'd gone to the north, but he tracked down Evans, found out her married name and started off for Marchbolt.

Things were getting serious. If Evans identified Mrs. Templeton and Mrs. Nicholson as one and the same person, matters were going to become difficult. Also she'd been in the house some time and we weren't sure quite how much she might know.

I decided that Carstairs had got to be suppressed. He was making a serious nuisance of himself. Chance came to my aid. I was close behind him when the mist came up. I crept up nearer and a sudden push did the job.

But I was still in a dilemma. I didn't know what incriminating matter he might have on him. However, your young Naval friend played into my hands very nicely. I was left alone with the body for a short time— quite enough for my purpose. He had a photograph of Moira—he'd got it from the photographers, presumably for identification. I removed that and any letters or identifying matter. Then I planted the photograph of one of the gang.

All went well. The pseudo-sister and brother-in-law came down and identified him. All seemed to have gone off satisfactorily. And then your friend Bobby upset things. It seemed that Carstairs had recovered consciousness before he died and that he had

been saying things. He'd mentioned Evans—and
Evans was actually in service at the Vicarage.

I admit we were getting rattled by now. We lost
our heads a bit. Moira insisted that he must be put
out of the way. We tried one plan, which failed. Then
Moira said she'd see to it. She went down to Marchbolt in the car. She seized a chance very neatly—
slipped some morphia into Bobby's beer when he
was asleep. But the young devil didn't succumb. That
was pure bad luck.

As I told you, it was Nicholson's cross-questioning
that made me wonder if you were just what you
seemed. But imagine the shock that Moira had when
she was creeping out to meet me one evening and
came face to face with Bobby! She recognized him at
once—she'd had a good look when he was asleep that
day. No wonder she was so scared she nearly passed
out. Then she realized that it wasn't she whom he suspected, and she rallied and played up.

She came to the inn and told him a few tall stories.
He swallowed them like a lamb. She pretended that
Alan Carstairs was an old lover and she piled it on
thick about her fear of Nicholson. Also she did her
best to disabuse you of your suspicions concerning
me. I did the same to you and disparaged her as a
weak, helpless creature—Moira, who had the nerve
to put any number of people out of the way without
turning a hair!

The position was serious. We'd got the money.
We were getting on well with the Henry plan. I was
in no hurry for Tommy. I could afford to wait a bit.
Nicholson could easily be got out of the way when
the time came. But you and Bobby were a menace.
You'd got your suspicions fixed on the Grange.

It may interest you to know that Henry didn't commit suicide. I killed him! When I was talking to you in the garden, I saw there was no time to waste—and I went straight in and saw to things.

The airplane that came over gave me my chance. I went into the study, sat down by Henry, who was writing, and said: "Look here, old man—" and shot him! The noise of the plane drowned the sound. Then I wrote a nice affecting letter, wiped off my fingerprints from the revolver, pressed Henry's hand round it and let it drop to the floor. I put the key of the study in Henry's pocket and went out, locking the door from the outside with the dining-room key, which fits the lock.

I won't go into details of the neat little squib arrangement in the chimney which was timed to go off four minutes later.

Everything went beautifully. You and I were in the garden together and heard the "shot." A perfect suicide! The only person who laid himself open to suspicion was poor old Nicholson. The ass came back for a stick or something!

Of course Bobby's knight-errantry was a bit difficult for Moira. So she just went off to the Cottage. We fancied that Nicholson's explanation of his wife's absence would be sure to make you suspicious.

Where Moira really showed her mettle was at the Cottage. She realized from the noise upstairs that I'd been knocked out, and she quickly injected a large dose of morphia into herself, and lay down on the bed. After you all went down to telephone she nipped up to the attic and cut me free. Then the morphia took effect and by the time the Doctor arrived she was genuinely off in a hypnotic sleep.

But all the same her nerve was going. She was

afraid you'd get on to Evans and get the hang of how Savage's will and suicide were worked. Also she was afraid that Carstairs had written to Evans before he came to Marchbolt. She pretended to go up to a London nursing home. Instead she hurried down to Marchbolt—and met you on the doorstep! Then her one idea was to get you both out of the way. Her methods were crude to the last degree, but I believe she'd have got away with it. I doubt if the waitress would have been able to remember much about what the woman who came in with you was like. Moira would have got away back to London and lain low in a nursing home. With you and Bobby out of the way the whole thing would have died down.

But you spotted her—and she lost her head. And then at the trial she dragged *me* into it!

Perhaps I was getting a little tired of her. . . . But I had no idea that she knew it.

You see, she had got the money—*my* money! Once I had married her I might have got tired of her. I like variety.

So here I am starting life again. . . . And all owing to you and that extremely objectionable young man Bobby Jones. But I've no doubt I shall make good!

Or ought it to be *"bad"* not *"good"?*

I haven't reformed—yet.

But if at first you don't succeed, try, try, try again.

Good-bye, my dear—or perhaps au revoir. One never knows, does one?

Your affectionate enemy, the bold, bad villain of the piece,

ROGER BASSINGTON-FFRENCH

News from the Vicarage

Bobby handed back the letter and with a sigh Frankie took it.

"He's really a very remarkable person," she said.

"You always had a fancy for him," said Bobby coldly.

"He had charm," said Frankie. "So had Moira," she added.

Bobby blushed. "It was very queer that all the time the clue to the whole thing should have been in the Vicarage," he said. "You do know, don't you, Frankie, that Carstairs had actually written to Evans—to Mrs. Roberts, that is?"

Frankie nodded. "Telling her that he was coming to see her and that he wanted information about Mrs. Templeton who he had reason to believe was a dangerous international crook wanted by the police."

"And then when he's pushed over the cliff she doesn't put two and two together!" said Bobby bitterly.

"That's because the man who went over the cliff was Pritchard," said Frankie. "That identification was a very clever bit of work. If a man called Pritchard is pushed over, how *could* it be a man called Carstairs? That's how the ordinary mind works."

"The funny thing is that she recognized Cayman," went on Bobby. "At least she caught a glimpse of him when Roberts was letting him in and asked him who it was. And he said it was a Mr. Cayman and she said, 'Funny—he's the dead spit of a gentleman I used to be in service with.' "

"Can you beat it?" said Frankie.

"Even Bassington-ffrench gave himself away once or twice." she continued. "But like an idiot I never spotted it."

"Did he?"

"Yes, when Sylvia said that the picture in the paper was very like Carstairs, he said there wasn't much likeness really—showing he'd seen the dead man. And then later he said to me that he never saw the dead man's face."

"How on earth did you spot Moira, Frankie?"

"I think it was the description of Mrs. Templeton," said Frankie dreamily. "Everyone said she was 'such a nice lady.' Now that didn't seem to fit with the Cayman woman. No servant would describe her as a 'nice lady.' And then we got to the Vicarage and Moira was there and it suddenly came to me—*Suppose Moira was Mrs. Templeton?*"

"Very bright of you."

"I'm sorry for Sylvia," said Frankie. "With Moira dragging Roger into it, it's been a terrible lot of publicity for her. But Dr. Nicholson has stuck by her and I shouldn't be at all surprised if they ended by making a match of it."

"Everything seems to have ended very fortunately," said Bobby. "Badger's doing well at the garage, thanks to your father. And also thanks to your father, I've got this perfectly marvellous job."

"Is it a marvellous job?"

"Managing a coffee estate out in Kenya on a whacking big screw? I should think so. It's just the sort of thing I used to dream about."

He paused. "People come out to Kenya a good deal on trips," he said with intention.

"Quite a lot of people live out there," said Frankie demurely.

"Oh, Frankie you wouldn't!" He blushed, stammered, recovered himself. "W-w-would you?"

"I would," said Frankie. "I mean I will."

"I've been keen about you always," said Bobby in a stifled voice. "I used to be miserable—knowing, I mean, that it was no good."

"I suppose that's what made you so rude that day on the golf links."

"Yes, I was feeling pretty grim."

"H'm," said Frankie. "What about Moira?"

Bobby looked uncomfortable. "Her face did sort of get me," he admitted.

"It's a better face than mine," said Frankie generously.

"It isn't—but it sort of haunted me. And then, when we were up in the attic and you were so plucky about things—well, Moira just faded out. I was hardly interested in what happened to her. It was *you*—only you. You were simply splendid! So frightfully plucky."

"I wasn't feeling plucky inside," said Frankie. "I was all shaking. But I wanted you to admire me."

"I did, darling. I do. I always have. I always shall. Are you sure you won't hate it out in Kenya?"

"I shall adore it. I was fed up with England."

"Frankie."

"Bobby."

"If you will come in here," said the Vicar, opening the door and ushering in the advance guard of the Dorcas Society. He shut the door precipitately and apologized. "My—er—one of my sons. He is—er—engaged."

A member of the Dorcas Society said archly that it looked like it.

"A good boy," said the Vicar. "Inclined at one time not to take life seriously. But he has improved very much of late. He is going out to manage a coffee estate in Kenya."

Said one member of the Dorcas Society to another in a whisper: "Did you see? It was Lady Frances Derwent he was kissing!"

In an hour's time the news was all over Marchbolt.